BLACK
JACK

GINA EASTON

This is a work of fiction. Names, characters, places, and incidents are products of the author's imagination or are used fictitiously and are not to be construed as real. Any resemblance to actual events, locations, organizations, or persons, living or dead, is entirely coincidental.

World Castle Publishing, LLC
Pensacola, Florida
Copyright © Gina Easton 2020
Paperback ISBN: 9781953271440
eBook ISBN: 9781953271457
First Edition World Castle Publishing, LLC, December 21, 2020
http://www.worldcastlepublishing.com

Licensing Notes

Cover: Karen Fuller
Editor: Maxine Bringenberg

PROLOGUE

Whitechapel. The summer of 1888. Not as sweltering as the heatwave of 1887, which had left the beleaguered inhabitants of London and its districts longing for a reprieve. The sultry weather only accentuated the squalor of this East End slum, adding to the oppressive atmosphere of poverty. Dilapidated buildings sprawled onto dusty streets, their sordidness highlighted by the brittle sun. A thick coat of grime lent an almost palpable presence of shadow. Although the heat pounded the city less cruelly than the preceding summer, the constant odor of decay was as overpowering.

The rats that crawled the alleyways were just as ravenous. Watching from underneath abandoned carts of refuse, their beady eyes glared at the street urchins who played in their midst. Whiskers twitched in response to the tantalizing smell of tender flesh so near at hand. Hunger drove them to be bolder and dangerous. Indeed, the number of children attacked by vermin had doubled this summer. Several fatalities occurred amongst younger children and infants who succumbed to the razor-sharp claws and teeth of their attackers.

Even among slum areas, Whitechapel was notorious for its inhospitable environment. Crouched in London's East End, it was commonly referred to as "the world's end." Superstition whispered that its confines exerted a strange and unsettling influence upon those who lived there, leaving a dark stain upon their souls. Thus it came as no surprise that a celebrated author would, in the not too distant future, christen it "the abyss."

A stranger entering Whitechapel from another part of London

might well find the stench of refuse, sewage, and unwashed flesh overwhelming. The claustrophobic dwellings and narrow sinister streets were sufficient to evoke dismay, even trepidation, as were the tortuous alleys which often led abruptly to dead ends. An apt metaphor this proved to be for the unfortunates who called Whitechapel home. Many had reached their own dead end along the road of life, spirits broken by poverty's relentless assault. Despair hung in the city air and clung to every man, woman, and child. It seeped in through their pores, taking up parasitic residence in their souls, where it fed off the remains of dead hopes and dreams.

No one remained immune to Whitechapel's perils. Streets hostile enough by day were stalked by danger when darkness fell. Many a nefarious deed was obscured by the fog which nightly shrouded the gas-lit streets. Robberies, assaults, rapes, and murders all threatened solitary travelers who braved the forbidden alleyways. Fog and darkness, allies of old, combined to confuse unwary individuals who wandered the labyrinths and paths. Distorting the yellow illumination of the lamps, the fog created bizarre and menacing shadows, transforming the night street into surreal landscapes. If not a thief or murderer lurking in the shadows to strike one down, then it was poverty and disease which claimed their victim.

Half the children born in the Whitechapel and neighboring Spitalfields districts died before the age of five. Those who survived wore the scars of childhood for a lifetime, often having witnessed the ravages of death upon siblings and parents alike. Orphans, often unclaimed by relatives, were placed in government-run institutions, where conditions were harsh and deprivation rampant. Children old enough to enter into employment were dispatched to poorhouses where, along with indigent adults, they earned their keep with whatever jobs were available.

Life was arduous and brutally exhausting. Overcrowding was common, accompanied by appalling sanitary conditions and squalor. Frequently, outbreaks of serious, sometimes lethal infections, such as cholera and typhoid fever, would first erupt in these poorhouses before spreading to the population at large. If truth be told, childhood was a myth in Whitechapel. No child retained its innocence for long, quickly learning that innocence was the price one paid for survival. For many, this price was too dear, and they perished on the unforgiving streets or in the cesspit conditions of brothels specializing in child prostitution.

Sadly for humans, there are places upon this earth which create and perpetuate misery in all its forms, such as poverty, disease, corruption of hope, manifesting their crippling impact not only in a physical decline but in an erosion of spirit as well. Whitechapel was such a breeding ground. Its denizens were hollow souls, haunted by dreams unfulfilled and desires unrealized. A toxic miasma of spiritual malaise seeped from the area's very foundations.

Thus it came to pass that by the late summer of 1888, Whitechapel flourished as a spawning pool for evil. Within its boundaries could be accessed any vice known to man or any perversion or act of depravity which man, in his darkest imagination, could conjure. Little wonder then that this slum served as a magnet to draw other forces of darkness. A perfect blend of the most wicked ingredients, it was a smorgasbord of vileness and a tempting repast to those creatures who derived sustenance from spiritual decay, the carrion feeders of the soul.

Evil waited in the shadowed alleys and backstreets of Whitechapel. But it was not content to linger in the shadows for too long. The servants of wickedness, instruments of chaos and destruction, bided their time, awaiting the summons from human hearts and souls.

Whitechapel now issued its invitation. Soon enough, it would be answered by one who would descend upon the hapless inhabitants with a malevolent and insatiable appetite for suffering. This evil was destined to strike terror in the hearts of those who wandered through the twilight existence of Whitechapel.

An existence soon to be ripped apart.

CHAPTER 1

"Ow, cor, that hurts like bloody hell!" the man yelled, flinching from the bandage that Emma Hollander was trying to wrap around his injured hand.

"Of course it hurts," Emma replied matter of factly. "You failed to seek attention at once, and now the wound is infected. Fortunately, it is only a minor infection; otherwise, you might have lost a finger or two. Now stay still and let me wrap it for you." She reached for the hand, green eyes smiling despite her admonishment. "I shall never understand why people don't attend to their medical problems more expediently." She raised an eyebrow. "Especially men."

The man shrugged and attempted a charming smile, an impossible task due to a mouthful of rotten teeth. "Ah now, miss. I would have come sooner, honest I would, but me wife wouldn't let me on account of you, you see."

"Me. What's it to do with me?"

"Well now, she is jealous, isn't she? 'Oh, you just want to see that young nurse at the infirmary,' she says. 'The one I hear is so pretty.' 'Ah, you mean Miss Emma,' I says. 'Is that her name?' she says. 'Well, is she pretty?' 'Pretty,' I says, all innocently. 'Not so I noticed.'" He chuckled slyly. "So you see, it is really me wife's fault I got infected."

"Oh, I suppose it is your wife's fault too that you injured your hand in the first place?"

He grinned sheepishly. "No, miss. I wish I could blame it on her, but it was me own carelessness." He leaned closer to Emma and lowered his voice conspiratorially. "Of course, I was fibbin' when I told her."

"When you told her what?" Emma tried not to flinch from the fetid odor of his breath. She finished bandaging his hand.

"You know when I said I hadn't noticed about you being pretty."

Emma rolled her eyes and waved dismissively. "You're all done, for now, Tom, but please come back tomorrow so we can change the bandages and apply more salve to the wound. It is very important."

Tom stood up and flipped his cap. "You bet, miss. I'll be here tomorrow, only don't tell me wife." He winked and turned as if to leave, then grinned back at her. "The truth is, I think you are the prettiest woman in Whitechapel."

Emma watched his retreating form exit the infirmary.

At twenty-two years of age, she was indeed a striking young woman. Curly chestnut hair with a hint of red fell to her shoulders, but it was always bound up tightly when she was at the infirmary. Still, despite her studious attention, the occasional tendril or two would escape from the massive curls underneath her nurse's bonnet.

Her eyes, wide apart and green as the sea under the noonday sun were lively and did not flinch from the sights before them. They seem imbued with a life of their own, drinking in every experience afforded them. And Whitechapel life provided ample opportunity to experience a multitude of sights, sounds, and smells.

As Emma waited for the next patient to present at the casualty ward, she reflected upon the women of Whitechapel, the haggard, diseased prostitutes who wore the ravages of poverty and hardship like an accessory to their threadbare clothes. And the exhausted wives and mothers who struggled to care for the families as they battled the twin ills of poverty and despair.

Emma felt the familiar sensation of guilt descend upon her like a cloak of thorns pricking her conscience. Why was her life so much better than theirs?

She pondered the capricious nature of fate, which had

allowed her to be born to middle-class parents who nurtured and cherished her. They had taught her that life was essentially just, and if one was a good Christian, one should expect a decent life in return. The ultimate reward, of course, was attaining everlasting life with God in Heaven.

However, two years in Whitechapel working amongst the desperately poor and sick had shattered that illusion. Emma now realized that life was neither that simple nor predictable, and that try as one might to control one's destiny, there were always obstacles to thwart one's goals.

The people who came to the infirmary seeking attention were, for the most part, good, law-abiding citizens who struggled, despite the continuous daily battle for survival, to retain some meaning and purpose in their lives. Yet, they were afforded no respite. Opportunities for good fortune did not present themselves. Indeed, they counted themselves fortunate if they could support themselves and live independently, thus avoiding being sent to the poorhouses, the last vestiges of the desperately impoverished.

Emma wrestled with these matters, finding no satisfactory answers. During working hours, she was able to suppress her frustration, but no such defense was available to her at night. In her dreams, she wandered aimlessly through the fog-filled streets of Whitechapel, confused and lost. A profound uneasiness gnawed at her. She would never find her way through this maze, and so was condemned to walk the streets until she dropped from fatigue and despair. Invariably, she woke from these dreams with a sense of depression and a heaviness in her heart.

Sighing audibly, Emma switched her focus to the bandages and basin, the medical instruments on the tray before her—solid reminders of the job she was there to perform. She loathed feeling helpless, an emotion with which she had become uncomfortably familiar since working at the Whitechapel Infirmary.

As a nurse, she was only too aware of the shortcomings in medicine, but when one was forced to contend with poverty and chronic ill health, not to mention rampant alcoholism, the battle seemed grim indeed. For that was how she viewed medicine and nursing. She and her colleagues were engaged in a relentless fight against the effects of disease and mishap. Their goal was to provide the best care possible, even if they failed to find a cure or remedy. Ultimately, death was the victor in this ongoing battle. The challenge was to evade the final outcomes as long as one could and to avoid asking oneself the question: Why did people have to suffer so?

***

Emma's mood was subdued. She had no inkling that she would soon be faced with a far greater challenge. Life in Whitechapel, precarious at best, was to become decidedly more perilous; and getting lost in the foggy streets would only be a prelude to the horror that was to menace the East End in the weeks to come.

CHAPTER 2

The young woman glanced around the shabby room, her gaze absorbing the worn brown carpet that was threadbare in places. The muslin curtains, once a rich caramel color, had now faded to a dusty beige. The solitary window, grime encrusted, reflected minimal sunlight. None of this seemed daunting to the young woman. She nodded with a satisfied air, ignoring an obvious rent in the brown and gold fabric of the roomy, lopsided armchair. Part of the stuffing, like a portion of exposed bone, was visible from a distance.

"Yes, this is adequate. Thank you," she said to the landlady.

Mrs. Grouse regarded with some suspicion the young woman's attire, which rivaled the room in terms of shabbiness.

"Well, I hope you can afford it," she said bluntly. "I know 'tis more dear than some, but our location is excellent, bein' so close to the city center and all. The rent is cheaper in Whitechapel and Spitalfields, you know—"

The young woman interrupted her with a haughty glare. "I have already told you," she said, her husky tone authoritative. "I will pay you weekly as we agreed. Here's the first rent money now." She dropped some coins into the landlady's palm.

"Right then," Mrs. Grouse grudgingly responded. "The room is ready when you are Miss…uh…."

"Boyd," the woman said. "Bessie Boyd."

A thinly veiled look of contempt was directed at the landlady as the young woman brushed past her and descended the stairs.

Well, la-dee-da, thought Mrs. Grouse as she watched the figure flounce ahead of her. *We're certainly puttin' on airs, aren't we? Miss*

Bessie Boyd thinks she's foolin' me; she's only foolin' 'erself. That story about takin' a room until her brother's house is ready to move into is just a bleedin' lie. She ain't no lady, not with those clothes. Does she think I don't know a whore when I see one? She shrugged her shoulders as she followed the woman down the stairs. *Well, 'tis nothing to me so long as the rent is paid proper and she don't bother the other lodgers. I will have to watch that she don't bring her men here, though. I run a respectable rooming house.*

As the woman who called herself Bessie Boyd reached the main floor landing, she turned and faced the older woman. A rather nasty smile was on her lips.

"Don't worry," she said in a frosty tone. "There won't be no sneakin' any men here, except for your gentleman caller who sneaks in through the scullery door at night." So saying, she turned and exited the building.

Mrs. Grouse stood in the doorway, watching until the woman disappeared from sight. She was dumbfounded, her mind reeling in shocked disbelief.

How could that hussy know about Mr. Hendricks, the kindly widower next door who visits several times a week? she wondered. It was all very secretive. She was certain that none of the other lodgers entertained any suspicion. The scullery entrance had proven perfect to maintain the utmost discretion.

She looked at the money in her hand, a profound uneasiness taking root inside her. She should be happy she'd rented the room. It was always a challenge to let due to the dearth of sunlight and the dampness that crept in through the cracks and windowpane. However, she felt anything but satisfied. The money in her palm somehow made her feel dirty like she was the whore instead of Bessie Boyd.

She suddenly wished with all her heart that she could cancel the arrangement—wait until the Boyd woman arrived tomorrow with her belongings and coolly inform her that there had been a change in plan and the room was no longer available. But she knew with a sinking feeling that she would not do that, for the uncomfortable truth was that she was more than just a little frightened of Bessie Boyd. A menacing air, though subtle, emanated from the woman, as if she could easily be malevolent if challenged.

As long as she keeps to herself, the landlady thought in an effort to raise her sagging spirits. *The less I see or know of that woman, the better.* She shuffled back to her kitchen, her expression preoccupied as she tried in vain to banish her trepidation.

CHAPTER 3

Nightfall in Whitechapel. The bustling din of the working day was ending. As street vendors packed up their wares, the poorhouse and factory whistles blew to signal the completion of another day's labor. Soon the men who had been cooped up all day would head to the numerous public houses in the district, there to relax into the evening's leisure hours.

At the Princess Alice Public House at Wentworth and Commercial Streets, a young woman stood at the glass-fronted doors looking out at the deepening twilight sky. It was her habit to stand here nightly, time permitting, waiting for the first stars of the evening to appear. She was a lovely girl of seventeen, with cornflower blue eyes and golden hair that fell in curls to her shoulders. Her creamy skin was smooth and fresh, and her face held a sweet softness in marked contrast to the sharpened features and care-worn faces of many Whitechapel women, even those no more than girls themselves.

She sighed, cherishing these brief moments of quiet, the calmness before the storm. Soon the pub would be teeming with customers—men sore and tired from the day's work would file into the pub and greet one another with hearty hails and congratulations for having survived yet another day of drudgery. Thus would begin the nightly quest to forget for a few hours the burdens of life and to search for solace in the company of others just as miserable and downtrodden.

Men, however, were not the only ones to frequent the pubs of Whitechapel. For now, their work time, the whores of the East End prepared to begin their nightly trade. Only two types of whores worked the streets by day; the very young ones blessed with the freshness and stamina to sell themselves both day and night, and the desperate ones. These were the women who had too many mouths to feed and left the children at home to fend for themselves while they worked the streets. At night they would sit at home nursing their babies while their husbands drank themselves into a stupor at the local pub.

And then there were the truly pathetic whores, too dissipated and disease-ridden to face the night time competition or to tolerate the rough trade which operated under the cloak of darkness amidst the back alleys. These bottom-of-the-barrel whores frequented the docks and wharves where the unskilled laborers were not, as a rule, fastidious about their women. The whores were an easy commodity, their homeliness and physical debilitation rendering them cheaper by far than their night-time colleagues.

Prostitution was grueling work any time of day, but it became fraught with new dangers once night descended. Life, cheap in Whitechapel to begin with, was that much cheaper for whores who frequently became scapegoats for much of the anger and misogynist attitudes of their customers. But it was not solely the local men who targeted these women.

The darkness, filled with menace and forbidden allure, enticed the fine looking gentlemen from the rest of London, whose proper manners and suave smiles often concealed a taste for the most unsavory perversions. Many a whore suffered serious injury or maiming; some were even accidentally murdered during an amorous encounter, which got a little out of hand, according to the gentleman involved. The bodies were often unceremoniously dumped into the Thames or left in back alleys beside refuse bins.

But the young woman standing in the doorway of the pub had no knowledge of such things. Though born and bred in Whitechapel, she was carefully shielded from this menacing reality by her father, the proprietor of the pub. She was forbidden from venturing into the streets after dark, her father preferring her to work in the pub where he could keep a vigilant eye on her.

"Sarah-Jane, where have you got to, girl?" A man's voice shattered the peace of her reverie.

"Out front, Da," she called in response.

"Well, come on then, no lollygagging. We've work to do."

A middle aged man, lean of build with graying hair at the temples and sparse on top, emerged from behind the bar wiping his hands on his smock.

"For the life of me, I can't understand what you are staring at every night." His eyes narrowed suspiciously. "You'd not be waiting for a beau now, would 'ya?"

Sarah-Jane blushed. "Of course not, you know I don't have no beau."

"Hmm. Well, a girl like you can't be too careful. I know what men are like," he nodded emphatically. "I've seen the way them blokes in here look at you. 'Tis a good thing you've got your father to watch out for you. Nobody dare lay a hand on my girl."

Sarah-Jane frowned, pretending annoyance. "Most of them barely talk to me once they find out I'm your daughter."

"And that's how it should be," her father replied. "No daughter of Joe Mullen is going to end up with a babe in arms and no husband, or worse, be out in them streets like a common whore."

"Oh, Da!" Sarah-Jane exclaimed, rolling her eyes in exasperation. "You do worry unnecessarily."

"And if your poor mother, God bless her soul, were still alive, she would be proper proud of what I do for you." He shook his head in sadness. "She was so concerned about you—made me promise to look after you proper. 'Swear on your soul, Joe, and may you be damned to hell,' she said, 'if you don't do right by our daughter.' So you see, child, I will burn in eternal damnation if some man does you harm."

"Well, at least you'll have lots of company down there," Sarah-Jane laughed as she skipped by her father, deftly avoiding the hand reaching out to slap her. She ran to the bar, her laughter echoing through the house. Joe Mullen shook his head, an indulgent smile on his lips. The girl was the apple of his eye, his heart's delight, but he would die a hundred deaths before admitting that truth to anyone.

***

In the weeks to come, he was to spend many a fretful, sleepless night worrying about his daughter, trying his best to ignore the urgent voices whispering from the shadows in the dead of night, telling him all the unspeakable things that they would do to his lovely daughter. They were to taunt him relentlessly as other inhabitants would be similarly plagued, and some driven to the brink of madness by the abomination that was to visit Whitechapel.

CHAPTER 4

Twilight deepened into night as Emma returned to the Whitechapel Infirmary. It had been a long exhausting day. Her head and feet ached, and she longed for her cozy bed-sitting room. She wished she was at this moment curled up in her favorite chair, awaiting Andrew's knock on the door. Emma smiled as she thought of her fiancé, soon to arrive back in London after a business trip to India. She eagerly counted the days until he was once again in her arms. How she missed him.

Emma hurried up the steps and into the infirmary, anxious to file her report and be done for the day. Fortunately, only a few patients were waiting for assessment. However, that number would increase as the night progressed, accompanied by the usual drunken brawls, domestic mishaps, accidents, and assaults.

The night nurse, Mary Simonds, smiled when she saw Emma. "You've had a long day, haven't you, love?"

Emma sighed as she sank wearily into a chair beside the small alcove which served as an office. "My feet feel like they are on fire," she said, rubbing her left boot as though that would soothe the aching foot inside. "Is Dr. Mackenzie still here?"

Mary nodded. "He is still here. Can't very well leave until that new surgeon, what's-his-name, arrives, and he's late again."

"Pelham," Emma murmured, now rubbing her temples, eyes closed.

"What?"

"His name is Pelham." Emma opened her eyes and shook her head to clear it. "I wish Dr. Mackenzie to check on Margaret Bowens over on Gouldstone Street. I'm worried about her. She is feverish and probably getting septic."

"How's the babe?"

"He's fine so far, sleeping and suckling well, but if Margaret should become too ill to nurse him...." Emma's voice hardened. "I am sick to death of seeing this complication of childbirth. The confinement is difficult enough without this extra suffering."

Mary patted her hand, a sympathetic expression on her round, plain face. "I know, love. You've worked long and hard with Margaret Bowens and her brood. It's difficult to think of losing her, and possibly the babe as well."

Just then, the door opened, and Dr. Mackenzie's tall figure strode into the office. He was a big man, in girth as well as height, in his early forties, with unruly ginger hair and a bristling mustache. His bushy, auburn eyebrows lent him a forbidding look, and he was gruff and stern with patients when necessary. However, he was also a kind man who, no matter how busy or fatigued himself, never refused a patient in need.

"Any sign of Pelham?" he demanded, looking flushed and harried.

Mary Simonds shook her head. "Not yet, Doctor."

"Where the devil is he?" Mackenzie scowled, then noticed Emma. "Why are you still here?" he brusquely inquired.

"It was a long day," sighed Emma. "Doctor, I am very concerned about Margaret Bowens. I think she may have contracted the birthing sepsis."

"Hm. When did she give birth?" Mackenzie asked, heavy brows knitted together.

"Yesterday afternoon. Today she is feverish and starting a delirium."

"I shall go and attend her," he frowned in irritation, "just as soon as Pelham gets his—as soon as he arrives," he finished haltingly. He turned and exited the room, but not before the two women noted the furious flush to his face and neck.

Emma and Mary looked at one another, then laughed, albeit quietly so as not to be overheard.

"He is such a dear," Mary whispered. "Gentleman he is,

always mindful of his language."

"As well he should be," Emma replied in a mock, haughty tone. She tilted her chin up, nose wrinkled distastefully in a parody of London's pretentious upper class. "After all, we are ladies of society, are we not?"

Mary giggled. "Too right you are, love. You know, I think I half fancy him."

Emma rolled her eyes. "You half fancy any man with a fine mustache. Besides, the good doctor is happily married."

Mary raised her eyebrows skeptically. "Who told you that?"

"He did and does so every chance he gets," Emma laughed. "He is forever talking about his wife. Edith this and Edith that. I think he's afraid I fancy him or some equally silly notion."

"Ha, not with the delectable Andrew Hewitt-Brown to occupy you." Mary winked and licked her lips lasciviously.

Emma dismissed her with a laugh and a wave of her hand. "Enough frivolity. I must finish this report lest I be here all night."

Smiling, Mary headed towards the door just as a wailing and keening issued from the adjacent casualty room. "Duty calls," she said and exited to attend to the commotion.

CHAPTER 5

Nine o'clock at night. Fog enveloped the streets like a small moving tide, distorting and obscuring familiar landmarks. So began the nightly metamorphosis of Whitechapel into an alien landscape. The fog tampered with sound as well as sight. The hollow echo of footsteps on cobblestones might sound much closer than it was. A shout, seemingly from a distance, might, in fact, emanate from just around the corner. A perfect environment for those who wished to remain unseen and vanish without a trace, blending in with the fog-enshrouded shadows.

As with other Whitechapel public houses, business flourished at the Princess Alice this evening. Raucous laughter permeated the sweaty, smoke-filled main room. Drunken laborers and tradesmen comprised the majority of patrons. They were rough-spoken men in simple work clothes, dirty and grime-coated as those garments might be.

A case in point was Fred, the Duke Street butcher, who, though he had removed his bloodstained apron, reeked with the stench of fresh gore, which clung to him like a second skin. Sarah-Jane Mullen approached the butcher's table, drinks tray in hand, her small pert nose wrinkling in distaste at the rancid odor, although the other men at the table appeared untroubled by it. She set the tray on the table and waited for the men to help themselves. The conversation slowed a little, the men eyeing her appreciatively while they reached for their glasses of ale.

Fred the butcher, a stout middle-aged man, winked at the others and said, "Sarah-Jane, my dear, why don't you come and sit on old Fred's lap for a while? Rest those pretty feet of yours." The others laughed, slapping one another on the back and shoulders. "Come on then, just for a minute."

Sarah-Jane tossed her curls dismissively. "With the smell coming from you, I doubt you could convince a pig to sit in your lap." She sniffed loftily, turned heel smartly, and glided away. Uproarious laughter followed her receding figure, the men at the table, including Fred, doubling over in mirth.

"The girl has a sharp tongue to her," William the fishmonger said. "Wouldn't I like to get me hands on such a spirited young thing."

"Ha!" Jimmy exclaimed. He was a youth who had recently taken his first paying job at the railway yard. "She is too fair for the likes of you. She needs a proper gentleman, that's what."

"Oh ho, a gentleman such as yourself, I suppose," chortled Fred, foam from the ale coating his bristly mustache.

Jimmy blushed. "True, I'm no gentleman, but one day I will have me own business in London itself." The other men laughed again.

"Poor Jimmy, you would be the biggest dreamer around these parts," remarked Albert, who had worked as a gravedigger for over twenty years. "Just how do you fancy you'd manage that?"

Jimmy's blush deepened, a frown creasing his brow. "I'll work real hard, saving me money, not waste it on drink and such, and then I'll move to London proper and get a better paying job. I hear the wages are higher in the city." He surveyed the men at the table, seeing the skeptical yet indulgent expressions on their faces like they were listening to a child's flight of fancy. "What?" he challenged. "You think I can't do it? Is that it?"

"Now Jimmy, tis nothin' against yourself, boy," Albert soothed. A look of regret fleetingly crossed his face. His voice softened as he gazed with an expression akin to pity at the young man. "Don't you know, nothin' ever comes of these dreams? Look at us. You don't think we had dreams, too, when we was your age? Everyone wants to leave Whitechapel for a better life. The trouble is, nobody ever gets out of Whitechapel. You're born 'ere, and 'ere is where you'll die."

Across from the butcher's table sat a group of tawdry women, greedily consuming cheap gin, the cheapest the house provided. They were, without exception, women of limited skills, accepting the odd job here and there, none of the work permanent or sufficient to keep them out of the poorhouses. Barely able to provide for themselves, they often ended up living with men who were only marginally better off, in the poorest and seediest rooming houses, and that was if they were fortunate.

The majority of these women were obliged to turn to prostitution in order to obtain a roof over their heads and food in their stomachs. Still, that did not deter most of them from drinking their earnings away. And snared in the downward spiral of alcoholism and destitution, they were forced to return to the streets over and over.

Driven by desperation to sell their bodies, they risked disease or abuse at the hands of a stranger. If they had looks, to begin with, it wasn't long before alcohol and ill health took their devastating toll, leaving them mere shadows of their former selves. Hair and nails dry and brittle, teeth rotten, skin sallow and sore-infested, they fought a losing battle against malnutrition and vitamin deficiency.

And for most women, the greatest danger of all, an unwanted pregnancy, was a fear they lived with daily. Such an occurrence would necessitate a clandestine visit to an abortionist, most of whom had inadequate training. Physicians and midwives who had failed proper licensing were prohibited from practicing at any reputable infirmary. They worked in appallingly filthy conditions with the most rudimentary medical instruments. The more fortunate whores were attended by qualified midwives who risked the loss of their professional status, usually out of sympathy and pity for the prostitutes. Their skills were often superior to the back alley abortionists. The women they tended usually fared better, as the midwives continued to monitor them postpartum for signs of infection. Still, many a whore died of sepsis after an abortion, lying alone and terrified in her own blood and infectious waste.

Mary Ann Nichols, known as "Polly" on the streets, raised a glass of gin to her lips. Her hand shook badly. She was hardly ever sober anymore, and just yesterday had been evicted from yet another boarding house, unable to furnish this week's rent. She was a small woman, just over five feet in height, with brown hair and mild grey eyes. She looked younger than her forty-three years, the alcohol not yet having destroyed her appearance.

Unlike many Whitechapel prostitutes, Polly Nichols had once known a better life. She had been married and raised a family, but her marriage had fallen apart eight years previously. Her husband had decided to run off with a midwife who attended Polly's fourth confinement. After that loss, Polly began drinking, and over time drifted away from the remainder of her family.

Feeling herself a profound failure as a wife and mother, she tried to obliterate that period of her life, but the painful memories surfaced often. She stumbled into a series of menial jobs, the last one as a domestic to a family in London. Here was a chance for a better life, but Polly was not able to stay away from drink and was finally dismissed from the position. After nicking a few household items, she left the place in London and headed to Whitechapel. She ended up at various lodgings, the most recent being a boarding house on Thrawl Street and a room shared with three other women.

One of her roommates and friend, Ellen Holland, sat with Polly and the other women. Ellen rubbed her foot, a pained expression on her face. "Ooh, this blister is causing me grief," she complained.

"I told you them shoes were too small for you," Polly said with a smirk.

"Ha, it's not like I can afford new ones," Ellen snapped back.

Polly drained her glass in one thirsty swallow. She gestured toward the front door of the pub. "Well, maybe if you spent more time out there and less in here, you could afford 'em."

Ellen glared at her. "You're a fine one to talk, Polly Nichols. Look at ya. The night not yet old, and you're pissin' drunk. Not enough money for a roof over your head."

Polly thumped her glass on the table and wiped her mouth with the back of her hand. "That's about to change right now. Before the night is over, I'll have money for a room and enough left over to buy meself a new bonnet. You wait and see."

She stood unsteadily, hands gripping the table edge for support. Her grey eyes were already glazed over. She carefully arranged the ragged shawl around her shoulders and walked with slow, deliberate steps toward the door.

Ellen sighed and nudged the woman next to her. "I just don't know what's going to become of her. She was a good respectable woman once upon a time. But then, I guess we all were." She stared at her drink and was quiet for a long time.

CHAPTER 6

The woman belched drunkenly, weaving slightly in the shadow of the infirmary doorway. She cursed herself, as usual, for drinking too much gin. She didn't even like the stuff. It left a foul aftertaste, rending her belches sour and stale. "Well, Martha, me girl, you never learn, do you?"

She grinned crookedly and put a hand out to steady herself against the infirmary wall. Her luck was quickly running out. The Whitechapel Infirmary was her last chance. If they didn't let her stay, she would be forced to spend yet another night sleeping outside. Not so bad at this time of year, but Martha shuddered as she thought ahead to the long autumn and winter nights.

"You're getting too old, me lass, to be sleeping outdoors. I don't think these old bones will stand another cold season." She shook her head, a baleful look in her eyes.

She sifted through the pockets of her ragged and dirty petticoat. Like many of Whitechapel's poor, she was often forced to wear all her clothes at one time, not having a place in which to safely keep these items. The extra insulation of multiple layers helped enormously to keep one warm in the cold weather, but in the summer heat, one could suffer quite miserably. Martha huffed with exertion as she finally located the object of her search.

"Aha!" she cackled, peering at the coin in her hand. Not enough for even the cheapest room to let, but enough to buy another drink of the abominable swill that passed as gin in the public houses of Whitechapel. She secured the coin in a little pouch she concealed under her petticoat and around her waist, guarding the single coin as if it were a valuable treasure.

Sobering her expression as much as she was able, Martha turned to the infirmary door and pulled on the large brass knocker three times. The door was opened a few moments later by Mary Simonds, the night nurse, lantern in hand.

"Please, nurse," Martha said in a plaintive voice. "Me stomach is hurtin' somethin' awful." She gripped her abdomen, bending almost in two.

Mary Simonds sighed and peered more closely at the grubby woman. She was clearly a transient and almost certainly a whore. She stood about five foot three inches and had brown eyes and hair. Her face was round and attractive in a bland way. She looked to be about forty years old.

Suddenly, the nurse frowned and drew back. "Is that you, Martha Tabram?" she asked suspiciously. "Weren't you here about a month ago with a similar complaint?"

Martha silently cursed herself for a fool. She had obviously not kept good track of the various infirmaries to which she had sought admission. She'd forgotten that she had been to the Whitechapel Infirmary as recently as last month.

"Ah, no, nurse. It 'twasn't me. Me name's Edith, Edith Turner, that is. I don't know no Martha what's 'er name. Please, I need to see the doctor. Oh, the cramps, the cramps."

Mary's frown deepened, but she opened the door wide, allowing the woman to enter. She tsked as she detected the strong odor of alcohol. "You've been drinking," she said disapprovingly.

Martha looked up at her, eyes glistening with tears as she shuffled into the entranceway. "Only so's to dull the pain," she said earnestly. "'Tis the only thing that 'as 'elped at all; strictly for medicinal purposes."

Mary Simonds glared at her sternly. "You had better not be malingering. We shan't stand for that, old girl." She sighed again, this time in consternation. "Come with me then to the casualty room." She turned on her heel, not looking to see if the woman followed.

Still clutching her stomach, Martha allowed herself a sly smile. So far, so good.

She was led to a small, dingy room and instructed to wait for the doctor. In a few moments, the door opened, and a youngish man with a bristling black mustache entered. He looked at the woman skeptically and then said, "I am Dr. Pelham. What seems to be the matter?"

"Oh Doctor, 'tis me stomach. It's painin' me somethin' terrible," Martha complained in her most pathetic tone.

"Mmmm. Too much drink, I should say," the doctor responded.

"Ah, no. I only took the drink, a small amount mind, to ease the pain."

"Really?" Dr. Pelham inquired in a sarcastic tone. "Well then, let's check that bothersome stomach. Just lift up your skirts, please." He approached her gingerly, aware of the possibility of lice and other vermin which habitually infested the unhygienic masses of Whitechapel. He pressed his hands against the warm, sweaty skin of the woman's abdomen. "Does that hurt?" he asked.

"Ow, ow, oh yes, it hurts a lot!" Martha wailed as convincingly as possible.

Dr. Pelham continued to palpate and probe her abdomen. Martha reacted with suitable howls of discomfort.

"Ah ha, just as I thought," the doctor concluded, his examination completed. Martha's cries were cut short as she waited with hopeful anticipation for the physician's next words. "A simple case of constipation," declared Pelham.

Martha's jaw fell open. "What?" she cried indignantly.

Pelham shook his head. "Nothing to worry about, old girl," he reassured her. "I could give you a tonic to help nature along."

Martha looked at him in annoyance and disgust. "What if you're wrong?" she demanded. "What if tis somethin' serious? I think I should stay overnight just in case."

Dr. Pelham pretended to consider this proposal. "Well, on one condition only. I shall prescribe large quantities of laxative during the night. The nurses shall supervise the procedure. If that is not effective, we may have to implement some more drastic measures to alleviate the problem — "

"All right, all right," Martha grumbled, interrupting the physician. She smoothed her crumpled skirts and patted her lank, greasy hair, carelessly gathered in a knot to keep it away from her face. "Tis a fine state of affairs when a person can't get the proper 'elp what's needed," she said haughtily as she brushed past Pelham on her way out the door.

Mary Simonds was waiting outside in the corridor to escort her. "Come on, love, this way." She ushered Martha towards the front door. Martha turned and looked at the nurse, noting the woman's kind expression. "Well," she said as she stepped outside, "at least 'tis not rainin', not even a lot of fog tonight."

Martha reached the Princess Alice just as the last patrons stumbled or were pushed out. She cursed aloud. Bad luck plagued her tonight. First, her customers had been few and far between. In fact, she'd had no blokes since she and Pearly Paul, another prostitute, had picked up those two soldiers just before midnight. Secondly, being turned away from a decent and free bed and missing her last opportunity for a drink before the pubs shut down.

She fairly ran towards the doors of the pub, hoping to persuade the landlord to sell her a drink, only one drink and she would be on her way. Her route was blocked by a comely girl, whom she recognized as the proprietor's daughter.

"Closin time," Sarah-Jane announced as the bedraggled woman approached.

"Oh, come on, ducks, just give us a little nip of gin," Martha pleaded in a wheedling tone. "I got money, see." She fumbled through the voluminous folds of her clothing to reach the pouch at her waist. She brought up a coin and waved it triumphantly before the girl's face.

Sarah-Jane was unimpressed. "Sorry, missus. Rules is rules. We're closed." Without another word, she shut the door. The sound of the bolt being drawn seemed to emphasize Martha's ill fortune.

She turned away from the Princess Alice and began to trudge

eastward along Wentworth Street. Time to look for a place to sleep, she thought resignedly.

A rustling sound followed by a short cough issued from ahead and slightly to her right. The gas lamps were sparse along this section of the road as compared to the busier Commercial Street. Martha could see very little in the yellowish gloom ahead.

"Who's there?" she demanded, wishing to avoid any trouble.

A woman lurched drunkenly from a doorway, almost tripping over her feet before steadying herself with a hand against the wall of the building.

"'Ello dearie," the woman greeted her in a throaty, slightly husky drawl.

She was dressed similarly to Martha, although the latter noted with some resentment that the woman's burgundy colored bonnet was newer than her own. From what Martha could see in the shifting shadows, the woman was a good deal younger than herself, probably no more than twenty-five or six compared to Martha's forty years. Like most whores, she was heavily painted, although not garish like some. Her features were even, and in this light, her skin seemed good. All in all, an attractive woman, Martha thought begrudgingly. She sighed to herself. Competition was not what she needed right now.

"Got a place to sleep?" the young woman inquired in a friendly manner. Martha shrugged. "Me neither," the young woman said and laughed aloud. "But I do have a treat." She reached into the grimy and tattered bag she carried and pulled out a bottle. "Got enough for a couple more drinks. Fancy a nip yourself?" She waved the bottle enticingly at Martha.

Martha ran her tongue over dry lips. "Well, I am a bit thirsty. Maybe just a little." She reached for the liquor, but the woman quickly stuck the bottle back into her bag.

"Not 'ere. Never know who might come along." She winked conspiratorially. "This way," she pointed. "Over there is a building. The back door is usually unlocked. We can 'ave our drink and then go and sleep inside. No one will bother us." She linked her arm through Martha's, and the two of them moved their way slowly down the deserted road.

Martha smiled to herself. Maybe her luck was about to change after all. She would at least have another drink before sleep claimed her. She was familiar with the rundown dwelling that was her destination. She occasionally used it as a private place to conduct her business instead of the alleyways. She glanced at the woman beside her.

"Me name is Martha. What's yours?"

"You can call me Bessie," the woman replied. She smiled back at Martha as she pushed open the iron gate leading to the George Yard building. "After you, my dear."

***

Mary Simonds trudged home in the early morning hours of August 7. The night shift at the infirmary had just ended, and Mary was thankful for the cool breeze blowing in from the river. She hoped to catch a few hours of sleep before the sweltering heat of midday drove her from the refuge of her dreams. She passed a news vendor on the street. Quite a crowd had already gathered to hear the latest stories. The vendor waved a copy of *The Star*, a popular London daily.

"Read it right here," he proclaimed. "Right here, ladies and gents. 'Orrible murder in Whitechapel! Woman stabbed thirty-nine times!"

A collective gasp came from the crowd. Mary shuddered as she drew nearer. Murder in Whitechapel was a common enough occurrence, yet this sounded particularly terrible.

Most murders in the East End were as a result of robbery, drunken brawls, and occasional domestic troubles. Not that murder was pleasant under any circumstances. But as a rule, the killings were not especially vicious, compromising a single knife wound or blows to the head. She could not help wondering who would wish to stab someone thirty-nine times. The insane anger and hatred involved was enough to make her stomach queasy. Try as she might, she could not picture in her mind what such a monster would look like. Surely he must be more beast than man.

She recalled a patient who had been incarcerated in an insane asylum where she had been nursing. This man, who had killed his wife and her sister, had been deemed to suffer from sexual insanity. She clearly remembered the doctors saying that those afflicted with this disorder preferred stabbing or suffocation as their method of murder. This particular patient had used a knife to wreak terrible damage to his victims.

"Here lad, tell us more," a man shouted from the crowd, snapping Mary's attention back to the present.

"Aye, who did it? Did the coppers catch the fiend?" Other voices joined in demanding answers.

Mary knew that many of the people gathered here were dependent upon whatever tidbit of information the newsvendor disclosed, for illiteracy was common in varying degrees. Therefore, any news that they could glean by word of mouth was invaluable.

The newsvendors, of course, took advantage of this fact. Holding court in the middle of a busy intersection, they waited for a suitable crowd to gather and would then proclaim the most sensational stories that caught their fancy; the worse the crime, the better for the news selling business. The crowds clamoring for details were given just enough to tantalize but not satisfy their curiosity until enough people were enticed into buying the newspaper to find out for themselves.

"Now, ladies and gents," the vendor cried. "You might want to get the answers to your burning questions by purchasing a newspaper. Get 'em while you can. Everyone wants to know about the gruesome murder in Whitechapel."

Mary pushed through the crowd, jostling for a position close to the newsvendor. Eventually, she obtained her copy and, fighting her way out of the mob, fled to a less congested area where she could read the story with minimal distraction.

"Mother of God," she gasped as she finished reading. "What is the world coming to?" She thought of the many whores who frequented the East End. They came to the infirmary only when they were too ill to walk the streets. Daily she witnessed the ravages wrought upon them. Many were so weak from malnutrition caused by alcohol abuse that they could barely maintain their balance, often collapsing to the floor of the casualty room.

She understood why her friend Emma was so angered by the injustices these women suffered, but being older and of a less tolerant disposition, she dealt with her own frustration by rationalizing that the women were themselves responsible for their sorry plights. Granted, life was hard, more so for some than others. Still, respectable employment for women was available. Her own mother had worked as a seamstress for as long as Mary could remember. Except for a very few, Mary believed, women had the choice to avoid the streets. All they had to do was stay away from the alcohol, and they could be spared a similar fate to the unidentified victim of the most brutal assault in Mary's memory.

As she folded the newspaper and continued her walk home, her mood now subdued, she wondered fleetingly whether she might have ever encountered the murdered woman at the infirmary.

CHAPTER 7

The train rocked gently along the tracks, its rhythmic cadence exerting a soothing effect on the sole and weary occupant of the carriage. The young man closed his eyes, allowing himself a few moments' respite. The journey abroad had been long. He was glad to be returning to London. He stretched his legs, his six-foot frame settling comfortably in his seat.

There was no mistaking the fact that Andrew Hewitt-Brown was a gentleman. His stylish and elegant attire notwithstanding, he exuded a quiet self-confidence and strength of character, which had little to do with his privileged status and much to do with his remarkable self-possession. He was clearly a man comfortable with himself, yet not in the least self-absorbed, unlike so many of his class. On the contrary, he expressed a keen interest in many subjects and enjoyed the company of his contemporaries. A quick smile and keen wit made him an attraction at social events and soirees, as did his good looks.

Although recently he'd sported a mustache, he was now clean shaven, and his fair hair was worn rather short. His features were sharp and bold; cleft chin, aquiline nose, and generous mouth. His most striking feature, his eyes, were an unusual slate gray color. His gaze was intense and often penetrating, disconcerting to those who sought to conceal things from him. This quality afforded him much success in business, for others found it difficult indeed to deceive him.

His sense of humor was notorious, if not at times irreverent. His charm was an innate part of his character, as was his candor, although this last quality was not always appreciated. But he made no apologies, believing if others asked questions or solicited his opinions, they inevitably wished for the unequivocal truth. Those who were his friends or colleagues held him in high esteem. Many aspired to that friendship, but due to his discerning nature, few were granted that privilege. At ease in business and social circles, Hewitt-Brown was able to discourse knowledgeably on a diversity of issues.

He was well educated and well-traveled. Nevertheless, he also cherished his solitude. Craving opportunity for reflection and quiet contemplation, he would frequently withdraw from social functions for days and occasionally weeks at a time. Those who knew him well respected this behavior. They never questioned him, somehow recognizing that there was an aspect of himself which he deliberately withheld from others.

Now, still with eyes closed, he smiled, allowing his thoughts to turn, as they often did, to Emma Hollander, the woman he loved dearly and desired to make his wife. He applauded her enthusiasm and passion for life, her dedication to the diseased poor of London's East End. Her conviction that compassion and care could penetrate even the toughest skin of those impoverished ones was admirable, if somewhat naïve by most standards.

However, Andrew knew differently. For people such as Emma, natural healers, this task was possible to achieve. More than that, it was necessary to allow them that opportunity, for if denied, they would remain emotionally and spiritually unfulfilled. He respected that some, her parents, for example, perceived this commitment as evidence of a willful and stubborn disposition. Emma had confided to him that her parents' lack of understanding of the value of her work in Whitechapel was a source of deep disappointment to her. They viewed her decision to nurse in that district with disapproval, hoping that with maturity, she would come to her senses and engage in a more worthy pursuit.

They had no quarrel with her choice of profession—nursing as embodied by Florence Nightingale was a vocation with noble and selfless aspirations. They simply would have preferred that her patients belonged to the upper well to do class of society. It was incomprehensible that their daughter should choose to work in such an unsavory and often dangerous environment. Therefore, Emma maintained somewhat of a distance with her parents, knowing she could rely upon them if necessary, but hoping that in time they came to accept her decision. She found engaging in futile arguments a most disagreeable task.

Andrew was aware that nursing was a vocation which had beckoned strongly to Emma since childhood. He supported her passion for her work, recognizing her as one possessed with the qualities to nurture and assist the sick of spirit as well as body. She was able to guide them in the healing process, no matter the ailment, whether the result was a complete cure or the acceptance of their affliction.

He had witnessed firsthand Emma's comfort and quiet strength when she administered to his own mother two years ago. It was a time in Henrietta Hewitt-Brown's life when both physical and spiritual strength were at their nadir. Plagued by chronic pain and weakness, his mother had despaired of recovering her vitality. Her physicians were puzzled, unable to provide a suitable diagnosis. They eventually concluded that at the age of sixty, she was more than likely a victim of the afflictions of advancing age. They had suggested that she resign herself to being a semi-invalid, engaging in only those activities which did not cause her undue distress.

This was a devastating blow to a woman of Henrietta's character. Throughout her married life, she played an active role in social crusades and charitable causes, dedicating much of her time and energy to advocating social reforms for women of less fortunate means. Consequently, Henrietta, struggling with the assault on her sense of purpose, withdrew into a self-pitying shell. She became self-absorbed and demanding, begrudging her family's refusal to accept her capitulation to defeat. Anger was now the feeling which motivated her, and she flew into a rage whenever her husband and children challenged her defeatist behavior.

Even Andrew, who among four children was closest to his mother, grew intolerant of her black moods. No amount of humor or cajoling succeeded in alleviating her despair. Soon, the once closely knit family relationship began to unravel.

Then, at Andrew's insistence, Henrietta's physician had arranged through the London Hospital to engage a private duty nurse. It was the hope of her concerned son that an independent party, someone outside of the family unit, might be beneficial to Henrietta's recovery. Thus, Emma, fresh out of nurse's training, was selected. Henrietta got along with her from the beginning, appreciating the young woman's kind and gracious nature.

It wasn't long before Henrietta asked her nurse to move in with the Hewitt-Browns under the pretense that it would be more convenient for Emma if she didn't have to travel to and from her parents' home. Wisely, Emma recognized the threat of her patient becoming dependent upon her and politely declined the offer. She was attentive to Henrietta's needs, and at the same time, encouraged her to perform as many tasks as she was able for herself.

She assisted Henrietta in exercising her aching swollen limbs, helped her to walk along the corridors in the house twice and three times a day, and applied soothing poultices afterwards to relieve the strain of sore muscles. All the while, Emma talked to her patient, offering gentle support and reassurance when Henrietta's spirits faltered. She suggested that they keep a written record to mark Henrietta's progress in all activities, concrete evidence to prove that she was indeed getting stronger. With much skepticism, Henrietta agreed, but as the days and weeks passed, she grew more enthusiastic as she accomplished goal after goal.

Andrew observed his mother's transformation with pleasure, noting her steadily increasing physical vigor and emotional vitality, and he recognized Emma's formidable healing abilities, although she herself was blithely unaware of their existence. They were such an innate part of her that she failed to recognize them as special and unique. Her charm and beauty, her generous and loving nature, captivated him beyond words. The first time he set eyes upon her, he knew she was the woman he desired above all others.

After Henrietta's recovery, when Emma was no longer employed by the Hewitt-Browns, he began a gentle courtship, and to his delight, Emma returned his sentiments. They had been romantically involved ever since and just recently had become engaged to be married. No date had been set for nuptials.

Andrew wisely discerned that Emma was still restless, yearning to fulfill a purpose which presented itself as a daunting challenge of caring for the sick and most destitute inhabitants of London. It would be imprudent and ultimately damaging to Emma's growth was he to distract her from her Whitechapel phase by pressuring her to marry. She was where she was needed, where her destiny had decreed she should be.

Thus he bided his time. He was not certain exactly what manner of events would unfold, but he knew Emma was to experience a momentous challenge to her beliefs about herself and her world and that her fortitude would be tested to the utmost degree. He vowed to be there to support and guide her through whatever fate held in store for both of them.

CHAPTER 8

Rain was falling in the warm London evening as Andrew's hansom stopped in front of the family home. It had begun to rain just as his train pulled into the station. He descended from the cab and moved up the steps to his front door, and was about to insert his key in the lock when the door was opened by Alice, the housekeeper, who had been with the family since the children were young.

"Why, Alice, you must have a sixth sense," he exclaimed.

A smile spread across the older woman's face. "I only wish, Mr. Hewitt-Brown. Alas, I must confess it was the sound of the horses' hooves which alerted me."

"Your hearing is as acute as ever," Andrew remarked as he entered the large foyer.

Welcome light glowed softly from two sconces on opposite walls.

"I remember as a child, how you always caught me whenever I tried to sneak outside at night, no matter how quiet I thought I was."

"Oh yes, and you with the surprised expression on your face pretending you were only getting a drink of water or using the lavatory." Alice chuckled fondly at the memory.

Andrew smiled as well. "But you always knew better, Alice. There was no fooling you. Still, I appreciated the fact that you never told my parents."

"Well now, Mr. Hewitt-Brown," Alice responded in a conspiratorial hush. "What would life be without our little secrets to spice it up?"

"Well said, Alice."

Andrew removed his lightweight coat and handed it, along with his hat, to the housekeeper.

"I trust things have been quiet here."

"Relatively speaking, sir, Mr. Hewitt-Brown is as busy as ever with his political meetings. I heard him saying to Mrs. Hewitt-Brown the other day that things were starting to get worrisome again in the East End. But as far as I can tell, it has never really settled down ever since the riots last year."

"And how is Mother?"

"Her usual self. Run off her feet, she is." The housekeeper shook her head. "I don't mind saying I don't know how she has time for all those causes, but she seems to thrive on it."

Andrew smiled. "Dear old Mother," he said fondly. "One can always count on her to be in the thick of the fight." He yawned and excused himself. "I must be more tired than I thought. How long have I been away?"

"Nearly eight weeks, sir."

"Eight! I have lost complete track of time. And how are my sister and her brood?"

"Miss Amanda is fine." Alice's face lit up. "And the children are such dears. Why just the other day, Master Robin—"

"Andrew, is that you, darling?" Henrietta Hewitt-Brown's voice beckoned from the sitting room at the end of the corridor.

Andrew raised his eyebrows and glanced at the housekeeper. "Excuse me, Alice. I shall hear of Master Robin's exploits another time." He proceeded to walk along the corridor. "Yes, Mother, I'm home," he called.

Henrietta sat in her favorite seat, a large sprawling armchair of deep burgundy velvet. Although her pose was relaxed, there was a regal air about her. Indeed, Henrietta could trace her lineage back far enough to have discovered an ancestral link to royalty, of which she was quite proud.

She stretched out a hand to her son, her fingers long and tapered. "I am so glad you're home." She was a handsome woman approaching sixty-three years. Her silver hair retained some golden highlights. In her youth, she had been as blonde as her son. In fact, the resemblance between mother and son was pronounced. He had inherited her fine bone structure and patrician features. As with Andrew, her eyes were most striking—piercing as her son's, and the same steel gray color. At five-feet-eight inches, she was tall for a woman, her figure lean and angular.

Andrew bent to embrace her. "You're looking well, Mother."

She gazed at him intently. "And you, my son, look tired. I trust your journey was productive."

He shrugged non-committally. "More or less. Is Father still out?"

Henrietta glanced at the grandfather's clock in the corner beside the mantel. "He should be home shortly. He is attending a lot of those council sessions of late."

"So Alice mentioned."

"Yes, well, at least it keeps him occupied." She waved her hand dismissively, much as she might have had they been discussing her husband's penchant for gardening. Andrew chuckled as he poured himself a cognac from the drinks cabinet.

"Emma came to visit today."

"Oh, yes." A tender smile graced his lips. "And how is my love?"

"She looks tired, too. I think she works too hard, but there is no telling her that."

"Don't I know it," Andrew murmured, taking a seat opposite his mother. "She will do what she must."

"Yes, she is willful and determined, there is no doubt." A frown creased Henrietta's brow. "She was quite distressed, actually. One of the local prostitutes was murdered last night in Whitechapel. Found in an alleyway with her throat cut from ear to ear; a ghastly business indeed."

Andrew stared thoughtfully into his drink. "Hmm. Was the woman perchance a patient of hers?"

"Not as far as I am aware. But Emma did say she knew who the woman was; had seen her quite often about the neighborhood.

This murder has shocked most of London with its brutality."

"Understandably so. Has the murderer been apprehended?"

"According to the newspaper reports, he has not. Scotland Yard is apparently without a clue," replied Henrietta sardonically.

Andrew frowned. "Every perpetrator of a crime, no matter how skilled, leaves at least one clue at the scene. The trick, of course, is to recognize it."

"Yes. Well dear, unfortunately for us, the men of Scotland Yard are not possessed of your superior intellect," Henrietta said in complete seriousness. "If they were, there would be a lot more criminals in prison than about the streets."

Andrew raised his eyebrows. "You haven't confidence in the Yard, then?"

Henrietta sighed. "If this murder had occurred anywhere but the East End, then perhaps I would. But the detectives of Scotland Yard have no more affinity than anyone else for that district. Ever since the riots last year, they have been keeping their noses well clear of Whitechapel. One can only suppose they must be somewhat vexed to have been called in by the local constabulary."

Andrew pursed his lips thoughtfully. "Scotland Yard has some very capable investigators. I wager that they should solve the crime before long." His eyes clouded. "But it is unfortunate that Emma is upset. I shall call on her tomorrow."

"Oh, do, Andrew. She's a strong girl, yet I can't help worrying about her like I would my own daughter. Whitechapel is so unsafe, as this incident last night highlights all too well. In spite of all her bravado, she needs the protection of a man such as you." A troubled look came into Henrietta's eyes. "I have been experiencing disturbing dreams for the last couple of weeks. Nothing concrete, just a collection of impressions and images, but sometimes the uneasiness carries over into wakefulness. I find myself feeling apprehensive, yet for no clear identifiable reason."

Andrew listened carefully to his mother's words. "Dreams often alert us to situations our waking minds won't allow us to examine. I would pay attention to these dreams, Mother, for you and I both know the power and truth which they contain." He laid his empty cognac glass on the table and arose. "As far as Emma is concerned, don't fret, for I shall see her tomorrow and hopefully bring a smile to her face. I made you a promise when Emma started working in Whitechapel that no harm would come to her. I fully intend to honor that promise. Now, Mother, I bid you good night, for I am indeed weary." He kissed his mother's forehead.

Henrietta waited until he reached the doorway. "Andrew?" He turned to face her. She stared at him as if searching his face for something. A sober look remained in her eyes. "How is Pradeep?"

Andrew sighed. "His spirit is stronger than ever, although his body grows weaker by the day. He believes his time in this world is close to an end, and he is correct."

"I am truly sorry to hear that," Henrietta said. "He is nightly in my prayers."

Andrew smiled gently before leaving the room and quietly closing the door behind him.

***

Henrietta sat quietly in her chair, listening to her son's footsteps retreat up the stairs. She sighed, staring into the crackling fire, and allowed her thoughts to drift back to the past to her children in their formative years in India.

As always, her thoughts first came to rest upon Andrew. From the start, he had been and remained the most interesting and enigmatic person she had ever known. This perception was no idle fondness of a devoted mother, but a sentiment echoed by many who had met her son through the years.

Since early childhood, Andrew had been different from any other child. True, he played the usual childhood games with his brothers and sisters. He engaged in the same daily routines as the rest of the family, but the air of self-possession he exuded was exceptional. He seemed almost eerily independent, quickly learning to care for himself on a physical level. As far as his emotional development was concerned, it pained Henrietta to recognize how little support he required from either of his parents. It was as if he were already an adult, albeit, in a child's body, Henrietta often thought.

She could almost believe that he had merely adopted the guise of a child, mimicking the appropriate behaviors, all the while devoting his thoughts to issues which had nothing to do with the trappings of childhood. Often times he was preoccupied and withdrawn. Henrietta could come upon him during one of these reflective states and pause, fascinated by this strange enigma that was her flesh and blood.

Perched in the window seat of the drawing-room, staring out at the lush garden of their house in Bombay, Andrew would be completely still. No muscle twitched to signal movement; even his breathing was barely detectable. He seemed to be in a trance state, unaware of anything outside of himself. Softly, as not to startle him, Henrietta would call his name, not once but usually two or three times. Finally, he would turn to her, an unfathomable expression in his eyes. In these moments, he looked older, graver, with a wisdom and awareness no child should possess.

Unease would clutch at her heart, and a vague fear settle at the base of her spine. Whether this fear was for her son or because of him, she could not decide. She knew only that at these times, the beloved son to whom she had given life was as alien to her as the dusky skinned natives of this country to which they'd moved. Then he would smile at her, and suddenly he was Andrew again, her charmingly precocious gifted son. Sometimes she wondered if living in India had cast a spell over her, but that was before she learned the truth about her son.

Andrew was the first of the Hewitt-Brown children to be born in India. Amanda, four years his senior, had been born at home in England, but when Henrietta was pregnant with their second child, George had decided that if he wished his import business to bring in more profits, he should move his family temporarily to India.

Although less than pleased with this news, ever the loyal wife, Henrietta, agreed to travel. The risk to her pregnancy was considered minimal. She was still in the early stage, and any ocean sickness she might experience on the voyage could not be worse than the bouts of nausea which daily plagued her. Besides, George assured her that she would have access to the very best English midwives and physicians in Bombay. In fact, she would almost certainly feel like she'd never left English soil.

This, of course, proved untrue, the intense heat alone a constant reminder of how foreign a land this was. She did find, to her relief and delight, many of the English amenities and luxuries to which she was accustomed.

Their house on the outskirts of Bombay was airy and spacious, built in a sprawling plantation style, designed to minimize the effects of the extreme humidity and extensive erosion caused by the heavy monsoon rains. The servants, most of whom spoke English, were reserved and respectful. The Hewitt-Browns were graciously and effortlessly embraced by the thriving British society so that in some ways, indeed, one could believe that a portion of England had been transported to this exotic land.

However, tragedy struck soon after their arrival when Henrietta went into premature labor and produced a stillborn boy. Devastated, she fell into a depression which seemed interminable, made even more difficult by living in a strange country far from the comforting surroundings of home. Eventually, her grief ran its course, receding to a dull ache in place of the sharp pain of the initial loss.

Slowly, she began to show interest in managing the household and spent more time with Amanda. The little girl had been cared for throughout her mother's paralyzing depression by her nursemaid, Cecilia. Prior to leaving England, Henrietta had insisted on engaging an English nursemaid to care for Amanda and any subsequent children. This was somewhat contrary to the fashion of the day, wherein most British families living in India employed local women to act as amahs for their children.

The following year, on May 4, 1857, Andrew was born. Life flourished for the Hewitt-Browns. George's import/export business, which shipped tea and spices to England, was very successful. Amanda and Andrew were healthy and contented children. Henrietta was delighted with her family and devoted herself to various social causes, such as improving educational opportunities for Indian children.

The subsequent years were highlighted by the birth of two more sons; Malcolm in 1860 and Reginald three years later. At the age of fourteen, Amanda was sent to finishing school back in England. Andrew set foot in his home country for the first time at the age of sixteen and was admitted to Oxford College. In time the family business was so well established that George felt it was time to return to England. He had carefully selected his most capable Indian employees to continue the work and set up his younger sons to manage the business. Over several months, George completed the transactions necessary to ensure the smooth operation of the company.

After graduating with honors from Oxford, Andrew joined his father and brothers, quickly becoming indispensable to the business. The long-term plan was for Andrew to assume control of the company after George retired, with his brothers continuing to manage the day to day operations.

Henrietta and George joined Amanda and her new husband in England in 1880, this time to stay. Andrew traveled back and forth between England and the subcontinent. His ambitious plan to boost productivity without increasing business costs was pronounced brilliant by his brothers. They wasted no time in implementing the creative strategies proposed by their older sibling. Hewitt-Brown's ideas were unerringly right and always profitable. Reginald occasionally teased him, calling him the oracle of business management.

Andrew tolerated his brother's good natured banter, but when Malcolm tried to extract information as to how he formulated these ideas, he always deflected the conversation, deftly avoiding the avid curiosity of his siblings. Thus he remained as he forever had been, an enigma to his brothers, albeit one they admired intensely. If truth be told, they were more than a little awed by Andrew's pure intellect as well as his elusiveness. They had long ago accepted that they would never really understand, never truly know their older brother. Yet his qualities, especially his staunch loyalty to family, were sufficient in their eyes to mitigate his eccentricities.

In actual fact, Andrew's visits to his brothers were only part of the reason for his sojourns to India. His main purpose was to spend time with a much-esteemed friend, a man whose teaching and wisdom he respected more than that of any other—a man who possessed the key which unlocked the mysteries of Andrew's identity and his destiny.

CHAPTER 9

Twelve-year-old Andrew's first encounter with Pradeep Bhirati occurred during one of the boy's many forays to the bustling city center of Bombay. Sometimes, when he was supposed to be at the British school with the other children, he would cut classes to spend half a day roaming the colorful streets of the city. Bombay was vibrant, alive with a plethora of sights and a rich variety of olfactory experiences which threatened to overwhelm the senses. The heady aroma of exotic spices such as cinnamon, cardamom, and tamarind was tempered by the pungent odor of excrement, both animal and human. One could walk past a street stall offering the most mouth-watering delicacies, only to find one's self about to step into a fresh steaming pile of human waste by the side of the road.

Andrew was captivated by the alluring and dichotomous aspects of Bombay. Every time he ventured into its depths, he discovered a new and titillating experience. He felt connected to the city, keenly aware of its vibrating hum that surrounded him. He had stumbled upon the secret heart of Bombay and marveled at its unique rhythm.

In later years, he was to appreciate this special quality as peculiar to individual centers as fingerprints were to humans. Each city exhibited its own personality. Some radiated a welcoming energy, receptive to the stranger who wished to embrace their wonders. Others, dark and brooding, were inhospitable and forbidding places, usually visited by those with more sinister appetites. This was not to deny that Bombay lacked a sordid side. To be sure, it contained its share of unhealthy and desperately poor areas, but compared to its dangerously corrupt sister city, Calcutta, it was less pernicious indeed.

One afternoon during one of his ventures to Bombay, Andrew happened upon a game of chance being played in the street. The players were men, with a few late adolescent aged boys. Officially, children were prohibited from participating in gambling; however, the authorities rarely intervened in these activities, rampant as they were. The good citizens of Bombay, it seemed, did not discriminate against children gambling, especially when a child's pockets bulged with rupees, as Andrew's plainly did.

These men were oblivious to the fact that this particular twelve-year-old was not as naïve as the average child. In truth, Andrew possessed a keen competitive edge and remarkable poise and judgment, especially when it came to card games. However, he did not limit himself to cards but explored all manner of gambling. He already had a fierce reputation among his school mates, for his uncanny abilities had enabled him to amass a formidable collection of prized possessions from those unfortunate enough to have challenged him and lost.

So it came as no surprise when the men on the street accepted Andrew into their gaming circle. The game itself was a modern variation of an old Indian pastime. Andrew had never played it, although he had previously watched a game or two as a spectator. An astute observer and avid learner, he required little time to familiarize himself with the nuances of the game.

Curiously, he paid little or no attention to his fellow players. It was the game itself on which he focused. His mind sought and found the subtleties and rhythm of the game. He deciphered the emerging patterns as he felt the flow of energy in and around him, absorbing its cadence. Like a space suddenly opening up in his mind, clarity shone. He was illuminated by knowledge. Patterns unfolded with startling predictability, revealing their secrets. It was then simply a matter of acting upon this knowledge and waging his bet accordingly.

Whenever he followed these intuitions, victory was assured, no matter the challenge. Sometimes, though, he refrained from using this skill, for there was a disadvantage to having the ability to win all the time. For one, it didn't do to discourage his opponents. It was important for them to believe they had a chance of being victorious, and he did not wish to gain a reputation as a cheater. Therefore, from time to time, he would lose a game.

This particular day, whether it was the intense noonday sun beating down on the back of his head or the natural exuberance and carelessness of youth, Andrew permitted his judgment to falter. He became absorbed with the game within the game, challenging himself to see how many consecutive rounds he could win.

The result, of course, was a group of disgruntled and hostile men whose deflated pride led them to the one reasonable explanation of how a mere boy, and a foreigner at that, had soundly whipped them at their own game. Obviously, the little wretch was cheating. Somehow he had managed to deceive and swindle them out of their hard earned rupees. One of the men was especially irate.

"Scoundrel!" he yelled, waving a threatening fist at the boy. "You think you can cheat us and get away with it?"

Andrew's gaze was steady, his voice cool. "Sir, you are mistaken. I did not cheat."

"Aha, and a liar too is he," the man challenged, looking at the others for support. "I have heard that Englishmen have honor. Apparently, that is something your father failed to teach you."

Andrew's face darkened with anger, yet he stood his ground, keeping his voice calm. "On the contrary, sir, it is you who show weakness by failing to recognize the truth. Your pride prevents you from accepting defeat at the hands of a superior player."

A few of the men looked taken aback by the boy's temerity, and some chuckled, but the angry man spat on the ground in disgust.

"Ah, as Siva is my witness, were you not the son of a foreigner I would —"

"Careful, Sharma," one of the others cautioned. "I would not be so quick to utter such words. Let us accept our losses and be done with it."

He turned a stern countenance towards Andrew. "Go now, boy, but be warned that you are no longer welcome to join us."

Without another word, Andrew turned and walked away, silently chastising himself for being such a fool. Now he would never again be accepted by any street players. The men would spread word of him, and he would be shunned, treated as a pariah by every street gambler in the city. Head down, he trudged along the street, wrestling with his anger.

"Well now, an interesting situation. What are you going to do?" A well-modulated voice spoke to him from a shadowed doorway to his left.

Frowning, Andrew squinted up into the gloom. "Who's there?"

A man emerged from the shadows, tall and slender, dressed in finely woven Indian attire. His dark-skinned face was striking; high cheekbones and chiseled plains, his eyes deep set and velvety brown. A short beard failed to conceal a strong cleft chin. He was perhaps thirty-five years old with a distinctly patrician air about him. He wore his turban like a crown. He bowed, left arm sweeping in an expansive gesture, conveying a subtle irony which did not escape the boy's attention.

"I am Pradeep Bhirati, Master Hewitt-Brown."

Andrew started. "Sir, how do you know my name?"

The man smiled. "Your family is held in high regard in this city, and there are many things I know about you," he replied in an exquisitely cultivated tone. The British inflection was quite pronounced. It was the voice of a well-educated Indian gentleman of high caste, one accustomed to privilege. Yet, something about the man contradicted this conclusion. It was as though he were a brilliant actor playing a role, a disguise which concealed his true and secret nature.

Andrew was wary yet intrigued. He raised a skeptical brow.

"For instance, I know that you just walked away from the game with all of those men's earnings and that you used deception to win."

The boy flushed angrily. "I did not cheat them!" he exclaimed.

"Ah, I did not say you cheated. I merely inferred that you employed superior skills of which they were completely ignorant. Skills they could not have believed one as young as you could possess. Therefore, they were deceived only by their lack of imagination."

Andrew's eyes narrowed suspiciously. "And just how would you know that?"

The man smiled, displaying startlingly white teeth. "Suffice it to say that I possess abilities similar to yours. Come, walk with me a bit, and I shall explain." He indicated for the boy to fall into step beside him.

"Where are we going?"

Bhirati glanced down at him. "To my establishment, my place of business. You shall see." As they proceeded down the dusty road, he began to speak. "I watched you with those others back there. I have seen you engaged in similar activities throughout the city. For some time now, I have been acutely aware of your presence." He looked appraisingly at his listener. "Does that make you uneasy?"

"Should it?" Andrew countered sharply. After a moment, he shook his head. "I think curious would be an accurate word to describe my emotional state."

Bhirati nodded. "Yes, of course. What have you to be anxious about when it comes to others? Your innate superiority protects you for the moment. But it shan't always be so. Greater challenges await you, which you are not ready to master. However, the time approaches when you must choose your path."

Taken aback by these words delivered in this matter of fact tone, the boy faltered in stride. He made no attempt to hide his consternation as he turned to face the stranger. "Who are you?" he once again demanded harshly.

Bhirati dismissed the question with a wave of his hand. He hadn't slowed his pace when the boy abruptly halted; therefore, Andrew was obliged to move quickly to make up the distance between them. As he pulled up along side Bhirati, the man resumed speaking, his tone conversational.

"So tell me why today you chose not to use your customary discretion while gambling?" He glanced at his companion out of the corner of his eye. "You have always been careful to ensure that, while successful, you were not overly fortunate, even purposely allowing others from time to time to claim victory though you knew you could win if you so desired. Today, however, you were unwise, and that carelessness led to your unmasking. No great harm ensued; a few bruises to the self-esteem of those men, but it could have been worse."

He paused, allowing his words to sink in. "You thought they reacted in such a manner because they thought you were a cheat, which is true. But how do you think they would have responded if they had any real suspicion of the truth?" Bhirati had allowed his intense gaze to focus directly on the boy. "They would have killed you. Stoned you to death where you stood before you would have had a chance to properly defend yourself. Men instinctively fear what they don't understand, and they envy that which they cannot control or possess themselves.

"Fear and envy are dangerous foes, and you would do well to remember that, young master. And do not console yourself with the idea that that scenario would be the worst that could happen. Imagine if you were confronting others who possessed similar skills to yours, for rest assured, they do exist. Your behavior would have alerted them to the presence of your own abilities, and they would consider you a threat to be dispatched. You, my boy, must be on your guard at all times, for you can be certain that if I know of your existence, so, unfortunately, do others, those who bear you great ill will.

"You're unique, a fact with which you are already familiar; however, even you do not recognize as yet the potential of the wonderful special abilities you possess, abilities others would avidly destroy. I know you think you have sufficient knowledge to protect yourself, and while you can circumvent certain dangers without fully realizing or understanding the process, many other perils exist against which you have inadequate defenses. I, young master, have been appointed to be your protector and your teacher if you so accept."

Andrew scowled at the man, his skepticism more blatant now. "Appointed," he echoed derisively. "Appointed by whom? How do I know you are not simply a madman trying to lure me into your lunatic delusions, or conversely, one of the nameless enemies you so eloquently describe scheming to gain my trust so as to do me harm?"

Bhirati was unperturbed. "Your questions please me, as they indicate your thoughts are traveling in the right direction. You have every reason to be suspicious of me based upon what I have told you. You must be wary of others. They must always earn your trust. It has always been thus, although you do not remember. As you do not recall that it was you, young master, who appointed me to be your teacher." He interrupted Andrew's bewildered protestations to add, "The time fast approaches when you shall be called upon to do your work."

"Work?" Andrew echoed. "I shall most likely assist my father in his business after I have completed my education in England."

Bhirati laughed shortly. "Yes, you will learn the appropriate skills and behavior to survive in this world and to prosper in it, I daresay. But it is not of your function in man's world that I speak, but of your true purpose, the reason you possess such extraordinary abilities as reading others' thoughts, shaping future events, access to knowledge which is forbidden and beyond the grasps of ordinary men."

The boy's gray eyes were as hard as flint. "Sir, this is the last time I shall pose this question before I walk away. Who are you, and what do you want with me?"

Pradeep Bhirati regarded the boy with pursed lips. Then he nodded to himself as if arriving at a decision. "I am from the tribe, or clan if you prefer, of spiritual beings — the Excala. The quest for knowledge is perpetual amongst my kind. I can provide assistance and guidance to you in the refinement of your skills."

Andrew shook his head, lips thinly compressed. "Am I supposed to believe that you, a prosperous businessman, also a member of some mystic Indian sect, are offering your services as a teacher to me, the son of an affluent English family?" His expression grew indignant. "Sir, you insult me by presuming a naiveté I do not possess."

Bhirati laughed again with genuine amusement. "No, no, no, you misunderstand me, Master Andrew. I think you far from naïve, but until you have developed certain skills, you shall remain vulnerable to your enemies."

"My enemies! You keep speaking of my enemies. Tell me who they are, these phantoms of the night. Am I to assume that you are the only one who can assist me, whatever that means?"

"Your discernment is correct. I do not expect you to understand all at once. I also realize that you require proof to affirm what I say." His eyes narrowed, growing darker, although no shift in the sunlight occurred. "I can tell you something no one else can. I can tell you about you, your ancestry and the wonders of magic.

"I know about your so-called dreams, the ones you experience nightly when in your sleep you travel to a mystical realm. You cannot name this place, yet it is achingly familiar and comforting. It feels like home in a way this world never will. The natural beauty of this realm is equaled by the profound harmony and serenity that permeate every aspect of it. Your heart swells with joy as you gaze upon its wonders. There is a gate you come upon of simple wrought iron, yet intricately woven with figures and symbols of many varieties. You know that each of these represents a story, a tale of this wondrous world, yet you have not the means to decipher them. So you stand by the gate knowing not for whom or what you wait, knowing only that one day that gate shall open before you and usher you into what lies beyond."

By the time Bhirati had finished uttering these words, Andrew's face had drained of all color, leaving even his lips with an ashen hue. The silence lengthened as boy and man locked gazes, the one with a multitude of questions, the other perhaps with the answers.

Gathering his wits about him, Andrew whispered, "I have

never spoken of my dream to anyone. How could you know?"

"Because it is not a dream. It is your home. It is my home also." A bittersweet smile lit his features. "It is a world which, for now, exists only in our spiritual memory, which means we remember with our hearts, not our minds. Only those who belong to our clan, the Excala, may journey to that realm, for in a far distant time, it belonged to us and we to it.

"We are not of man's world, bound by physical restrictions. We are beings of spirit and magic. We are Excala. Not, as you thought, an obscure 'Indian sect.' In fact, nothing at all in connection with India or any other place in this world." He scrutinized the boy with his keen gaze. "We possess many abilities referred to as 'magic,' which our human counterparts lack. We may leave the physical plane at will, protecting ourselves spiritually whenever we desire. This knowledge has always resided within you, Andrew. You simply required someone to bring it to your awareness. If left to your own devices, you would have retrieved the memory at some point, but having a teacher to assist you expedites the process."

"Are you saying that we were destined to meet?" asked the boy.

"I assure you that destiny had nothing to do with it. We encountered one another because I deliberately searched for you."

"But how did you know I existed, let alone where to look for me?" Andrew queried, intrigued.

"You have numerous questions now, and just as you think you have all the answers, more questions will arise. You shall have a lifetime of questions to keep you occupied. The short answer to your question is that my function—my destiny, if you will—is to seek out other Excala, also known as Insiders, and assist them in their spiritual development. Not all Excala, of course, but certain ones who are destined to play a significant role in mankind's development. I shall explain this in greater detail at a later date. I teach the mysteries of creation. If you permit me, I shall guide you in pursuit of knowledge and the enhancement of your magic.

I will also act as your protector, for your spiritual journey will be fraught with peril. If you wish, you may accompany me now to my establishment, where we can speak without distractions."

"You said earlier that I was the one who appointed you to be my teacher. But how can that be since I never met you before today?" Andrew asked perplexed.

"That answer, you shall know in time. Come now, if you will." Bhirati set off once more at a brisk pace.

"One last question then," Andrew interjected. "When shall my lessons begin?"

Bhirati's expression was enigmatic. "They have already begun."

CHAPTER 10

Emma paced distractedly along the length of her sitting room and back again. Her fiancé had sent a message that morning that he had returned from his trip and wished to call on her today. She had agreed and was looking forward to the appointed time. However, as the morning progressed, she felt increasingly ill at ease. This was her day off work, and she had a list of tasks she wished to accomplish, but she had only completed a small portion. It was difficult to focus, to keep her mind on the task at hand. Her thoughts kept straying to the prostitute murdered in Whitechapel two nights ago. Along with most Londoners, Emma was horrified with the savagery of the crime.

The woman, known as Martha Tabram, had had her throat slashed in a deserted laneway. As if that wasn't brutal enough, her assailant had proceeded to mutilate her in unspeakable ways. Although the murder occurred in the early hours of the morning, around three o'clock, there were always nocturnal goings on in Whitechapel. One would have expected at least one person to have heard or seen something of a suspicious nature.

Although she had never attended to the woman at the infirmary, Emma recalled seeing Martha Tabram loitering outside various public houses, often appearing very intoxicated. The woman was well known in the area for her boisterous rowdy nature. Once Emma had assisted her when Martha tripped and almost fell outside the Princess Alice. Martha thanked her and grinning drunkenly, then continued to weave a precarious path along Commercial Street. Emma shuddered as she conjured up an image of the dead woman, alone in the darkness, stripped of dignity, body partially exposed, abdomen slashed by vicious knife strokes. What had Martha Tabram ever done to deserve such a fate?

A knock at the front door below her window startled Emma out of her morbid imaginings. She heard the heavy tread of the landlady, Mrs. Barclay, as she walked to the door and opened it. Her heart soared at the familiar, dear tone of her beloved. Without waiting for the landlady's nasal voice to summon her, she flew out the door and down the stairs and into Andrew's arms.

"Oh my love, I have missed you so much," she cried, snuggling deeper into his embrace despite the disapproving frown of Mrs. Barclay.

"And I have missed you," Andrew murmured, caressing her chestnut curls. "But you are trembling, my dear. Is something the matter?" He held her gently at arm's length, anxiously searching her face.

Tears glistened in Emma's eyes. "It is simply that I am overcome with joy at seeing you," she declared.

"I, too, have looked forward with great anticipation to this moment," he said and smiled tenderly at her.

"Ahem," interjected Mrs. Barclay. "If you would be so kind as to make use of the parlor for your visit." She ushered them to the large room at the front of the house.

"Ah yes, the parlor," Andrew remarked, secretly winking at Emma as they followed the landlady. "I even miss the parlor, it being the site of so many pleasant visits."

Emma suppressed a smile as they entered the room. The furniture, although somewhat shabby, was functional and comfortable. She wondered what Mrs. Barclay would say if she were aware of other visits, those which clandestinely took place in Emma's room when the landlady was asleep. Fortunately, Mrs. Barclay was a heavy sleeper, and Andrew was an agile climber so that gaining entrance to Emma's chamber via the window presented no great challenge. The door closed discreetly behind them, and the sound of Mrs. Barclay's footsteps receded down the hall.

Emma smiled at Andrew as he opened his arms to her. They kissed for long minutes, mouths hungry for one another. Finally, they moved apart and, clasping hands, sat together on the settee.

"Tell me, how was your trip?"

"It was necessary, but I would much rather talk about how you longed for me every single day as I did for you."

Emma closed her eyes in delight. "Oh, my dear, you know I longed for you. My heart ached so; I dreamt of you every night." She opened her eyes and squeezed his hand. "The dream felt so real I thought I could reach out and touch you. I felt comforted and happy."

Andrew smiled and stroked her face with gentle fingers. "I'm glad, Emma. It pleases me that you felt my presence. I sent my love to you every night."

She smiled, eyes aglow. "We have a special bond, you and I. Sometimes I think it is a love like no other."

Andrew nodded, his expression now serious. "You're right, Emma. One day you shall realize how true your words are."

"I know already that my life changed forever the day I met you."

Andrew raised her hand to his lips, softly kissing her knuckles. "Mine too, dear Emma. Both of us have been blessed with this love." He cupped her chin in his hand and stared into her luminous green eyes. "But something is troubling you. I see it in your eyes, hear it in your voice, hiding beneath the pleasure of this moment. What is wrong?"

Emma sighed, momentarily lowering her gaze as Andrew released her chin. "How well you know me, Andrew. It is this foul murder in Whitechapel. You've heard about it?"

"I've read the newspaper accounts."

Emma rose from the settee and began to pace. "It's all so senseless and barbaric," she blurted. "This poor woman. What could she have done to merit such hatred?"

"Hatred?" echoed Andrew.

"Yes," Emma declared emphatically. She stopped pacing and stood in front of the settee. "Oh, the police have some ridiculous theory that she owed money to one of the local gangs, the Hawkston High Pips, and they killed her. But all one has to do is consider the way in which she was murdered to conclude that the crime was motivated by hatred. A gang would have slit her throat, but I can't believe they would mutilate her like that."

Andrew's expression was thoughtful. "An astute observation, Emma. It occurs to me that nursing might not be the best profession for you, after all. It's a pity that women can't join the constabulary, for you should make a fine detective indeed."

Emma looked closely at him to determine whether he was being facetious, but his expression was sober. "The savagery involved suggests to me that whoever did this was not content with simply killing her; he wanted to annihilate her."

Hewitt-Brown considered this statement for a few moments. "Emma, I believe you offer some extraordinary insight into this crime. I, too, do not consider this to be a routine murder, but one that contains some highly unusual aspects. It's true that hatred is a very compelling emotion, capable of inciting men to acts of great ferocity and violence, which then begs the question; why would anyone feel such hatred towards this woman, by all accounts a lowly prostitute merely eking out an existence, one amongst many in this district? Why choose her?"

Emma frowned and shook her head. "That's the question I have puzzled over since I heard the news."

"Unless…." Andrew fixed her with his keen gaze.

"Unless?" Emma prompted.

"Unless she wasn't deliberately chosen," he said. "Maybe it wasn't so much this woman as what she represented."

"You mean someone who has an aversion to prostitutes?" Emma asked.

"That would be a convenient excuse or cover," he mused. "What if there was no other motive than the desire to kill, to cause suffering and terror, by someone who has an aversion, as you say, not to prostitutes in particular, but to life itself?"

Emma stared at him. "I don't understand," she murmured.

"Ah, but I think you do, a little. A glimmer of understanding is there. I see it in your eyes. You don't really wish to consider it, but the more I ponder this idea, the more convinced I am that it is correct. We are talking about true evil."

Emma flinched slightly. "I suppose one could use that term. It's easy to fathom that one capable of inflicting such brutality upon another is acting upon evil intentions. However, you are right that it makes me uncomfortable to dwell on it, for I can't understand, as I might if it were discovered that a raving lunatic committed this murder. And in fact, it appears that most people do think the killer is a madman, at least from the talk I have heard at the infirmary and on the streets."

Andrew nodded. "As you say, the concept of a madman is easier to accept than one who is deliberately evil. It should be interesting to see how Scotland Yard handles the case."

"It should focus more attention on Whitechapel and the problems in the East End," Emma responded. "Perhaps the government, at last, should be persuaded to provide increased services to the poor. A murderer running amok, even in Whitechapel, won't sit well with popular opinion."

"That's possible," Andrew agreed. "So something positive might yet emerge from such a heinous act."

"It should not be so," Emma declared passionately. "Politicians have no right to be apathetic to such a degree that it takes an incident of this shocking nature to stir them to action."

Andrew nodded. "I agree with you. However, I don't believe this trait is exclusive to those in public office. People, in general, are so preoccupied by the minutia of their own lives that they have no concern for others unless something sensational like a murder occurs. The closer it is to their own lives, the more affected they are. The same murder, say in Paris or Bombay or Rome, wouldn't have caused a ripple in London. But when it happens on their own streets, people are uncomfortably reminded of their own mortality."

He regarded Emma's somber expression. "Come now, my love, enough morose musings. It's a glorious late summer day. Let's hail a cab to St. James's Garden and take a stroll through the park. I want to see you smile in the sunshine. We have an entire afternoon and evening to spend together. And tonight, of course, you shall dine with Mother and me."

Emma smiled as she reached for his hand. "It would be a pleasure to forget the woes of Whitechapel for a time. A change of environment and your company shall lighten my heart." Arm in arm, they exited the room.

CHAPTER 11

Weak light from the early morning sun crept through the quiet streets. Whitechapel never truly slumbered, but a brief respite occurred just after the breaking of dawn. Taverns discharged the last customers, some of whom wandered the streets in a drunken haze while others, in a stupor, sprawled in alleyways and courtyards. Tired whores scuttled back to their lairs like night creatures fearful of the harsh daylight and what it might reveal.

Laborers, dock workers, and market vendors ventured out at this early hour in preparation for the long day ahead. Stalls were erected in the marketplace, produce and wares removed from freights and readied for display. Cobblestones rang with the sound of horses' hooves as the animals were led from the stable yards and harnessed to carts.

Emma walked towards the infirmary, enjoying the relative quiet of the city streets. One could almost forget the sordidness and squalor, the cramped ugliness of the buildings. It would not be long before the interlude ended, and Whitechapel would once more burst its seams in a whirlwind of activity.

As she neared the infirmary, she glimpsed a movement out of the corner of her eye. The wrought iron gate was shrouded in darkness. Even so, she was certain that something lurked in the shadows off to her right. Emma had never cared for the imposing front gate. It struck her as vaguely ominous, the gate which might guard the entrance to a prison instead of an infirmary. She often wondered whether if she were ill, she would wish to enter a building whose façade was so intimidating and devoid of comfort.

Why must our hospitals and infirmaries, places where the sick come to heal, be so uninviting and dismal? she thought. Not lacking in imagination, she sometimes fancied that the spirits of those who had died within the infirmary's confines now haunted this very space, warning prospective patients to stay away lest they, too, met with a similar fate.

She stopped in her tracks and stood very still. Her eyes scanned the darkness, searching, trying to penetrate its layers, ears keenly attuned for any sound. The fine hairs on the nape of her neck stood to attention, and she half expected to see a ghostly form gliding towards her. Her heart beat fast. She felt the pulses galloping at her throat. A few moments passed before she dared to speak.

"Who's there?" she demanded with the sharpness of apprehension in her tone. For several seconds there was no reply, then without a sound, a form emerged from the shadows. "Stop right there! Approach no further!" Emma commanded harshly. Poised to run or scream for help, a small sigh of relief escaped her as the figure, heeding her words, halted his approach. "Identify yourself," she ordered.

"If you please, madam, it was not my intention to frighten you," a pleasant male voice responded.

"Indeed, then why are you hiding in the shadows?"

The voice chuckled softly. "I am not hiding. Rather, like you, I should imagine, indulging the opportunity to walk along the streets at such a peaceful hour. It is a unique time of day, and I find it useful to organize my thoughts and plans for the day ahead. In addition, I have the chance to observe the fine architecture of this old building, which is to be my new place of employment as of today."

Still wary, Emma asked, "You are to start work at the infirmary?" Understanding dawned in her eyes. "Then you are the new apprentice physician...."

Her words trailed away as the man left the shadows and approached the gate. He stopped a few feet from Emma and bowed. "John Dennys, miss, at your humble service."

He was of medium build and slender, standing five feet seven inches tall. His brown hair was thick and curly and worn curiously long for the fashion of the day, just brushing his collar. He was clean-shaven, his skin smooth and unmarked, his features even. Remarkably, not only did he still possess all of his teeth, but they appeared intact and were of a healthy white in color. He looked to be about twenty-eight years of age, certainly not more than thirty, although if one were to search the record books, no official birth information would be discovered.

He looked at Emma, dark eyes unfathomable. Then he smiled, a smile that failed to reach his eyes.

For reasons which were puzzling, Emma continued to feel uncomfortable. Perhaps it was simply the shock of the last few minutes affecting her, but Emma was prey to a profound unease in the presence of this stranger. There was no hint of menace or malicious intent emanating from John Dennys, yet Emma felt vaguely threatened. She had to stifle the impulse to flee, to put as much distance as possible between herself and the young physician.

Attempting to regain her composure and return Dennys's smile, she said, "Yes, I was a little startled by your presence, Mr. Dennys. I do not usually encounter others on the infirmary grounds at this early hour."

"I truly regret any discomfort I may have inadvertently caused, Miss...."

"Hollander," Emma replied quickly. "Emma Hollander. I am one of the nurses."

Dennys extended his hand. "It is a pleasure to meet you, Miss Hollander."

Emma hoped he did not notice the brief hesitation before she gingerly put her hand in his. She suppressed the urge to cringe as he held her hand and bowed over it. She bit her lip to conceal the involuntary expression of distaste on her face.

At last, he released her hand, but not before she saw the look in his eye that told her he was fully aware of her unease. Emma felt her color rise and said to herself in vexation, *I must not show any weakness, for here is one who would turn such weakness against me.* She was puzzled by her own thoughts—not the thoughts themselves, but her certainty that they were absolutely true.

She smiled more naturally this time, forcing her apprehension deep down inside.

"I hope you shall find your apprenticeship rewarding, Mr. Dennys. The Whitechapel Infirmary presents some unique challenges."

"I trust that is so, as I look forward to mastering challenges," Dennys replied. "In fact, the bigger the challenge, the more determined I am to conquer it. That was one of the reasons I requested to serve this part of my apprenticeship here in Whitechapel."

What other reasons had you for choosing Whitechapel? Emma wondered. Somehow she was convinced there was a more important yet secret reason for John Dennys's foray into this godforsaken slum land. She slowly retreated from the gentleman in front of her. "Well, I must attend to my duties. I am sure that we shall work together at some point."

"I look forward to that immensely, Miss Hollander," Dennys responded.

Emma had great difficulty turning her back on John Dennys and hurried up the steps to the infirmary doors. An unpleasant shiver ran up her spine, and she quickly shut the door behind her, swallowing the taste of bile in her throat.

CHAPTER 12

Emma finished laying out the instruments on the tray in the post-mortem examination room. No matter how distasteful a procedure, an autopsy was indisputably an excellent opportunity to learn about the intricacies of human anatomy and physiology. Medicine was an intriguing and challenging science, Emma reflected, and the human body a fascinating mystery of complex systems working in harmony to sustain life. This delicate balance was so easily threatened by disease or injury. Any disruption could result in serious, sometimes even irreparable damage to a part of the body or, indeed, the entire being itself.

In opposition to the social dictates of Victorian society, Emma had longed to become a physician. As this goal was not attainable, she had become a nurse instead. While content in her womanhood, there were times when she regretted that her femininity was considered an impediment to achieving her desires. Astute enough to recognize that this widely espoused discrimination was a misjudgment of society rather than a reflection of the limitations of women, she nevertheless was frustrated by the prevalent attitudes towards the feminine portion of society.

And it was not only men who were at fault, she mused, but women as well, particularly those who blindly lived for and through their husbands, having learned at a tender age to suppress their own yearnings. Of course, there were always a few notable exceptions — the so-called freethinkers or radicals, those who questioned and sometimes even rejected the popular tenets of society...men such as Andrew Hewitt-Brown. From the moment they'd met, he treated her with a genuine respect, not the patronizing mix of deference and arrogance most men demonstrated towards women. The majority of men gave the impression that women were considered as treasured but fragile children, requiring protection from the hard realities of the world.

Emma had nothing in common with such women, whose only knowledge of the day to day world came through the carefully filtered information given to them by their husbands. Emma was determined to experience life for herself, not secondhand, even through someone as wonderful as Andrew. And Andrew not only recognized that need in her, but he also respected and encouraged the independent traits of her personality. He regarded her as an equal, was interested in her opinions, and engaged in lively discussions and arguments about a variety of subjects. He never dismissed her inquiries or derided her lack of knowledge in certain areas but provided her with the necessary information. He was so unlike other men, Emma thought. He had the ability to make her feel special, not to just make her think she was.

She only wished that her father might be as opened-minded as her fiancé. Though she loved and respected her father, their relationship was not as close as she would have liked. As a child, she felt cherished and protected by him. But as she grew to womanhood, the willful streak which had induced amusement and indulgent laughs from her parents suddenly became problematic and was denounced as unsuitable for a young lady.

Her parents thankfully had no argument with her choice of profession. Nursing was a respectable employment for a young woman of Emma's social standing. They had expected their daughter to seek employment as a private nurse-come-nanny in an affluent household, but Emma, to their great chagrin, had other designs.

She did not waste her time and her training to be a nursemaid to snotty-nosed children. She wished to be of greater service to society, to nurse where she was truly needed. Thus when a position in a poorhouse infirmary became available, Emma seized the opportunity to care for those who were destitute and ill.

Both her parents strongly objected to this decision, especially since the infirmary was in the heart of Whitechapel, which along with neighboring Spitalfields, had one of the worst reputations for poverty, disease, and violent crime in all of London. Her father had actually referred to Whitechapel as a cesspool harboring the scum of society. Her mother, too, had professed her horror that their daughter had wished to degrade herself by associating, even on a professional basis, with the filthy and corrupted inhabitants of that notorious place. And they had nearly disowned her when she informed them that she would no longer live at home, as the distance to Whitechapel was too great to travel on a daily routine.

When she told them of her intention to rent a small bed sitting room on the outskirts of Whitechapel, her father even threatened to have her put away in a lunatic asylum, for surely she had taken leave of her senses. It was only the Andrew Hewitt-Brown intervention, which salvaged the precarious relationship between Emma and her parents. Ever the voice of reason, Andrew had reassured the Hollanders that their daughter had not lost her sanity but was merely asserting her independence as a young adult. He suggested that rather than trepidation, they might show satisfaction that they had instilled in their offspring a strong desire for self-sufficiency. He further alleviated their concerns by promising that both he and his mother, Henrietta, would keep a watchful eye on the impetuous young woman.

Somewhat mollified, but by no means content with their daughter's decision, the Hollanders' reluctantly agreed to abide by a trial period of six months. They secretly hoped that after six months of working in and living near such squalor, Emma would be only too happy to return home and decide on a more sensible course of action.

Alas, for the distraught parents, a year had passed, and this event had yet to occur. Although nursing at the infirmary yielded heartbreak and sorrow in equal measure to satisfaction, Emma reveled in the challenges she faced on a daily basis. After the initial horrified panic she experienced in her first few days at the infirmary, Emma knew she'd made the right decision. She had never been this close to abject poverty and misery, never felt so keenly the needs of others or the care she could give.

She would never forget the first time she held a seriously ill child in her arms. She gazed in shocked dismay at the wasted limbs and emaciated torso, watching as fever shivers racked his frail body, hearing Dr. Mackenzie, sorrow in his eyes and voice, say to the drink-besotted hollow-eyed mother, "There is nothing we can do. The infection has traveled through his blood and poisoned his heart. We shall put him in a cot on the infants' ward. You may stay with him until it is over."

One of the attendants had gently pried the child from Emma's clenched embrace. Wordlessly, eyes brimming with tears, she watched the attendant carry the prostrate boy away, the mother meekly following. A few seconds passed before she whirled about to face the physician.

With a mix of anger and distress, she said in a low but furious tone, "Why did you not chastise that woman? Dear God! Didn't you see her? Drunk as a sailor, probably never sober. She isn't fit to care for that child. He has obviously been getting sicker for days. The deplorable condition of him! Almost starved to death. If it wasn't for the infection, then he would surely have died from malnourishment and neglect."

The doctor quietly interjected, "Yes, Miss Hollander, I am aware of that."

"Emma sputtered passionately, "How can you so calmly admit this and so complacently accept this child's death? His mother is responsible for his well-being. She should be held accountable. At the very least, the authorities should be notified."

Mackenzie spoke in the same quiet voice. "If the authorities were to arrest every mother in Whitechapel who in someway neglected her children, the jails would be overflowing." He shook his head. "It is not unusual for poverty-stricken children to die prematurely, Miss Hollander. In fact, if a child attains its fifth birthday, it is considered a milestone of sorts. Is the mother to blame, or is she merely another victim caught in the crushing grip of deprivation? What of her life? She faced the same hardships growing up as a child, one of the fortunate children to survive into adulthood. She probably has too many children herself, as well as a husband who either works himself to the bone and still can't meet his family needs or else has given up all hope and is slowly drinking himself to death every night at the pub.

"You saw that woman; the look in her eyes. Mark that look, Miss Hollander; you shall see it often in Whitechapel. It is the result of poverty and poverty's offspring, despair. Now, try if you will to cast yourself in that woman's place. Is there really a more severe punishment than the life she is forced to endure? This world is vastly different from London. Whitechapel abides by its own rules, its own social values, and, believe it or not, its own retribution for those who transgress the limits. It would be wise for you to learn the ways of Whitechapel, Miss Hollander; otherwise, I suggest you return to the familiar and comfortable lifestyle of London."

Dr. Mackenzie turned from her abruptly and headed down the opposite corridor, but not before Emma had glimpsed the sorrow and compassion in his eyes. She had a strange idea that the compassion had been directed towards her.

CHAPTER 13

That incident was a crucial one, for it sparked Emma's realization that if she were to continue this work in a meaningful manner, she would have to cast aside her judgmental attitudes. Dr. Mackenzie had helped her to understand that if she were to exact any positive effects through her nursing, she would have to accept the way in which the inhabitants of Whitechapel lived. She would refrain from condemning them for choices she herself was not forced to make.

Gradually, she began to understand that the people of Whitechapel were not different from other Londoners. Fate had simply dealt them a cruel blow, saddling them from birth with the burden of poverty. By the time they reached adulthood, it was too late for them to escape the devastating effects of poverty. A few fortunate ones were occasionally spared this miserable fate, perhaps sent away as children to distant relatives in the countryside or as orphans adopted by affluent Londoners.

Emma had heard whispers about a clandestine scheme whereby some East End parents actually sold their children through an intermediary to childless couples in London and further from the city limits. Newborns and infants were in highest demand, and it wasn't unusual for an infant-broker to be present along with the midwife at the birth of a child. Emma had never knowingly attended a birth where an illicit transaction had occurred; however, she had been suspicious on a number of occasions when a gentleman in the room had been hastily introduced as an uncle, a clergyman, or even the father himself.

Emma knew from experience that the last place most men

wished to be was in the confinement room; most of the time, they could be found at the local pub, basking in the congratulations and well wishes of their mates. A wholesome and numerous brood was considered clear evidence to all of a man's virility so that despite the practical problems with respect to clothing, feeding, and housing their offspring, it was important for a man to impregnate his wife as often as possible.

Human nature being as greedy as it is, the black market business of child procuring soon became so lucrative that the brokers — usually members of local gangs, desperate to maintain the supply to meet demands — realized they could eliminate a third party transaction and thereby pocket the entire sum of money themselves. They began the practice of snatching infants without consent, as well as young children. The advantages, of course, were enormous; no drunken, squabbling parents to haggle over money, plus the turnover time from the snatching of the children to delivery to the new parents was considerably shortened. This allowed the brokers to complete more transactions for more financial profit.

Eventually, it became apparent to the authorities that children were going missing, kidnapped from the streets to and from the way to school, sometimes even taken from their own doorsteps and from prams left briefly unattended. However, it was a crime of low priority for the weary constabulary of Whitechapel, most of whom were aware of the activities of the infant brokers.

The police, unfortunately, had more pressing problems, such as controlling the daily and nightly brawls, whether on the streets or in the pubs, as well as solving the latest round of assaults and murders and generally remaining vigilant to signs of social unrest. No one wished a repeat of last year's riots, and though serious violence had yet to occur this year, tensions and hostilities simmered just below the surface. It would not take much of a spark to ignite a full-fledged conflagration.

Alas, missing children became an accepted part of life in the East End. And if the truth be told, there were some parents who secretly breathed a sigh of relief when their child disappeared, for it meant one less hungry mouth to feed, as well as the sympathy and attention briefly afforded them by neighbors and friends.

Emma watched and learned in those first months of work. She felt a growing respect and fondness for Dr. Mackenzie, who unfailingly administered to his patients with tolerance and professional equanimity. She came to understand the underlying sense of humor and optimism, which allowed him to approach each situation with forbearance and equilibrium. Even when admonishing a patient who failed to take medicine or follow treatment directions properly, he was not harsh.

Despite the bushy eyebrows which lent him a gruff appearance and an expression that was sometimes stern, Emma recognized it was a concern for his patients' well-being which motivated his behavior. And the patients in turn respected and trusted Dr. Mackenzie more than any other physician—no mean accomplishment for those who were by nature mistrustful of and hostile to any perceived authority.

Emma observed with disappointment that not all the physicians who served the required placement at the infirmary considered the patients as did Dr. Mackenzie. Some were quite dismissive and did not bother to conceal their disdain or distaste for certain patients. Their attitude was one of minimal tolerance, and Emma always breathed a sigh of relief when their allotted time at the infirmary had expired.

She found herself emulating Dr. Mackenzie's approach, and to her delight, not only was it successful with her patients, but it felt comfortable and natural to her personality as well. She soon discovered that those who sought attention at the Whitechapel Infirmary, no matter how filthy or smelly, were not to be pitied or feared but treated with dignity and consideration. While many of them neglected their health out of ignorance or indifference, there were those who succeeded in maintaining their self-respect, a quiet pride in their refusal to submit to life's harsh rigors.

The door to the examination room opened, and Mary Simonds interrupted her reverie.

"Almost ready, love? They are in a frightful hurry to get

started on this one." Mary privately thought Emma's interest in post-mortems peculiar. Nevertheless, she was more than content to let Emma take charge of these unpleasant procedures and the cleanup afterwards.

Emma glanced around the room, then nodded. Everything was ready. All that was needed was the cadaver, and that would be brought in by the attendants. Usually, one attendant remained, who assisted the physician and cleared up when the examination was completed. However, when Emma was on duty, this task, upon her request, fell to her. She and Dr. Mackenzie had engaged in a raging battle of wills over the issue initially, the physician extremely reluctant to allow Emma anywhere near a post-mortem procedure. The autopsy room was no place for a woman, he had maintained. Emma had argued that male attendants were not always available and that it would be beneficial to the physicians if she were trained as an assistant.

Mackenzie had been skeptical of this logic, but Emma's irritating determination showed no sign of abating. Finally, weary of the incessant badgering, he permitted her to attend a post-mortem strictly as an observer. He had been firmly convinced that one look at a decomposed corpse even before the first incision of the scalpel would be sufficient to silence the persistent young woman, who would then run in horror from the room; that was if she didn't swoon into a dead faint first.

However, much to the physician's surprise and even chagrin, no such incident occurred, and Emma stoically endured the autopsy, using all of her considerable will to maintain her composure. Save for an unhealthy pallor, there were no visible signs of the discomfort she endured. Forcing herself not to flinch, she watched as the first surgical incision was made down the center of the abdomen, dividing it neatly in half.

Her awareness of her uneasiness began to decrease as fascination took hold and layer upon layer of the human body was exposed. Emma discovered the ability to depersonalize the corpse in front of her, to avoid thinking of it as a human being, and instead as an interesting specimen. In this way, she was able to focus on the procedure itself, to marvel at the mysteries of the body as it revealed some of those answers.

The smell, however, was another matter. No amount of mental preparation was sufficient for her to cope with the abominable stench of decomposition or the decay related to certain diseases of the internal organs. During that initial autopsy, she had to continually press a lavender silk handkerchief over her nose and mouth. It had helped only to the extent that it had prevented her from being overcome by the noxious fumes and falling senseless to the floor. However, it had not prevented the traumatic rebellion of her stomach afterwards, nor had it permitted her to take in nourishment for the remainder of the day. The smell seemed to have lodged in her nostrils. She caught whiffs of it throughout the day, causing her to gag from time to time. Dr. Mackenzie had lightly assured her that one never became accustomed to the odor of death and that some corpses stank much worse than the one they had dissected that day.

Emma viewed this as a new challenge. She knew that Dr. Mackenzie and the others expected her to fail; indeed, she knew that some of them laughed behind her back. There were even those few nurses who regarded her with umbrage, referring to her persistence as temerity in the extreme, seeking to elevate herself beyond the role of a nurse.

Emma paid no heed to their concerns. She was determined to succeed, not only for her own sake but to prove her point that women could cope with such situations. Her major obstacle was the smell. There must be some way to make it more tolerable for everyone.

She observed many a young inexperienced physician needing to be escorted from a post-mortem, looking almost as deathly as the corpse itself. Rising to the challenge, she'd gone to work to create a salve which minimized the noxious odors as much as possible. The unguent was a combination of menthol, camphor, and a base mixed into a paste. A hint of ground ginger root contributed to a calming effect on the bilious activities of the stomach. When rubbed under the nostrils, the salve greatly reduced one's sense of the offensive odors, camouflaging them with its own clean and pungent smell.

To her surprise and pleasure, the salve proved a blessing in disguise. When she offered a sample of her concoction to Dr. Mackenzie, he lauded it as highly effective in neutralizing the post-mortem vapors. Her salve was a huge success with other physicians as well. There was now no doubt that Emma had endeared herself, and her presence at future autopsies was secured.

CHAPTER 14

The door opened once more, and the corpse was wheeled in by two attendants. The body had earlier been washed and prepared. However, as the men transferred it from the trolley to the examination table, the pristine whiteness of the covering sheet was a sharp contrast to the odor of decomposition.

Dr. Mackenzie, followed by the new apprentice physician, John Dennys, entered the room. The doctor's manner was brisk as usual. "All right then, what have we here this morning?"

"A floater," one of the attendants replied. "The coppers pulled 'er out of the water durin' the night. Been in there a few days by the looks of 'er."

Mackenzie frowned at the foul odor. "Miss Hollander," he said as he turned to wash his hands in a basin. "I fear we shall require an additional quantity of your post-mortem salve."

"Certainly, Doctor," Emma replied. She extended the jar to Mackenzie, who gratefully accepted a generous portion of the fresh smelling unguent to apply beneath his nose. Emma also helped herself. When she offered the jar to John Dennys, the latter shook his head dismissively, a look of unabashed disdain in his eyes.

"Ah, fancy yourself a stoic, do you, Dennys?" queried Mackenzie. "Well, you may change your mind after a couple of these procedures. Understandably, one wishes to prove one's mettle at a first post-mortem. But I assure you it is by no means unmanly to accept whatever assistance is available to render the procedure as tolerable as possible."

Dennys allowed himself a slight smile. "With respect, sir, I assure you that I am in no such need. You are correct in your statement that this is my initial attendance at a post-mortem. However, I am familiar with death and find neither the sights nor odors associated with it distressing."

Dr. Mackenzie raised his right eyebrow quizzically. "Well, we shall see," he said in a skeptical tone. "But I warn you, all physicians must endure trial by fire of sorts." He turned a stern gaze upon the younger man. "If you faint, I shall not interrupt the procedure to collect you off the floor." He gestured for the attendant to lower the sheet from the body.

Emma noted the faint but derisive curl to Dennys's upper lip. He said nothing, but as his eyes came to rest on the corpse, she could have sworn that she saw a mocking gleam of amusement in them.

As predicted, the body was in deplorable condition, having been submerged in the river for a number of days. Pieces of tissue had been gnawed away, evidence that fish or perhaps a water rat or two had feasted on portions of the dead meat. The decomposition was in full progress, the body grotesquely swollen with the pressure of internal gases. In some places, the skin had burst, exposing layers of fat and muscle covering the internal organs.

It was female, somewhere in the third decade of life. The face was grossly bloated, features blackened and distorted, barely recognizable as human. The right eyeball had exploded from gaseous pressure. It lay on the woman's cheek, loosely attached to the socket by thin strands of tissue. Viscous yellow fluid had seeped from the eye, forming a congealed sticky mess. The left eye had been chewed, mutilated by scavengers, and the eyeball itself missing. The skin of the brow and upper cheek was torn away in strips, exposing muscle and fragments of gleaming white bone.

The fingers and toes also bore ragged bite marks, some digits completely severed and presumably devoured. The rest of the body looked intact, the skin a vivid shade of greenish black in places where putrefaction was advanced. The stench was almost unbearable.

Mackenzie cleared his throat a couple of times as though to dislodge the foulness which had invaded his nose and mouth.

"Post-mortem of an unidentified female," he announced. "Appears to be mid-thirties. Time…," he checked his pocket watch, 7:40 on the morning of August 15. Usual inspection reveals the body to be relatively intact except for some obvious scavenging of animals. More details on this later. The body was extricated from the river at approximately…," he glanced at the police report on the nearby table, "…3:50 this morning. It appears to have resided in the water for several days, but no longer than one week, I should say, judging from the fact that the abdomen has only ruptured in some places instead of the entire cavity.

"No wounds indicative of assault or injury on the anterior aspect of the body. No obvious ligature or stricture marks, only a minor contusion to the back of the head consistent with a fall perhaps, but not severe enough by itself to cause death.

"Hang on, what's this?" Mackenzie gingerly raised the cadaver's chin. A jagged gash sliced the throat from ear to ear. "Strike the last sentence from the record, Miss Hollander," he instructed Emma, who was writing notes on the procedure. "This woman's throat has been slashed, likely the work of a knife. It is now apparent that the cause of death was not drowning as was first suspected. In any case, we must now consider this case to be a murder. The victim was most definitely assaulted. Death resulted from massive blood loss from the major vessels in the neck having been severed."

Bending closer to the body, he inserted his fingers into the wound, gently prying apart the edges of the skin. "Hmm, no wonder this injury escaped notice upon cursory examination. See here, Dennys, this is most peculiar." He shifted his position to allow the apprentice physician a better view. "Note the skillfully straight cut. One would expect a wound of this magnitude to have caused a great mess with torn wound edges and ragged ends of blood vessels spattered haphazardly, but that is not the case. The major arteries and veins have been completely severed, such was the force of the attack. However, instead of hanging exposed from the wound, they are neatly tucked inside the edges of the skin."

He raised his head and looked at the younger man in bewilderment. "Bloody hell. I'll be damned if I have ever encountered anything so bizarre. Whoever cut this woman's throat made sure he did as neat and tidy a job as possible by pushing the sliced pieces of blood vessels back into the wound. Confound it, why? What possible motive could there be?"

Dennys peered at the wound. "A precise incision — unusual in a cut so deep. Instantaneous death from massive exsanguination." He glanced at Mackenzie. "A highly efficient manner in which to dispatch someone, don't you agree?"

Mackenzie shook his head. "Bloody strange is what it is. In all my experience, I have never observed such a phenomenon. Why go to the trouble of concealing the wound if that indeed was the murderer's intention? He would have realized that it would have been discovered during the post-mortem." He stepped forward once more. "Here, lad, help me turn her over."

Together he and Dennys hoisted the corpse onto its side, attempting to avoid pressure to the fragile abdomen. However, even the slight jarring caused by this movement precipitated the rupture of the distended tissue. The abdominal cavity burst open, a loop of intestines sliding onto the table and discharging rotting fecal matter.

"Bloody hell!" Mackenzie sputtered, retching and turning his face from the sickeningly foul odor.

Emma backed away, raising her apron to her face in a futile attempt to avoid the putrid stench. Her eyes stung with tears as acrid gastric juices burned the back of her throat, and she fought to quell the turmoil in her stomach.

Only Dennys failed to react. He continued to support the body in a lateral position, its back toward him. He glanced almost casually over the corpse's shoulder at the coiled intestine, mottled greyish green with decay and gas bubbles.

Mackenzie, handkerchief shielding his nose and mouth, stood well back from the cadaver as he gestured for the attendant to clean away the excrement. It took several minutes before the attendant, coughing and gagging, removed the mess.

"A bit of nastiness that," Mackenzie stated, stepping up to the examination table once more. Quickly he assessed the back of the corpse. A terse shake of his head indicated that there were no other significant wounds, only the occasional contusion. He nodded at Dennys, who returned the corpse to a supine position. Even without the excrement, the stench of putrefying flesh was barely tolerable.

"We could open the window and door a little," Emma ventured, breathing through her mouth as much as possible.

The physician nodded. "Normally, I believe in maintaining privacy during these procedures, as you know, Miss Hollander. However, I agree that we must take measures to prevent the asphyxiation of all present." So saying, he walked to the opposite end of the room to open a window while Emma did the same with the door.

The attendant who had removed the mess now returned through the back door, which led to the mortuary. He brought with him some disinfectant. Generally, the disinfectant was reserved for the post-procedure clean up. However, it was on occasion necessary if the autopsy were to proceed without its participants being forced to withdraw from the room. The attendant, a decidedly greenish cast to his pallor, wrinkled his nose in distaste at the odor which still reeked in the air.

"Here, try some of this under your nose," Emma suggested, proffering a jar of salve.

The man regarded it suspiciously. "I don't know, miss, if it is the right thing to do. Mr. Biggs is always after us to get used to the smells." Biggs was the attendant in charge of the mortuary. The man continued, "He says that if you are going to work with the dead, might as well accept how they smell, for it don't go away ever." He shook his head, ruefully. "I've been tryin' for a while to get used to it, but that don't seem to be happenin'."

"Perhaps Mr. Biggs should be asked to join you in the cleanup," Emma said acidly. "Maybe then he could show you and us what his secret trick is to adjusting to this foulness."

Both Mackenzie and Emma breathed a sigh of relief as the carbolic acid began to neutralize the stench. The chemical exuded a harsh, unpleasant smell, but it was definitely preferable to the other odor. Emma became aware that her entire body had tensed as she had struggled to prevent her stomach from regurgitating its contents. Now, as her muscles started to relax, her attention focused on John Dennys.

The young man was remarkably self-contained, she mused. He appeared completely unfazed by the noxious fumes and grotesque sights. In fact, she thought there was some amusement in his expression as he observed the weaknesses of others. Emma felt a second of pique at his attitude of cool superiority. What had he alluded to earlier, something about his familiarity with death?

Because of her irritation and wish to annoy him, she asked with heavy sarcasm, "I trust this does not cause you too much ennui, Mr. Dennys?" Mackenzie scowled at her, but she paid no attention. "I mean to say that you appear rather blasé of the post-mortem," she continued. "Is it that death fails to interest you?"

Dennys's dark eyes fixed on her, but to Emma's consternation, they reflected not anger but more of the same contemptuous amusement.

"Not at all, Miss Hollander," he replied amiably. "On the contrary, I find death a fascinating subject. Isn't that a trait common to all humanity?"

"It is true that death is the greatest mystery of life," Mackenzie interjected. "And the biggest challenge that we in the medical profession face."

Emma turned her gaze to the older man. "I believe our biggest challenge is not death itself, but the alleviation of suffering in as much as we are able. We can't prevent death, but it is our duty to ease the pain, both of body and spirit, so as to render the transition between life and death a less frightening event."

"A noble aspiration indeed, Miss Hollander," Dennys's voice gently mocked her. Glancing down at the corpse before them, he continued, "But what about this unfortunate woman?

Presumably, her death was a sudden occurrence, not an event for which she could prepare. In such a case, there is no facilitating a 'transition' into death, as you so quaintly phrase it."

Emma blushed and bit her lip, trying to control her indignation at Dennys's condescending tone.

Before she could respond, he added, "I would vouchsafe to say that this woman's death was not only sudden but brutal and terrifying. And that in her last moment of life, her soul cried out for a salvation that was denied."

Despite her best efforts to suppress them, tears rose in her eyes as she felt the truth of the physician's words. As loathsome as she found this man, she had to admit that in this instance, he was probably right.

"Hmm…yes…well…. We should continue with the post-mortem," Dr. Mackenzie said gruffly, visibly uncomfortable with his apprentice's words. "As the odor is more tolerable now, we shall proceed with the internal examination and organ inspection."

Emma endured the remainder of the autopsy in tight lipped silence. She kept her gaze focused on the procedure, deliberately ignoring John Dennys, although she was aware of his watchful eyes on her. Afterwards, while she was tidying up, she was approached by Dennys. The attendant who assisted her with the cleanup had just left the room. Her back was to the door, and she had not heard any footsteps. Nevertheless, she knew that John Dennys stood in the doorway.

"Yes, Mr. Dennys?" she inquired, her voice neutral, keeping her back to him.

"Why, Miss Hollander, have you eyes in the back of your head?" His tone was tinged with amusement.

No, just the hairs on the back of my neck which stand to attention every time you are near, she thought. Out loud, she replied, matching his tone. "Surely not, Mr. Dennys. It is my womanly intuition which alerts me to your presence."

She turned to face him, catching a glimpse of an unfathomable expression in his eyes. In the time it took to blink, his eyes resumed their normal appearance. She noticed, not for the first time, how dark and flat were those eyes, and how deep the coldness which emanated from them. The effect was quite unsettling.

His posture was relaxed as he leaned against the side of the doorframe. There was no reason for Emma to feel uneasy, except for the smile on his face, which was devoid of any warmth. *He could trap me.* The thought intruded suddenly into her mind. *Standing thus, he could impede my egress from this room.* The first stirrings of fear scratched at the bottom of her stomach. *Emma,* she scolded herself. *Don't be such a fool. There's no reason to think such a thing. You can leave this room anytime you choose. Just because you dislike this man, there is no cause to fear him.* Deliberately straightening her shoulders, she rearranged her expression, banishing the frown from her brow.

"Is there something with which I may be of assistance?" she inquired.

With a gesture similar to her own, Dennys straightened up and pushed away from the doorway. "No, Miss Hollander. I have returned to offer my apology, as I fear I have offended your sensibilities. It was not my intent to cause you distress." He watched her as a cat eyeing a mouse.

Emma's color rose, and she clenched her fists to her sides in vexation. *Liar,* she thought. *That is exactly what you meant to do.*

Nevertheless, she refused to rise to his bait. She silently counted to ten, willing her anger to subside, then responded in a voice as steady as her gaze. "While your views on death seem harsh to me, you are obviously entitled to express them."

Dennys smiled in acknowledgment. "Perhaps they are harsh, Miss Hollander. But then the truth is often unpalatable to those who must, for the sake of their own peace of mind, maintain a falsely idealistic belief."

Emma eyed him coldly. "I do not believe death need be as terrifying as you say. We can approach it with compassion and equanimity, especially if we have faith in an afterlife, as many people obviously do."

"Ah, the so-called 'paradise' of many conventional religions," answered Dennys, shrugging his shoulders dismissively. "A panacea for the masses so they can live their lives free from the paralyzing fear of what will become of them when their mortality claims them."

Emma shook her head. "It is no panacea, but a test of faith that God wishes us to endure so that we may earn our heavenly reward."

Dennys chuckled softly. "You sound so sure, but what if you and those other God-fearing people are wrong? What if the existence you hoped for isn't a paradise at all? What if your religion has fed you nothing but lies, and what awaits is similar to this life, only infinitely worse?"

So saying, he bowed and left the room, leaving Emma gaping in astonishment.

CHAPTER 15

Andrew's departure for England at the age of sixteen heralded the end of one phase of his life and the beginning of another. As he grew into young adulthood, he continued to perfect his skills, practicing his craft and allowing his spirituality to flourish. To be sure, there were times when he wrestled with his weaknesses, impatience being one of them. It was often difficult to sit back and permit a situation to evolve to its natural resolution when all one had to do was focus one's will to bring about a desired result. However, Andrew was true to his mentor's admonitions and resisted the temptation to indulge in arbitrary adjustments.

He was an accomplished, if somewhat distracted, student. The formal education system had never provided him with more than the rudimentary necessities, and this continued at Oxford, but due to his superior intellect, it did not require much effort on his part to assume the role of an honor student. Andrew's most important discoveries occurred independent of Oxford's hallowed halls and dusty tomes.

He found England to be vastly different from India. The pace of daily life was faster and more pressured. Britons worked longer hours, sometimes for more money, but they didn't, in general, seem happier than the people he'd known in India. In the streets of Bombay, he'd encountered some of the happiest, albeit dirt-poor people. Not that every pauper in India was content with his lot in life, but overall the poor seemed to accept their plight with less anger and bitterness than their British counterparts. Perhaps the predominant religious belief in reincarnation played a role. People could hope for a better chance next time around on the cycle of life.

Traveling the streets of London afforded no such glimpses of well being among the impoverished classes. These disenfranchised people resented anyone whose fortune was better than theirs. Many a time while in London during hiatus from Oxford, he wandered into less respectable sections of the city. He would become acutely aware of the unfriendly glances, even open hostility, directed toward him.

Occasionally ruffians hurled abuse, and once a group of ragged urchins mocked his gentleman's attire. They pelted his coat with raw eggs before running off in great delight. Another time, he was accosted by three mates on their way to the pubs. They approached him with the intent to rough him up a little, maybe rob him for a few quid. They calculated that the lone gentleman they were approaching would be no match, supposing he'd rather capitulate than risk the marring of his fine attire. After all, it wasn't the first time one of his sort had risked life and limb for illicit diversions on the streets of Whitechapel and paid dearly for that risk. If these dandies insisted on presenting such easy targets, who could blame hardworking blokes for capitalizing on the opportunity?

This one more than likely had more money in his pockets at this very moment than they would see in months of back breaking toil. Armed with these thoughts as well as their eager fists, they sauntered toward Hewitt-Brown with easy arrogance.

Since attaining maturity, Andrew's intensity of character had grown to a great magnitude. Sometimes the very air around him seemed to hum and vibrate with a vast amount of energy awaiting release. He could soften and camouflage this quality when desired. Rarely did he access its full strength, and never with humans.

Andrew had assessed the thugs approaching as easily as they thought they had him. One didn't require any special skills to fathom their intent. Thus he didn't even bother to listen in on their thoughts. On this particular evening, he was somewhat out of sorts, certainly not in the mood to deal with outsiders who wished him harm. He decided that a blast of his anger was precisely what the situation demanded.

The men were a few meters away when the first sensation struck them. A strange oppressive quality overtook the air so that extra effort was required on their part to simply move through it. They began to pant with the exertion, glancing at one another in surprised bewilderment. Andrew's gaze narrowed, focused intently on the men as they faltered in their approach. He saw fear rise in all three pairs of eyes as they staggered and began to weave, as though trying to ward off a physical assault. Indeed, to the men, it seemed as if they were under attack, as wave after wave of negatively charged energy bombarded them, pounding like a relentless sea.

Only one thought consumed them; they must run, escape this angry force which they understood emanated from the stranger in front of them. However, while the assault lasted, they were powerless to break the spell exerted on them. They could only pray they would survive it. One of the men fell to his knees and began to vomit uncontrollably, unable to stem the acute sensation of nausea threatening to overwhelm him. Another's nose bled spontaneously, gushing as though he'd received a punch in the face. The third one began to shake spasmodically, tremors ripping through his body as he stood rooted to the ground.

Then, as quickly as it had started, the assault was over. The air returned to its normal pressure as it does in the aftermath of a storm's unleashed fury. The men were once again in control of their bodies; although the first man's nausea remained, the vomiting ceased. The second one's bleeding slowed to a trickle, but his nose was grossly swollen and crushed to one side of his face. The third's tremors abated, but his muscles continued to ache for a long time, and thereafter he was forever plagued by a severe stammer.

They fled in terror, disappearing into the darkness. They never spoke of the incident to others or amongst themselves. Indeed, their friendship soon dissolved, each too haunted by the experience to want to be reminded by others who shared it.

Andrew, on the other hand, simply shrugged his shoulders and continued on his way, no more vexed than as if an annoying pest was no longer a bother.

During that long and lonely first year in England, there were times when Andrew was tempted to return to India. Though of British blood and heritage, he felt like a stranger in these unfamiliar and unfriendly streets. The dampness of the cold weather disturbed him. The fog which nightly cloaked the sky and obscured the stars irritated him. He was accustomed to clear Indian skies, the stars visible in bright clusters. He longed for the heavy scent of jasmine and other night blooming flowers, craving the exotic aromatic atmosphere. He even missed the ferocious monsoon rains. At least that rain was warm, not like the bleak English version, which dampened one's spirits as well as one's skin.

Through the ensuing years, after graduating from Oxford with honors' degrees in philosophy, languages, and history, Andrew decided to remain in England for the time being. He devoted his days to assisting his father with the business and marketing the merchandise his brothers sent him from India. He planned trips to his boyhood home with anticipation, always eager to visit his mentor. Bhirati's health had deteriorated over time. Though not so advanced in years, he now suffered from a heart condition which restricted his physical activities. Nevertheless, he continued to manage his profitable gambling business in Bombay.

The Hewitt-Browns were aware of their son's concerns for his former teacher. They had come to regard Bhirati as a family friend, pleased at the way Andrew had matured under his tutorship. His parents understood that their son's frequent trips to the subcontinent only in part involved business interests.

Bhirati was untroubled by his ailing health. "Remember," he stated to Andrew, during one of the latter's visits in 1883. "The human body is only a vessel, and a weak one at that, for the spirit. I have used my physical energy to achieve spiritual harmony and to perform the magic required to complete my duties to the Creator. This body has been pushed far beyond the endurance of humans. It is tired, prematurely depleted."

His dark gaze held a hint of sorrow as he looked at the younger man. "You too shall burn out sooner than humans do. It is one of the conditions we accept by agreeing to take on the flesh. Therefore, heed this warning. Employ your magic judiciously, for you pay a price every time you use it."

His former student nodded. "Yes, so you continue to impress upon me. I do heed your words, Pradeep, for you are the wisest man I know. My trust in you is absolute."

Bhirati's pale lips parted in a ghost of a smile. "I have never lied to you, Andrew, nor shall I. I may not always have an answer, but I always know the truth."

Andrew clasped the other's cold hand. "You are more than a mentor. You are my dearest friend. It saddens me to see you in ill health, for I thought we would have more time."

Bhirati laughed softly. "My young master, there is never enough time. Shall we reach the point where we have said enough, learned, laughed, or loved enough?"

Andrew smiled wistfully. "Yes, that is the truth of every lifetime, as I recall. Still, it remains a difficult condition to accept, an impossible concept for those who exist solely in the flesh."

"Humans' understanding of mortality and eternity is severely limited," Bhirati said. "It is only when one leaves the flesh and exists in spirit that absolute comprehension comes to pass. What's difficult for Excala to accept is that such dichotomy exists between flesh and spirit. Despite the fact that we live in man's world and are prohibited from full knowledge, we nevertheless retain this spiritual memory of all our experiences in the realm of spirit.

"Lesser beings could not remain sane in both worlds, for humans are not meant to compare one world to the other. How could they possibly be content or attach any purpose to their lives in this world if they had but one glimpse of existence in the Creator's realm? But enough now of such things." Bhirati struggled from his seat yet managed to rise gracefully, politely but firmly declining the younger man's offer of assistance. "It is time to switch focus to more worldly matters. We both require a distraction. Would you care to join me at the gaming table?"

CHAPTER 16

Pradeep Bhirati ran a gambling house in the heart of the city. Situated unobtrusively on a side street, it was thus removed from the chaos and distraction of the congested thoroughfares. On their first encounter, when Andrew was but a boy, they entered through a side door, Bhirati ushering the boy into a spacious office. The décor was an intriguing combination of English practicality and Indian craftsmanship.

"Please sit down." Bhirati indicated a comfortably appointed chair embroidered in rich green silk. "Wait here while I attend to some business. I shall only be a moment." So saying, he exited through the main door of the office.

Young Andrew surveyed the room, admiring the lush colors of the rugs and cushions strewn on the floor. Despite the years they had spent in India, his parents had never become accustomed to the delightfully informal manner of lounging in comfort on divans and oversized cushions. Andrew, however, thought it a wonderful practice and had arranged his bedroom at home accordingly. He smiled in pleasure as he noted ornaments of various sizes and shapes adorning the shelves behind an imposing mahogany desk.

He walked over to the desk, marveling at its beauty. The luxurious wood was polished to a bright gleam, detailed carving rendering it one of the handsomest pieces of furniture the boy had ever seen. Andrew waited a few moments before impatience triumphed over good manners. He opened the office door and peered into the long dimly lit corridor, at the end of which hung a large bamboo curtain. From behind the curtain issued the steady hum of voices punctuated by occasional raucous laughter or an excited shout.

He ventured down the corridor, his curiosity roused. As he neared the curtain, his nostrils detected the unmistakable odor of clove cigarettes; the aromatic spicy scent mingled with the heavier musty smell of regular cigar smoke. This close to the action, he was aware of more subtle sounds — the clink of glasses on tabletops, an anxious murmur or nervous cough here and there.

Andrew grasped the curtain and, pulling it aside, received his first look at a professional gaming room. Filled to maximum capacity, the room had men crammed into every available seat. Those unable to find a seat stood behind or around the tables, patiently waiting for a player to falter so a coveted seat could be seized. A cloud of blue gray smoke hovered above the room, silent observer of the spectacle below.

Andrew felt on the threshold of another world. He sniffed the air, then drew in a deep breath, allowing the pungent aroma to fill his lungs — a tingling sensation coursed through his nerve endings. The atmosphere of the room was intoxicating, a heady blend of high-strung anticipation and gut-wrenching trepidation. He smelt the grime and sweat emanating from the men, and beneath, the fear seeping from their pores — fear of failure, of losses, financial and emotional; fear of being overpowered by desires and hungers beyond their control. Fear was a potent and seductive stimulant, culminating in the evitable sweet surrender to a force greater than themselves. The boy absorbed all these sensations, digesting and processing the meaning of each one. He, too, was mesmerized by the allure of the game, but his attraction was not based on fear or victory over others but in deciphering and manipulating the energy pattern of the game itself.

He spotted Bhirati in animated conversation with one of the patrons. The man was either upset or excited, gesticulating wildly as they spoke. Their words were lost amidst the incessant din; however, after a few minutes of intense interaction, the man appeared calmer. Bhirati clapped him lightly on the shoulder, smiling easily; the patron, now smiling as well, backed away, bowing before heading for a table of noisy acquaintances.

Bhirati saw Andrew and crossed to where, half-concealed behind the curtain, the boy stood watching. "I see the temptation to have a look at my humble establishment was too great to resist," he remarked. "What is your opinion?" He glanced sideways at the boy, amused by his wide-eyed expression.

"It is fascinating, magnificent," responded Andrew enthusiastically.

Bhirati turned to face the room, proudly surveying it like a sovereign might his kingdom. "It is indeed. You can feel the exhilaration, can you not? This room is alive with an energy, an appetite."

"Truly, that is so," Andrew agreed. "I feel the energy humming through my body as I stand here."

Bhirati nodded. "I am pleased that you find favor with my establishment. But now, let us return to the office, for we have much to discuss." He observed the boy's crestfallen expression. "Fear not, young sir. You shall return soon to this room. In fact," a knowing look twinkled in his eye, "I would wager that you will spend a great deal of time here."

Thus began Andrew's initiation into the mysteries of spirituality and mysticism. Every day he would slip away from school in the afternoons to spend time with the man he soon came to regard as his most important teacher. Bhirati was a remarkable individual, highly educated and esoteric in thought. The lessons were conducted in the library, a room adjoining Bhirati's office.

The first time Andrew entered this library, he was overcome with a sense of wonder. Hundreds of books covering a multitude of themes peered out from the voluminous shelves; historical books, social and political commentaries, philosophical treatises, were only a few examples of the diversity of subjects contained within those four walls. A large section covering one entire wall was devoted to studies of mysticism and magic, religions and spirituality. Some of the tomes were obviously quite ancient; others were in foreign languages. Andrew recognized the titles in Latin but could only guess at some of the others, a number of which appeared to be in Arabic. There were, as well, Greek books dealing with mythology and more obscure old European and Hebrew texts.

"Can you read all these languages?" asked the boy in amazement.

Bhirati shrugged eloquently. "Some better than others, but yes, I have read every book on these shelves at one time or another."

Wide-eyed, the boy gazed with reverence at the shelves crammed with information and knowledge.

An amused expression appeared on the man's face. "Everything that is of importance can be found within the pages of these particular books. They contain the essence of mankind, the embodiment of man's monumental struggle to understand the conflict between good and evil. Many questions are posed, many mysteries unveiled."

"And the answers?" asked the boy. "Can they too be found in those books?"

Bhirati shook his head slightly. "There is only one place where answers are found. It is here." He placed his hand over his heart. "The books are tools to guide us to those answers. The words written on their pages, penned by wise men through the ages, may assist us in our enlightenment. Ultimately, however, it is the individual who must discover the truth for himself."

They sat and talked for a long while. Andrew quickly deduced that being in Bhirati's presence was an experience akin to no other. The library was both comfortable and peaceful, an oasis in the midst of the chaos outside that was the city. A surreal quality permeated the room. It seemed as if the library and its two occupants were suspended between this world and another. Time passed slowly in this space so that Andrew was startled when his teacher informed him that he must leave if he wished to return home before sunset.

It was during Andrew's second visit that Bhirati remarked, "It is an interesting phenomenon, is it not? One would swear that no more than an hour has passed since you've walked into this room, yet as time is measured in this reality, it has actually been over five hours. Humans would simply dismiss this as losing time. What say you, young master?"

Andrew's brow furrowed as he pondered the question. "I could say that time is different, meaning that we presently occupy a different reality than those outside."

Bhirati's expression was neutral. "How do you arrive at this conclusion?"

The boy hesitated before replying. "It seems the logical conclusion to draw is that you have cast a spell to alter reality."

Bhirati's gaze was sharp. "Why alter reality? Why not alter time itself?"

Andrew concentrated, biting his lip. "I do not believe it is possible to alter time," he responded slowly.

"How can that be? Cannot anything and everything be accomplished through the use of magic?" Bhirati challenged. "You must know the answer, for those who practice magic must be aware of its strengths and limitations."

The boy sighed. "I don't know the explanation. I only know that I am right."

"Indeed. However, it is not sufficient to know the answer. You must also understand it. Magic is a force both wondrous and dangerous. If you wish to be a superior magician, you must be well-versed in its properties. Magic demands respect from the practitioner, and if the respect is not forthcoming, it may well destroy those who foolishly attempt to harness it.

"Andrew, you have the ability to be a powerful magician, but you must first learn wisdom, which comes from spiritual growth. A magician who is not wise may be corrupted by evil influences. You are learning that the universe of which this world is a part is a combination of energies which exist in balance. Opposing forces maintain a delicate harmony, which is constantly threatened by disruption. The concept of equilibrium and opposition is an essential one to comprehend.

"It explains the existence of good and evil, and highlights the reason why all man's choices can be reduced to this most basic level, and it accounts for why the Creator gave man the gift of free will so he might play a pivotal role in the natural balance and evolution of his world and, by extension, the universe. If one understands that every decision, every choice in one's life is based upon this premise, then one recognizes the importance of opposition in maintaining balance. Balance is necessary for survival. We have only to examine mankind's history to realize that this is so. Any great turmoil or state of chaos is a significant threat to man's survival. Wars, pestilence, civil insurrections, and natural disasters are all examples of extreme disruption. It is simple, really; all you need to remember is that there is a duality to existence.

"Take good and evil, for instance. Humans have been taught that evil is a negative force. Yet if evil did not exist, neither would good, for there would be no context in which to understand it. Opposition is necessary for survival. The difficulty arises when that balance between forces is disrupted. Intervention is required to restore the balance. That is the role of a magician; to be a restorer of equilibrium. Depending on a magician's motives, he may either eliminate the chaos or add to it."

Andrew listened attentively to his teacher's words. "Then I suppose there must be rules that govern the use of magic," he said pensively. "If only to maintain order and balance."

"Precisely," agreed Bhirati. "That is why a master magician must be on intimate terms with his magic. He must be cognizant of its limitations. These limitations are often not impossible to transgress — they are forbidden by the universal laws as decreed by the Creator. To explain more fully, an example of the limitation is the following: Can one cast a spell of immortality?"

"No, I should think not," the boy tentatively responded.

"You are correct. But why is it so? Because the flesh is finite. It has a beginning and an end; birth and death. It cannot endure indefinitely. Therefore not even magic can prevent the natural dissolution and decay of the human body. Thus immortality does not exist. Correct?"

"Correct," Andrew echoed.

"Ah, but it does indeed exist; an immortality not of the body, but of the spirit. Excala are spiritual beings. We had our beginnings in spirit, and it is to the spirit that we return when our mortal lives end. You shall learn the rules of magic, Andrew."

He gestured towards the collection of books behind him. "Some knowledge you will gain from these books. Other knowledge, of a deeper, more secret nature, you will apprehend from me directly. You will come to understand that despite the restrictions of magic, there are ways to compensate. Ways in which a magician may achieve a desired result by using a different approach than the one that is forbidden.

"Like the issue of time alteration. Time is not static. It is a continuum composed of past, present, and future. We cannot change events that have occurred, for that would only result in a level of chaos so intense mankind would be crushed beneath its mass. So the question is as follows; how can I, as a magician, bring about the same outcome to an event as would be achieved if time could be changed?" Bhirati paused as if waiting for a reply.

When Andrew merely shrugged, a perplexed look on his face, the man continued. "What if I were to adjust *your perception* of the passage of time; say, for example, make you believe that only one hour has passed when, as defined by man's measurements, five hours had actually elapsed? Time itself would remain as constant as always, the only difference being that you would believe it to be something it was not, and you would respond accordingly."

The boy nodded. "Yes, I understand how that can occur. One may manipulate circumstances to achieve one's goal."

"Excellent," Bhirati said, smiling. "You understand this concept. You must keep this information, store it in your mind, to be evoked when it is necessary. The question you may ponder for next time: Did I use magic to adjust your perception of time? Or did I, in fact, shift us into another reality or dimension wherein time is measured differently from the method used in man's world? I wish you to reflect upon this issue, and we shall discuss it next time in detail."

CHAPTER 17

Thus, Andrew's instruction progressed. He proved a keen student, swift to comprehend new ideas, possessed of an insatiable need to challenge both himself and his teacher. Many a lively discourse ensued for hours on end as the boy's knowledge expanded in great strides.

One day Bhirati announced, "It is time for you to learn about the Excala."

The boy tensed with anticipation. Over the past several weeks, his numerous inquiries about this subject had been dismissed by Bhirati. He would only respond with his typical eloquent shrug, claiming that there were other lessons which must be learned first.

On this particularly sultry Bombay day, they had been lounging on the cushions strewn across the floor, drinking carafes of chai, a tea blended with cardamom and other native spices, which was refreshing in the sweltering Bombay summer. Andrew scrambled to a sitting position. He focused attentively on his teacher, noting that his eyes were darker and even more penetrating than usual.

"What I am about to tell you, the legacy of the Excala, will clarify many of the issues that have preoccupied your thoughts. As I have said before, we are not human in the typical sense, although we occupy human flesh. The fundamental differences between Excala and humans exist because we're not originally of man's world.

"At one time long ago, our world coexisted with the human world here on the physical plane, until certain events occurred, which resulted in the severing of ties with the physical. From that point onward until this very day and forever beyond, ours is a spiritual world, never again to occupy an existence within a physical realm. But long ago, time was a wondrous period for Excala. Because we weren't human, we flourished in absolute harmony with our spirituality and our magic. We bore no animosity towards mankind, but neither did their affairs or their world interest us particularly.

"As for humans, they were aware of our existence, but equally indifferent, being too self-absorbed in pursuit of material acquisitions. We took care of our families, tended to the necessary daily tasks, taught our children the mysteries of creation. Magic was as natural and essential to us as the air we breathe. We were blessed with insight and wisdom. On rare occasions, we traveled to man's world, as, for example, when we attended the birth of the Creator's son."

"The three wise kings!" Andrew exclaimed.

Bhirati nodded. "Yes, they were Excala certainly, the most recognized but by no means the only ones to venture to man's world. But humans could not enter our world. We were wise enough to understand that because they lacked spiritual purity, any interference on their part could have a negative impact on us. Occasionally we were forced to defend our borders from intruders who, having heard tales of our wondrous realm, desired to conquer and plunder it for themselves. But they were no match for our magic.

"Everything was idyllic. We could not have been more happy. The only weakness from which we suffered was a collective naiveté or unshakeable belief in the safety and security of our world. For were we not superior beings? As long as we kept humans out, they could not threaten us — or so we thought."

Bhirati's eyes clouded with sorrow. "Alas, like Achilles, we dismissed our weakness, and like the ancient Greek, we paid dearly for our error in judgment. And when the danger was upon us, we were slow to recognize it, for evil often masquerades in benign, even friendly guise. It started innocuously enough when three members of Excala visited man's world. The very fact that they chose to conceal their visits from the rest of us would have been cause for great concern had we been aware. Deception and subterfuge are not characteristics of Excala. These traits remain to this day inherent to humans.

"It was an ominous portent of things to come had we been discerning enough to perceive it. Alas, these Excala were in a state of metamorphosis, which had caused irreparable damage; in essence, bringing about the demise of our world. Despite being Insiders, they did not possess the fortitude or spiritual integrity necessary to resist the temptations of the human world. However, it is imperative that you recognize that they were not victims; on the contrary, they willingly sacrificed their spirituality in exchange for the human vices of greed and power. They permitted themselves to be seduced by evil. The seeds of corruption took root, and the spiritual decay was swift to follow.

"Like many humans, these traitorous Insiders lusted after power and became swollen with its toxic effects. Not content to dominate mankind, they conceived a scheme to overpower the Excala as well, thereby gaining control of both worlds. This presented a grave danger, for the marriage of human vice with magic was a potent and deadly union. So completely had these Excala surrendered to evil that they would not hesitate to unleash their diabolical forces against their sisters and brothers.

"They might well have succeeded in decimating us had it not been for the intervention of one particular Excala. Gifted with enormous discernment and insight, he discovered the betrayal and organized a contingent with exceptional combat skills to dispatch the traitors. Remember, never before had we engaged in battle with an adversary who rivaled us in ability, so who could say how well prepared we were for such conflict?"

Bhirati paused momentarily to sip his drink. Andrew stared at him, enthralled by the story's compelling events.

Bhirati continued, his expression sober. "A fierce battle ensued on a level plain known as the Fields of Ambrosia. It is almost impossible to imagine the scene. Two sets of warriors pitted against one another, each possessing phenomenal magic. Evil had complete mastery over the traitors, and they attacked with all the fury and power their magic contained, now intent on total annihilation if they failed to subdue us. For the first time in our history, evil had blighted our world, casting a shadow across the sun and a chill over the land. The struggle was so intense it could not endure for long. All combatants were destroyed. Not one was able to withstand the terrible onslaught of deadly magic.

"The presence of evil had a powerful effect, a poison which spread across the land and through the heart of our people. In mounting horror, we watched nature's beauty wither and die, unable to resist the devastation inflicted by the corrupt magic. For now that it had been wielded against us by our own kind, it no longer afforded us the protection we had heretofore experienced from ill health and death. The immortality of Excala had been destroyed forever.

"As Excala sickened and died, so did our world. The product of our passion and magic, it could not escape the fate poised to claim it. The skies turned dark with sorrow and shed torrents of tears upon the land. We were powerless to save our beloved world. For many, the misery and horror were too much to bear. Some literally lost their minds, sinking so far into the depths of madness they could never surface again. There were even those suffering such intense despair that they were driven to take their own lives, an act so unspiritual that no Insider had ever before contemplated it.

"Those of us determined to survive realized there was one choice. We had to abandon our world or perish along with it. The human world was closest to ours, both in distance and physical composition. Therefore, we decided to rebuild our lives in that world. Hearts heavy with grief, we undertook the sorrowful task of leaving our home. Though in mourning for our world, we had to ensure our survival in this one, so we developed new skills in order to function efficiently in the human realm. As we had conjured up our world upon the physical plane in order to have a tangible manifestation of our inner spiritual existence, so now we were able to preserve it in a spiritual realm. We used our magic to visit it.

"To this day, we journey home when we have the need or desire, most notably through our dreams. And there are those among us who may travel at will in spiritual form to any location. However, as we are restricted by our fleshly existence, we must inevitably return to the corporeal world. The Creator did not forget us in our time of tribulation. He presented us with an offer. Having witnessed over time the struggles of mankind, the Creator concluded that humans could benefit from the presence of Excala in their world. There was an opportunity for Excala to become spiritual guides and to assist man in the improvement of himself and his world.

"The following was proposed. We could choose to live out the remainder of our earthly existence and return to the world of spirit forever. Or we could serve the Creator and remain in man's world. If we chose the latter, we would be assigned a specific function—for example, the role of a teacher or warrior or healer. But there was one important consideration. Given the momentous scope of our tasks, it would not be possible to achieve our goals in a single human lifetime. When one considers the millennia of years this earth has existed, what could be accomplished in a mere sixty or seventy years? Therefore, we would be allotted multiple lifetimes, as many as we desired or required to fulfill our duties."

"Multiple lifetimes," Andrew echoed, bemused. Then an understanding registered in his eyes. "You speak of reincarnation. A belief that is prevalent in this country."

Bhirati nodded. "Yes, there are religions, not only here in India, but elsewhere, which share this belief. However, as man is wont to do with any issue pertaining to spirituality, he has distorted the concept of multiple lives. So called reincarnation, while retaining an essence of truth, has been altered to complement mankind's misshapen idea of spirituality. This highlights another fundamental difference between Excala and humans. Excala search for pure knowledge, accepting the answers we find, as we are not fettered by preconceived notions. Humans, however, when confronted by the unknown, approach it with fear and trepidation, then attempt to fit it into their perception and structure. They will do so even if this necessitates a blatant disregard for logic or truth. They are extremely adept at self-deception and will obstinately cling to their beliefs no matter how flawed these may be. Excala see truth clearly. We look at the universe and all its wonders with open eyes, unlike humans who stumble and falter in their self-induced blindness.

"Most Excala were too heart-sickened and weary after the destruction of our world to remain one moment longer than was required in man's world. The desire to return to the spirit state burned hungrily in their souls. Not that the others were immune to those flames of longing, but for individual personal reasons, we chose to stay and accept the Creator's offer. That position was based in part upon our strong loyalty to the Creator, and on assessment of our own spiritual development and the lessons we still wished to master. Our freedom of will was paramount.

"After completing a lifetime, one could decide to remain indefinitely in the world of spirit, whether for respite only or for eternity. All that was asked of us was a sacred pledge of loyalty and obedience to the Creator. Each Excala who continues to exist among humans helps in some manner to maintain order in this world; most importantly, the tenuous balance between the forces of good and evil. As Satan has his infernal servants to carry out his bidding, so the Creator counters with Excala.

"We are the guardians of spirituality, appointed by none other than the Creator Himself. But lest you think that we exist with impunity, let me say that this is not so. The risk we face is indeed great. Notwithstanding our magic, in all else, we are human, born of flesh and blood, subject to frailties and temptations of mankind. Daily we face the threat of spiritual loss, not only the result of evil's assault on mankind but also of the inner struggles to avoid temptation."

"But one would think it would be the opposite," Andrew protested. "The more spiritual one is, the less chance of succumbing to temptation. Isn't that so?"

Bhirati shook his head. "As the Creator's trusted servants, bound by our sacred oath, we are on the contrary favored and relentless targets of evil in its many guises. Thus as one succumbs to the destructive and seductive influence of evil, one fails in one's pledge to the Creator. Betrayal of the Creator is an unforgivable transgression. A disgraced Excala is banished from the Creator's light. He becomes an Outsider, stripped of his magic and rendered mortal as other humans. Such a one is condemned to wander aimlessly in a world of man, with no hope of returning to the Creator's presence. If he is fortunate, he will live out his allotted lifespan until death claims him. Then, because he is spiritually bereft, he is doomed to return to the human plane, there to repeat yet another meaningless existence, never to partake in the joys of the spiritual realm."

Andrew frowned in consternation. "But I have been taught that God is a loving being who can forgive any offense."

Bhirati raised his eyebrows. "There is no doubt that the Creator is love itself. Nevertheless, if an Excala discards his spirituality, the greatest gift bestowed upon us, it is tantamount to performing spiritual suicide. It is a loss from which he can never recover, and because spirituality is so closely linked with free will, once the choice is made to forfeit spirituality, an Excala must then accept the consequences. It may seem harsh, but that is how highly the Creator values and wishes us to value our free will."

"Hmm," Andrew mused, processing this information. "Does the same also apply to humans?"

"Ah, you are now using your discernment, young master. Humans are different, remember. Their spirituality is not as highly evolved as ours. Therefore spiritual expectations are not, shall we say, as rigorous as they are for Excala. Humans may be forgiven certain transgressions, where Excala are not. Let us not forget that we have undertaken the task of the spiritual guidance of mankind. We must, of course, be held more accountable than they are."

"But what about those who, in addition to forfeiting their spirituality, decide to call upon evil forces in order to regain their magic?"

"A splendid question," Bhirati responded approvingly. "You raised the issue of what transpires if a fallen Excala becomes totally corrupted by evil. One can only assume that if such an Excala rejects the Creator, it follows that he would be attracted to the Creator's opposite. Thus, he casts his lot with Satan, forfeiting his soul to the devil. It is an unfortunately accurate description, for the devil doesn't need to gain mastery over the soul of one who enters into a pact with him.

"Because this earth is the domain of Satan, the fallen Excala is given whatever he desires in terms of material acquisitions, power, and perhaps most importantly, the reinstatement of his magic skills. These dark magicians about whom humans whisper are feared and hated, and with good reason, for they are inordinately dangerous. Alas, they have tarnished the reputation of magic, reinforcing a common misconception of humans that magic is evil."

Andrew nodded. "Yes, I understand, Teacher. Magic is a force, neither good nor evil. The will of the one who wields it dictates to what purpose it shall be used."

"Precisely," Bhirati agreed. "It is imperative that you be prepared against attacks from these evil ones, Andrew, for they will do everything in their power to destroy you. They might try to precipitate your physical demise, but one of the fundamental aspects of evil is that it revels in suffering. Thus, the actual death of the individual, while involving some degree of pain, is all too brief an interlude. Physical suffering affords some pleasure, but the servants of evil have a propensity for the extreme anguish of the spirit. If they succeeded in instilling doubt about spirituality or the Creator, then Excala might indeed succumb to corruption.

"From this day forward, you must be vigilant against evil attacks. The evil one's spies and servants will be aware of your every move, and they will strike where you are most vulnerable, for you pose a great threat to their activities, and you shall become even more dangerous once you have fully matured and gained the necessary knowledge and wisdom. There are a multitude of lessons for you to learn. Many of them require skills that you already possess. I shall teach you to fine hone them and to gain complete control of them.

"You will become a master of spells and incantations of all sorts. I shall assist you to use your mindreading ability to a good advantage. This will afford you the opportunity to influence the wills of humans in an expertly subtle way. I shall teach you one of my favorite interventions, the art of 'adjustment.' This involves the manipulation of events to achieve a desired result. It includes the skill of discernment to know when and how to intervene in a situation. There is an order, a pattern which accompanies the rhythm and energy of the universe. Events unfold in a specific sequence. The ability to foresee the sequence, to perceive it before it occurs and intervene accordingly, is an enhanced skill which you shall develop."

Silence ensued as Bhirati observed the boy, who sat very still and deep in thought. The teacher's eyes reflected the melancholy tenderness he felt as he contemplated the future of his student, for whom so much wonder and heartache lay in store. His voice was gentle when he spoke. "I understand the magnitude of what you have heard today will take some time to assimilate. That is why I am here, to assist you to develop your remarkable skills."

Andrew regarded him with an intense and solemn expression. "Your description of the Excala's battle against the traitors was so vivid I feel as if I were there. I can see the battlefield in my mind's eye, hear the cries of distress from fallen horses and men, and inhale the unmistakable stench of carnage and death."

"You were there," Bhirati said quietly.

Andrew nodded. "Yes, I know. I am remembering it more clearly as we speak." Understanding flashed through his steel-gray eyes. "I was that warrior of whom you spoke. The one who discovered the betrayal and led the Excala into battle."

"Yes," Bhirati agreed. "Since that very first lifetime, you have been a warrior in one form or another. It is one of, but by no means the only function you serve. Because you are an Excala, you can accept with equanimity the vast knowledge and skills you must yet acquire, but over the past several weeks, a spiritual transformation has occurred within you, as subtle as it is powerful, and it will continue throughout your earthly existence.

"It is now time to experience firsthand some of the wonders I have described. Tonight, when you journey to our world, take a walk down the stone path which leads to the wrought iron gate; wait there for me. Together we shall open it and enter the Garden of Mysteries. I promise that you will find all the answers you seek, and some which you don't even know you seek."

CHAPTER 18

Polly Nichols stumbled along Whitechapel High Street. Though the early part of the night had been fine, a light rain now misted the streets, and the fog was rolling in heavily off the river. Polly had just been turned away from her lodging on Thrawl Street, not having sufficient money to pay for her room. She really didn't care about that. She had made enough money so far tonight to pay for her room three times over but preferred to spend it on more important things such as drink, and a new black straw bonnet with black velvet trim, now slightly soggy from the rain.

She came to the corner of Osborn Street, where she spotted her friend Ellen Holland in the company of two other women.

"Hey, Pol," Ellen hailed her.

Polly waved drunkenly. "See me new bonnet," she said proudly.

"'Tis nice, Pol. Where you headed now?" asked Ellen, noticing how intoxicated her friend was.

Polly laughed and gestured vaguely. "Wherever the road takes me."

"Blimey, it's after two-thirty. Why don't you come home then?"

"Can't; the deputy won't let me in. No money left."

Ellen clicked her tongue in annoyance, looking at the other women. "Well, Pol, I don't want to make this no habit, but maybe I can help you out tonight. Why don't you come back with us?"

"Oh, Ellen, you must have struck it rich tonight," Polly chortled. "Finally working your ass off like I told you." She held up a hand, nails cracked and grubby. "No need, no need. I'll get me some more money. Don't you worry about old Pol now."

"You sure?" asked Ellen doubtfully.

"Of course, I am." Polly bent forward in a mock bow. "Good night, duck, see you in the morrow."

Polly turned from the others and continued east on Whitechapel High Street. She trudged along for perhaps ten minutes before she became aware of footsteps behind her. She glanced over her shoulder but could see nothing in the thick shroud of fog closing around her. Polly shrugged and quickened her steps as much as her inebriated state would allow. She tripped and fell to the cobbled pavement, tearing a corner of her skirt on some loose stones. Cursing, she staggered to her feet.

"Here, love, need some help now?" a voice inquired out of the fog behind her.

In her alcohol-muddled mind, Polly didn't know whether to be relieved at the female's intrusion or irritated that her would-be rescuer was not a potential customer. As she regained her balance, Polly peered at the figure emerging from the fog.

The woman was tall, several inches taller than Polly's five-foot-two. A shabby green skirt and brown green apron covered a seemingly slender build. She wore a shawl, dark brown and threadbare, carelessly draped around her shoulders. In the eerie glow of the gas lamp, Polly saw that beneath the woman's green bonnet, her dark hair was thick and curly, reaching the nape of her neck. Her features, even and unremarkable, provided an overall attractiveness, as did her relative youthfulness.

"A little too much to drink, dearie?" the stranger inquired in a sultry tone. She was indeed a stranger to the East End, Polly knew, for she had never come across this woman before. Polly walked the streets a lot and was familiar with all the other whores, at least by sight, who frequented Whitechapel and Spitalfields.

Polly chuckled in response to the question. "Well, me feet seem to think so anyways."

The younger woman smiled. "I'm heading towards Buck's Row. Me friend told me there's good trade over there tonight.

You know...." She sidled up to Polly and winked. "One of them special gentlemen's pubs which stays open all night."

"I heard of 'em, but they're bleedin' 'ard to find," Polly said doubtfully.

"Unless you know someone like I do. Care to come along?"

"Why not? I can always use an extra quid or two," Polly snickered. "For me new fashions, of course."

The stranger smiled again. "Let's hurry then."

They walked less than a quarter mile to Buck's Row, situated near the railway yard.

"Over this way," the woman gestured. She indicated a row of darkened doorways. "Tis one of them doors. Number two is the address, I believe."

"It's awful quiet." Polly slurred her words and felt somewhat winded from hurrying to keep pace with the other woman. "You're sure we'll find some gentlemen 'ere?"

"Tis what me friend says," came the reply. "And he should know, being a gentleman himself and all."

"Blimey," exclaimed Polly as she lurched over to the spot where she thought the woman was standing. "You know a proper gent, do you?"

"Indeed, I do. Would you like to meet him, Pol?"

Polly stopped in confusion, eyes straining to see in the swirling fog and darkness. She knew her mind was befuddled from drink, but she could have sworn the other woman had stood right here a moment ago. But if that were so, why did her outstretched arms encounter only empty space, and why did the stranger's voice seem to emanate from several different directions at once?

A prickle of uneasiness started in the pit of her stomach. She didn't like this situation one little bit. Something wasn't right. In fact, it was terribly wrong, but she didn't know what it was. Perhaps if she hadn't been so intoxicated, she wouldn't have wasted time trying to ascertain what was wrong. She might have just reacted to instinct and tried to flee, and she might have succeeded, for if she had been sober, her feet might have been able to respond to her brain's command. As it was, she could barely manage to maintain her balance. A chill crept over her as another thought occurred to her.

How does she know me name? I don't remember telling 'er me name. I know I didn't tell 'er — or maybe I did.

"Where are you?" she asked, surprised at the fear in her voice. Polly's apprehension grew in the ensuing silence. As the seconds ticked by, she became aware of the darkness around her, filled with restless voices, muffled and whispered mutterings, unintelligible yet vaguely ominous.

"Come on now, ducks," she quavered. "Quit trying to scare old Pol, now will ya?"

A throaty chuckle issued from behind her. Polly Nichols had no time to react before strong hands grasped her throat and began to squeeze.

"Well, here I am," a cultured male voice whispered in her ear. With smooth malice, he continued. "Glad to make your acquaintance, Polly. You may call me Jack."

Polly, barely conscious, was yet able to register the object which now appeared in the hand pressed against her throat. Its silver gleam was the only flash of brightness in all the darkness. The last thought in her dulling mind was of her new pretty bonnet and how she'd really had no time to enjoy it. No time at all. Then a quick surge of pain as the knife slashed through flesh and final darkness descended.

***

Constable John Neal whistled softly as he patrolled his regular route at just past three-thirty in the morning. The night had been quiet except for the usual half-hearted drunken skirmishes after the pubs closed their doors. Only a couple of more hours before his tour of duty ended. He looked forward to going home and wondered if his wife was even now busy cooking the kidney and potato pie that was his favorite. He imagined the juicy aroma, and his mouth began to water. He could almost taste that first spicy spoonful of pie.

As he turned the corner into Buck's Row, his pleasant reverie was disrupted by the sight of a still form stretched out on the pavement.

"Blimey, what's this?" he asked aloud.

It was a woman; that much he could tell in the dim illumination of a nearby lamp. He approached the woman and gingerly nudged her with the toe of his boot.

"Missus. Missus." To his consternation, the woman did not move or give any indication she even heard him. "Damnation," Constable Neal muttered. He bent over the still figure and shone his lantern directly on her to get a better look. "Merciful Lord!" he exclaimed, recoiling in horror. The woman was obviously dead, eyes staring vacantly. Her throat had been viciously slashed from ear to ear.

Neal straightened up and immediately blew hard on his whistle. Within a few minutes, another constable came running to his assistance. He had been alerted to the gruesome discovery by two passersby who happened upon the body just prior to Constable Neal. Soon, other officers and the police physician flocked to the scene. After a cursory examination of the body, Dr. Llewellyn directed that it be transported to the mortuary at the old Montague Street Workhouse Infirmary to undergo a complete post-mortem.

As the corpse was lifted onto the casualty cart, Constable Neal noted the large pool of congealed blood which had collected beneath the body. The cart had begun to move forward when the constable spied an object on the ground next to where the unfortunate woman was slain.

"Hang on a moment," he called to the driver, who paused.

Neal retrieved the object and brought it over to the cart. It was a black bonnet with velvet trim. Despite the dirt and bloodstains, it looked to be in fairly new condition, like it hadn't yet molded itself to the contours of its owner's head. It crossed his mind that his wife might fancy such a bonnet. With a grim expression, Neal placed the bonnet next to the sheet clad figure in the cart. In silence, he watched the vehicle lumber away.

CHAPTER 19

The first of September was another hot and sultry day. Mary Simonds and another nurse were in the casualty room of the Whitechapel Infirmary, checking and restocking supplies. Mary sighed as she counted rolls of linen bandages.

"My eyes are itchy and burning from this heat," she complained.

Anne Martin smiled in sympathy. She was a woman in her fifth decade and had worked amongst London's impoverished for many years. "Just think in a few months how cold it will be. Remember we had to wear gloves last winter when we did the inventory?"

Mary laughed shortly. "'Tis true. I thought we certainly would come down with consumption."

The other woman was about to reply when the door banged open, and Emma burst in, waving a newspaper in the air. "There has been another prostitute most foully murdered!"

"Anyone we know?" Anne inquired, interest piqued.

"Mary-Anne Nichols, known as Polly. I have seen her around the streets and at the Princess Alice."

Mary shook her head. "Can't say the name is familiar to me. Who keeps track of all the whores who pass through the infirmary, especially when half of the time they won't even tell you their real names?"

"Well," Anne prompted. "Tell us the details, Emma."

Emma shook her head. "They are gruesome indeed. Polly Nichols was found in the early hours of the morning with her throat slashed. Sliced from ear to ear, *The Star* says."

Anne frowned in distaste, and Mary exclaimed, "That is horrible indeed."

"Wait, there's more," Emma cautioned. "Her abdomen and private parts were severely mutilated, and she had been eviscerated."

Mary and Anne exchanged horrified looks.

"What monster would do such an unspeakable thing?" Anne asked incredulously while Mary covered her face with her hands, severely shaken.

"The police have no clues," Emma said, scanning the news story. "But they hypothesize that it might have been a deranged customer. Sound familiar?"

"Why yes," agreed Mary, removing her hands from her face. "Martha, what's-her-name, murdered earlier in August. The whore who came to the infirmary here the night she was killed."

"Precisely," Emma concurred. "As soon as I read the account, I was reminded of Martha Tabram. Didn't the police in that case announce it was probably a customer as well?"

"That's right. They thought it likely a soldier or a navy man on leave was responsible," Mary said.

"So it is possible the same murderer killed them both?" Anne asked disbelievingly.

Mary shuddered. "This is very disturbing. If it is true, then—"

"Then there is a vicious murderer at large in the East End preying on defenseless women," Emma finished.

"But what a ghastly murder even for this district," commented Anne. "I find it hard to believe such a crime was committed with no witnesses to hear or see anything. More likely, no one is willing to come forward to talk to the police. This is Whitechapel, after all."

***

Throughout the streets of Whitechapel, people stopped to listen to news vendors proclaim the sensational story about the foul and perverted murder of a prostitute in Buck's Row. They gathered in small impromptu groups, exchanging opinions and offering suggestions as to how the authorities might apprehend the murderer. Constables on patrol were approached by helpful citizens ready to share their theories and advice. Many voices were raised in anger and outrage, but under the surface, fear lurked, biding its time before emerging with a vengeance.

The police had released the grisly details of Polly Nichols' murder to the public but minimized their lack of progress in tracking down the killer's identity. As well, they attempted to dismiss the similarities between this murder and that of Martha Tabram in George Yard. They hoped to diffuse public speculation that a madman was stalking the destitute and unfortunate of society.

The last thing the authorities desired was renewed and focused anger amongst the populace of Whitechapel. The memory of last year's East End riots was still fresh in the minds of the constabulary. They wished to avoid provoking increased ire on the part of the citizens. Thus, officially there was no connection between the murders of the two prostitutes. Privately, however, many policemen were of the opinion that the same individual was responsible for both acts, and they were apprehensive that a madman was running amok, for the criminally insane were highly unpredictable and therefore more dangerous than the average killer.

But it was too late for deception. Fear and trepidation had already taken root in the inhabitants of the East End slums. There was no doubt that this brutal murder had shaken them from their torpor. Most believed the killer was a madman, for what other explanation could account for the savagery of the act? They also believed this ordeal would soon end with the capture of the murderer, not because they had great confidence in the local constabulary, but because the killer, being a lunatic, would aid in his own downfall by committing a fatal mistake.

***

However, the citizens of Whitechapel, like their police force, were mercifully ignorant of the magnitude of danger invading their city. Perhaps this was indeed a blessing, for had they glimpsed the hideous truth, they might have been driven to great panic and desperation. They might even have decided to take a plunge into the Thames, thus allowing the river to claim their souls. Then again, it would have been preferable for the river to take one's soul than have it ripped from one's being by the Dark One, who was already in their midst.

CHAPTER 20

Waves of laughter crested and reverberated off the walls of the pub's interior, most of it issuing from the table in the corner near the bar. Eight women of varying ages and looks, but sharing a common occupation, raised their glasses full of gin in acknowledgment of the unspoken bond between them.

One of them, a young woman of twenty-five, possessed of an infectious laugh which invariably brightened even the glummest of countenances, sat with the others. When she was very drunk, which was often, her laughter took on a raucous tone and could be irritating to others. But at this time of the evening, the sun just dipping below the horizon, she was still sober.

Her above average looks and exuberance set her apart from the other women. Whereas most Whitechapel whores displayed the ravages of poverty and disease, this young woman fairly glowed with vitality and vigor. She had a slim figure with a small waist and shoulder length honey blonde hair, which she often wore swept up in the French style. Tonight, as most nights, she was without a bonnet, and her hair was tied back in a thick plait. Her dark blue eyes crinkled to little slits when she smiled. Her mouth, wide and generous, displayed slightly crooked teeth. They were intact except for a couple of lower molars whose absence went unnoticed. Her voice was light, a charming Welsh lilt enhancing its musical quality. That voice now rang out merrily as she regaled her listeners with one of a multitude of humorous stories.

"That's what I told him about the dress I wanted. How it was the most beautiful dress I 'ad ever seen, and how I would be ever so grateful if he could get it for me." She coyly batted her eyelashes, to the delight of her companions. "I described the dress down to the last detail, then 'e asked me what shop I'd seen it in. So, I gave 'im the name and 'e frowned and said in that snooty voice of 'is, 'I am not familiar with that shop. Where exactly is it?'

"So I looked at him all innocent like. 'Why in Paris, of course. Where else?'" She broke up laughing while the others joined in. "But the best is," she waved her hands excitedly. "He went to Paris and bought it for me."

There was a collective gasp of astonishment from the other women.

"You're lying, Mary," declared one. "No man would do that for the likes of you unless he was a bit batty."

The young woman flushed with indignation. "'Tis the truth, I swear. Mary Kelly is no liar." She sneered at the other woman. "Just because it could never 'appen to you, Nelly Carson, is no reason to doubt me. Don't forget, I once lived in Paris with just such a gentleman."

"Ah, so you keep telling us. And where is he now?" Nelly snorted. "In case you 'adn't noticed, this ain't Paris."

A couple of the others snickered. Mary stared at each, in turn, an injured look on her features, lips pouting. "I didn't fancy Paris all that much. I prefer our good British soil. 'Omesick I was, so back 'ere I came. I may 'ave fallen on 'ard times of late, but at least I've known better in life, which is more than I can say for some of you." She tossed her head and straightened her shoulders.

Another woman, Lizzie Foster, snorted her amusement. "Well, I tell you, Mary, at least your stories are entertaining, true or not."

Mary sighed dramatically. "I really don't care if none of you believe me. I know it's true."

"I believe you," said Sarah-Jane, who had been collecting empty glasses at the next table and had overheard the spirited conversation.

"Ah, there's a good lass who knows the truth when she 'ears

it," Mary exclaimed triumphantly.

Sarah-Jane turned and faced the women, one hand effortlessly balancing her tray of glasses. "I know it's true because it's happened to me too. I have gentlemen come in here and ask me to go abroad with them. They want me to be their lady companion, is 'ow they say it."

Lizzie howled at that. "Ha, lady companion, my arse. That's precious. And what do you tell them, girl?"

Sarah-Jane smiled. "I tell them that me dad is standing right over there behind the bar, and why don't they just go over and ask 'is permission."

The others chuckled.

"But 'ave you never been tempted to say yes just to see what it would be like?" Mary inquired.

"Why," Nelly challenged. "So she can end up like us, old before our time and thrown to the gutter when 'er looks fade away?"

Sarah-Jane shrugged. "It would break Da's heart if I was to run off. 'E is constantly worried about that 'appening even though I tell him it won't."

"Do you have a beau?" asked Mary.

"No, Da wouldn't let me. Besides, there is no one around 'ere I fancy. Who wants some factory lad who can barely look you in the eye, all the while blushing and stammering when he is talking to you? Unfortunately, all the interesting men are spoken for."

Mary giggled. "Oh, come now. There's lots of fine Whitechapel men available, right girls?" There was laughter all around. Mary looked speculatively at the young barmaid. "In all seriousness, lass, I don't doubt that you could earn yourself a decent living. Fair hair and good complexion are much in demand, as I should know. Lots of men love women whose beauty reminds them of angels, as long as their behavior ain't angelic too. There are some classy brothels where the wages are good and no freezing your arse off on the streets neither."

"'Ere 'ere, I'll drink to that!" Nelly exclaimed, drinking greedily with lip smacking haste.

Sarah-Jane frowned in distaste. "No offense. But I don't think I could do what you do."

Mary laughed once more. "Oh, it's not so bad. Kind of queer at first, but you get used to it. One big advantage is that you get to leave Whitechapel. If you go to one of the brothels in the west end, like where I was, you'll see 'tis completely the opposite of Whitechapel, and the customers are true gentlemen. They treat you like a lady, not like a cheap whore. They're 'appy to pay for your services. It wasn't a bad place at all."

"Then why did you leave if it was so great?" Nelly demanded.

Mary looked at her with mild irritation. "I told you already. I met a gentleman who offered to take me to Paris with 'im. It was too good an opportunity to turn down. Then when I came back to London, I just sort of got stuck in Whitechapel, and 'ere I remain."

Nelly smirked derisively. "And now you are no better than the rest of us, Mary Kelly. No matter what fancy airs you put on, at the end of the day, you're scrounging like us all for a roof over your 'ead."

Mary tossed her braided head dismissively. "Not exactly. At least I 'ave me own lodging and don't 'ave to sleep in some smelly vermin-infested rooms like some I could name. I also 'ave a decent man in Joe Barnett, whereas some people at this table couldn't keep a man if their life depended on it."

Nelly stood up, weaving slightly before gaining her balance. She shrugged as she said, "Just as long as you remember you're the same as us."

She walked from the table towards the exit. At the doors, she collided with Emma as the latter tried to enter the pub.

"Pardon me," Nelly said with a loud belch as she brushed past Emma.

Emma paid her little notice as she waved at Sarah-Jane. Her gaze fell on the women with whom the barmaid was conversing — an expression of recognition mixed with consternation registered on her face. In quick strides, she crossed the room to the table in the corner.

"Mary Kelly!" she exclaimed. "I might have guessed I'd find you here."

The young woman smiled good naturedly. "Miss 'ollander, 'ow nice to see you. Will you 'ave a drink with us?"

Emma ignored the snickering of a couple of the whores. "Thank you, but no. I'm here to see my friend." She gestured toward Sarah-Jane. "However, since our paths have crossed, I must ask why you failed to keep your appointment at the infirmary today?"

"Truth be told, I never remembered until it was too late. Me mind is sometimes a little scattered like that."

Emma sighed. "But Mary, you know how important this appointment was. You and I talked about the necessity of another health check."

"But I'm feeling so much better," Mary said earnestly. "That concoction you gave me cleared me insides straight out. There is no sickness left, I daresay."

"And where did you receive your medical training?" Emma asked sternly. "That's why physicians and nurses exist, to make those assessments. Just because you are feeling better doesn't mean the infection is gone completely. If even a small bit remains, you can get sick again, likely even worse this time. Won't you come in, Mary? Dr. Mackenzie can see you tomorrow."

Mary let out an exaggerated sigh. "I suppose I will 'ave no peace from you until I do. Can't 'ave you following me around to all the pubs now, can I? All right, I'll come in tomorrow."

Emma smiled warmly. "Good. Let's say just before tea time, shall we?"

Mary nodded. "Whatever you say, Nurse." She raised her glass in salute.

Emma acknowledged the gesture and walked away to join Sarah-Jane.

"Was she really following you?" a woman named Meg asked.

Mary shrugged. "Who knows? With 'er, anything is possible. She's all right, although a bit stubborn."

Liz smiled sardonically. "I guess she would have to be to

deal with the likes of you."

Mary's attention was claimed by a woman who had just entered the Princess Alice. Waving her hand in greeting, she called, "Maria, over 'ere."

The woman joined them, an anxious look on her face. "I can't stay too long," she said. "One drink only."

"That's what you say now," Mary laughed. "But I 'ave never known you to walk away from a pub anywhere near sober."

"Well, not this evening," Maria Harvey replied in a serious tone. "I plan to keep me wits about me."

"Why? What's so special about tonight?" asked Liz.

"What do you mean? The Whitechapel murders, of course!" exclaimed Maria.

"Oh blimey," Liz scoffed. "A couple of whores get themselves killed, and you're all upset. This is a dangerous trade. Some of us are bound to end up dead. Not me, of course," she hastily added, "but others."

"It's not only me. A lot of people think it's the same killer that murdered them two back in August," Maria responded.

"Pshaw," Liz exclaimed.

"Do they now?" asked Mary with interest. "Just what 'ave you 'eard, Maria?"

"Well…." Maria leaned in closer to the others and lowered her voice as if she were about to disclose a great secret. "A friend of mine told me 'e 'eard a couple of coppers talking down by the market, and they seem to think it was one and the same murderer that killed them whores."

"Coppers love to talk. Makes 'em feel important," Liz said in derision. "It doesn't mean they know anything different from the rest of us."

"You can believe whatever you like, but I, for one, will not take no chances out there on the street," retorted Maria.

"A whore has to be able to take care of herself," declared Liz. "I always carry protection with me. You can never tell when you might come across a bad egg. If you're prepared, you're a lot safer."

"That's what I mean," Maria stated emphatically. "A girl has to keep 'er wits about 'er. It's no good carrying a weapon if your senses are so dulled by drink you can't think proper."

"Too right you are," Mary agreed. "Tis best if we all cut down on the grog." Smiling, she lifted her gin in a toast.

Talk of the murders gradually subsided as other topics surfaced to claim the women's interest. After a while, one by one and in pairs, they drifted out to the streets until only Mary Kelly sat alone, staring thoughtfully into her drink.

"A halfpenny for your thoughts," said a voice near her shoulder.

Mary looked up into Emma's lively green gaze. She straightened her shoulders, sitting back in the chair, a small grin playing at the corners of her mouth, enhancing the dimples in her cheeks. "Oh, nothing too important," she said. "Just thinking about me life."

"Is that all?" Emma asked, irony coating her words.

"Aye, thinking of things that 'ave turned out so different from what I expected."

"And what you've hoped?" Emma gently inquired.

"In some ways," Mary replied, reflecting. "I never saw meself living this kind of life, but I daresay not many of us do. I guess I thought it would turn out different for me; like I'd meet some gent who would take me away from this life, set me up in a nice 'ouse, maybe even marry me instead of treating me just as some whore."

"What about the time you spent in France?" asked Emma. "You mentioned that to me once."

Mary's smile faltered, and she sighed. "Oh, that. I made it sound really good to entertain the girls. They find it amusing to think of a man doing that for me."

"You mean it never happened?" queried Emma.

"No, no, it 'appened all right. For a couple of weeks, everything was fine. Then 'e started to get nasty, short-tempered and such, like nothing I did was right. Then 'e started 'itting me, knocking me around. I decided to do better by coming back to

London, so I did."

"I'm sorry it didn't work out for you, Mary. But you did the right thing getting away from that situation."

"It's true," Mary agreed. "Besides, I don't 'ave to go to Paris to find a man who would abuse me. There are plenty here at 'ome to choose from." Her mouth twisted in an ironic smile. "But I don't tell me friends 'ow it really was because they like to 'ear the stories and have a laugh."

"And you tell them what they wish to hear," Emma stated.

"I do indeed. There's no 'arm in that. After all, it's important to 'ave something to dream about," Mary said wistfully.

"You're right, Mary. It is good to have dreams, especially as it is so difficult to sustain them in a godforsaken place like Whitechapel."

Mary registered the anger in Emma's voice. "Why do you work 'ere, Miss 'ollander? I mean, you could be a nurse anywhere. Why 'ere?"

"Why Whitechapel?" Emma echoed. "Believe me, I have asked myself that very question on several occasions. There may be not one particular reason, but I think part of it is that I am needed here. There is work for me to do." She struggled to express her feelings. "It is difficult to explain. Did I choose Whitechapel, or did it choose me? The clarity of this issue often eludes me. Still, every once in a while, I catch a glimmer of what it's about, like seeing the sun's rays poke through the clouds. Briefly, I understand that I am where I am supposed to be, doing what I am supposed to do. I have no idea how long that conviction shall last, but I suspect that when it is no longer there, I shall know it is time for me to depart Whitechapel."

"Blimey, that's deep." Mary looked at her, keenly. "I've never felt anything like that, but I wish I 'ad. Makes you feel like you've a purpose in life, doesn't it?"

"Yes, I guess it does," Emma acknowledged.

"And it helps to know you are not trapped here either."

"Trapped? You mean trapped in a life of poverty?"

"Well, that too," Mary replied. "One is connected to the

other, right? I mean, the ones who live in Whitechapel are poor. Otherwise, they would live somewhere else." She shook her head. "You must 'ave 'eard the superstition about Whitechapel. People 'ere believe that them what's born and bred in Whitechapel, and even anyone who becomes a part of Whitechapel's poverty and disease, is trapped 'ere for life. No matter 'ow 'ard you try, you can never leave Whitechapel. It won't let you go."

Emma frowned. "Granted, poverty does limit one's options, thus making it that much more arduous to better one's self. However —"

"No, that's not it exactly," Mary interjected. "It's the effect Whitechapel 'as on them who lives 'ere. It doesn't want us to leave. It won't allow us to leave. There's them who tried it, of course, but it never works."

Emma stared at Mary, nonplussed. "That's poppycock! Anyone is free to walk away from Whitechapel without fear that they should be smitten by the hand of God."

Mary gazed back at her with a strange expression. "Who said anything about God? I think God is about as far away from Whitechapel as I am from Buckingham Palace. Besides, you could leave anytime, but not me. I belong 'ere with the rest of them."

Emma shook her head in consternation, distressed by the bleak expression that had taken over Mary's face. She decided to shift the conversation, which had become decidedly queer. "What about the man you live with now? Does he treat you well?"

"You mean Joe. Aye, 'e is quite fond of me. A bit gruff, but 'e 'as a good heart. Like most men, though, 'e is a little jealous."

"But he knows what you do? How you make a living?"

"Oh, that," Mary laughed. "Of course 'e knows. I've been straight with him from the start. 'E's not too 'appy naturally, but 'e knows we can't live on 'is pay alone. We got to have some things for ourselves. For me, it's decent clothes and boots. I couldn't stand to parade around in some of the rags the other whores wear." She shrugged her shoulders. "Guess it is an old 'abit from me brothel days."

Emma smiled. "Well, there's nothing wrong with having

good taste." She glanced at the pocket watch attached to her skirt. "Goodness, look at the time. I must go." She stood up. "I shall see you tomorrow, right?"

Mary nodded. "Don't worry, Miss 'ollander. I'll be there."

"Good night then," Emma said and departed the pub.

Mary sighed once more. She knew she should go home before she got any drunker, but Joe was out with his mates, and she didn't want to sit home alone; too many shadows, both external and inside her head. Being alone with shadows was a dangerous prospect. There's no telling what dark path her thoughts might wander down. Better to stay here where there were distractions aplenty. She raised her hand to signal the barmaid.

CHAPTER 21

Dense fog gripped London in a shrouded embrace. Though it was but early September, the night air was damp, presaging the bone-chilling cold that would besiege the city.

Annie Chapman, known as Dark Annie on the streets, plodded down the alley along the Whitechapel Spitalfields border. She felt weak and lightheaded, perhaps because she had eaten a scarce amount throughout the day. She shivered in the dank air, wishing for a good strong cup of tea with lots of milk and sugar. She felt a bit queer like she had been drinking, yet she hadn't had a sip of rum for a couple of days. Lately, she had noticed the sensation, the lassitude which overtook her without warning, sometimes leaving her momentarily befuddled, her thoughts unclear. *Perhaps it is old age taking its toll*, Annie reasoned.

She was forty-seven years old and had never enjoyed the best of health. She loathed going to the infirmary for medical checks and avoided doctors like the plague. But last week, she'd felt so poorly she actually found herself on the steps of the old Montague Street Infirmary. The doctor had wanted to admit her for observation and rest. He didn't like the sound of her lungs, but Annie didn't agree to that. In her experience, once a poor soul entered those infirmary walls, he or she never again saw the light of day. Annie coughed harshly, disregarding the twinge of pain in her chest. Better to die in the streets, she thought, than in some ward with strangers hovering around and the cries and moans of the desperately ill creating a macabre chorus.

This was a miserable night; hardly anyone about the streets. She longed to be in her lodging at 35 Dorsett Street, but as misfortune would have it, she was unable to afford this night's rent. Sighing heavily, she turned the corner onto Hanbury Street. Maybe she would find shelter near one of the buildings where she could hunker for a while and collect her thoughts.

The backyard gate of Number 29 Hanbury was ajar, so she went through into the small courtyard. It was a shabby tenement with flats rented by the week, but this time of night, no one stirred. Anyone lucky enough to have a roof over his head was safely ensconced in bed. Annie lowered her weary body to the ground and rested her back against a set of steps. She thought she would take just a few minutes to catch her breath, but before she was aware of it, sleep claimed her. She woke with a start, muscles stiff and aching.

Oh, I must 'ave drifted off, she thought, aware that the darkness was brightening as night crept towards dawn. She rubbed her eyes and yawned. There was a sound off to her left, a light rustling as if someone was moving about.

"Blimey, what time is it?" a husky female voiced asked softly.

Annie shifted her sore bones, craning her neck to see beyond the stair banister. She was able to make out the shape of another woman sprawled on the ground, obviously, like Annie, in the process of awakening.

Must have come in after me, she thought, *since I am sure no one was 'ere when I lay me down.*

The woman looked over at Annie and smiled as she sat up. "Morning, dearie. Restful sleep, was it?"

Annie shrugged. "I've 'ad worse."

"I daresay you 'ave," the woman laughed. She was perhaps in her late twenties, with attractive but unremarkable features. "Got any money?" she inquired.

Annie looked at her askance. "If I did, do you think I would be sleeping outside?"

The woman yawned and stretched luxuriously, catlike. "Well, I for one 'ave got to get some money. I am famished." She rose to her feet, smoothing and dusting off her skirts. She was a good height, perhaps five-foot-seven with a slender yet solid figure.

Annie was uncomfortably aware of the churning and gnawing sensation in her own stomach. A wave of dizziness nearly overcame her as she struggled to a sitting position. The stranger knelt before her, peering at her with a concerned expression.

"Poor dearie, you look 'alf done in. Need some 'elp getting up?"

Reluctantly, Annie nodded. Chagrined that her weakness was so apparent, she was nevertheless grateful for the woman's offer of assistance. As she extended her hand, the woman ignored it, instead shoving her backwards heavily with both palms. Annie sprawled on the ground, momentarily stunned. Her thoughts whirled in confusion, the only coherent idea emerging that the woman believed she had money and meant to rob her.

"I told you I don't 'ave no money," she yelled plaintively.

The woman's face had been transformed by a feral sneer. She spat at the prostrated whore and then pounced on Annie, grasping her by the throat. Annie moaned, her neck feeling like it was caught in a vise, the grip more powerful than anything she had ever imagined, let alone encountered. She was completely immobilized, unable to use her arms or legs.

In her many years on the streets of Whitechapel, Annie had found herself in precarious situations, but none as life threatening as this. She'd never seen such a malevolent expression or such depraved glee in someone's eyes. She tried to scream for help, but no sound could escape, trapped by the lethal force crushing her throat. In agony, the pressure built, extending from her throat up into her head, causing a pain so fierce she was sure her brain would burst apart. As the hands tightened and squeezed, the constriction became unbearable. Her body went limp and numb.

She felt nothing below her neck, her entire essence concentrated in the exquisite pain radiating from neck to head. Spots danced before her eyes as she struggled to remain conscious. Then, miraculously, she was able to breathe again, but that brought little relief. Each inspiration was more torture to her traumatized throat. She was as helpless as a fish out of water, tremors racking her body as her assailant leaned over her. The woman fixed her malevolent gaze upon Annie's face, locking eyes with her victim.

Spurred by terror, Annie sought in vain to close her eyes, sensing that though her body was already lost to this fiend, she might yet save her soul if she could only protect her eyes from the darkness of that gaze. But all her strength had drained away so that even a simple action such as this was beyond her. Too late, she comprehended a flash of silver as her instrument of death.

With tremendous force, the blade slashed across Dark Annie's neck, almost severing her head. A brief yet intense pain seared her body. Horror engulfed her as she registered the gaping edges of jagged flesh, literally feeling the blood vessels, sinews, and nerves unraveling from her neck. A geyser of blood spurted from the wound, drenching her in seconds. The spots before her eyes exploded into dark pools, drawing her into them. Deeper and deeper, she fell, plummeting to their depths. By the time she realized she would never surface, Annie Chapman was no more.

**

The killer stood well back from the blood, waiting for the death throes to subside. The whole process was remarkably swift. The gurgles and gasps, the struggles and convulsions ceased abruptly. When it was over, the woman looked around, scanning the environment for any sign of alarm. All was quiet.

The murderer knelt to the right of the corpse, a contented smile on her lips as she gazed at her victim. Then she picked up the blade once more and began to slash and rip the body of Dark Annie. Working with remarkable speed and dexterity, the knife seemed imbued with a will of its own. In perfect harmony with the hand that wielded it, the knife rose and fell in a mesmerizing dance. A strange fluidity of grace accompanied the motions, killer and knife intimately joined; the blade slicing through layers of fat and sinew, muscle and tendon with tremendous force, masked by the skill and artistry of the mind behind the knife.

At last, the buried treasure exposed, the abdominal cavity with the glistening internal organs beckoned enticingly, awaiting the crimson kiss of the blade. Dawn was about to break, and still, the mutilations continued; knife strokes deft and deliberate, no frenzy evident — a fact the newspaper reports would cite. Carnage ceased only when the desecration of the flesh was absolute when the body resembled nothing more than a carcass laid open. As a slaughtered animal's corpse was cast to rot, so were the remains of Annie Chapman stripped of any human dignity. Dark Annie no more resembled a woman than dead meat hanging in the butcher's window.

At last, the murderer sat back, her work complete. She eyed it critically, a demonic artist surveying her macabre masterpiece. An expression of undiluted malevolence glittered in her onyx eyes. She rose and quickly removed her outer layer of clothing, which was bloody and spattered with gore. These she bundled into a neat ball and stuffed in the battered bag she carried. The knife was safely hidden in its sheath away from prying eyes.

Bessie Boyd smoothed her skirts and straightened her hair and new bonnet. She exited Hanbury Street by the back gate, disappearing into the welcoming shadows.

CHAPTER 22

The interior of the club was a combination of luxury and practical décor. Designed like a huge drawing room with a large stone fireplace against one wall, the room contained tasteful furniture and harmonious colors. Comfortable velvet and brocade armchairs were grouped around tables for those gentlemen who wished to socialize and enjoy the company of others. For those who desired privacy, secluded alcove spaces were available.

The room's colors were rich yet muted, from the elegant tapestries adorning the walls to the dark beam of polished oak and mahogany tables. Intricately patterned Persian rugs sprawled across the floor, muting the sound and enhancing the tranquil atmosphere. Men came here to dine, to meet with friends or business associates, to debate politics and discuss issues of law, medicine, philosophy, or whatever subject claimed their interest. But mostly, they came to be with other men, to celebrate and congratulate one another on their various successes, whether professional or personal in nature. Every man, albeit unaware, looked to his neighbor's face hoping to see the reflection of his own achievements and tacit confirmation of self-worth—except for one man, who had no need of affirmation from others.

Andrew Hewitt-Brown, self-contained as a fortress, sat at his accustomed table, strategically placed to allow him an unobstructed view of the entire room. Ever vigilant, he wished there to be no opportunity for those who might wish him harm to sneak up on him unawares. He lifted his glass, swirling the amber colored liquid gently before raising it, allowing the heady aroma of the cognac to penetrate his senses. He sipped, savoring the smoldering delight as the liquid slid smoothly down his throat.

Across the table sat his good friend, Montague John Druitt, whom he had met when they were both students at Oxford College. Normally quite gregarious and sociable, Druitt was unusually subdued this evening. He drank his whiskey and smoked a cigar in silence. Hewitt-Brown had attempted to initiate a flow of conversation, but Druitt appeared distracted and soon lost interest in whatever topic was being discussed.

Hewitt-Brown eyed his friend speculatively. "Come now, Monty. All evening long, you have been under a thundercloud. Something is troubling you. You wish to talk about it?"

Druitt looked up from his drink, a half-hearted smile on his lips. "Just my inner demons letting me know they are still present, lurking in the recesses of my mind, clamoring for attention." He briefly made eye contact but looked away.

"You are concerned about your mother?" Andrew suggested.

Just this past July, Ann Druitt, Montague's mother, had been certified insane and confined to Brook Asylum. The sad smile widened a little.

"Astute as always, old chap," Druitt sighed heavily. "It seemed that she was making progress, nothing spectacular, but a steady improvement nonetheless. Her sleep was less disturbed, and she experienced periods of lucidity and was generally calmer. But I went to visit her the other day, and as God is my witness, Andrew, I swear she is deteriorating again. She didn't even recognize me at first. She thought I was one of those plotting to electrocute her. It took me forever to convince her that I was her son, and even then, I could see the distress in her eyes as if she only pretended to believe me." He pounded his fist on the table. "It is so bloody distressing to see her like that. No way to reach her, to make her see reason, no way to calm her fears and make her feel safe." He gripped his glass tightly, teeth clenched in a grimace of despair.

"I can see that it is most upsetting to you," Andrew said. "Disease of the mind is so much more complicated because its elusive quality prevents men from truly understanding its components. Men may look at a gangrenous limb or see visible ravages of disease upon the body itself, but the mind — now, that is a mystery. What causes the mind to snap like a delicate violin string stretched too tautly? Why are treatments so inadequate that the only recourse is to lock people away, so they do not harm themselves or others?"

He leaned closer to Druitt, the intensity of his gaze compelling the other man to look at him eye to eye. "I know this is small consolation now," he whispered. "But rest assured, hope is not abandoned. There shall be important advancements in the understanding and treatment of mental infirmity."

Druitt gazed at him in wonder. "How can you know this, Andrew? My god, you are a strange fellow, and have been since first we met all those years ago. Always coming up with bizarre ideas and pronouncements. And yet…," his tone softened, "You have spoken the truth every time, and have a wisdom and foresight that are remarkable indeed. For reasons incomprehensible to me and against my better judgment, I believe your words." He shook his head, puzzled.

Andrew smiled. "That is no mystery, my friend. However, I believe the concern for your mother is not the only issue that occupies you."

Druitt sighed again, this time with a hint of exasperation. "Confound it, Andrew! No matter how I try to push things aside, you always know. Have you the ability to probe my heart, to hear the echo of my darkest secrets? It is true that I also worry about myself and my siblings. As you may be aware, diseases of the mind are prevalent in my family. My mother's mother committed suicide. My mother has attempted the same, as has her sister, my aunt, who has also, from time to time, been confined to an asylum.

"I fear that whatever defect of mind plagues them may also affect me. If that should occur, I know I couldn't go on living. When I see how Mother has suffered, I can't condemn her for trying to end the pain of her existence. I only pray that I should have the fortitude and determination to complete the act rather than submit to the indignities of an asylum. It is a fear that haunts me continuously, a menacing phantom, and as it steadily grows, I wonder if it is a sign that I am already disturbed.

"Every time a strange thought intrudes into my mind, or I misinterpret what someone says, I ask myself, is it starting? Yet, I have heard that one is usually oblivious of the signs of encroaching madness. Thus will I even recognize its onset or be the only one blind to it? I tell you, Andrew, I am haunted; yes haunted." Druitt sat back, a sheen of perspiration on his forehead and trembling noticeably as he raised his glass to his lips.

Compassion softened the intensity of Andrew's gaze. "It is indeed a terrible burden to bear."

Tears glistened in the corners of Druitt's eyes. "Andrew, you are a man whom I trust absolutely. Promise that you will tell me if you observe any strangeness of thought or disturbance of behavior on my part."

Andrew's expression was subtle. "I can assure you of one thing, Monty, and that is, should your fear come to pass and you begin to descend into the abyss of madness, you shall recognize it yourself, requiring no confirmation from other sources."

Druitt nodded. "Yes, I see that you understand. Then we shall speak of this no more." He drained his whiskey in one swallow. "Look there, Hastings and Carruthers have arrived." He stood and hailed the other men. "Hey, good fellows, over here." Hearty greetings ensued as the four shook hands and sat down at the table.

Andrew signaled to their server. "I took the liberty of ordering drinks for you gentlemen. The usual for you both, I presume."

Carruthers laughed. "Ah yes, good chap. That was thoughtful of you." He nodded in satisfaction as the server deposited the glass of port and a selection of cheeses in front of him.

Sebastian Hastings murmured his thanks as he raised his snifter of brandy. "Cheers." The others lifted their glasses in salutation, Druitt having replenished his whiskey.

"So, how go things in the import-export business?" Carruthers inquired of Hewitt-Brown. "I heard you were recently in India."

Andrew inclined his head in assent. "Yes, I was. The business is flourishing. Malcolm and Reginald both, fortunately, possess good management sense, and things are running smoothly."

Carruthers smiled. He was in his early thirties, with brown curly hair and a round, cherubic face that lent his countenance an innocent cast, an attribute which often proved a surprise advantage for him over his opponents in court. He worked as a barrister for one of London's prestigious law firms. "Ah, but they always call on their big brother to help them over a spot of trouble," he remarked.

Andrew shrugged. "Once in a while, I offer suggestions as to how certain aspects of the business might be improved. But over the last year or so, I have had less and less of a hand in things. I see my role more as a consultant than an actual partner in the company."

Carruthers laughed loudly and slapped his knee. "Aha, I suspected as much. You plan to go off and start your own business quite separate from the family. Right enough?"

Andrew smiled enigmatically and sipped his cognac. "Now, James, what gives you that idea?"

"Because, you scoundrel, I know how your mind works," Carruthers proclaimed. "You have become bored with the import-export trade. You require a new challenge to stimulate your interests."

Hastings nodded in agreement. "James is right, Andrew. You constantly seek new experiences, new creative enterprises, and your ideas are unfalteringly brilliant."

"Here, here," Carruthers acknowledged, toasting Andrew. "Perhaps you would be willing to entertain the idea of a partner in your business venture."

Andrew chuckled. "Why, James. Are you offering your services? I should think a successful barrister like yourself would not have the additional time or energy to invest in such an endeavor."

"While it's true that my career demands are significant, I am never averse to a potential lucrative business prospect,"

Carruthers replied.

Hastings reached for the cheese tray, helping himself to a slice of Stilton. "I fear that you are in for it, Andrew. James will not be easily dissuaded now that he has hold of this idea."

"Well, that remains to be seen," Andrew responded. "If indeed I have in mind a venture, the time is not yet right to discuss it. Therefore, let us turn to another topic."

Carruthers smiled. "Very good. But as Hastings says, I am as tenacious as a dog with a bone."

"Which, my dear fellow, is not in question," stated Andrew. "It is, in fact, one of your better qualities."

Hastings and Carruthers laughed heartily while Druitt remained glum, a distant expression in his eyes.

"I say, Monty, you are uncommonly taciturn," Hastings remarked. "You aren't feeling ill, I trust?"

There was a momentary pause before Druitt responded. "No, no, of course not, Sebastian. I am simply preoccupied."

"Oh, with what?" Carruthers inquired, ignoring Hastings' frown.

"These damnable Whitechapel murders," Druitt replied.

"The prostitute murders?" Carruthers asked incredulously. "Why do you bother yourself about that, old fellow? A few whores less never hurt anybody." He shook his head.

A flash of anger briefly flared in Druitt's eyes. "Whores they may be, but the savagery of the killings is most disturbing."

Carruthers shrugged dismissively. "Only if one allows it to disturb one. A hazard of the trade is how I see it, old chap. Prostitutes, particularly those in the East End, place their lives in jeopardy every single night, presumably."

"Yes, but these women are especially targets of one individual," Druitt countered. "They are stalked and slaughtered like animals simply because they are whores. No decent woman has been victimized."

Carruthers chuckled. "One would be hard pressed to find a decent woman in Whitechapel."

"Careful where you tread, James," Hastings cautioned.

"Andrew's betrothed works in the area, doesn't she?"

"Indeed she does," confirmed Andrew.

"Why, dear chap. You know I meant no offense," Carruthers, in a fluster, protested.

Andrew raised his hand in a conciliatory gesture. "You haven't offended me, James. However, Monty has a point, one which is shared by my fiancée, Emma. She works with these people, tends to their needs, teaches them ways to improve their health. These women, however downtrodden and unfortunate, are human beings, and they have been brutalized in the most appalling fashion."

"Yes, if one gives credence to the newspaper accounts," Hastings concurred. "The mutilations of the corpses are particularly horrific. The popular opinion holds one man responsible for all three murders, as Monty stated. It's causing quite a stir and having a negative impact on the businesses and trades in Whitechapel.

"There is talk that these murders, especially if more were to come, could disrupt the precarious economical state of the entire East End, and that would inevitably affect the rest of London adversely as well." Hastings worked for his father in a respected financial institution, and so was privy to this information.

"So there is one madman running around Whitechapel wreaking fear and havoc," Carruthers said. "Scotland Yard will catch him soon enough. Believe you me, after last year's riots, Sir Charles Warren doesn't relish any further trouble in the East End. The police will find this lunatic or heads will roll."

"They say he leaves no clues behind, none at all," Hastings mused. "Vanishes without a trace. No one has ever seen or so much as heard him."

"Nonsense," Carruthers exclaimed. "If the police are saying that, it is merely to cover up their own incompetence. What say you, Andrew?"

"It is indeed a mystery shrouded in shadow and fog, much like Whitechapel itself. How apropos this killer should strike the East End where the most vulnerable population resides. People with no names, no faces, no homes, no identity. Here one day, gone the next. The transient quality of their lives so brilliantly suits the killer's purpose; no one to even notice their absence, save when a mutilated corpse is conveniently discovered."

The men were silent as they contemplated Andrew's words. Then Hastings, with a puzzled frown, ventured, "It's true what you say, Andrew, but no one would even realize that those women were murdered were it not for the discovery of their bodies. Why then doesn't the murderer dispose of the remains? That would be easily accomplished by simply dumping the body in the Thames. It would be ages before they would be found, if ever."

Druitt said quietly, "The answer is simple. He wants the bodies to be discovered."

Hastings' frown deepened. "Why on earth would the killer want that? There is much more chance of him being apprehended that way."

Druitt shook his head. "You said so yourself, Sebastian—he leaves no clues behind. What fear does he have of apprehension? It's obvious he doesn't want the killings to remain a secret, for what would be the point of these murders? No, this murderer obtains satisfaction from the reaction of the public. He thrives on the notoriety and, more importantly, the fear that his actions arouse." He turned to Carruthers. "Why do you think he is mad?"

"What other explanation is there?" replied Carruthers. "I don't pretend to understand the poppycock you just said, but unless he knows these women personally and they all somehow have grievously wronged him, the only conclusion to draw is that he is insane."

Druitt looked down at his drink. "He has a reason for his behavior. Whether it is understood by anyone else or not, his actions, these murders, are intended to evoke fear, even terror in the populace. On the whole, his plan has been rather a smashing success, don't you think?"

"Ha," Carruthers slapped the table. "I rest my case. For if fear is his motive, along with infamy, then indeed, madness has claimed him and disrupted his perceptions. What sane man would wish to be known for heinous acts of murder? You know how madmen are; no matter how disturbed they may be, in their own minds, they rationalize their actions. Sometimes they may even present themselves in a somewhat normal and sound manner. But it only works for a time.

"Take you, for instance, Monty. You could be stark raving mad, yet sit here and have drinks with us, all the while plotting our gruesome demise." He chuckled at this idea as he delved into a delicate piece of Camembert. "Why, for any of us knows, you could be the dreaded Whitechapel fiend."

Andrew, who had keenly observed Druitt throughout the proceeding interaction, now saw his friend start and his color fade to a ghastly pallor. For a moment, he seemed to look as though he might faint, but the moment passed. His hand that gripped his glass tightly now began to tremble. He seemed to want to speak, his mouth opening and shutting. Unable to maintain eye contact with any of the others, he lowered his head, but not before shooting Andrew a look of pure panic, as though he were a drowning man begging rescue.

Hastings and Carruthers both stared at Druitt with perplexed, slightly alarmed expressions. Hastings was about to say something when Andrew intervened to shift focus from the panic-stricken man.

"I believe that Monty has a valid theory about this murderer," he said. "It would appear that the nature of his crimes is designed to disturb and frighten ordinary men and women. It isn't that Whitechapel is unfamiliar with murder and other violent crimes, but that these crimes are perpetrated with a deliberate intent of causing fear and revulsion to a degree where normal daily life is disrupted."

It was apparent that Carruthers was tiring of the subject. "It may be as you say," he said with a shrug. "But I for one shan't lose any sleep over the matter." He gazed surreptitiously at Druitt, who still sat with bowed head.

Andrew deftly steered the conversation away from the disturbing topic. As talk drifted to less provocative subjects, he carefully monitored Druitt's response. The tension gradually drained from the latter's face, the frown moving from his forehead, stress lines fading from the corners of his mouth, clenched fists slowly relaxing. The discussion, by tacit agreement, was kept light, staying clear of murder and madness. After a while, Druitt attempted in a half hearted manner to rejoin the conversation, but it was clear that any interaction at this point was a strain on him. Finally, he rose from the table and bid his farewell.

"I apologize for my dismal manner this evening," he said. "It was ill advised on my part to have sought company while in this mood. I trust I haven't spoiled the evening for any of you, and I promise when next we meet to be a more congenial companion."

Carruthers waved his hand in an expansive gesture. "Don't distress yourself, Monty. I hope you feel more like your old self soon."

Hastings nodded. "Here here, my sentiments exactly. We shall see you in a fortnight, old fellow."

As soon as Druitt had exited the club, Carruthers shook his head. "My God!" he exclaimed. "What the devil is wrong with the man? He would jump at his own shadow."

Hastings concurred. "He is certainly most high strung. Do you have any clue what troubles him, Andrew? I seem to recall some sort of illness with his mother."

"Yes, he is quite concerned for his mother's welfare," answered Andrew. "It's no secret that she was recently confined to an insane asylum. She had been ill for many years but had deteriorated markedly and could no longer be cared for at home."

Carruthers whistled. "So that explains his reaction to the subject of madness. No wonder he was so defensive during this discussion. Old Monty's mother in the madhouse! Poor sod, he is probably worried that he could become a lunatic as well."

"That does appear to be a preoccupation of his," Andrew acknowledged. "Monty has always been acutely sensitive, so it is no surprise that he has become fixated on the Whitechapel murders. The subject seems to hold a fascinating allure for many."

"But it's rather odd, don't you think?" Hastings inquired.

"On the one hand, he seems truly appalled by the murders, yet on the other, he displays an almost sympathetic attitude toward the murderer." He frowned. "Perhaps he believes the murderer should not be held accountable for his actions if he is insane."

"Right you are, Bastian, especially if he has seen firsthand the effects of madness," Carruthers agreed. He shook his head in chagrin. "I wish I had known about his mother. I would never have taunted him with that ludicrous talk about him being the East End murderer." He looked at his friends accusingly. "Why didn't one of you simply tell me to shut my bloody mouth?"

"That would have only inflamed the situation," Andrew responded. "By calling attention to his family's plight, we would have embarrassed him most horribly. Besides, the damage was already done long before tonight's conversation. It was merely unfortunate that you had to articulate some of Monty's worst fears."

"What? That he is going to go insane and embark on a murderous rampage?" Carruthers exclaimed in amusement. "That was a jest, admittedly in very poor taste, I belatedly realize. I didn't for one minute mean to infer that I believed such a tale—"

"No, of course, you didn't," Andrew interrupted. "And indeed Monty is not running amok killing whores in Whitechapel. But, contrary to popular belief, the Whitechapel murderer is not insane."

"He is not?" Hastings echoed dubiously.

"Whatever do you mean by this pronouncement, Andrew?" Carruthers protested.

"A man who commits such heinous acts is not necessarily deranged. He is undoubtedly evil."

Both men stared at him, perplexed. "You may call it evil, but one could argue that insanity is a form of evil," Carruthers said.

"The interesting question is, did their insanity lead them to evil actions, or did the evil which possessed them eventually drive them insane? I firmly believe, gentlemen, that those who open themselves to evil influence receive that which overpowers their will, thus leading them on a path to destruction from which there is no salvation. Whoever this murderer is, he is not a raving lunatic who attacks at random and kills in a frenzy. Quite the opposite, in fact; he is level headed, well organized, and plans his attacks with care and cunning. If he were a lunatic, he would have been apprehended by now."

Hastings continued to look puzzled. "But if he isn't insane, what purpose has he in killing in such a brutal manner?"

Andrew shrugged. "Evil's purpose is quite simple. It exists to disrupt and destroy the spiritual equilibrium of man. Monty's observations weren't far off the mark. This murderer definitely intends his victims to be discovered while his identity remains shrouded in mystery. His desire is to create an atmosphere of fear and horror, and what more fitting means than to show his diabolical cleverness by eluding capture by the best police force in all of Britain, and some might say in all the civilized world?"

Hastings shook his head in wonder. "I don't profess to have as keen a sense of the intricacies of the human mind as you, Andrew. However, I must concede that you present a convincing scenario when a short while ago I, along with most Londoners, thought a blood-thirsty maniac skulked the streets brandishing a knife whenever the fancy struck him. Now I am certain that he is a clever, calculating bastard who has a perverse motivation to kill and to taunt us all in the process. Perhaps you and James should switch positions. I think you would make an excellent barrister and present your arguments brilliantly."

Carruthers was mildly perturbed by the last comments. "You forget one thing, dear chap," he said irritably to Hastings. "As brilliant as Andrew may be, this is all still supposition on his part. He is not privy to information issued from Scotland Yard, at least not to my admittedly meager knowledge. Or have the inspectors called upon your services to assist them in tracking the murderer?" His tone was mocking now as he turned to Andrew. "I know," he snapped his fingers. "You have received a personal invitation from Sir Charles himself, asking you to share your pearls of wisdom with the police."

"Sarcasm and churlishness are two of your less appealing

characteristics, James," Andrew admonished lightly. "And perhaps it would be wise of Sir Charles to heed my words."

"That's precisely the sort of statement which irks me," Carruthers said in exasperation. "You are so damned smug, so convinced that what you have to say is more valuable than that of anyone else."

Andrew smiled in amusement. "Only if one values the truth above deception and prevarication."

"Ha, I knew it!" Carruthers exclaimed triumphantly, slapping the table for emphasis. "You mean to say, Andrew, that you always speak the truth?"

"If the truth is known to me, then yes, I speak it," replied Andrew in a more serious tone.

"Ah." Carruthers shook his head in frustration. "I simply abhor trying to win an argument with you. You are so perturbing, Andrew. It's like trying to argue with the oracle at Delphi. You could never be persuaded to any other point of view."

"But there is no other point of view," Andrew objected. "There is truth, and there is deception. Your points of view are rationalizations of lies. Either something is true, or it is not. Just because one disguises the falsehood as truth doesn't render it so."

"Come now, James," Hastings urged, laughing. "You must concede defeat. As always, Andrew's logic is impeccable. You have yet to confound him at any discourse."

"I didn't think we were engaged in intellectual rivalry, James. Certainly, I do not view it as such," Andrew said. "What I enjoy is good, stimulating conversation between friends. Isn't that sufficient?"

Before Carruthers could reply, Hastings interjected. "Didn't you know that James perceives everything in terms of victory and defeat? His mind naturally operates that way. It serves him well as a barrister. Must keep a keen sense of competitiveness, right old chap?"

Carruthers shrugged. "Of course, I look forward to our conversations. The differences of opinion enhance the exchange, don't you agree?"

"By all means," acknowledged Andrew. "We can't all have the same ideas and thoughts. Otherwise, there would be no point in sharing the experiences. However, I don't believe there must be winners and losers, for when ideas are presented, there is always something to be learned; new knowledge and insights are gained. And what is knowledge if not the greatest acquisition, and its brother wisdom, the purest form of power?"

"Well said, good fellow, I'll drink to that." Hastings raised his glass in salute.

The flow of conversation soon reached its natural ebb. The three men prepared to go their separate ways, agreeing to meet again in a fortnight. Once on the street, both Hastings and Carruthers hailed cabs.

Andrew decided to walk home. The evening air was crisp, not cold. For once, the dampness and fog were in abeyance. The night should have been pleasant, but Andrew's keen senses detected an undercurrent of tension trembling beneath the city streets, deep in the labyrinth and heart of London itself. Continually in tune with the unique energies around him, he was acutely cognizant of the habitual rhythm of the city's heart being disrupted. In other words, London was under siege.

***

In the unusually quiet streets of Whitechapel, shadows played with echoes of whispers, phantoms shifted shapes, cavorting in alleyways; wraiths shivered, pale forms draped in lacy tendrils of fog as they glided along the cobblestone paths. A gateway to this world had been opened for them, and they came, eager to follow the dark master who had summoned them. Their single-minded purpose was to propagate and feed off human misery, offering in return devastation and chaos. Spiritual scavengers and parasites, their existence was dependent upon the number of souls they could claim. Each broken soul was another dead blossom on the funereal garland the dark master would wear as a symbol of his supremacy over mankind. Nothing could stop him from satisfying his dark cravings. The day of reckoning was fast approaching.

CHAPTER 23

The Whitechapel Infirmary was busier than usual this September evening. An accident down by the docks at the end of the workday had injured several men who had been unloading heavy cargo. Three of the injured were presently in the urgent casualty section, while the remainder had been carted off to other infirmaries in the East End. In addition to these serious casualties was the usual motley assortment of complaints ranging in nature from significant to minor.

The inhabitants of Whitechapel were not renowned for their pleasant and tolerant dispositions, especially when sick or in pain. The mood in the general casualty ward was one of high disgruntlement, with many complaining bitterly and loudly about the long wait and their neighbors' less urgent ailments.

One particularly irate patient, an elderly woman with a stooped gait, waved her cane in the air, swiping it at anyone who came near her space in line. "I'm next, I'm next," she yelled repeatedly. "No one is getting ahead of old Gertie."

"Stop your caterwauling, you old crow," a man shouted. "There are some really sick people here, so shut your mouth and wait like the rest of us."

"I'm sicker than any of you." The old woman whipped aside her ragged mud spattered skirt to reveal misshapen hobnail boots. She stuck one foot out, kicking off the boot. "See," she cried triumphantly.

She pointed to the grossly swollen foot wrapped in bandages saturated with a purulent fluid, which gave off an appalling odor. Several people in the vicinity shoved and pushed one another to get away, running from the reeking and festering wounds.

Gertie surveyed the crowd in satisfaction. "You see, me old foot is covered in them sores, hurts something terrible. I needs to see a doctor now." She banged her cane on the floor for emphasis.

Meanwhile, in the adjacent urgent casualty area, Emma and two other nurses worked furiously with the physician to try to stabilize the injured workers. Two of them, though seriously hurt, were not critical. However, the man Emma attended had sustained a grave injury to his left leg. A heavy crate had fallen on it, completely crushing the limb. He already had lost a dangerous amount of blood from the ruptured vessels. The man was still conscious but in a delirium of pain. Emma did her best to calm him while Dr. Pelham quickly assessed the mangled limb.

Pelham shook his head, a deep frown creasing his brow. "Prepare for amputation, and hope that the blood loss has not been too great."

The man's eyes grew round with terror as he registered the physician's words. Through his haze of pain, he began to scream frantically. He attempted to sit up but was too weak to do more than thrash feebly on the narrow cot. Emma grabbed him by the shoulders, holding him securely in place.

"Please, Mr. Donnelly, you must try to calm yourself. We must perform this procedure if you are to survive."

Tears of dread and agony cascaded down the man's face. "Don't cut me leg off, please. I'd rather die!"

Pelham continued to frown as he momentarily turned away from the patient. "The other two are fairly stable. Miss Martin...." He beckoned to one of the other nurses. "Could you help Miss Hollander prepare the patient for surgery?"

"Yes, Doctor," Anne Martin replied. She quickly collected the items and towels necessary for the procedure while Emma endeavored to clean the wound, hoping to minimize the threat of deadly infection.

Dr. Pelham clicked his teeth in frustration as he selected his surgical instruments. "I could do with another pair of hands. Someone get Mr. Dennys. Where in damnation is he anyway?"

"He is doing a post-mortem," Emma replied.

"Well, get him in here. We really need his services more than the dead, and someone attend to that commotion in the waiting area," Pelham ordered irritably.

"Right away, Doctor," the attendant said as he hastily retreated through the door.

Emma continued to soothe the frightened man as Dr. Pelham began to wash up.

Anne Martin approached Mr. Donnelly with a cup of strong spirits. "Drink this," she instructed, pouring the liquor into the man's mouth a little at a time. "It will help dull the pain."

Emma looked at her in dismay. "Where's the chloroform?" she demanded.

A grimace appeared on Anne's face. "There's none left," she said helplessly. "The supply has not arrived yet."

Emma clenched her teeth in consternation. This was the worst situation in which to find oneself without the anesthetic. But unlike the larger hospitals, the infirmaries in Whitechapel were not always assured of the steady supply of the drug. It was true that the number of surgeries had increased over the last month or so. Still, Emma cursed silently, for if there was any time she wished oblivion for her patients, it was the procedure which awaited the hapless Mr. Donnelly.

She noticed that the other nurse had stopped the administration of the alcohol. "Give him more than that," she instructed sharply. Anne looked at her dubiously, but in a fierce whisper, Emma interrupted. "Do as I say. Better that he should be rendered insensible from the alcohol than from the pain."

Anne nodded and hesitantly offered more drink to the man. He spluttered and tried to refuse the foul tasting liquor.

"Open your mouth, Mr. Donnelly," Emma commanded. "It will be worse for you if you do not."

Despite his agony, the man understood and obediently drank more. Just then, the door burst open and an attendant, harried and flustered, announced urgently, "Doctor, come quickly. A child has gone into convulsions, and the mother is hysterical."

Pelham swore in irritation. "Where the devil is Dennys? I need him here now. Miss Hollander, is the patient ready for surgery?"

"Yes, Doctor."

John Dennys entered the room, his relaxed manner at odds with the frantic atmosphere of the casualty area. He grabbed an apron from the pile of clean linen and approached the others.

"Ah, Dennys, at last," Pelham stated. "I need you to attend a child in the waiting area whilst I perform an amputation."

Dennys examined the stuporous man on the cot. "A complete amputation, I gather?"

"I am afraid so," Pelham concurred. "All the bones, including the femur, are crushed."

Dennys turned to him. "Doctor, since surgery is to be my specialty, may I propose that I perform the amputation while you attend to other matters?"

Pelham considered momentarily, then shrugged and nodded. "I have no objection. Dr. Mackenzie has instructed me to afford you as much opportunity as possible to hone your surgical skills. Proceed. I am off to assess the child."

Anne Martin indicated the instrument tray. "Everything is ready, sir."

She and Emma began to drape the patient, now mercifully quiet, ensuring that additional towels and buckets were strategically placed around the operating site.

"Once the pressure bandage is removed, we must work very quickly to sever the limb before there is more blood loss." Dennys frowned as he eyed the man critically, sniffing the air. "Is this man stuporous from blood loss or too much liquor?" he demanded.

Anne Martin hesitated. "Well, I intended to give him only a small amount, but—"

"I asked her to give him more," Emma finished.

"You did." Dennys turned to her, a quizzical look in his dark eyes. "Are you aware of the deleterious effects of large amounts of alcohol upon the body of someone who is in shock?"

"Yes, I am aware," Emma responded steadily. "As I am cognizant of the effects of excruciating pain, which often exacerbates the severity of shock, sometimes causing intolerable stress upon the body and mind. In my judgment, given the severity of the injury and the fact that the patient remained conscious while experiencing agonizing pain, further depleting his strength, it seems more prudent to over rather than under sedate. Besides, if we had administered chloroform, we would not be engaged in this conversation."

"You are correct in that assumption," Dennys snapped. "For this patient would have undoubtedly succumbed to his injuries under the even more nervous depressive effects of chloroform." Dennys's expression was stony, his lips compressed to a thin line. "Your judgment has nothing to do with the situation," he said scathingly. "Did you ask Dr. Pelham's permission to administer the alcohol? Or are you in the habit of making medical decisions yourself?"

Emma felt her anger rise, but she was determined to suppress it. "It is an accepted practice at this infirmary to sedate patients in this manner when chloroform is not available," she stated in a coldly controlled tone. "You may confirm this with Dr. Pelham and Dr. Mackenzie."

"Emma is absolutely right, sir," Anne interjected. "It's simply that I tend to be a little more cautious with administering sedation."

"And you are to be commended for that, Miss Martin," Dennys replied. He looked penetratingly at Emma. "Rest assured, Miss Hollander, I shall pursue this matter."

"In the meantime, we are wasting our patient's valuable time," Emma said frostily.

Dennys refocused his gaze on Mr. Donnelly. "I shall now remove the pressure bandages. Miss Martin, please endeavor to rouse the patient."

"What?" Anne exclaimed, pausing in her tracks.

Emma stared at him, anger reaching a boiling point inside.

"Snap to it, Miss Martin," Dennys exhorted impatiently. "I

desire this patient to be more alert. That way, his system shan't be too depressed by the alcohol to combat his injuries."

"Oh, I see." Anne glanced surreptitiously at Emma, unnerved by the seething fury in her colleague's eyes. "Well then...." Still hesitant, she approached Mr. Donnelly and tentatively shook his shoulders, then lightly tapped him about the face.

"Forcefully, Miss Martin. We haven't all night," Dennys barked.

Emma bit her lip, fighting to subdue the rising angry torrent building inside. *I must be professional,* she cautioned herself. *This man's life is at stake. If I am to be of any use to him, I must keep my emotions under control.*

So she watched in silent condemnation as Donnelly was reluctantly coaxed out of his oblivion. He was obviously resisting the journey back to consciousness, but within a few moments of the nurse's efforts, he had surfaced enough to moan feebly and grab at the air.

Dennys's lips twitched with satisfaction. "That is better. We shall now begin. Mr. Donnelly, can you hear me?" The man moaned in response, his eyes fluttering open. "Mr. Donnelly, look at me. Yes. Good." His gaze bored into the man's pain racked stare. "Mr. Donnelly, I am now going to take your damaged leg to cut it off." He steadily unwound the blood drenched bandage. "Do you understand?"

The expression in Donnelly's eyes changed from blankness to stark terror in a matter of seconds.

"Yes, that's right," Dennys said, voice smooth as silk. "You must lose your leg to save your life. Unfortunately, it will be a painful procedure. You must remain very still. My assistants shall restrain you. It shall be over soon, I promise."

A horrified wail of pure anguish pierced the air as Donnelly was firmly held down by two attendants and Anne Martin. Even after they had strapped him to the table, it was necessary for the men to restrict his movements. Emma, standing to one side of Donnelly, shuddered, for she was uncomfortably reminded of the cries of a soul condemned to eternal torment. One glance at his eyes was enough for her to recognize that he was beyond any solace she could offer. Assaulted by unbearable pain and terror, he had retreated into his own world of suffering. His reality fragmenting, he could only scream mindlessly.

Emma tore her gaze away from Donnelly and his mangled limb, a ruined mass of flesh and bone. She struggled to force her emotions to the back of her mind, to focus on the task at hand. She reached numbly for the clamp which would be applied for the severed artery, handing the clamp to Dennys before he could ask, refusing to meet his gaze.

Dennys clamped the torn vessel, and immediately the flow of blood ceased. "The bleeding has been contained," he stated, "but for how long I cannot say. Therefore, we must make haste to amputate the limb." Turning to the instrument tray, he selected a saw-like blade with serrated edges. "Miss Hollander," he continued coolly. "I shall require you to remove any tissue which might impede the procedure, as well as to dispose of the amputated limb afterwards."

Out of the corner of her eye, she saw Anne Martin start. These unsavory and messy tasks usually were delegated to the infirmary attendants, not the nursing staff. However, Emma did not flinch as she acknowledged the instruction with a curt, "Very well, Mr. Dennys."

The stricken Donnelly's screams increased in volume as he glimpsed the gleaming surgical saw in the physician's hand. Unperturbed and seemingly oblivious to the man's torment, Dennys prepared to make the first incision.

"The idea, of course, is to complete the procedure in as few strokes of the blade as necessary. However, this surgery may take longer due to the severity of the mangling, crushing injuries."

The idea, of course, is to inflict as much suffering as possible.

Emma started at the sound of Dennys's voice inside her head. She gasped for one dizzy moment, believing that he had actually spoken the words aloud. But no, a quick glance at the others confirmed that those words were intended for her ears alone.

I must get hold of my senses, she thought, her dismay increasing.

I must focus on the task at hand instead of listening to imaginary voices.

As the first edges of the blade sliced into the patient's decimated flesh, his wails reached a heart wrenching crescendo. Unable to watch the suffering, Emma instead fixed her gaze upon the surgeon. Almost imperceptibly, a predatory expression crept across Dennys's face. His eyes looked almost black as something dark gleamed and flickered briefly in them.

A shiver raced through Emma, her hands trembling in response. In dawning horror, she thought, *He's enjoying this; he is savoring this man's pain and terror.*

She felt the solid earth crumble beneath her feet, opening to reveal a gaping chasm which offered only endless darkness.

The word that described what she felt at that precise moment was dread. Rooted to the spot while the agonized wails of Donnelly reverberated off the walls of the room into her head, spatters of bone and shredded tissue pelting her face, the stench of gore permeating her nostrils, she recognized this as the most dreadful moment of her life. And she knew something else. The one responsible for this travesty was a monster, merely assuming the guise of a physician. For the first time in her life, Emma had come face to face with pure unadulterated evil, but it was not to be her last encounter.

CHAPTER 24

Emma sat in the staff room, sipping her cup of tea. Despite the warmth of the liquid flowing down her throat, she felt ice cold; her hands still trembled. She wondered bleakly if she would ever feel warm again. She could not banish from her mind the gruesome surgery she had seen. The incident repeated itself, painful image upon image.

Despite the surgical intervention, the patient had died from hemorrhage, according to the official report. However, Emma understood that Donnelly had succumbed to a lethal combination of terror and unendurable pain, resulting in irreversible shock. She recognized full well that had he been properly sedated, the outcome might have been no different, but at least he could have passed in quiet oblivion, his dignity intact, instead of as the howling madman he had become, writhing in his own excrement.

Emma would never forget the expression on Donnelly's face as he breathed his last. The stark terror had driven him beyond the fringes of sanity into madness. What she had seen in his eyes was the agony of the hopelessly lost and insane, the realization that a monstrous evil had come to claim him, body and soul. She had barely suppressed a horrified gasp before turning away in distress. It had taken more than a few moments to regain her composure. Behind her, the cleanup procedure was in progress, attendants wrapping the body and removing blood drenched linens.

When she turned around again, she caught Dennys looking at her as he washed the traces of blood from his hands. His saturated apron had lain where he carelessly tossed it on the linen heap.

His expression was inscrutable, save for a transient gloating look in his eyes, as though he understood how profoundly this experience had shaken her. Though every fiber of her being urged her to run from the abomination in that room, Emma exerted her willpower, forcing her gaze to remain steady as she returned Dennys's stare. She worried that Dennys could somehow sense her fear and loathing, so she deliberately unclenched her fists and willed her hands to stop shaking.

At that moment, Dr. Pelham returned and was apprised of the situation by Dennys. He clasped the younger physician on the shoulder. "Bad luck, old chap. It happens to the best of us. This patient's chances for survival were grim indeed, but at least it was good experience for you." He noticed Emma observing them. "Come now, Miss Hollander, don't look so distressed. You know we can't save every patient."

Emma cleared her throat of its dryness. "No, sir, I am aware of that."

Dennys, his tone only slightly ironic, said, "Miss Hollander is very sensitive, I fear."

"Yes, well, we have many patients yet to see," Pelham stated firmly. "Miss Hollander, you may return to the waiting area and continue with assessments."

"Very good, Dr. Pelham," Emma replied. She was about to leave the surgical theater when Dennys's voice stopped her.

"Oh, Miss Hollander, one little favor before you go." She turned to face him as he presented her with the object wrapped in linen. It took several seconds for her to register the amputated limb of the late Mr. Donnelly. "Would you take this to the specimen room posthaste?" Dennys asked politely.

Wordlessly, Emma accepted the severed body part. As she left the casualty area, she breathed deeply to steady her nerves for the task ahead.

The specimen room was located in the subterranean level of the infirmary, adjacent to the morgue. As its name implied, this storage chamber housed body parts, tumorous growths, and various medical anomalies, all of which had been removed from the good citizens of Whitechapel. Sometimes the parting was a happy one, as was the case of an old gent who had a growth the size of a melon incised from his neck. More often than not, however, the loss was traumatic in nature, involving limbs and organs the owners would have dearly loved to have kept.

Emma found the specimen room more forbidding than the morgue. The idea of dead bodies was less disconcerting to her than that of dismembered pieces. Most of the specimens housed here were sent to the hospitals in London to be used to train physicians and medical students. The specimens were carefully wrapped and loaded onto carts and transported to the hospitals twice a week, if there was enough supply, for there was always demand.

Emma fumbled with her key, finally locating that which would unlock the specimen room door. She held her breath as she opened the door, wishing to avoid as long as possible the pungent odor of formaldehyde which permeated the room. She hoped to place the tagged specimen in the chemical bath before she was required to breathe again. She also hoped the large vat in the corner of the room already contained sufficient formaldehyde; otherwise, she would be obliged to drag over one of the canisters and perform the odious task of filling it herself.

Relief flowed through her as she approached the tub and saw that there was plenty of chemical inside, as well as a hand, an arm, and a foot. Obviously, the other workers injured at the dock's accident had likewise lost some body parts to amputation. She prayed they had been spared Donnelly's horrific fate.

Emma unwrapped the mangled limb, gingerly lowering it into the vat. She was careful not to splash any chemical on herself, experience having taught her that even a few drops would ruin one's clothes. She quickly exited the room, locking the door behind her. Once in the corridor, she released a sigh of relief and stood breathing deeply of the comparatively fresh and odorless air.

The door to the staff room opened, and Anne Martin popped her head in, interrupting Emma's thoughts.

"Sorry to disturb your tea, love, but Dr. Pelham wants to see you." Her troubled, sympathetic expression indicated that she assumed that Emma was to be reprimanded for her altercation with Dennys. Emma sighed and hastily swallowed another sip of tea. She stood, smoothing the clean, freshly starched apron she had quickly flung over her uniform after the amputation fiasco.

One way the nurses gauged how busy they were was the number of apron changes they made during their hours of work. Thus, one nurse might remark to another, "It has been a five-apron day for me. How about you?"

Tonight, Emma had lost count of the number of times she changed her apron, until one of the attendants had informed her that the supply was rapidly being depleted; therefore, the nurses would require limiting their use.

When Emma reached the casualty room, Dr. Pelham beckoned her over. She was too emotionally exhausted from the evening's events to feel even the slightest apprehension.

If I am to be reprimanded, she thought, *I shall say nothing in my defense, for I know not what my tongue might retort before my tired mind could prevent it.*

"Miss Hollander," Dr. Pelham greeted her. "We have need of your excellent communication skills. The wife of the unfortunate Mr. Donnelly has just arrived and is seeking information regarding the deceased. Would you speak with her?"

Emma squared her shoulders and drew in a deep breath. "Isn't Mr. Dennys available?"

Pelham frowned. "Mr. Dennys is completing the postmortem we interrupted to assist me in casualty. Besides, you are very adept at handling situations with family members. You possess a definite sensitivity for that sort of thing, as Mr. Dennys remarked earlier."

At the mention of these last words, Emma bristled yet managed to hold her anger in check. "I do not believe Mr. Dennys's use of the word was intended as yours are, Dr. Pelham. Besides, shouldn't Mr. Dennys develop skills in communicating with families?" she challenged. "Presumably, he shall have to tolerate grieving families on occasions such as the loss of a loved one."

Although she endeavored to moderate her sarcasm, enough was evident in her tone for the physician to register.

Pelham's expression grew stern. "Miss Hollander, you are being impertinent. Mr. Dennys's skills as a *surgeon* are singularly relevant to his practice. As with most physicians, he has not the luxury of time to console grieving widows. That is your task."

Emma sighed in resignation, biting her lower lip. "Very well, Doctor, I do not wish to debate with you. I shall attend to Mrs. Donnelly."

Pelham nodded. "Good," he said, curtly dismissing her.

Emma steeled herself for the impending ordeal. How, in the face of what she had witnessed, could she comfort this poor woman? She shook her head, deep in thought, as she traversed the corridor to the ill lit cubbyhole which served as a waiting room for relatives.

I cannot tell her that her husband suffered needless agony, she reflected. *Mrs. Donnelly cannot know that his pain and fear were exacerbated by the physician who attended him, who refused to let him die in merciful unawareness. I must shield her from that knowledge. It shall remain my secret until I decide what to do with it.*

Emma reached the narrow, wooden door, its paint scratched and cracked in many places. She knocked softly, then entered. A painful throb began in her heart as she saw the frail, care-worn figure sitting uncomfortably straight and stiff in the chair.

Mrs. Donnelly was probably no more than thirty-five, but her face was marred by lines of worry and strain. Her skin was pale, its only color the smudge of shadow under her eyes. In those eyes was an expression of hope mingled with dread.

As Emma approached her, the woman's hands clenched and unclenched. She rose from her chair. *She still clings to hope*, Emma thought miserably. *Now I must crush that hope to dust.*

"Mrs. Donnelly," she said gently. "I am so sorry."

Before she could continue, Mrs. Donnelly burst into sobs and threw herself into Emma's arms. Emma cradled the grief-stricken woman, talking in soothing murmurs as one does with a child. She felt the fragile bones tremble in their scant casing of flesh as sobs ran through the woman's body. Although no words were spoken by Mrs. Donnelly, Emma was painfully aware of the desperate thoughts which must be circling in her head.

"How are my children and I to survive? Shall I find work to keep a roof over our heads and food on the table, or will we be forced to throw ourselves upon the mercy of the poorhouses? What will happen, what will become of us?"

As the distraught woman continued to pour out her sorrow, Emma wondered about how many thousand upon thousands, perhaps even millions of tears the human body could produce, and if it were possible to ever run out of them. Blood and tears, she thought. Life was not possible without these two fluids, and neither was death. First came the blood, a life sustaining river, followed by tears, the manifestation of heart and soul arriving in the wake of that river running dry. In the end, it always came down to blood and tears.

CHAPTER 25

Emma lay supine, stretched out on a hard surface. Confused and disoriented, she didn't know where she was or how she had come to be there. Her head felt thick, her senses muddled, as one emerging from a deep slumber. It was dark, but a weak light emanated from the far corner of the room, its flickering glow indicating that fire was its source. Sufficient illumination was cast for her to discern the silhouette of a man crouched in front of the fireplace. From the angle of her view, Emma concluded that the structure upon which she lay was several feet above floor level, similar in height to a surgical table or a postmortem table, she thought and shuddered.

She tried to sit up, but to her complete surprise, she couldn't summon even one muscle twitch. She fought to move her arms, then her legs, to no avail. With mounting agitation, she discovered that the only part of her body she could move was her head. She appeared to be in the grip of some sort of paralysis; whether induced by trauma or drugs, she couldn't discern. A wave of panic struck as she realized how profoundly helpless she was.

She struggled to calm the fear and gain control of her emotions and thoughts.

There must be a rational explanation, she told herself. *I must settle down enough to think this through. Perhaps I have had an accident of some sort; that would account for both the amnesia and the paralysis. Dear God, let me be able to cope with this tragedy, for I fear that I shan't have the strength.*

Or, and this idea was more comforting, it could simply be a bad dream.

Her frightened mind seized upon this thought and clutched it tightly.

Yes, I am having a nightmare. Of course, that's what this madness is. She frowned, however, doubt forcing its way into her thoughts. It didn't feel like a dream. It lacked the usual disjointed, surreal quality. Colors, textures, the sound of crackling flames, everything was so vivid. She could even smell a heavy, unpleasant odor. It was nagging, familiar, and after several frustrating moments, she identified it as a combination of blood and feces.

What was happening? The idea of an accident took firm hold. Had she been gravely injured? Was this a hospital? It was impossible to obtain answers to these vital questions as the limited movement of her head prevented her from assessing for any injuries. She tried to call out to the figure by the fire, but no sound issued from her. Dear Lord, even her vocal cords were paralyzed.

She lifted her head off the table, craning her neck as far as she was able. The figure was still crouched by the fire, its back to her. She couldn't be positive, but she had the impression it was male. From his movements, he seemed to be cooking something over the fire, and sure enough, within a minute or two, the smell of roasting meat and juice began to rival that other darker odor.

Emma was more bewildered than before. What in heaven's name was going on? Who was that man, and why did he attend to his meal while she lay helpless and possibly even dying? Anger sparked within her, soon overpowering panic for control of her emotions. She began to bang her head against the table, desperate to attract the man's attention in the only way available to her. As she thrashed her head to and fro, her peripheral vision caught an object to the left of her. With effort, Emma slowed her movements and once again lifted her head, this time straining the muscles in her neck to lean to the left side. Her eyes grew wide in horror, mouth agape in a silent scream.

The lifeless body of a woman was laid out on the table next to Emma, and it was her corpse which emitted the abominable stench. She had been gutted like an animal, abdomen ripped open, globs of fat and muscle scattered haphazardly around the table. Glistening loops of intestine were strung over her left shoulder, the other portion absent, along with the mesenteric artery that supplied blood to the abdominal organs. The torso had been savaged, the contents of the abdominal cavity casually plundered. Emma's horrified gaze was next drawn to the deep crimson gash across the woman's throat, from which stringy sinews and remnants of blood vessels hung. Gleaming white bone from the cervical spine peeked out from the depths of the mutilated flesh of the neck.

Emma's gasp of revulsion was soundless. Her fear was nauseating in intensity, and she swallowed several times, convulsively to repel the bitter taste of bile. Briefly, she closed her eyes against the ghastly sight, but she couldn't close her ears to the sounds issuing from the creature by the fireplace. Contented sounds of chewing, swallowing, and lip smacking attested to the gastronomic bliss enjoyed by the mysterious stranger.

Emma opened her eyes to peer at the crouched figure as he skewered yet another piece of roasted meat from the fire. As though finally aware of Emma's gaze, the man turned around. His face in shadow; his features were indistinguishable. She watched in fascinated loathing as he extended the skewer with its steaming link of intestinal meat in a grotesque salute to her.

Butcher, Emma raged, her voice echoing loudly inside her head. Her mind leapt to the sickening connection before she could suppress the appalling thought of this fiendish butcher sampling his own wares. Unable to express herself in any other fashion, Emma spat violently at the figure's feet, with all the hatred she could muster.

A throaty, gargled chuckle issued from him. Shrugging dismissively, he drew the meat from the skewer and devoured it with relish, savoring every bite. Emma now understood with mounting dread that this was no dream. Somehow reality had flipped over on itself, distorted beyond recognition. She concluded with shocking certainty that she was a captive of the Whitechapel murderer, for this monster could be no other

By what manner of alchemy he had captured her, she didn't know. With increasing fear, she watched as, having sated his appetite for the moment, the creature stood and began to walk towards her. She recoiled mentally in abhorrence as he emerged from the shadows, and she clearly saw the misshapen head with sparse tufts of hair. The nose was a flattened lump of tissue, the rictus mouth stretched wide to reveal sharp, crooked teeth the color of pus. Black eyes, flat and reptilian, focused on her with the total absence of emotion, chilling Emma to the marrow. Although the shape and size of a man and incongruously clad in formal attire, there was nothing remotely human about this monster. Its thickened skin, heavily marred with blemishes and lesions, was gray in hue. The hands displayed long and strangely elegant fingers, which tapered to curved lethal talons.

Thoughts rushed through Emma's head in a tide of terror. No wonder the police had failed to catch the Whitechapel murderer. They were searching for a man, not a demon from the nightmare depths of hell with a predilection for human flesh, a monster whose deadly talons could rip and shred that flesh as if it were paper.

The creature reached the table and bent over her. She nearly fainted from the fetid odor of its breath. Gagging, she once again battled the urge to vomit. She clenched her eyes shut, praying that the terror would soon end and death claim her. In her mind's eye, she glimpsed a fleeting image of her severely mutilated corpse lying in a deserted courtyard in Whitechapel, rendered a spectacle upon which horrified onlookers would gawk.

If only I could scream, she thought desperately. *I shall surely suffocate in these pent up screams. If only I could....*

An ear-piercing shriek awoke her. Emma bolted up in bed, gasping and tremulous. Her heart pounded savagely, and sweat dripped down her back and between her breasts. Confused and shaken, she tried to collect her scattered thoughts. What was the sound that had so abruptly awakened her? It had sounded vaguely like a scream, but if so, from whence did it issue? Could the Whitechapel murderer have claimed yet another victim?

Suddenly her stomach clenched and heaved mightily. Nightmare images inundated her mind, loathsome and terrifying.

Dear God, she cried silently. *I can move. I am not paralyzed.*

She surveyed the room.

And I am safe and sound in my own bed, with the gas lamp burning low so I could sleep with the assurance of being undisturbed by unpleasant dreams. She chuckled in bitter irony. *Obviously, keeping the light burning was not a guarantee to a peaceful slumber; now I understand why those plagued by nightmares so dread going to sleep. It is my fervent prayer that I never experience another dream as disturbing as this one.*

A discreet knock on the door interrupted the frantic cascade of Emma's thoughts.

"Miss Hollander," her landlady's voice tentatively inquired. "Are you all right?"

Emma started as she realized that she had been the one to scream. She cleared her throat. "Yes, yes, Mrs. Barclay, I'm fine. Merely a bad dream. I regret having inconvenienced you."

"Yes, well then, right. Good night."

"Good night," Emma whispered to Mrs. Barclay's receding footsteps.

A shiver ran through her, and she was suddenly aware of how cold her body felt. Quickly pulling the sheets and heavy counterpane around her shoulders, she huddled against the headboard. She longed for a cup of tea but had no desire to leave her bed. Reaching over to the bedside table, she turned the lamp up a notch. Her anxiety was lessened slightly by the increased brightness.

"There, that's better," she said aloud as the last shudders began to subside. Comforted by the sound of her voice, she continued speaking softly. "It was only a dream. Strange how the mind tries to warn one. If only I heeded my own words, I would have realized I was, in fact, dreaming. For how often does one suspect one is dreaming while actually awake? That sort of confusion between reality and fantasy occurs in the mentally disturbed, not in normal people. Then again, I suppose one is in quite a vulnerable state when one is asleep. Therefore one's reasoning is apt to be less reliable too." She bit her lip as she recalled how helpless and frightened she'd felt in the dream and how easily she convinced herself of its reality.

In her heart, Emma cursed the Whitechapel murderer, the cause of her terror. She despised him for his reprehensible acts, of course, but also for the vulnerability and insecurity which his existence had unearthed in her.

Look at me, she thought in vexation, *reduced to night terrors like a child who, victimized by the phantoms of her imagination, is obliged to leave the light burning.* And as much as she tried to rationalize her fear, she could not persuade herself to extinguish the light.

CHAPTER 26

It was the evening after the day of Emma's horrendous shift in the urgent casualty ward. She was having dinner with Andrew and Henrietta in the Hewitt-Browns' tastefully appointed dining room. Andrew's father, as was his custom on Thursdays, was breaking bread with associates at his club.

"Do have some more Yorkshire pudding, Emma," Henrietta urged. "I know it's your favorite, but you have hardly eaten at all."

Emma, who had indeed only picked at her food, managed an apologetic smile. "The food is superb, as always. It is simply that I have little appetite today." She took a sip of wine.

"You are subdued, my dear. Not your usual self," Henrietta remarked. "Don't you think so, Andrew?"

Andrew wiped his mouth with his napkin. "Yes, I do. Are the Whitechapel murders still troubling you?"

"No," Emma replied hesitantly. "Of course, they remain a source of anxiety, and I do fervently hope that the police apprehend the murderer soon. It's just something to do with work, that's all."

Henrietta frowned in distaste. "Yes, dear. You know what I think about you working in that place."

Emma smiled wanly. "Oh yes, Henrietta. You have expressed your opinion on many an occasion. I am abundantly clear about your thoughts regarding my work."

"Not your work, Emma," Henrietta admonished. "Where you choose to do your work. You could seek employment anywhere else, and you would have obtained a good position too, of that

I—"

"Mother," Andrew interrupted gently, but firmly. "I believe we have had this discussion before. Do you really feel it is necessary to repeat it?"

Henrietta sighed. "No, of course not, Andrew. I simply hate to see Emma unhappy." She raised her wine glass to her lips, a ruby ring on her finger gleaming in the candlelight.

"As do I, Mother," Andrew responded with a smile. He turned to Emma. "Tell us, my love, what disturbs you?"

Emma sat back in her chair, no longer even pretending to enjoy her meal. "Well," she began hesitantly. "There was an incident last evening that upset me." She related the details of Mr. Donnelly's injury and amputation.

"I can certainly appreciate how distressing it can be to do your best, and still the patient dies," Henrietta said empathetically.

Andrew watched Emma closely. "Is that the entire story, love? I have a sense that it is incomplete."

Emma nodded. "You are correct, Andrew. The death, whilst tragic, did not in itself upset me unduly. If one is to nurse, one must be capable of handling difficult, distressing situations. No, it was instead something I witnessed which so disturbed me, I don't know if I can speak about it."

Henrietta glanced at her son as Emma remained silent. Andrew acknowledged the concern in his mother's eyes with a slight nod. "Sometimes talking about an issue is actually easier than one assumes," he said softly. "If it upsets you to this degree, then it is obviously significant and worthy of attention. Sharing the burden may help to alleviate some of your consternation."

Emma's face clouded with anxiety. "I am sure that's true," she acknowledged, "and it would be helpful to hear what the two of you, whose opinions I hold in such high esteem, have to say." She drew in a deep breath. "Everything was moving along as it should until the surgeon in training was called in. I have had occasion to work with him and find his manner arrogant and offensive. Anyway, he persuaded the attending physician to let him perform the surgery. The first intimation I had of something untoward was when he questioned me about over sedating the patient. I had done nothing out of the ordinary, adhering to the standard in the infirmary practice for the relief of severe pain. Mr. Dennys felt that the patient's condition was too unstable to tolerate that level of sedation, or so he said."

"You didn't believe him?" Andrew asked.

"At the time, I simply thought it was a disagreement based upon differing points of view. My perception was that the patient wouldn't be able to withstand that level of pain, let alone an increase, without experiencing a potentially lethal shock. Mr. Dennys, of course, overruled my decision and instructed the other nurse present to rouse Mr. Donnelly out of his stupor, which she did.

"It was that action to which I objected, not understanding how an increase in his consciousness at this stage could be of any benefit. Mr. Dennys then proceeded to tell the patient that he was to lose his leg. It was the quality of his tone, which sparked an uneasiness in me. One could argue that he was merely emphasizing the details for the patient's understanding, but somehow I knew that wasn't the case."

Emma leaned forward intently, elbows on the table, her agitation evident. "And then when the amputation actually began, and Mr. Donnelly's pain became excruciating, it distressed me so I could not gaze upon his suffering. I looked instead at Mr. Dennys, and as God is my witness, I saw him smile. It was a sly, ghastly smile. I was sickened by it and frightened because the horrible revelation came to me that Dennys enjoyed Mr. Donnelly's pain, deriving pleasure from his torment and that he deliberately manipulated the poor man into an alert state so he would feel his pain as acutely as possible, all for Dennys's unspeakable pleasure."

Emma sat back, face flushed, a light sheen of perspiration across her brow. "It was terrible. No one else seemed aware that anything was amiss; they were all so focused on the task at hand, I should guess. But I saw, and oh, how I wish I hadn't! I felt so helpless, unable to stop the abomination before my eyes, scarcely daring to believe it myself. However, I couldn't doubt what my intuition was telling me."

Andrew's slate colored eyes narrowed as he focused on Emma. "What else did your intuition tell you?"

A strained look appeared on her face. "I felt a tension in the pit of my stomach, a revulsion so strong it was akin to nausea, and I knew that I was in the presence of great evil."

Henrietta drew in a breath sharply.

"I know how strange it sounds," Emma said. "If I had not experienced it myself, I am sure I would have difficulty believing it."

"Yet, you don't doubt it?" inquired Andrew.

"No, how can I? I know what I saw and felt. That man is evil. He is loathsome."

Andrew pursed his lips thoughtfully. "I'd wager that this surgeon is rather new to the infirmary, is he not?"

"Yes, he is," Emma nodded. "And he is very confident for an apprentice."

"Did you confront him afterwards?" Andrew asked.

"No. I wanted to, but after dealing with Mrs. Donnelly and her grief, I confess I lacked the mental energy to confront Dennys."

"Just as well. It would have been an exercise in frustration, and perhaps one which would cause him to focus his attention upon you as one who would potentially cause trouble for him. You must not give him any reason to be concerned about you."

Emma sighed. "We have already exchanged words that were less than amicable. I am certain he is aware of my animosity."

"Your animosity isn't the issue. If he thinks your pride has been wounded by his public chastisement of you, all the better. But you must not challenge him, or even intimate that you believe his motives are evil in nature."

Emma frowned. "Why ever not?"

Andrew reached over and clasped Emma's hand. "Think for a moment how he would respond if he were to view you as a threat. He would act swiftly and ruthlessly to eliminate that threat. It would be quite easy for him to succeed, too. All he need do is express enough concern to cast aspersions on your character and your competence as a nurse. Who do you think the medical establishment would support? You would be the one sanctioned, your profession as a nurse over."

"But I can't remain silent," Emma protested in indignation. "He should be sanctioned, prohibited from ever practicing medicine anywhere. He betrays that noble profession, and if the price to be paid for accomplishing this is the end of my nursing, then it is worth it."

Andrew shook his head. "Emma, listen carefully to what I have to say. You could not win against him, for he is as clever at manipulating others as he is replete with evil. Why do you think you were the only one present to observe his behavior, to sense the wickedness in him? You, like Henrietta and myself and a small percentage of others, are extremely sensitive to the presence of evil, whereas others suspect nothing. We intuitively recognize evil when we are confronted with it. We must also recognize its danger and never underestimate its potential to harm us."

"Then what am I to do?" Emma asked helplessly.

"Subtlety of action and patience are required when dealing with one such as this Dennys. I have many acquaintances in London. As a matter of interest, your Dr. Mackenzie is a regular at my club. He appears to be friendly with some distinguished physicians who are also members. It would not be inconceivable for me to have a few words with the good doctor, and in the course of the conversation, to mention very discreetly a rumor or two concerning Mr. Dennys. Nothing concrete, merely whispers and insinuations, but with enough details to sow the seeds of doubt regarding Dennys's character."

Emma's face brightened. "Oh, Andrew, that's brilliant." She frowned momentarily. "And of course, your words would have considerable credence over mine, no matter how unfair it is that by simply being a woman, I have less credibility than any man."

Henrietta reached over to pat Emma's hand. "While I commiserate with you wholeheartedly, one cannot let that fact of life shackle one's desire to see justice done. As women, we must use the art of manipulation to achieve our goals. Although regrettable, it is necessary. However, Andrew has generously offered to act on your behalf, so there is no need for you to expend energy, trying to persuade him to do so. I wish all men could be as accommodating." She smiled fondly at her son.

"Ah, Mother, you speak from experience, do you not?" Andrew inquired, laughing slightly. "If Father were only aware of how often he has been persuaded to make one decision over another or to change a decision already decided upon." He turned to Emma. "My mother is correct when she describes manipulation as an art, for one must be very skilled in order for it to be successful, which means the person being manipulated must never realize that this is occurring." His tone turned serious. "Now then, Emma, you must promise me that you will leave this matter in my hands."

Emma lifted her sea green gaze to his. "I promise that I shan't lose my temper or voice my concerns to anyone, including Mr. Dennys. Most especially Mr. Dennys."

"You have my word too, Emma. Dennys shall pay the price for his actions."

Emma noted the determination evident in the strong set of his jaw and the unflinching purpose in his eyes. For the first time in a couple of days, she felt her spirits brighten and her hope restored.

CHAPTER 27

With dinner long over and Emma escorted back to her flat, Andrew sat alone in the drawing room savoring a brandy. The rest of the household had retired for the night. The silence was absolute, save for the shifting and settling of the house itself. The gaslight was turned low, leaving most of the room in shadow.

Andrew allowed his thoughts to drift as he leisurely puffed on his cigar. Emma's story was compelling. It intrigued him, demanding his attention. In light of certain revelations this evening, he now understood why the Whitechapel murders—or to be precise, the murderer himself—were about to become his major concern. Clearly, this fiend posed an enormous threat not only to the populace of the East End but in particular to the woman he loved more than life itself. And tonight, Emma had unknowingly revealed the identity of this killer.

From the moment he had arrived back in London from abroad, he had been aware of a sinister change in the city. From a physical perspective, the atmosphere was no different, but on a spiritual level, it was as though a poison invaded the city, creeping stealthily towards London's heart. This toxin emanated from Whitechapel and from the creature who menaced the darkened streets masquerading as a man.

Such a being was dangerous as no other. In return for dark favors, he willingly acted as Satan's instrument of torment and destruction. He crossed into forbidden territory, no offense too heinous or deed too abominable. Master of the occult arts and taster of forbidden fruits, he was saturated with the reek of evil. Powerful, hungry for suffering, he would not rest until

Whitechapel was laid to spiritual waste.

Andrew was no stranger to this evil. As ancient as the universe itself, it negated all life and light. It understood only terror and death. Andrew had confronted its hideous power when, long ago, he stood before the gates of Hell, a point of entry from man's world into the netherworld. He challenged this evil to come forth and engage in mortal battle with him, but it had chosen to decline; a wise decision on its part.

It had remained in the netherworld these many years, biding its time, waiting for the right moment to emerge from the bowels of hell. That moment had now arrived. He decided that it would be opportune to seek out more information about the creature who called itself John Dennys.

Closing his eyes, he entered a trance state, separating his spiritual consciousness from his physical self, leaving his body a temporarily empty shell. He was free to journey where he wished, and as before, he ventured down the streets and alleyways of Whitechapel. But once again, there was no sign of his elusive quarry. So the Whitechapel murderer was not about any gruesome business this night. Well then, he would cast his net wider to track down the killer. His body relaxed in its chair as his consciousness hurtled through space and time until he happened upon the subject of his search.

A formal soiree at Dr. Ian Mackenzie's house in north London. Many distinguished guests were in attendance, including the chief surgeon of London Hospital, the eminent Sir William Gillespie. With a drink in one hand and a cigar in the other, he was engaged in conversation with several other physicians. Nevertheless, he cast an occasional glance toward the group assembled in front of a large bay window.

The window overlooked an immaculately kept garden. In the center of the group, his back to the window, stood John Dennys. He apparently was the focus of the others' rapt attention as he spoke compellingly upon some matter. There was much laughter and nodding of heads as he delivered his words, followed by exclamations of delight and spontaneous applause as he concluded. He smiled and bowed graciously in acknowledgment of his listeners' appreciation before excusing himself to replenish his glass.

Gillespie turned to his host. "And how is our popular young friend making out at the infirmary?" he asked, gesturing toward Dennys.

"Ah, very well, indeed." Dr. Ian Mackenzie beamed. "He has the makings of a very fine surgeon. Nerves of steel, that one."

"Mmmm, sounds promising. He came highly recommended from Paris, as I recall. Did some clinical training in medicine there. When do you think he should be ready to apprentice at the hospital?" Gillespie inquired.

"Very shortly, I believe, although we shan't be glad to see him leave the infirmary. He has been invaluable, very keen on the postmortems as well. He takes great interest and precision with them."

"A true surgeon, aye? Well, some men are born to wield the knife. Cutting is in their blood." Both men chuckled and then turned to greet an approaching colleague.

As John Dennys lingered at the drinks table, he was joined by an attractive, handsomely attired woman. Dark of eye and hair, she wore a green silk gown. The green jeweled clasps secured the chignon at the nape of her neck, the perfect match for her silk embroidered slippers.

Andrew hovered close, the better to hear what was said.

"Why Mr. Dennys, I do hope you are enjoying yourself," the woman remarked, smiling.

Dennys turned to her with an answering smile. "Immensely, Mrs. Mackenzie. I am indeed grateful to you and the good doctor for inviting me to your lovely house."

"It is I who am honored by your presence," Edith Mackenzie replied, extending her hand.

Dennys took the proffered hand and held it briefly to his lips. "And you are an enchanting hostess."

She smiled again, a hint of archness in her expressive eyes. "I very much hope that you will attend more of our soirees," she said warmly.

"I should welcome the opportunity," he responded.

"Is there a Mrs. Dennys?"

He chuckled. "No, I am afraid not."

Her smile widened, and an eager gleam shone in her eyes. "How fortunate," she said, her gaze lingering a moment before she turned and glided away.

Dennys returned his attention to the table, reaching for his glass of whiskey. His smile vanished. His upper lip curled in a sneer, and he whispered disdainfully to himself. "Whore. The sparkle of greed and lust in your eyes is so blatant. This is not the first time your mind has strayed in such fashion, but it could very well be the last."

A hand clapped him on the shoulder from behind. A smooth smile once more in place, he turned to greet Dr. Mackenzie and Sir William Gillespie.

"Dennys, my boy," Mackenzie began. "I should like you to meet the distinguished Chief of Surgery of London Hospital, Sir William Gillespie."

Dennis shook the man's hand heartily. "It is a great honor to meet you, sir."

Gillespie smiled haughtily. "Quite. Mackenzie has been telling me some very flattering things about you. In fact, he has recommended you for a position in my surgery apprenticeship program. What do you think?"

Dennys continued to smile with ease. "I daresay, sir, it would be a wonderful opportunity, and I should feel the utmost privilege."

"As well you might," Gillespie agreed. "It is a rare opportunity to study under one as qualified as I. This is no idle boast. It is simply that I have an unquestionable gift for producing the most highly skilled surgeons in all of England. Only those physicians who exhibit superior abilities and knowledge are accepted into the program." He glanced at his host. "Dr. Mackenzie believes you are a suitable candidate. Would you agree?"

"Sir, as Dr. Mackenzie's judgment is above reproach, I cannot but humbly agree with his learned opinion," responded Dennys.

"Ha!" Gillespie exclaimed, amused. "We shall see how the remainder of your apprenticeship at the infirmary transpires. If Dr. Mackenzie is still of a favorable opinion, you may be considered for the surgery program."

"Thank you, sir. I shall look forward to that event."

Gillespie eyed him speculatively. "And what do you think of Whitechapel?"

"It is a disagreeable place, but the practice of medicine is very challenging there," Dennys replied.

"Indeed," Gillespie said. "Infested with poverty and disease as it is, the East End can be an extraordinary learning experience for the resourceful physician. Well, lad," he continued. "Keep up the good work." He nodded courteously and turned his attention to a frail looking elderly man. "Lord Dubarry! How good of you to join us this evening."

Mackenzie beamed at Dennys. "Well, John, I think you have made a good impression. Sir William seems quite keen on having you in his program." He raised his glass in salute to the younger man.

"Thank you for recommending me, Dr. Mackenzie," Dennys responded.

"It is, of course, an immensely exciting prospect. Sir William has an uncanny sense when it comes to choosing good surgeons. You know what he said about you? Born to cut, the lad is," Mackenzie laughed.

"An astute observation," Dennys remarked, an ironic smile twisting his lips.

Andrew had heard and seen enough. Within the blink of an eye, he was back in his own drawing room, his spirit reunited with his corporeal self. There was no doubt in his mind regarding Dennys's identity, nor had there been since he first learned of the man's existence. He simply had to see for himself to observe his enemy's actions. The evil emanating from John Dennys was of a magnitude equal to that which he experienced at the gates of Hell. This was no ordinary sorcerer, but one with demon blood coursing through his veins.

While spying in the Mackenzie house, Andrew had been aware of a tide of sibilant voices issuing from the shadows, voices which whispered the words "black" and "Jack." Faceless and formless, they were nonetheless faithful minions of Dennys, their purpose to serve him and alert him to possible dangers. Andrew's more powerful magic had allowed him to evade their detection.

It made perfect sense that Dennys chose Whitechapel for the working ground of his devastation. The overabundance of desperate indigent prostitutes assured him a steady supply of easily attainable victims. Despite the fact that prostitutes had thus far been the only victims, all of Whitechapel was sullied by the taint of evil. The rest of the populace, helpless to stop the evil contamination, were victims as well, albeit of terror and chaos.

The police, both the Metropolitan and Scotland Yard forces, had clearly demonstrated their inadequacy in tracking this elusive killer. In a district such as Whitechapel, where mistrust of law enforcement was already rampant, these murders further eroded the tenuous relationship between the police and the populace. Evidence of mounting unrest fueled by panic could easily result in insurrection and riots. As the public's fear and outrage swelled, the burgeoning anger required a target, and the police were obvious scapegoats.

The police commissioner, Sir Charles Warren, along with Chief Inspector Swanson and Inspector Abberline, had already received heavy criticism for their handling of the case. Mindful of last year's Bloody Sunday riot, the last thing these men wanted was social upheaval and calls for resignations. The police were in a precarious position, their manpower under enormous duress. Street constables worked extra shifts at night, all hoping against hope for the big break, one vital clue which would enable them to close in on the Whitechapel murderer.

Andrew was aware of the acute stress of the police departments, not only because he read the newspaper accounts, but because of his magic. He used his ability to focus his thoughts on the individuals concerned and glean necessary information from their minds. His telepathic skills were as highly developed as his other abilities. Therefore, he understood the anxieties and doubts harbored by these three men in particular.

For example, he knew that all three were concerned about the declining morale of the police, especially amongst the Metropolitan force. Frustration was at a peak level as the weeks passed with no leads to pursue. There was also an aspect of this case, prohibited from the public, which worried those in charge of the investigation.

Rumor had surfaced amongst the police members that they were dealing with no ordinary killer but one who possessed supernatural abilities. Of course, no constable or officer would openly admit to such thoughts, nor would either police force condone such speculation. It was annoying enough that some of the general populace favored a supernatural theory. However, whispers circulated through the ranks and the inspectors caught wind of them. Inspector Abberline was particularly troubled by these insinuations, as his wife had voiced similar thoughts.

She considered herself a spiritualist and professed a firm belief in the influence of supernatural forces in the world. She was convinced that the Whitechapel murderer was not even human but some type of demon or other evil being. She spoke so passionately on the subject that Abberline worried she was becoming obsessed with the murders, and he even began to secretly worry for her sanity. Thus, he found it expedient to quell any hint of the supernatural and forbade his men to indulge in such womanish fancies.

The Whitechapel murderer, he said, was no more supernatural than Abberline himself. They were facing an intelligent, crafty, calculating killer who, thus far, had had good fortune on his side in evading the police. But the good fortune would not last indefinitely, he warned, and this murderer would make a mistake, as all murderers must, and then he would be apprehended. All this, he told his men with confidence. But Andrew looked deep into Abberline's mind and even deeper into his heart and saw that the inspector had grave doubts about ever capturing this killer.

And he saw something else in Abberline—fear.

CHAPTER 28

Sarah-Jane glanced up from the beer mug she was polishing behind the bar counter. What tedious work this was. How she wished life was more exciting than this daily drudgery. She couldn't imagine working in her father's pub year after year, her world restricted to the oppressive confines of Whitechapel streets. She desperately longed to escape from this life, but how? That was the question that preoccupied her thoughts.

She was aware that most girls she knew had no such aspirations. Docile and accepting of life in Whitechapel, they seemed resigned to the limited options available. Most would be fortunate if they married a decent man with steady employment, if they survived the many perils of pregnancy and childbirth, and had enough money to afford tolerable lodging and keep their children from starving.

All too frequently, women, whether single or married, were forced into sweated labor, toiling long and exhausting hours in appalling conditions in poorly ventilated factories and warehouses. They received only a daily pittance for all their hard work. To Sarah-Jane, this prospect was frightfully depressing. She had watched it happen to girls she knew, her age and slightly older. Their youth, beauty, and vitality gradually drained away, leaving them bone dry, brittle husks. Sarah-Jane vowed that this fate would never befall her. She swore on her mother's grave that somehow she would rise above the adversity of life in this dead end hole, and then life would truly begin.

She thought of Emma, so different from these other girls. Emma was blessed with purpose and determination. She didn't hesitate to voice her opinion and was passionate about many aspects of life. More than any other reason, Sarah-Jane admired her because Emma was doing what she wanted. She was involved in work that demanded she not only care *for* people but *about* them as well. She let nothing deter her from her goals. Sarah-Jane looked to her friend as inspiration and proof that a woman could be successful despite the many obstacles society placed in her way.

"A penny for your thoughts." She started at the intrusion into her reverie. Glancing to her left, she met the amused eyes of Andrew Hewitt-Brown.

"Oh, Mr. Hewitt-Brown!" Sarah exclaimed, cursing herself silently for her awkwardness. Even though he had instructed her to address him by his Christian name only, she had great difficulty complying, for despite being her best friend's beau, he was also an important gentleman in London society.

He chuckled. "I apologize, Sarah. I didn't realize you were so preoccupied."

"Oh no, that's all right. I mean, I am not doing anything important. Just putting the clean mugs away, ready for the crowds later on."

"Ah, yes," Andrew remarked. "It's still quite early, isn't it?" He looked around at the sparsely occupied tables. A few dedicated drinkers were already ensconced at their tables, but otherwise, it was quiet as usual at six o'clock in the evening, the working crowd not yet having arrived.

Sarah-Jane watched him intently, observing his fine attire, so discordant in the slum district, and marveled that he took such a risk of being robbed, especially as evening approached.

But Andrew never encountered any trouble, he had once told her smilingly when Sarah had expressed concern. She gazed at his manicured hands, fingers slender and strong, noting the ring on the fourth finger of his right hand. Her eyes were drawn by the smooth stone setting, a rich blend of swirling gold and brown.

Andrew was aware of Sarah-Jane's scrutiny. "I see you have

noticed my ring. What do you think of it?"

"Blimey, it's beautiful!" she exclaimed. "I have never seen a ring like that before. Special, isn't it? Is it gold?"

"The band is, yes. The stone is exotic to you because it is not found in England. This ring is from India, and the stone is called a tiger's eye. I imagine because it resembles a tiger's eyes in its colors."

"Tell me about India," Sarah-Jane said eagerly. "Is it true that the snakes are so big they can swallow a man whole?"

Andrew laughed heartily. "My, such exaggeration. Where did you hear this tale? Never mind, it's not important. Nevertheless, I am sorry to disappoint you, Sarah. The snakes are not versed in that particular skill, for which I can assure you, the populace is very grateful. However, there are a few decidedly nasty species, the giant cobra, for example, whose poison is invariably fatal."

"You wouldn't catch me near one of them. And the wild animals like elephants and tigers roam the streets?"

"Elephants are the most common mode of transportation, especially for goods. So, yes, one can usually see an elephant or two in the cities and more, of course, in the countryside. But in the bigger cities like Bombay and Calcutta, the rickshaw is by far the popular choice for people to travel quickly. As for tigers, generally speaking, they are not found in highly populated areas. Occasionally, the odd rogue tiger attacks a village, and I have heard tales of tigers in the city, but never have I witnessed this phenomenon."

"And is it true that the natives have darker skin than us because they never wash, and so the dirt keeps gathering on them?" Sarah-Jane asked.

Andrew laughed again. "That sounds more like a description of an inhabitant of Whitechapel, many of whom seem to have a peculiar aversion to soap and water. Indian people have dark skin because that is the color of their race, just as Africans have even darker skins, while it is normal for us to be light colored."

"I'd like to travel someday," Sarah-Jane said wistfully. "But I don't think I would go to India. I might catch a horrible disease or get eaten by a disgusting animal. I'd rather go someplace more civilized, like Paris or a city in Spain."

Andrew smiled sardonically. "I venture to say that in many ways, Whitechapel is just as dangerous as Calcutta or Bombay, except that the wild animals here come in human form."

Sarah-Jane pursed her lips thoughtfully. "You would know, Mr. Hewitt-Brown. 'Tis true there's lots of sickness here at home, but you tend to pay not too much attention until it's someone you know. Emma was telling me the other day about a girl who came to the infirmary by the name of Eliza Madison. Well, it so happens that I went to school with an Eliza Madison, and sure enough, this girl was my age, so I guess it was her. Emma said that she was so sick and weak; she collapsed right there on the floor before they could even find her a bed in the casual ward. She died a few hours later. The doctor said it was most likely lead poisoning from the tile factory where she worked, and her just seventeen years old."

Andrew nodded gravely. "It would seem that working in your father's pub might not be so bad when compared to other types of employment."

Sarah-Jane was silent.

"Life in Whitechapel is a game of chance," he continued, "with the odds stacked against survival." He looked intently into her eyes. "You, Sarah, are a survivor. You shall not let Whitechapel defeat you, of that I am certain."

Sarah-Jane felt a thrill at the base of her spine as she stared into his sharp gray eyes, turbulent and mysterious as any ocean. She felt lost in those eyes, as though a current pulled her down into their depths, but there was no fear in this. Instead, she saw hope and promise for the future swirling in the tides. A giddy disorientation swept through her, followed by a surge of warmth as her worries dissolved under the hypnotic influence of those strange eyes.

Andrew smiled gently. Sarah-Jane floated in the tranquil waters. Though it felt like a long time, it could have only lasted a few minutes. She blinked, and the room snapped back into focus.

She felt calm and refreshed, a feeling of well-being one might experience after a relaxing bath in the sea.

A spontaneous smile lit up her face, which glowed with good health. She suddenly felt much better than she had all day, although she couldn't quite remember the events of the last several moments.

"Are you seeing Emma tonight?" she inquired.

"Yes, I'm just on my way to her lodging now," Andrew replied.

"Would you like a drink then before you leave?"

"No, thank you, Sarah. I really stopped by to say good evening."

Sarah-Jane blushed and lowered her eyes. "That's very nice of you, Andrew," she said. "You can stop by anytime."

"I shall," he promised. "We shall be seeing more of one another in the times ahead." He tipped his hat in farewell and reached the door in a leisurely stride.

Sarah-Jane barely restrained her squeal of delight as he exited the pub. Now, what could Andrew have meant by that parting comment? She was aware of several pairs of curious eyes turned upon her. Some of the patrons had watched and possibly overheard the conversation with Andrew. She shrugged and turned her back to them dismissively, pretending to busy herself with arranging glasses and bottles on the bottom shelves behind the counter. She hoped indeed that she would see more of Andrew.

Ever since she was introduced to the dashing young gentleman over a year ago, she had occasion to lament that he was Emma's suitor. Would that she, Sarah, had met him first. She had heard stories about fine gentlemen marrying below their station in life, especially if a woman was strikingly attractive. Sarah-Jane knew she was an extraordinarily pretty girl. She received enough admiring glances from men of all sorts to corroborate this fact. So it wasn't really far fetched to believe that someone like Andrew might fall in love with her.

Just my luck that he is already spoken for, she sighed to herself.

It was difficult not to envy, even sometimes resent Emma for the life she led. Once she married Andrew, she would live like a lady; no more work, residing in a fine house in London. It would be easy for her to forget about Whitechapel. She, unlike Sarah-Jane, had not been born and raised in this slum. Whitechapel was not part of her blood.

But Emma was a true friend, and Andrew had promised to see more of Sarah, so they wouldn't leave her behind, would they? She chided herself for such silly thoughts. It was not as if London was all that far away, although at times it seemed a different world entirely; one that she might glimpse, but of which she could never be a part.

CHAPTER 29

Andrew awoke with a start. He was not alone in the room. Something stood in the corner at the foot of his bed, silently watching him. Shape concealed by a dark hooded cloak, face shrouded from view, it neither moved nor uttered a sound. He knew it was evil.

He sat up in bed, keen vision adjusting instantly to the dark. Fixing the intruder with a steely gaze, he said, "If you have something to communicate, do so at once, otherwise begone with you. I have no interest in cat and mouse games."

A soft rustle emanated from the figure as it shifted. An image flashed through Andrew's mind, vivid and repulsive. Corrupt flesh stained with foul excrements appeared before his eyes. The dank, musty odor of the tomb assailed his nostrils.

A gaunt claw-like hand emerged from the folds of its cloak, clutching an object which glowed with a faint illumination, the better for Andrew to see. A single lock of chestnut hair, the rich color highlighted with streaks of reddish-gold; it belonged, unmistakably, to Emma. Andrew regarded the curl at the same time, fixing his intent gaze upon the silent figure.

"You may tell your master that I do not take kindly to threats. I shall not be deterred from my course of action. Let him be forewarned. I shall find him no matter where he goes or what he does, no matter how long it takes. He can't hide from the wrath of the Creator. 'Vengeance is mine,' sayeth the Lord. I am the Lord's Avenger. From this day forward, your master shall know what it is to be the prey instead of the hunter. Now be gone from my presence."

The figure inclined its head slightly and then disappeared as unobtrusively as it had come.

Andrew lay back in bed, pondering his visitation. He had been expecting some such occurrence since his decision to pursue and destroy the Whitechapel murderer. Tonight's apparition represented the first overt communication from his enemy, an attempt to intimidate him through fear — not for himself, but for Emma. After tonight he should expect further escalation in threats against his fiancée.

The visitation confirmed not only that the Ripper knew Andrew's identity but also that his adversary's magic posed a significant danger to the Ripper's existence. No idle threats here; Jack the Ripper would strike with lethal force when the time was right. Tonight's theatrics were a warning to show Andrew that Emma was within the grasp of the Ripper's malignant reach.

He considered his next move. He wasn't in the least surprised by the Ripper's focus on Emma. Obviously, the demon had circumvented the protective spell cast by Andrew. Otherwise, his servant would not have succeeded in procuring a lock of Emma's hair while she slumbered. He pondered this latest action on the part of the Ripper.

The demon had apparently concluded that Andrew's vulnerability was connected to Emma's well-being, an assumption that was logical if not completely accurate. Andrew had deliberately cast a weaker version of the protective spell he normally used in order to test the demon's responses. He was intrigued by what had been revealed.

Not only did the Ripper understand his enemy's receptiveness to intimidation tactics, but he was also counting on Andrew's presumed weakness where Emma was concerned. Flawed deductions, he thought, for one who should be all too familiar with the fiery determination of the Avenger.

The Avenger had confronted this evil on a number of occasions, although its guise and presentation varied each time. The only explanation which occurred to Andrew was that the human, John Dennys, whom the demon occupied, suffered from the flaw of arrogance. This was something the Avenger could use to advantage, as the demon's arrogance made it more likely to underestimate his enemy's power. Andrew could easily prevent any *physical* harm from befalling Emma, but her spiritual well-being was a different matter. He could only provide a limited safety where spiritual issues were concerned, for he couldn't interfere in any way with Emma's freewill.

Emma must make the choices regarding her spirituality. The process of inner growth must be allowed to occur naturally, which would not happen if her ability to decide her own spiritual destiny was compromised. But therein, of course, lay the temptation for Andrew. With less effort than it would take to raise his hand, he could adjust circumstances so that Emma would not be confronted with this potentially hazardous spiritual dilemma. A threat, whether physical or spiritual, from a demon as powerful as this fiend was not to be lightly dismissed.

Andrew knew he was the only one who could circumvent the emotional and soul wrenching pain that lay in store for his beloved. For if one wished to embrace one's spirituality, there were lessons to learn, some more bitter than others. The lesson which leads to the most joy is also the one which demands the most sacrifice and suffering, namely the attainment of unconditional love. In order for Emma to acquire that capability, she would have to experience firsthand the pain and sorrow of self denial, something which the human component in her would rage against.

The demands on her fortitude of will, her desire and determination, would be enormous, as would the rewards awaiting her. The challenge would involve suppressing all those negative human emotions that would struggle within her for mastery, especially doubt, despair, temptation, and anger. It was a challenge that not all Insiders were able to meet.

Andrew knew the best way for Emma to learn the skill of unconditional love was for her to experience it herself. Since she met Andrew, she had been the recipient of his unconditional love, and she had blossomed like a flower on the vine. She understood what it felt like to be cherished; to feel safe and secure in her lover's embrace; to gaze into his eyes and feel the immeasurable depth of that love; to know that there were no words she could utter, no deed that she could perform, that would ever diminish the love bestowed upon her.

This love, the source of spirituality, was the purest, most selfless form of love, offering the perfect symbiosis of pain and joy, a reflection of the universal duality of which it was a part. The pain of wisdom must, on occasion, dictate a course of action against which human nature rebels, a decision based not upon the desires of a loved one but upon that individual's needs. The joy which comes from knowing beyond a doubt that one has bestowed a love which is unsurpassable, timeless, and limitless is an incomparable sensation. It is the closest man can come, while still in physical form, to the Creator.

It is the love which all men seek that they want to experience from the first awakening in the womb to the last breath of this existence. They may not know its name, but their hearts cry out for it. Only very few are fortunate enough to receive it; fewer still blessed enough to give it.

Thus reflected Andrew in the deep, still hours of the night. He was thankful for the love and wisdom entrusted to him through his pledge. He knew he would rely heavily on these attributes in the days and weeks to come, as he watched in silence Emma's spiritual trial by fire. He could only hope that though the flames might scorch, they would not consume her.

CHAPTER 30

London at midnight. Darkness blanketed the city, wrapping its inhabitants in a cloak of slumber. But in the black heart of London known as Whitechapel, there was indeed no rest for the wicked. Whitechapel hummed with restless activity, for this was the hour when violence flourished. Scornful of the meek and faint-hearted, it offered a haven to those whose hearts festered with malevolence. No act of kindness went unpunished, and injustice struck with swift and deadly force.

A dark energy prowled the fog enshrouded streets, searching to satisfy its terrible craving. It crept down darkened alleys, but not because it feared discovery; on the contrary, it was eager to reveal itself, to gloat and revel in its sinister glory. It moved with the darkness because they were allies, twins born of the same seed; darkness and evil enmeshed, inseparable one from the other.

Dead autumn leaves lined the streets, shrivelled corpses, paper thin, dry rustled in the wind like the whisper of ghosts. Fog flew quickly along the path, eager to meet its lover, the shadows, in this night gloomed world. Fog and shadows embraced, intermingled, then rushed as one to meet their dark master.

From his hiding place in the shadows, he watched the woman stomp her feet and rub her wind chapped hands together. It was a miserable rainy night, damp as only London could be. He knew the damp sent a chill up her legs and into her lower back, causing a sharp stabbing pain whenever she moved a certain way.

"Ow," he heard her exclaim as she massaged a spot on her back.

He'd been following at a discreet distance since her release from Bishopgates Police Station, where she had been detained earlier in the evening for drunk and disorderly conduct. Now, considerably more sober, here she was after one in the morning at Miter's Square, notorious for its prostitution trade. Tonight, however, due to the inclement weather, or perhaps out of fear of the Whitechapel murderer, the square was quiet.

Marked by an absence of its habitual lively transactions, it was eerie and lonely. To be sure, people were never far away. He observed three men walking past the square, laughing in easy camaraderie. They spared barely a glance for the whore stomping her feet to keep warm, although one of them would later identify her to police as the same woman he'd seen earlier in the square.

He watched and waited to make certain that no one else passed by. He had removed his disguise, for tonight, he wished for his victim to recognize him for who he was. The disguise, concealed in nearby bushes, awaited his return. The immediate vicinity was deserted, and his keen sense had conveyed to him that no one ventured this way. He emerged from the shadows.

Hearing his footsteps, the woman turned around. She peered nearsightedly only for a moment, then offered a simpering smile. "Hello, dearie. Want a bit of company this evening?"

He paused in his stride and pretended to consider. "Well, that depends."

The whore continued to smile. She was small in stature, only five feet tall. At forty-six, she looked her age, her fine auburn hair, slightly graying, tucked beneath her black straw bonnet.

"'Tis reasonable rates, sir, I assure you—" she began.

But he interrupted her, raising his black gloved hand. "Money is not the issue, my good woman. It never is. However, I wish you to answer a question for me."

The woman's smile faltered a bit, a look of uncertainty creeping into her eyes. But if she noticed the ironic emphasis of the word "good" in his slightly mocking tone, she gave no indication.

"Why, of course, sir. A gentleman like you has a right to ask a question or two, I'm sure. If it is sickness you're worried about, I can tell you—"

He stopped her once more with another gesture. "It matters not what diseased state you may or may not be in. My question is simply this. Do you miss your old life?" He took a few steps towards her.

The woman cast him a perplexed look. "What do you mean?" she asked, frowning.

"Well, presumably, you had some sort of life before you became a whore; home, a husband, children perhaps?"

The woman's frown deepened to a scowl. "What's it to you?" she challenged. "Anyways, that was a long time ago." She shrugged dismissively.

"You haven't forgotten that life," he says softly. "In fact, you dream about it almost every night, don't you, Kate?"

The woman started with surprise. "'Ow do you know me name?" she demanded, a note of alarm in her voice.

He smiled a flash of white in the darkness. "Oh, I know a lot about you, Kate," he replied in the same soft tone. He advanced a few more steps. "I know all your secrets, the good and the bad of your life.

"I know how your husband mistreated you and how you fought to keep your family together as long as you could. But the misery was too great, and so you took to drink in the hope that you would feel better and stronger. It worked for a while, as false comforts do; however, too late, you realized the demon drink had control of you. Because of it, you lost everything, including the love of your daughter Annie, she who is most precious to you.

"Your heart was irreparably broken the day you saw the scorn in Annie's eyes, her revulsion of her drunken mother. Your heart will never heal from that wound; it cries out in your sleep every night. It was all your fault, Kate. You brought your suffering, not only upon yourself but your family as well. You were too weak-spirited to save your daughter and yourself.

"You made a mess of your life, one bad choice leading to another, until here you stand in a deserted square in one of the most sordid places on earth, about to pay the final price for your cowardly, worthless life.

"Tell me, when you relinquished control of your life, who then took over that control? Surely you can see that such abdication has dire consequences. When one is no longer one's own master, one becomes a servant. Who did you invite to become your master, Kate? Who now controls your soul?" He stood only inches from her and extended his hand. His voice was barely an echo of a whisper, but she heard it clearly. "I see your pain. I touch it. I breathe it in, for its odor is sweet. Your pain makes me smile."

A vise-like grip clamped down on her wrist. She was too petrified to move, startled by the contrast between the whispered utterances, soft as a caress, and the iron fury behind his grip. She had listened in fascinated horror to him describing her life in all its sordid, shameful truth. She felt as though a growing chasm had opened up at her feet, and poised on its edge, she was doomed to fall into its dark depths. As his gaze locked onto hers with riveting intensity, the bewilderment and fear coalesced into abject terror.

"Ah, yes," he murmured. "The windows of the soul, at last, they recognize me. They hold the look that is worth waiting an eternity to see. The sweet, terrified knowledge when at long last, you face the embodiment of all the nightmarish pain you thought so safely buried. That pain now claws its way to the surface, demanding release.

"Can you allow it a voice, Kate? Do you dare?"

Panic consumed her as his eyes held her rooted to the ground. Helpless to look away, a magnetic force pulled her ever closer to those eyes, although she understood that no physical movement was involved. The entire scenario unfolded with nightmare intensity, yet sharp and clear. She knew it was real, the culmination of every event, both good and bad, in her life. The eyes of the man—who wasn't a man—glittered with an impenetrable darkness. With dreadful certainty, she realized she would fall into those black pits and keep endlessly falling while the shrieks and curses of the damned echoed into eternity around her.

With a last desperate effort, she tried to break away. She cried silently, her daughter's name on her lips. "Annie, Annie."

The grip on her wrist tightened with bone crushing force. The delicate bones were not so much broken as ground to powder beneath the sheer strength, so that later, during the autopsy, the broken wrist would be missed by the coroner—no telltale protrusion of bone, just a slight bruising of the tissues. And when compared to the extensive mutilations to the rest of the body, it would be no wonder that a mere broken wrist should be overlooked.

Her daughter's image blossomed before Kate's eyes. She finally opened her mouth to scream, but before the impulse could travel from brain to vocal cords, he raised his left arm and slashed with brutal force, his dagger slicing her throat from ear to ear. A bright flash of pain seared through Kate, and suddenly the image of her daughter was running red, a bright red rose opening up before her eyes. She tried to smile, but she was already dead.

Jack the Ripper stepped back as the body hit the ground with a thud. He watched the bright geyser of blood shoot up and outwards, drenching the sleeve of his coat. He took a moment to sniff the air—no human scent was detectable. He had time to complete his work. He spared a glance at the shadows, for some of his minions and lesser demons had gathered, drawn by the kill.

Mouth open, he breathed deeply of the night air, allowing the taste of fog and darkness to linger on his tongue. He savored the rancid, spoiled meat odor beneath it all, the stench of corruption that ran rampant in Whitechapel.

What a grand night, he thought, turning his attention to the corpse. The blood was already congealing in pools around the body, spilling onto the ground atop the sodden cobblestones. He wiped his dagger on the woman's apron, ready to begin the real work of the night.

It was not long before the silver blade dripped crimson once more.

The next day's newspapers screamed the headline, "Double Murder in Whitechapel," and "Murderous Fiend Strikes Twice in One Night." News of the double event murders of Liz Stride and Catherine (Kate) Eddoes traveled like wildfire through the East End and the rest of London.

Panic gripped the populous at the idea of the murderer claiming two victims in such a short space of time. Rumors escalated, especially regarding the murderer's identity. Many pointed to the double event as proof that a supernatural force was at work, for how else could the killer have evaded the clutches of the police, not once, but twice in the span of a few hours? The frenzy of fear churned around Whitechapel like an ominous pall, rivaling the fog in its intensity.

One individual chuckled as he read the newspaper accounts, for he was the only one who knew the truth. Two murders, true enough, but only one committed by the dreaded Whitechapel murderer — the other by a human killer in thrall to its demon master. He was also aware that the police had in their possession a letter and would soon receive another allegedly sent by the murderer.

In the letter, whose tone was macabre and taunting, though oddly jovial, the writer introduced himself as Jack the Ripper. It was destined to become the murderer's trade name and would continue to evoke horror and revulsion long after the killings had ceased. A blood-spattered legacy would remain shrouded in mystery, despite exhaustive searches for the killer's true identity.

A smile of satisfaction played about Dennys's lips. The letters could not be traced to him, for indeed it was not he who had written them. The author of the letters had served his purpose well, although the pathetic human, Druitt, had no inkling of the master who controlled him; merely another tormented, corrupted soul who had succumbed to diabolical influence.

And the Whitechapel murderer, from that day forward to be known as Jack the Ripper, had no intention of revealing his secret.

CHAPTER 31

"Push, push!" Emma urged the sweat-soaked woman lying on the bed. "You must not slacken. Come now, Amelia, push harder."

"Ah, oh, oh, oh!" grunted the woman, red-faced with exertion. Her oldest daughter, Penny, a girl of thirteen, stood at the head of the bed on her mother's left side, mopping her brow with a cool cloth and murmuring words of encouragement. Emma, straddling the woman's legs, exhorted her to even greater effort. Clean linen and towels were positioned between Amelia's thighs and around her buttocks.

"That's it," directed Emma. "Keep pushing. I can see the baby's crown. Come now, harder."

A neighbor, Alice James, was in attendance on the other side of the bed, ready with a basin of warm water to cleanse the newborn. Amelia's moans increased to piercing shrieks.

"Ah, no, I can't, no, no, no!" she screamed, face contorted in pain.

"Just a little more. Hold on a bit longer," Emma instructed. "Yes, that's it. The head is through. Now comes the easy part."

As the baby shot forward straight into Emma's waiting hands, the smile of anticipation playing about her lips abruptly vanished. Through the layer of blood that coated it, Emma could see the blue color of the body, tiny limbs flaccid and lifeless, the umbilical cord coiled around its throat. A stillborn child.

Emma pursed her lips. Her eyes met those of the neighbor, and she shook her head. The woman clamped a hand to her mouth, trying to stifle a gasp.

"What is it?" Amelia rasped, throat raw from screaming. "Is it a boy or girl?"

"Boy," Emma replied. She cut the umbilical cord and knotted it efficiently. Quietly, she handed the baby's body to Alice, who surreptitiously wrapped it in a towel.

"Amelia," Emma began. "I am afraid I must tell you—"

She was interrupted by a torrential gush of blood and fluid from between the woman's thighs. It was expelled with such sudden force that Emma had no time to avoid the deluge, which drenched the front of her dress, splashing up into her hair.

"Oh, the pain, oh!" cried Amelia, words ending in a wail as her body shuddered violently.

Wiping a bloody strand of hair away from her eyes, Emma lunged for the woman's distended abdomen and applied pressure to expel the afterbirth. She knew she only had a few moments to get the bleeding under control, or Amelia would hemorrhage to death.

"Quick, give me more towels," she urgently demanded.

Alice ran in a frenzy to do her bidding.

"Get anything—blankets, pillowcases, it matters not. Hurry!" Emma shouted.

Meanwhile, Penny crouched in the corner, gnawing at her hand, eyes wide in terror.

Emma looked down at the pool of blood between the woman's legs, and a coldness crept into her heart. The afterbirth lay in the mess. Ripped prematurely from the walls of the womb, the trauma had caused the death of the child and now threatened the mother as well. The blood vessels in the womb had ruptured. There was little Emma could do to save her, but instinctively she reacted as her training had taught her.

"Here, quick!" She grabbed some towels from Alice. "I need your help, Alice." She moved aside for the neighbor to approach. "I want you to press down on Amelia's abdomen," she directed, "whilst I try to staunch the bleeding. Now...." Emma moved her hands as Alice gingerly placed hers on the woman's abdomen. "No, no, harder than that," Emma urged, applying pressure to

Alice's hands. "There. Keep the pressure just so until I tell you to stop."

She paused for a momentary look at Amelia. The woman had lost consciousness, eyes rolled back, her ghastly pallor reflected in the gaslight. Time was running out. Emma began stuffing a towel into the woman's vagina, inserting it as high into the cervix as possible, hoping it would act as a tampon to compress the blood flow from the vessels, as external pressure to the lower abdomen and pelvic regions were simultaneously applied. There was a chance, however slim, that with sufficient compression, the torn blood vessels might be occluded and the bleeding cease.

It seemed to work. The flow of blood slowed noticeably before it finally stopped.

"It is working," Alice exclaimed.

But it might be too late, Emma thought. She might have already lost too much blood.

After ensuring the towel was tightly in place, Emma moved swiftly to the head of the bed. She bit her lip as she stared at the pale face below her. It was relaxed now, no longer creased by furrows of pain.

Emma touched the pulse at Amelia's neck. The beat was very faint and irregular, almost undetectable. As Emma kept her fingers in place, the pulse faltered once, twice, then stopped. She gently closed the woman's eyes.

"Is she...?" Alice whispered.

"Yes, she's gone," Emma replied softly.

A great sobbing wail erupted from the girl crouched in the corner. "Mamma, Mamma, no!" Penny cried, burying her face in her hands and sliding to the floor.

Emma approached the child and knelt beside her. She stroked the bent head as Penny continued to sob. Suddenly, the girl lifted her streaming face and threw herself into Emma's arms, trying, as a small animal might, to huddle against its mother, seeking warmth and comfort. Emma folded the girl tightly to her, murmuring soothing sounds in her ear.

Alice began quietly removing the blood soaked linen,

bundling it into a burlap sack to be burned. Then she set about preparing Amelia's body, cleaning and grooming the dead woman as best she could. She approached Emma and tapped her gently on the shoulder.

"Could you help me dress her?" she asked in a hushed voice.

Emma nodded, gently disengaging Penny, whose wild sobs had softened to a steady weeping.

"I shall return, Penny, but I must help Alice attend to your mother."

Lips trembling, the young girl unwrapped herself from Emma's embrace. She shivered, hugging herself, and started rocking back and forth. Emma reached for her nurse's cloak and draped it about the girl's thin shoulders. Then she crossed to the bedside and assisted Alice in dressing the dead woman in a fresh nightgown. They positioned her in bed and pulled the clean coverlet up to her shoulders.

"Where are the other children?" Emma asked.

Alice sighed. "Lord love'em. They're staying with another neighbor across the street. Nan Burkett. What's to become of them now?"

"Where's the father?"

Alice grunted disapprovingly. "Huh. More than likely down to the Frying Pan, drinkin' a good portion of his wages. He'll never be able to take care of them seven little ones," she said worriedly.

"No, I don't suppose he will," murmured Emma. "Are there any other relatives?"

Alice thought a moment, frowning. "It seems to me that I remember Amelia talking about a sister out in the country somewhere."

"Aye, that would be Aunt Mary," Penny interjected between sobs. "She lives in Surrey. She is a cook for a family there."

"Does she have children?"

Penny wiped her runny nose with the back of her hand and sniffled back her tears. "Three or four. But they're mostly grown up now. Aunt Mary is quite a bit older than Mum." Her face crumpled as a fresh spasm of grief shook her.

"It doesn't sound very promising, does it?" whispered Alice in an aside.

"No, it doesn't," Emma agreed. "Obviously, the child welfare authorities shall have to be notified."

"'Tis such a shame," lamented Alice. "They'll split the children up, won't they? It'll be so hard on them. How will – ?"

"Shh," Emma interrupted sharply, her voice low. "This is not the time to discuss that subject. Right now, the children require support and care, not concerns about the family being torn asunder. Can you take Penny back to your place for a while?" Emma still had to alert the coroner and other authorities.

"Surely," Alice agreed. "I will be glad to watch the poor child for a bit."

Emma went over to Penny. The girl had stopped shivering and rocking and now sat quietly on the floor.

"You need to go with Mrs. James now, Penny. She'll take care of you until your father comes home."

"Where is me dad?" she stammered.

"I'm not sure at the moment," Emma answered truthfully. "But sooner or later, he will return home."

"Come then, love, I'll make you a lovely spot of tea," Alice said kindly, putting a motherly arm around the girl and leading her to the door of the bedroom.

"Wait," Emma stopped them. She went to the wardrobe into the adjoining room, and after a bit of searching, brought out a shabby but decent coat. "I need my cloak back. This coat looks as if it might belong to you," she said, presenting the item for Penny's inspection.

The girl nodded. "'Tis mine." She quietly relinquished Emma's cloak in exchange for her own. She put it on and examined its flimsy sleeves. "I've just about outgrown it, Mum says. It'll pass to Jane – she is growing fast. Mum promised she would buy me a new coat for the winter. Mum said…." She trailed off as a fresh wave of tears assailed her.

"There, there, love, let's go," Alice soothed. She escorted the girl through the bedroom and out the front door.

Emma stood silently for a few moments, listening to the echo of their footsteps. Then she caught sight of her blood-spattered reflection in the old mirror on the wall opposite the bed. Brushing the tears from her eyes, she set about the task of cleaning up herself.

CHAPTER 32

A wave of laughter and merriment greeted Emma as she walked through the doors of the Princess Alice. It was almost ten at night, and most of the revelers had arrived at the pub much earlier in the evening. She fought her way to the bar, ignoring the appreciative whistles and shouted invitations of the predominantly male crowd. Joe Mullen was busy serving several loud voiced men at once.

"Come on here, Joe, slowin' down in your old age, are you?" one of them boomed, slapping his mate on the shoulder.

The landlord glared at him. "Show me where you will get quicker or better services, and I will give you a free drink, Stan."

Stan laughed good-naturedly. "Ah well, you win this one, Joe. At least you're not falling down drunk like some landlords I know. Plus 'e's got the best looking barmaid in all of Whitechapel," he said to his mate, but in a voice lowered so that Mullen couldn't hear. The landlord, known to be as ferociously protective of his daughter as a female bear with her cubs, had on more than one occasion soundly trounced an amorous patron who foolishly paid too much attention to Sarah-Jane.

Emma elbowed her way to the bar, her nose wrinkled in distaste at the heavy fumes exhaled from too many sour mouths. "Mr. Mullen," she called above the general din. "Where's Sarah?"

Mullen looked up briefly from the counter. He gestured toward the crowded, smoke-infested room. "Up there, somewheres." Turning back to his customers, he gathered their money in exchange for their pints.

Emma scanned the room for several moments before she

spotted Sarah-Jane. The girl balanced a tray of empty mugs in one hand while she slapped an unwelcome suitor trying to grab her about the waist. Twisting expertly out of his grasp, she hurried toward the bar. She saw Emma wave and nodded an acknowledgment as she headed in a beeline toward the raised curtain behind the bar. Emma followed her into the small alcove, which partitioned off the public area from the main floor kitchen.

Sarah-Jane set the tray down on a wooden shelf. Sighing, she brushed a hand across her brow, pushing back wisps of blonde hair from her smooth forehead.

"Well, Emma, 'tis good to see you."

Emma nodded. "Have you had your tea break yet?"

"No, but I think now is as good a time as any," Sarah-Jane replied. She wiped her hands on her apron, then peeked through the curtain at her father behind the bar. "Da, takin' a bit of a break now," she called to him.

Joe Mullen frowned in reluctant acknowledgment. "Not too long, lass. It's busier than usual tonight."

"Aye, I know," Sarah-Jane responded. "Come," she gestured to Emma and led the way to the kitchen at the back of the building. She put the water on to boil for tea, then unlatched the iron handle of the thick oak door. Together they stepped out into the courtyard.

It was relatively quiet outside, the noise from the public house a muted din. They sat on the stoop side by side. Neither one spoke for a moment, each taking pleasure in the gentle night air. Stars shone in the clear sky overhead, and a new moon cast a comforting glow into the shadowed recesses of the courtyard. Sarah-Jane finally broke the silence.

"I wonder what them stars look like up close? When I was a girl, I used to pretend I lived on one of them stars, the brightest and shiniest one." A soft smile played about the corners of her mouth. She turned to her friend and asked in a wistful tone, "Do you ever wish you could be somewhere else or someone else? I do."

"Where and who would you like to be?" inquired Emma.

"That's easy—anywhere but Whitechapel. And I would like to look the same, but be a different person, like a society lady with one of them fancy houses, who wears the latest fashions from Paris and throws lots of lavish parties. I would have a good and rich husband who would give me anythin' I wanted, and I would have a well-behaved little brood I could sing songs to in the nursery to help them fall asleep at night, and I would be happy."

Emma smiled. "That sounds like a fairytale version of life."

"But some people live those very lives," Sarah-Jane said.

"Yes, at least in the superficial manner you described. But how do you know there aren't aspects of their lives which leave them dissatisfied or lacking in some way?"

Sarah-Jane gaped at her in surprise. "Why wouldn't they be happy then? I know I would, and you too, I'm sure, Em."

"Perhaps," Emma acknowledged. "It is obviously easier to be happy when one is comfortable financially. However, I believe it is possible to be happy despite a lack of material acquisitions."

"Oh, aye," Sarah-Jane responded sarcastically. "You see a lot of happy people here in Whitechapel, don't you, Em? And streets just full of people shouting out their happiness every day."

"Very well, you've proved your point," Emma sighed. "Whitechapel is not a particularly good example. Poverty is worse here than anywhere else in London."

"That's what I mean," Sarah-Jane said earnestly. "Is it any wonder I long to get away from this hellhole?"

Emma patted her friend's hand. "You shall leave it behind you one day, Sarah. Of that, I am certain. Perhaps you and I will run off and live together in a nice cozy little flat in London."

"Will it be big enough for three?" Sarah-Jane inquired caustically. "'Cause unless you've changed your mind about marrying your gentleman, you will have to live with a husband."

Emma laughed. "Of course, Andrew and I shall be married, but I don't know exactly when. In that case, we shall just have to acquire a bigger flat."

"But won't you live in Andrew's mansion in London?"

Emma shrugged. "We'll see. It's not an issue we have actually discussed. The main thing is, Sarah, I would not leave you behind in Whitechapel by yourself."

Sarah-Jane threw her arms around Emma's neck and hugged her enthusiastically. "Thanks, Em. You're the best friend I could ever have." She stared warmly into her friend's eyes and caught a flash of the sorrow Emma struggled to suppress. "Something troubles you, Em? One of your patients?"

Emma sighed once more. "Yes. A woman I attended this evening died in childbirth, and so did the baby. One of her other children, a sweet girl of about thirteen years, witnessed the event."

"Oh, Emma, I am truly sorry!" exclaimed Sarah-Jane. She brought Emma's hand to her lips and kissed it softly. "And here am I complaining about me own petty problems when you are dealing with real tragedy. I don't understand how you can bear to do such work. If that was me, I probably would faint dead away."

"A lot of help you would be then," commented Emma with gentle sarcasm. "As much as we are friends and share much in common, we are totally different personalities. I could no more be a barmaid than you could be a nurse. I should have no tolerance for all those drunken men."

"But if they were sick, you would take care of them, wouldn't you?" Sarah-Jane challenged.

"Yes, without a doubt, I would and have. It is my professional duty to assist those in need of care. Therefore, I must put aside my feeling regarding their intoxicated state. However, it is often very frustrating to treat men when they are drunk, as they are too stupid to comply with reason or cooperate with the procedure."

Sarah-Jane laughed. "I see them at the beginning of the evening, help 'em get 'emselves messed up, then they get in a brawl or accident and end up seein' you at the infirmary." She laughed louder at Emma's distasteful expression. "You just have to know how to handle 'em. Laughing at their silly jokes and talking back is a good thing. Men like a girl who is witty and a bit cheeky, not some dullard."

"Oh, I don't know how you can abide them, forever clutching and pawing at you whenever you come near them. Fortunately, by the time I confront them, they are usually in too much distress to do anything of the sort."

"Better than have' em bleedin', shittin', or vomitin' all over me," retorted Sarah.

Emma laughed as well. "Touché, dear Sarah. You are right. My job also has its less appealing aspects, and it is heartbreaking at times. My only consolation is the belief that I can help, that I can make a difference in someone's life when he most needs it."

"As you do, Emma. But when they die, it must be so hard."

"Yes," Emma replied quietly. "It is terribly sad and tragic sometimes. I try not to become dejected, for as awful as pain and death are, when an ill or injured person recovers against all expectations, there is no feeling like the joy which invades one's soul; to see eyes, once dulled by suffering and grief, aglow with renewed hope and health. I tell you, Sarah, there is no more wondrous sensation than the knowledge that one has played a part, however small, in God's miracle."

Eyes bright with tears, Emma looked into her friend's eyes and clasped her hand tightly. "It is these moments which teach me that everything is worth the struggle, the loss, the suffering, the injustice; that hurtful, hateful things are balanced by the wondrous healing things. It helps me understand the rhythm of life itself, its ebb and flow."

Sarah-Jane's lips trembled, so moved was she by Emma's words. "Blimey, wish I felt such passion, such meaning in me own life."

"You shall, Sarah, in time. You are still so very young."

"Seventeen is not so very young," Sarah-Jane protested indignantly. "You are only a few years older, yet I feel like a child compared to you."

"Nonsense!" Emma replied emphatically. "When I was seventeen, I had not yet experienced such emotional revelations either. My understanding of the world was limited to my own segment of it. It was only when I began my studies in nursing that I perceived the diversity of other peoples' lives and experiences. It is one thing to comprehend the existence of disease and deprivation, another to witness these phenomena on a regular basis."

Sarah-Jane shrugged. "You get used to them things in Whitechapel. People don't know no different. All their lives, it's been the same struggle every day. What you said earlier about me leaving Whitechapel and livin' with you and your husband — now that's the fairytale! The only future I have to look forward to is marriage to some man who, if I'm lucky, won't beat me when he comes home after a day's work to find me fallin' asleep over the dinner I was supposed to have ready, and me dead tired after runnin' around with the little ones all day and bein' up all night with the baby who's been sickly. That's life here in the East End."

Emma looked at her with a stricken expression. "It is beastly of you to think I would break my word to you, Sarah. I should never desert you, no matter the situation."

Sarah-Jane bowed her head in consternation. "Forgive me, please!" she said in a tremulous voice, "for doubting your friendship, only I never met anyone like you before, Em." She raised her head, and there were tears in her eyes. "I never had a friend who I could share so much with. Someone who feels more like a sister than a friend."

"Neither have I," Emma said, smiling gently.

"Sarah-Jane!" a voice bellowed from within the pub.

Sarah-Jane jumped up, smoothing her skirt and apron. "Comin', Da!" she called. She bent down and gave Emma a quick kiss. "Make yourself a cup of tea. The water should have boiled by now."

Emma nodded. "Take the pot off the fire. I just want to sit awhile longer and enjoy the night."

Alone with her thoughts, Emma gazed up at the night sky ablaze with twinkling lights. She shared Sarah's affinity for the mysterious and beautiful objects. Sighing, she closed her eyes and enjoyed the delicious sense of warmth and calm flowing into her heart, recalling the day she had first met Sarah-Jane. Emma had only been nursing at the Whitechapel Infirmary for a few short weeks when Sarah-Jane brought her father in late one night after his forehead had been badly cut by broken glass while trying to throw out two drunks during a fight. Emma had been preparing to leave but stayed to comfort the scared girl as Mary Simmonds patched up her father.

One of Emma's first patient housecalls had been to come to the Princess Alice to check on Joe and make sure he was properly caring for his wounds. Her visits to the pub had been frequent since that day.

CHAPTER 33

"Right then, Mr. Ralston, you're done. Keep the bandage on and get your wife to change it only when necessary," Emma instructed. "That means should it become wet or messy looking. Otherwise, leave it alone, understood?"

The elderly man nodded and gave her a toothless smile as he limped away on his good foot.

"We will see you in three days," Emma called out. She wrote a brief notation in the ledge on the desk. "Who's next?"

Mary Kelly came forward and sat in the designated patient's chair near the desk. Emma smiled. "Well, Mary, what is the trouble?"

Mary sighed. "Ah, it's me bleedin' chilblains." She held out her hands for Emma's inspection.

"They do look rather nasty," Emma remarked as she examined the inflamed lesions. "I imagine they are quite sore."

"Aye," Mary said. "It's me cursed father's fault. His side of the family always have been thin skinned, with bruises and blisters easily."

"So you have had this before?" Mary nodded, and Emma continued. "It's not uncommon for fair-skinned people to develop chilblains and other skin irritations, especially when the weather turns cold as it has these last few days."

"But they are so unsightly! Men won't want to go with me, they'll think I have some kind of disease. I know—it's happened before. Can't you give me something for them, Miss?"

Emma considered. "I do have an unguent that you could use. It should improve those lesions significantly if applied properly."

"Oh, I'll try anything. Truly, I will," Mary responded eagerly.

"So you say. You must follow my instructions exactly, or the treatment will not work. It will necessitate you bandaging your hands to let the unguent absorb. I suggest you apply it before going to sleep."

Mary nodded. "I can do that. I have an old dress at home that I can tear into rags."

"As long as you make sure the dress is clean first. You must wash it thoroughly. Otherwise, you could develop an infection if you wrap your sores in dirty material." Emma peered closely at Mary's hands. "Most of the sores look all right. There is no sign of infection except for that one on the back of your hand there." She indicated a sore that was more inflamed and puffy than the others. "I want you to observe that one closely. If it becomes redder or starts to drain foul-smelling fluid, you must soak the wound with a warm compress at least three to four times a day, and, of course, you should come back to the infirmary. Any questions?"

Mary shook her head, and Emma continued.

"Good. Then shall I apply the unguent and wrap your hands now? That way, you can see how much unguent you need to apply." She saw the look of doubt on Mary's face. "I have an idea. The bandages are not at all cumbersome. You could easily slip on a pair of gloves over them. That way, no one need see them."

Mary pondered the suggestion. "Aye, that would work, I guess, at least for this evening." She sighed. "I shall just have to get used to keeping me gloves on."

Emma smiled. "Well, it is possible that you might start a new fashion in Whitechapel," she said teasingly.

"Ha, that'll be the bloody day," Mary replied, but a slight smile lifted the corners of her mouth.

"Let me go fetch the unguent, and we can get started. Oh, by the way, I should mention that the smell of the concoction is really quite horrid."

"Lovely," Mary murmured, rolling her eyes as Emma left.

Emma returned in a few moments with a glass jar containing

a pasty substance the color of congealed porridge. Mary's nose wrinkled in distaste as the jar's lid was lifted.

"Phew!" she exclaimed, waving a hand vigorously in front of her face. "You weren't exaggerating about the smell. It reminds me of the burnt boiled cabbage me mother used to cook."

Emma paused a moment to consider. "You know, I never thought about it. But now that you mention it, that is what it smells like, or at least what I imagine it smells like," she amended. "I have never actually smelled burnt cabbage before."

"Well, you are the lucky one then," Mary said. She held out her hands. "Go on, ducks, let's get this over with."

As Emma applied the ointment, she noticed the normally gregarious young woman was quite subdued. "Is something troubling you, Mary? You seem rather somber."

Mary glanced at her, then looked away. "Ah, it's just me nerves, that's all," she said with a shrug. "What with so many murders, it's got so a girl don't feel safe out there on the streets." A look of anxiety creased her features. "It's very eerie once darkness comes, do you notice? The air itself seems to change, become sinister. The wretched fog plays tricks with your eyes, makes you see things that aren't there and hides things what are." The anxious expression deepened into one of profound unease. "And you know he is out there, Jack the Ripper," she whispered. "No one knows when or where he will strike, only that he will."

Now she looked directly at Emma, dread in her eyes. "Sounds strange, but sometimes I hear his footsteps behind me, echoing on the cobblestones. I start to run, and the footsteps run too, only faster, gaining on me. So finally, I can't stand it no more—me heart would surely burst with fear—and that's when I stop dead in me tracks and turn around because I have to see. I have to get a look at him. But when I turn around, no one is there, just the fog and the wind rustling the dead leaves in the alleys. I tell meself it was just me imagination—I never really heard no footsteps— but I am still scared because I feel something bad lingering there, something dirty and foul—unclean, as me mother used to say— and filled with hatred. That's why I know for sure that's it real and not in me head, because I couldn't make up such an awful, horrid feeling. I'm a nervous wreck. See, I've bitten all me nails to the quick. I used to have such pretty nails," she added wistfully.

Emma gazed at her with concern. "Mary, your fear is well justified. A very real and terrible danger prowls the streets at night. All women are potential targets if they are out alone. I can't say whether you've been followed, but you do need to be extremely careful. You must avoid going to isolated areas or using the alleyways as shortcuts. Stay close to main thoroughfares as the police advise. Do you carry a weapon?"

"I always have my spike ready. See?" She pulled a large and lethal looking hatpin with a sharp point from her coat pocket. "I've used it to scare blokes away — not often, mind. Most take one look at it and leave me alone."

"Well, I guess this is of some assistance then," Emma replied hesitantly. Privately, she thought that it would require a great deal more than a hatpin to deter a fiend like the Ripper. However, she did not wish to add to Mary's disquiet; therefore, she didn't pursue the weapon issue any further. "Have you considered trying to obtain some other temporary employment during the day instead?"

"Ha!" Mary snorted. "What would you suggest, Miss Hollander?" she scoffed. "I don't have no skills. Can you see me sweating it out in some factory hole-in-the-wall earning less than half of what I make now, or hawking trinkets in the stalls? I tried that once, you know, but men still approached me there for one thing only." She sighed. "It seems I was born to be a whore, no matter what."

Emma shook her head. "Mary, you are smart, as well as pretty. You could do other things if you had a mind to." She held up a hand to forestall Mary's protest. "I realize the money might not be as good, but at least with more skills, you would have better choices. Right now, you are telling me you have no other option but to prostitute yourself. Is the money really worth the risks to your safety and well-being? There are some particularly horrid diseases you might catch. Besides, any extra money you have is wasted on alcohol, so how are you really better off by allowing men to use you?"

Mary looked at her, despondently. "I know you are only trying to help, but you don't understand my life, what it is really like to be me. We're from different worlds, you and me. We don't have anything in common, except we're both women and close in age. One lesson I have clearly learned, Miss Hollander, is that women can be divided into two types: the way society sees them — them women, which is considered to be respectable, and them what's not. Now, it can happen that a respectable woman might fall into disrespect through unfortunate circumstances, but it can't happen the other way around; once a whore, always a whore." She looked at Emma with a hint of bitterness in her eyes. "That's why I allow men to use me because these fine gentlemen which sneak into Whitechapel for a bit of fun with the likes of me pay well for my time. But they would never dream of taking me back to London and marrying me because they understand that here is where I belong, in this place and in this life."

She sighed, and the expression in her eyes changed to one of resignation. "I'll just have to keep me wits about me, and as Maria always says, 'Stay away from too much drink and be out in the streets as little as possible.' I'm lucky I have me own private lodgings. As long as Joe's not about, I can bring me men inside. I prefer not to, but 'tis safer than the dark alleyway."

After Mary's departure, Emma spent the remainder of the day preoccupied by the young woman's plight. It seemed her attention was constantly drawn to the Whitechapel murderer. His name was on everyone's lips, be it the staff and patients at the infirmary or people she overhead in the shops and markets. All of Whitechapel was mesmerized by the sinister style of Jack the Ripper. Notices were posted warning women of all ages and social status to proceed with extra caution. Reward posters were also in abundance, as the police attempted to induce the populace to share any information, no matter how trivial.

Conversations concerning the Ripper reached a peak in the pubs on any given night. One might have expected the pubs to suffer a decrease in customers during this period. Paradoxically, however, most were filled to capacity every night—a reflection, no doubt, of the need for people to receive comfort by sharing their fears with others in this common experience.

This was especially evident with the whores, who tended to linger longer than usual over their drinks and brave the streets in twos and threes. No one, regardless of age or sex, was immune to the thrall of terror which by this time gripped all of London.

Even the children were affected. A new verse of the popular child's game, hiders and seekers, emerged in which the seeker pretended to be Jack the Ripper and proceeded to hunt down his hidden victims. Accompanying this game was a rhyme Emma found particularly disturbing, and which sent a chill through her whenever she heard the high-pitched voices of the children in the tenement buildings at play.

"Run and hide
Run, run away
Naughty Jack's come out to play
If you're not tucked up safe in bed
He'll rip, rip, rip you till you're dead."

CHAPTER 34

Mary Kelly paced within the narrow rooms of her lodgings at Miller's Court. The flat was a step down from the one she had previously shared with Joe Barnett, the gloomy interior a forlorn contrast to the brighter, cheerier flat at Brick's Lane, just further evidence that her fortunes were in a downward spiral. She wrung her hands in agitation as she paced. The only good thing, she thought ruefully, staring down at her hands, was that the chilblains had almost disappeared. Only a couple of scabs lingered. Nurse Emma's treatment had been a success.

"A lot of good that does me now," Mary lamented aloud as she stopped to gaze out a grimy window. She noted with a shiver of dread that the sun had set, and the shifting shadows of early evening now had control of the city.

Since the double event murders of Catherine Eddoes and Liz Stride, Mary had become increasingly reclusive, venturing out mostly in the light of day. The night, once her ally, was now a mysterious enemy, shielding terrors that belonged to the realm of nightmare. Most evenings she spent alone in her flat, drinking steadily through the long hours.

Since Joe had moved out of their shared flat a couple of weeks ago, this had become Mary's solitary habit. Sometimes Joe came to visit, but Mary actually preferred that he go out with his mates. It seemed like they only bickered when they spent time together, and they both now drank more heavily than in the past.

All in all, life was a depressing affair, Mary reflected as she turned away from the dingy view. Whitechapel was a horrid place. There was really no good reason for her to remain in the squalor, especially with the terrifying specter of Jack the Ripper haunting the streets. Maybe she should just disappear, leave London entirely.

"And go where?" she asked herself. She didn't have enough money saved for travel expenses, but maybe Joe could lend her some. He was always giving her gifts, so he must have extra money from time to time. She stopped pacing, realizing she had to do something before she went crazy from her own fears. The walls of the flat were confining and the atmosphere oppressive. She would go across the way to her friend Julia's and persuade her to come along to the pub.

A steady rain was falling, and the November wind cut like shards of glass. She ran across the narrow courtyard to Julia's tenement basement flat. Pulling her heavy coat tighter around her, she knocked at the door. Impatient at the lack of response and the wind tugging at her, she knocked again, this time more loudly.

"Julia, Julia!" she called.

The window on the second floor opened, and an elderly woman stuck her head out. She peered down, nearsightedly at Mary.

"Who's there?" she demanded cantankerously.

"'Tis Mary Kelly from across the way, Mrs. Glidden," Mary answered. "Is Julia at home, do you know?"

"Ha!" Mrs. Glidden exclaimed. Whether in annoyance or satisfaction, Mary couldn't tell. "I warned her that she would get into trouble bringing men here at all hours of the night like that, and the noise! Someone must have told the landlord about her." Her small eyes gleamed in the reflected light from a nearby gas lamp. "She was tossed out earlier today. Don't know where she's gone. Most likely drinking herself silly at the pub." With that, she slammed the window dismissively.

Mary turned away from Julia's door. For a few moments, she simply stood in the courtyard, oblivious to the rain beating down on her. She felt both expectant and apprehensive, as she used to feel when as a child in Wales, she stood outside her family's house awaiting her father's return home from the ironworks. There was always a moment of doubt that he might not appear, that fate may have intervened to snatch him away from her. But then she would catch sight of her father's figure, the familiar long stride approaching the hillock upon which the house rested, and little Mary would run to greet him, relief and joy almost bursting her heart.

Then his warm embrace enveloped her, the tangy smell of sweat and tobacco reassuring, his rough hands dissolving at their touch all the little girl's anxieties and worries. He'd laugh and swing her atop his shoulders, carrying her up the path to the house. With its poverty, disease, and grimy streets, Whitechapel was a far cry from the fresh gleam of a Welsh countryside. And there was no man now in her life who could reassure her and give her the sense of safety and security for which her heart ached.

Biting her lip to keep back the tears, Mary ventured out onto Dorsett Street. She carried herself in a determined fashion, vowing to be stronger. She had to believe that life would improve, had to cling to that hope. That was one lesson that John Kelly had taught his daughter; that no matter how dismal life might be, one must never give up hope, for hope was what made the struggle for survival worthwhile.

It was still early evening, though darker than usual because of the rain clouds. She took some comfort from the fact that many people were out and about their business. Her destination was the Princess Alice. It had been a while since Mary had been there, but it was one of Julia's favorite pubs, so there was a good chance she would meet up with her friend inside.

A welcoming blast of heat struck her as she opened the pub's door and stepped inside. Her journey from Dorsett to Commercial Street had been uneventful, most people, as was she, hurrying to get out of the rain. She peered through a veil of smoke, looking for Julia. She saw several of the pub's regulars, but no sign of her friend.

Might as well get a seat and wait awhile, she thought, winding her way amongst the various tables. She finally spotted a chair at the very back of the room and a table occupied by a couple of women she recognized from the neighborhood. They nodded cordially as she gestured towards the empty chair.

Sarah-Jane was serving customers at the next table. When she turned around, Mary caught her eye and beckoned her over.

The young barmaid collected her money and walked to Mary's table. "Good evening, miss. What can I get you?" she asked.

"Ale, please," Mary answered.

Sarah-Jane looked inquiringly at the other women. "Nothing more for us, dearie," one of them with several missing teeth said. "'Tis time we got ourselves 'ome.''

"Don't want to be out on the streets too late," the other added. "What with Jack the Ripper out there and all."

Sarah-Jane nodded. "Aye. I heard the coppers tell the women to walk in groups of at least two and not be out alone at night."

All three looked pointedly at Mary.

"I'm waiting for a friend," Mary said defensively. "Besides, 'tis early yet. The Ripper don't strike until the wee hours."

"You never can tell. It could be that he will change his mind and go out at a different time," the toothless one said as she stood up to leave.

"It's true," the other agreed. "You can't expect a madman to be predictable, now, can you?"

The first woman leaned closer to Mary and lowered her voice conspiratorially. "There's them who say that he's not a regular human being, but some sort of phantom—that's why the coppers can't catch him. He's got special powers, so he just disappears into the air."

"Where did you hear that?" Sarah-Jane demanded frowning.

"Aye, there is talk on the street," the woman replied, shrugging. "But I heard that even some of the coppers believe it."

Sarah-Jane's eyes grew wide with wonder. "If it's true, then the coppers won't never catch him. Why, he could eventually kill all the women in Whitechapel!"

Mary slapped the table in irritation. "That's just a lot of

blarney! Leave me to enjoy me ale in peace. Off with you now."

The women hastily gathered their coats and departed, murmuring disapprovingly about some people being oversensitive like.

"I do hope your friend shows up," Sarah-Jane said as she turned and headed towards the bar.

Mary frowned. She was beginning to have second thoughts about this excursion out tonight. Maybe she should have stayed home. She shook her head in exasperation. Where was that cursed Julia? She closed her eyes and rubbed her temples, feeling an aching pressure behind her eyes.

"You alone, love?" a gruff male voice asked.

Mary opened her eyes and looked up in annoyance. A middle aged man with a dark mustache and dressed like a dockworker leaned across the table, a definite leer on his face.

"No, I am expecting a friend any minute," Mary replied in a haughty tone. "A gentleman," she added, looking the man up and down scathingly.

The docker's lips curled in a sneer, and he walked away. She heard him comment to his mates about the silly whore who thought she was "too good for regular folk." She shrugged dismissively in her best Parisian gesture.

Just then, the barmaid returned with her ale. Mary dug in her purse and handed the girl some coins. She took a sip of the drink, realizing how thirsty she was. The foam tickled her lips, and she licked traces of it from her mouth. She would have this one drink, and if Julia hadn't shown up by the time she finished, she would go home.

It would still be early enough to walk alone—after all, the Ripper had never struck before midnight. But he was an unpredictable madman who was capable of any irrational act. She tried in vain to prevent her thoughts from whirling in that direction; however, it was as though she was determined to frighten herself. That woman who had sat at her table had been right. Jack the Ripper could just as easily be waiting outside the pub for her right now, lurking in the shadows.

He would watch her leave alone, a solitary woman, obviously of dubious reputation. What other kind of woman frequented a pub by herself, drinking the night away? He would chuckle to himself where he crouched in the dark, a lunatic quality to his laugh, but quiet. Yes, he was so very quiet, a maniacal child playing a diabolic game of hiders and seekers. He would employ the utmost stealth and cunning, gliding silently along the street behind her, biding his time as he waited for the right moment to strike. A demonic smile would twist his mouth as he reached for his knife, a swift glint of silver in the absolute darkness. And then, her goal in sight, Miller's Court beckoning urgently, he would pounce upon her, turning her to face him so he could see her expression as he raised the dagger and plunged it into her throat.

"Excuse me, love, do you mind if I sit? Me feet are just killing me."

Mary started and almost spilled her drink; her hands were shaking so much. She looked up into a pair of dark brown eyes that registered concern.

"You all right, ducks? Didn't mean to give you a fright."

Mary blinked twice, the disoriented feeling quickly dissolving. She looked at the woman, who appeared to be around her own age, maybe slightly older. She had an attractive face framed by dark curls, which were visible beneath her brown velvet bonnet.

"No, I'm fine. Just off in me own world, 'tis all," answered Mary, with a self-deprecating smile.

The woman sighed contentedly as she sank into the chair. "Me feet feel like they're on fire."

What a unique voice she 'as, Mary thought. *That throaty tone must attract a lot of men to be sure.*

"I haven't seen you around before," she commented, swigging back a mouthful of ale.

"Been to the countryside, I have," the woman responded. "Only recently back in the city. Me last placement didn't work out."

"Domestic, were you?" Mary inquired. When the woman

nodded, Mary continued. "I know what that's like. Still, the countryside sounds like a nice place to be right now."

The woman shrugged. "Some of us just aren't suited to domestic service. I like to be in charge of me own life." She looked closely at Mary. "You wouldn't by chance be Mary Kelly, would you?"

Mary's eyes narrowed suspiciously. "Who wants to know?"

"A friend of yours, Julia, asked me to give a message to Mary Kelly. You fit the description she gave me."

"Aye, that's me. What did Julia say?" demanded Mary curtly.

"Something about losing her lodgings and having to find a place to sleep. She said she might stay with a friend tonight and that she might stop by the pub later."

"Mm," Mary said. "She'll most likely be off to Maria 'Arvey's for the night. She wouldn't stay with me on account of Joe. He never approved of her staying over, and even though he doesn't live with me no more, she knows he comes to visit a lot."

"Well, then would it be all right if I stayed at your flat tonight?" the woman asked. "I don't have no place neither, and the weather being as foul as it is, 'tis not likely I'll find a place now."

Mary looked at her askance. "Do I look like I run an alms house?" she snapped.

"I got a little money," the woman said. "Not enough for a sleep house, mind, but I could pay you something to put me up."

Mary nodded. "'Tis all right then."

The woman smiled. "Julia was right about you. She said you were a good sort, always willing to help out."

Mary waved her hand, dismissively. "What's your name?"

"Bessie Boyd." Her smile widened, revealing surprisingly white, even teeth.

Mary registered the smile and felt the realization that this young woman was her first serious rival to come along in a while.

Among the Whitechapel whores, it was no secret that Mary Kelly was the cream of the crop. She was younger and prettier than most. However, this Bessie Boyd was also attractive, with clear skin to compliment her good teeth. Country living had obviously enhanced her fresh looks. Mary compared it to her own skin, paler of late, its delicate rosiness lost to the city's harsh air and factory smoke. Recently, too, her teeth had been giving her trouble, especially in the damp of this late autumn. But, she noted with satisfaction, her figure was superior to that of Miss Boyd, for though the woman was taller, Mary's waist was more slender and her hips more rounded. Her spirits rising slightly, Mary smiled at the woman and raised her glass.

"Cheers," she said.

Bessie Boyd, in turn, saluted Mary with her glass of whiskey. "To friendship."

"Aye," Mary replied. Strange, she didn't remember the barmaid bringing a drink over to Bessie, but maybe the woman had bought her whiskey before approaching Mary's table? It mattered not anyway.

"To friendship," Mary repeated. "'A good drink and a good friend. 'Tis all a man needs in the end.' That's what me father used to say. Mind you, I think his taste in drink was better than his taste in friends," she chuckled.

"So, is this your regular pub then?" Bessie Boyd inquired, her gaze traveling around the Princess Alice.

"One of them. I have many regular pubs," Mary replied. "Though lately, I don't go out nearly as much as I did before."

"Why is that?"

Mary stared disbelievingly at the other woman. "Because of the murders, of course." At Bessie Boyd's questioning look, she said in exasperation, "You know, Jack the Ripper!"

"Oh," Bessie nodded. "Yes, I heard about that. Even at the country manor where I worked, there was talk, but I thought some of it might be exaggerated. You know, there are those who love to tell tales to frighten us women."

"Jack the Ripper is no tale," Mary muttered darkly. "He is all too real. It isn't only women what's frightened. Plenty of men don't fancy the idea of a lunatic killer running freely through the streets. Even the politicians in London is concerned, so the newspapers say. They don't want no more trouble in Whitechapel like what happened with the riots last year. I heard that the queen 'erself is shocked by the murders and has told the prime minister to solve the case quickly."

"Really!" Bessie exclaimed, suitably impressed by Mary's revelations. "How come the coppers haven't caught him then?"

Mary shrugged. "'Cause the Ripper's too smart for 'em. Never leaves a trace. Some say he disappears into the shadows."

"And he only kills whores?"

Mary's smile was bitter. "Sure, and why not? He likes an easy target. People don't care if the city is missing a whore or two."

"Yet people are upset," Bessie Boyd pointed out.

"Aye, and scared because this murderer is so mysterious. Look at 'ow many suspects the coppers have dragged in. But the Ripper could be anyone; your next door neighbor, your landlord, the fruit vendor you say hello to every day. Why, any of these men sitting at tables around us could be 'im. You've got to be wary of all men, not just the ones what look like lunatics. And the way he kills is so horrible. The poor women torn apart slaughtered like animals." Mary shuddered. "Why would he do that?"

"Maybe he does think that," Bessie Boyd said. "Or maybe it's easier to kill whores than regular people, or maybe it don't matter to him who he kills. It's the kill that's important, not the women themselves."

Mary's color had risen, and an angry flash had appeared in her eyes. "Maybe he does think whores are no better than animals." She took another long swallow of ale. "But whatever he might think, he's got no right to hunt us down in the streets."

She slammed her glass down onto the table and glared at the other patrons in the bar. Raising her voice, she loudly proclaimed, "Jack the Ripper is a dirty scoundrel! 'E has no right to murder us, and Mary Kelly is not afraid of 'im!" She shook her fist in the air.

A silence fell over the bar for several seconds. Then one or two men chuckled, and a male voice cried out, "That's a girl, Mary Kelly. You show them what Whitechapel women are about!"

More voices joined in, including other women, who, echoing Mary's statement, drunkenly asserted that they too had no fear of Jack the Ripper.

One inebriated prostitute, her dress in disarray, lurched from her seat and began to stumble from table to table. In a gin slurred voice, she yelled, "I were no scared, and if Jack the Ripper was to come up to old Molly 'ere I'd grab 'im by his 'air and box his ears something fierce." She gestured with both hands, showing the other patrons just how she would confront the Whitechapel murderer. Her display of bravado, comic as it was heartfelt, drew a round of hearty laughter and encouraging words.

"Too right, Molly! Jack the Ripper would do well to watch himself with Molly!"

"Hey Molly, maybe you could teach the other whores how to box so they could catch the Ripper, seeing as how the coppers can't."

A female voice chimed in. "Aye, maybe she could teach the coppers how to box too."

More raucous laughter greeted this last witticism as Molly obliged her audience by curtsying and promptly falling onto her backside with a gut-wrenching belch.

Mary ignored the shenanigans around her, staring gloomily at her glass and drinking steadily. She didn't remember ordering another ale, yet the glass she clutched was more than half full. It seemed she had been drinking out of the same glass forever. She shook her head and exclaimed, "Oh, how I hate this horrid place! I wish I could just get away. I want to feel safe again instead of trapped like a rat in the rat catcher's sack."

Sarah-Jane approached the table. "You ladies ready for another?"

Mary looked at her, balefully. "Now, lass, I think you've been filling me glass steadily without me noticing." She lifted her mug. "'Tis but half gone, and me drinking half the night away."

Sarah-Jane gave her an odd look. "Now, why would I do that, Mary? Me dad's strict on how we ration out the ale. You've had but the one glass unless you have been to the bar and ordered another yourself."

Mary waved her away. "Never mind, it isn't worth the argument." She pressed her fingers to her temples. "Blimey, me wretched head is starting to pound like when I've been drinking more than usual." Her gaze settled on Bessie Boyd. "So now that you've heard more about the Ripper, aren't you scared to be out on the streets alone?"

A haughty expression filled the woman's eyes, and her lips curved in a sultry smile. "Scared!" she repeated, a note of scorn in her voice. "I have no fear of the Ripper or anything else. Fear is for the weak, not for the likes of me."

"Blimey!" Mary exclaimed in vexation. "You mean there is nothing you are afraid of?" She slapped the table. "Cor, but you are a good liar."

Bessie Boyd shrugged. "'Tis no lie, Mary Kelly, but you can disbelieve me if you choose." She stared steadily into Mary's eyes, her dark gaze unwavering. "There is nothing in this world for me to fear."

Mary tsked in exasperation. "I give in," she gestured dismissively. "You obviously don't wish to tell me, so be it." She was silent a moment, then looked surreptitiously at her new friend and said slyly, "You mean if that vicious fiend was to grab you and drag you into the shadows and hold his dagger to your throat, you wouldn't be frightened to death?"

Bessie Boyd chuckled, the sound vaguely unsettlingly. "That would never happen."

"Ha, 'tis them what thinks it could never happen what actually gets it in the end. That's why I always remind meself that it could be me, so if I do believe it could happen, then it won't," Mary said earnestly.

The other woman shook her head. "What you believe or don't believe makes no difference. When you are marked for death, then it will find you." She leaned forward and stared intently into Mary's blue eyes. "There is no safe place. You can't hide from death."

Mary's lip trembled. She tried to look away, but she was

mesmerized, unable to break contact with the other woman's gaze. She was aware of the subtle shift in the air around her. A lightheadedness overcame her, and she experienced the sensation of things moving slower, but still, she could not resist the overpowering urge to stare at Bessie Boyd.

Her gaze fixated on the lean, vulpine face with the intensely dark eyes and generous mouth with its harsh red lip paint. That mouth now seemed predatory, and why had she not noticed before that the woman's lips were so very red? They were the color of blood.

No sooner did this thought cross her mind when, to her mounting horror, huge cracks appeared in Bessie Boyd's lips, jagged ugly scars crisscrossing her mouth. The blood gushed from those gaping cracks, flowing down the woman's chin, staining the bodice of her dress a bright crimson. Blood rushed forth, a torrent coursing faster, reaching the table and spreading across the center towards Mary, who watched in horror as the blood inched toward her, eager to engulf her. How could there be so much blood? How?

"Who are you?" Mary asked in a hoarse whisper. She gripped the edges of the table in an effort to steady herself, aware that she was swaying in her seat, her head spinning, a nauseated surge in the pit of her stomach. Her mind touched upon the answer but veered frantically away before her awareness could register it.

From the periphery of her vision, a darkness encroached, coming towards her as steadily as the tide of blood. Her visual field narrowed, and shadows leapt before her eyes. Blood and darkness gathered to claim her.

What's happening to me? she cried in panic, just before her mind shut itself down.

CHAPTER 35

Liquid, cool, pressed against her lips.

Blood! Her mind screamed in terror as she struggled to move, trying to flail her arms, but a heavy weight bore down on her, rendering her helpless. She wrenched her head to the side, away from the blood, squeezing her lips tightly together in a determined effort to prevent even a single drop of the treacherous liquid from finding its way past her lips.

"Here, love, come on now, take a sip," a voice urged.

Cautiously, Mary opened one eye. A woman she did not recognize, but with a kindly face and voice, leaned over her, holding a glass to her lips. Mary opened her other eye and saw more faces leaning over her. Sarah-Jane was there looking both concerned and apprehensive.

"That's right, love, keep your eyes open," the woman directed. "Now take a sip of water; there's a good girl."

Water! So it wasn't blood she was being offered, after all, only water. She squinted and saw, to her enormous relief, the clear, colorless fluid in the glass at her lips. She opened her mouth and drank greedily, enjoying the non-taste, the thirst-quenching flow easing the dry ache in her throat.

"Grab her head, dearie," the woman instructed Sarah-Jane, who obliged, albeit somewhat awkwardly.

Mary felt a wave of dizziness assail her as her head was lifted and then cradled in the barmaid's lap. The sensation quickly subsided. She became aware of the hard flat surface beneath her, realizing when she saw the collection of wooden legs of the tables and chairs that she was stretched out on the floor of the pub.

"I must have fainted dead away. Well, it wouldn't be the first time, but blimey, I didn't have that much to drink tonight, have I? What happened?" she croaked, her voice like a rusty hinge.

"You fainted, like a fit or something," Sarah-Jane explained, eyes wide with curiosity.

"I don't remember," Mary said, frowning.

"Do you think you could sit up, love?" the woman inquired. Gently she took hold of Mary's arms and assisted her to an upright position.

Mary blinked and looked around. "Strange, I don't feel like I had too much to drink." A vague unease rushed through her and was gone. She shivered once, twice, and that too dissipated. *Why did I think they were giving me blood to drink? Something about blood, but what?*

"Where's Bessie?" she asked, suddenly sitting up straighter.

"Who?" Sarah-Jane asked.

"The girl who was sitting at me table, that's who," Mary snapped impatiently.

Sarah-Jane shrugged. "I can't say. Perhaps your fit scared her off."

Mary shook her head. "No, she's not afraid of anything," she muttered in a low voice.

"Are you feeling lightheaded still?" the older woman asked.

"No, 'tis gone now. Maybe I did have more to drink than I remember."

"Well, let's get you off this floor and into a chair." The woman and Sarah-Jane helped Mary to her seat. "Do you think you should go home?" the woman queried.

"In a bit, I just need to sit a moment," Mary replied. She turned to the barmaid. "I'll have another whiskey, dear."

"But you was drinking ale," Sarah-Jane pointed out.

Mary shrugged. "Maybe so, but now I have a thirst for whiskey." She looked at the older woman who had come to her aid. "Thank you for your help, missus. It was kind of you."

"Ah, it was nothing, love." The woman patted her on the shoulder and walked back to her own table.

Sarah-Jane returned promptly with the whiskey. She waited patiently while Mary fumbled in her skirt pocket for money.

"That friend of yours, I've never seen her in here before tonight."

Mary shrugged. "She's just returned from the countryside. 'Tis the first time I've met her."

"That explains it then," Sarah-Jane nodded.

"What?"

"Well, I was thinking she wasn't such a good friend to leave you when you needed help."

"You know, it is a strange thing," Mary pondered. "I can remember her sitting here and talking to me, but I don't recall a thing we talked about."

"Mm, maybe you will later on. Me dad always says that if it is something important, it'll come back to you. If it don't, then stop worrying, 'cause it's nothing you really need to know."

Mary nodded absently as Sarah-Jane left to attend to other customers. The barmaid was probably right, she reasoned. Still, something stirred at the edges of her mind, gnawing through the alcoholic haze she assumed she was feeling. A vague unease overcame her every time she thought of the mysterious Bessie Boyd. But why? Had the woman said something to upset her? If that were so, then was it important that she remember? And why did the thought of blood disturb her now?

This was all a bit much, Mary reflected, disgruntled. She had come out to the pub to ease her tension and anxiety and ended up feeling more disquieted and jittery. And that fit she had, it wasn't like any fainting spell she'd heretofore experienced. Many was the time that she had been assisted from the floor or gutter in a drunken stupor, but she usually felt good and in high spirits and giddy with laughter. She didn't feel well at all tonight. Aside from her emotional distress, her stomach felt queer, and her head pounded with a fierce headache. Worst of all, she had to face the walk home, alone.

CHAPTER 36

It was close to midnight when Mary returned to Miller's Court. She leaned heavily into her companion, a stout, poorly dressed man with blemishes all over his face, sporting an orange-red mustache. He appeared to be in his thirties. Mary had encountered him just outside of the Princess Alice as she was leaving for the night. She quoted her usual price with the addition of an escort home.

She usually preferred to conduct business at her own lodgings. It was a lot more comfortable than being outdoors, but the man was insistent that they use the back alley adjacent to the Princess Alice. If Mary hadn't been so drunk, her better judgment would have caused her to refuse. However, the whiskey had brought a flush to her cheeks, a sparkle to her eyes, and a giddy exhilaration, so into the alley they went. When he was done, he kept his agreement and walked her to Dorsett Street. They met a neighbor, Mary Anne Cox, who was also returning home. Mary greeted her effusively.

"Mary Anne, me darling, 'tis a fine night, isn't it? A wonderful night for singing. Do you fancy a song or two, my dear?"

"Afraid not, love. I am too tuckered for anything but sleep," Mrs. Cox replied.

"I'll come in and sing for you, Mary," her companion offered eagerly.

"Ah, ah, ducks. You have had your fun tonight," Mary admonished, laughing gaily. "You be on your way now. Go on." She gestured at him, waving him away and making shooing noises, amused by his crestfallen expression. He dutifully shuffled away to the sound of Mary's laughter ringing out into the night.

Mary fumbled briefly with her keys, weaving slightly on the doorstep. She giggled at her clumsiness and jammed the key in the lock before mustering the coordination to unlock and open the door.

"'Tis me, I'm home," she shouted as she stumbled inside. "Blimey, it is colder than a witch's teat in here, as me father used to say. Ha!"

She lurched around, searching for and finally locating the gas lamp. She turned the lever until the blue flame jumped into being, followed by the yellow glow of light.

"Anybody home?" she called. "Joe, you here?"

Although no longer living with Mary, Joe Barnet retained a key to Miller's Court and sometimes stopped by. However, silence greeted her this night. She flung off her damp coat, wrinkling her nose in distaste.

"It smells like the bloody fog in here!" she exclaimed loudly, but the musty underground smell reminded her of a basement flat she once shared with another whore. The cold and damp infiltrated the building to such an extent that slimy mold flourished on the interior walls. Mary grimaced at the unpleasant memory.

"It was a wretched time in my life, to be sure," she said emphatically.

Crouching before the grate in the fireplace, she attempted to light a fire, but in her inebriated state, the fine motor skills required for this task eluded her. She gave up in resignation.

"'Tis not as if fire would do much good anyhow," she said, glancing ruefully out the window that was missing a pane of glass; neither the cold air nor a determined intruder could be kept out of the flat.

She weaved her way over to the bed in the corner, and kneeling, stretched her arm underneath the bed and pulled out a bottle of whiskey. It was still a third full. She stumbled to a semi-upright position and threw herself onto the bed. She grabbed a thin blanket and draped it over her shoulders before tipping back the bottle and taking a long swallow.

Then Mary Kelly started singing, "Only a wild rose I plucked from me mother's grave," in a loud, drunken tone.

***

"George! George, hello!"

George Hutchinson turned around, looking for the woman who had called his name. He grinned as he saw the familiar figure walking unsteadily toward him. "Mary Jane Kelly, 'tis good to see you."

"'Tis Marie-Jeanette, you know that." Mary frowned, then smiled in return. "Have you sixpence you can spare, George? Mary smiled, fondly recalling her stay in Paris.

Hutchinson shook his head. "Sorry, lass, I have nothing to spare tonight." He turned the pockets of his trousers inside out so she could see how empty they were.

Mary sighed. "Well, then I guess I'll have to earn me money the hard way." She brushed Hutchinson on the shoulder as she headed along Commercial Street toward Aldgate. Hutchinson paused to watch her.

A fine-looking lass, he thought, as he had many a time, *wasting herself on the likes of Joe Barnett. If I could only afford to keep her.*

He shook his head, sighing. That wasn't likely to happen on a laborer's wages. He frowned as he saw Mary approach a man at the corner of Thrawl Street. Her sweet, infectious laugh was easily discernible in the quiet night streets. The man laughed too, though his tone was more reserved. Hutchinson watched Mary link her arm through his, the couple then proceeding towards Dorsett Street. For some reason unclear to Hutchinson himself, he followed them at a discreet distance. This wasn't a usual habit of his. The thought of Mary with one of her gents caused him discomfort and left him with a sad feeling, but somehow tonight was different.

Mary and her companion entered Miller's Court walkway and proceeded to the doorway of her flat. The man grabbed her by the shoulders and lightly spun her around to face him. He kissed her for several moments before Mary, laughing again, disengaged herself. She had unlocked the door and let them both inside.

Hutchinson took shelter from the light rain under the arched entryway next to a lodging house across the street. He stood there, his gaze fixed on Mary's window, waiting for the man to leave. After forty-five bone-numbing minutes, the damp cold got the better of him, and he headed home. He never knew how long the man stayed.

CHAPTER 37

Three o'clock in the morning, the dark hour when the distance between the realms of the living and dead is bridged by sleep, and dreams are the vehicles by which those who wish may make the journey. It is the hour when the human body most closely mimics death. Organ systems are maintained at minimum power, energy is conserved, even blood flow is sluggish. Only the brain, always active, continues to operate at full capacity, but in a reality vastly different from the conscious state, the darkest hour of the night is when death waits patiently in the shadows for those who stumble and fall into its welcoming embrace.

Mary Kelly tossed restlessly, her sleep troubled by phantom images. Fragments of dreams carried by rushing waves dissolved into splinters as they crashed on the shores of consciousness. She was walking on a sandy beach, the sound of the breaking sea to her left. The sand captivated her attention, for it was like no other she had seen. As black as obsidian, it seemed intent on consuming all light around it. It was as if daylight, encountering this dark expanse, was swallowed whole. The sand was cold beneath her toes. The ocean was mysterious and forbidding, the murky turbid water encroaching onto the sand, greedily claiming each grain for itself. The sound of the waves was mournful, a lonely chorus decrying this wasteland.

The entire scene was redolent with a terrible beauty, and Mary was awestruck. Austere and self-contained, it evoked a vivid memory of the wild horses that had roamed the Welsh countryside during her childhood. Unfettered and magnificent beasts, possessed of a capricious will and strength, they were capable of delivering death with one effortless kick. Those elegant, deceptively delicate legs contained enough force to crush a man's skull. Mary's heart had always ached at the perfect beauty and freedom of these creatures. Now standing amid this stark landscape, her heart ached with a sorrow she had never felt before.

Suddenly, she recognized the forlorn vista, the knowledge striking her swift and sure. Perhaps it was whispered on the waves or absorbed through her feet from the sand. This was the shore of broken dreams, a place where dreams came to die, a place of hopes abandoned and desires lost, carried by the turbulent waters and discarded upon the barren shore to be consumed by the black sand. With a grief heretofore unacknowledged, Mary realized why she stood on this beach. She had given up hope, her dreams dashed to pieces on this very shore. Tragically she had lost the ability to create new dreams and hopes for herself, and so, here she stood, in this place of death, with a broken heart and a withered spirit.

In a moment of shattering insight, revelation claimed her. Whitechapel was responsible for her emotional and spiritual disintegration. For the first time, she discerned the glimmer of the malevolence, the gratuitous cruelties seething within its confines. How could she have been so naïve as to think she could survive such a hellish place? She had been doomed since she first set foot in cursed Whitechapel. Dulled by despair, she had failed to notice the trap set for her.

Too late, she now understood the source of all her recent woes and anxieties, the nightmares and fears of the dark. In sinister fashion, Whitechapel had lured her in, she the helpless fly now caught in the voracious spider's web. She had been expertly hunted and held captive. Tonight, Whitechapel was poised to claim its prey.

Sensing that she was not alone on the beach, Mary turned around.

A man approached; elegantly clad in jet black waistcoat and trousers, he seemed to rise out of the sand, a part of its forbidding mystery. Hatless, his dark curls blew gently in the soft breeze. Mary stood her ground. Although she knew he was the man of her nightmares, she also recognized that she could not escape her destiny. She might run along this beach with the shadow man in pursuit until she collapsed, clawing at the nightmare-colored sand. This tableau would never end. Her killer would proceed relentlessly, for he would never tire.

As he came closer, Mary's attention was drawn to the object he held in his left hand. She knew it was a dagger even before she saw the silver flash and carved ebony handle. What she hadn't anticipated was how beautiful an object it would be, as beautiful as it was terrifying. The handle was longer than most knives, and both it and the blade shone with a tremendous gleam like it had just been polished. It was no ordinary knife, as the man who wielded it was no ordinary man. Both weapon and man emanated an unspeakable evil, a monstrous symbiosis that enhanced their formidable power.

Mary had no idea how all this knowledge came to her, but she didn't question it, for she recognized it as the truth.

"Strange," she murmured, as her killer drew closer. "I always thought you'd be taller, like a giant. But you're not much bigger than me."

The man smiled nastily, revealing his strong white teeth, jolting Mary's memory of another smile she had recently seen, a mouth feral and dripping with blood.

"Bessie Boyd!" she gasped, her mind seizing the awful truth.

The man applauded her, his clapping hands the only other sound besides the susurrating restless ocean.

"Bravo, Mary. It may interest you to know that you are the only person privy to that particular secret of mine. Most of your kind, humans that is, lack the imagination to conceive, let alone appreciate, such a creative deception. Simple yet brilliantly effective, wouldn't you agree?"

Mary shuddered in horror as she considered how easy it was for this murderer to gain the confidence of his intended victims. He was free to roam wherever he chose, right under the very nose of the authorities. If any police were to see him, he would seem to be just another whore. To think that she herself had sat face to face with Jack the Ripper at the Princess Alice and had almost permitted him to share her flat. She experienced a sudden urgent impulse to leave the dreamscape behind. As dreams go, it was certainly one of her most interesting and revealing, but she felt a great desire to emerge from sleep.

She struggled to regain wakefulness, her eyes quickly flying open. She attempted to sit up, but she was pinned beneath a vise-like grip, a sturdy form straddling her body. She opened her mouth to scream but could manage only a feeble croak.

"Jack the Ripper!" she rasped, eyes widening in terror.

"Touché, my dear Miss Kelly," the Ripper replied.

His smile, formerly all charm and dazzle, was now revealed without disguise. Mary nearly gagged with revulsion when she saw the true face of Jack the Ripper. It was like admiring a beautiful apple, perfectly polished and enticingly red, only to bite inside it to receive a mouthful of writhing maggots.

The face that leered at her was monstrous, a foul corruption of the human mask of John Dennys and Bessie Boyd. Stinking decayed flesh hung in ragged strips, which were sloughed off in some areas. Gleaming fragments of bone poked through, glistening with putrefaction. The skull was soft and rotting. The mouth stretched wide in a death-grin rictus, opening to exhale breath which stank of charnel houses and refuse heaps, poisonous vapors that threatened to suffocate her.

Summoning the remainder of her waning strength, Mary again opened her mouth to scream, even though the futility of such an action was obvious. The sound died in her throat as the creature pressed its abominable mouth to hers. The overwhelming horror rendered her senseless, but she was only vaguely cognizant of the exquisite pain of the knife to her throat.

***

With one swift motion, the Ripper's blade slashed her throat, brutally slicing through flesh so deep that the spinal cord was exposed. She exsanguinated quickly, blood erupting geyser-like from the severed arteries, spraying onto the walls beside the bed.

The entity known as Jack the Ripper sat back on his heels and surveyed the tableau before him. Tonight he would give the inhabitants of Whitechapel a memento so horrifying it would forever haunt them in their nightmares.

"Sweet Mary Kelly," he said aloud. "You are fortunate, indeed, for tonight, you shall be immortalized. When your name is spoken, others will shudder in terror. You shall have a place in history. Your death shall cause more of an impact than your pathetic life could rival."

He stood up and carefully removed his immaculate black waistcoat, then folded and placed it beside the bag that contained his Bessie Boyd clothes. He intended to exit the flat in this disguise, sensing that this was perhaps the last time he would don this particular garb. He smiled as he saw that not a single drop of blood had stained the waistcoat.

Then, he turned his attention to the task of obliterating Mary Kelly.

CHAPTER 38

Emma walked briskly through the overcast streets of Whitechapel. There was more activity than usual at this hour on a Saturday morning, likely in preparation for the lord mayor's show. Festivities were to start at noon with a parade, followed by celebrations afterwards in the market squares and public houses.

Winding her way along the seedy routes, she couldn't help but notice the increase in police patrols. There were more constables about than in recent weeks due in large part to the Ripper terror, which continued to grip the city. However, the presence of the authorities held a twofold purpose, for Commissioner Sir Charles Warren was clearly unwilling to risk any social or political unrest which might arise from today's event. He'd ordered the metropolitan force to be extra vigilant for potential hooligan activity.

Emma frowned in consternation at the thought that, angry though they might be because of the social and economic inequalities between themselves and London's other districts, the citizens of Whitechapel would just as soon spend their time and energy drinking at the pubs rather than in pursuit of solutions to their woes. They lacked a decent organizer, Emma decided, a leader committed and charismatic enough to inspire them.

Someone like Andrew would be perfect. She often wondered why he hadn't entered politics. He possessed both the creative vision and the skills to implement his ideas, and he was a natural leader, quick and decisive, but never impulsive, able to command allegiance and respect. But whenever she had spoken with him about this issue, he'd merely smiled at her indulgently as if her suggestions amused him. Emma, however, was not one to give in so easily and concede defeat. She would talk with him again, persuade him to recognize the validity of her conviction. He could contribute more value to society than simply managing a successful family enterprise.

Deep in thought as she planned her fiance's political future, she turned from Thrawl Street north onto Commercial. She barely glanced at passersby on her way to Dorset Street until someone bumped against her, causing her to momentarily lose her stride. She glanced up quickly.

The woman who had stumbled into her looked like she had a rough start to the day. Her clothes were disheveled, and she stank of alcohol. Peering bleary-eyed at Emma, she said, "Pardon me, dearie. Just lost me footing, is all." She recognized Emma's navy cloak and bonnet with gray trim. Her expression brightened. "Ah, Nurse, me back's aching something terrible. Do you think you could give me something for it?"

Emma had wisely learned not to carry any medicines on her person when out on the streets of Whitechapel. There were too many thieves and desperate men, addicts who would stop at nothing to procure narcotics, especially laudanum, an effective painkiller rivaling opium in its popularity among the drug-addicted.

She shook her head in response to the woman's query. "I have nothing to offer you, but your ailment could be seen to at any infirmary."

"Ah," the woman spat on the sidewalk. "Infirmary. All they do is slap on a smelly poultice and tell you to wear proper shoes. Besides, them's for sick people." She grinned, showing a mouthful of stained and broken teeth. "Don't suppose you could spare a few pence for food, now."

"No, I am afraid not, but you can get a decent breakfast at —"

"Blimey, you're just full of information, aren't ya? I already know where them places is." The woman gestured dismissively, muttering to herself as she meandered down the street.

Emma shrugged and continued along Commercial, her

eyes alert for Dorsett Street. She had attended a confinement in this area sometime last year, and she remembered that Miller's Court was located at the back of Dorsett. She hoped to find Mary Kelly at home. Lately, she had been worried about the young woman, more so since Mary had failed to keep a scheduled appointment for a follow-up check on her chilblains. This had been set for Thursday and, although whores weren't renowned for their reliability or punctuality, Mary, amid some grumbling, usually kept her appointments with Emma. When she still hadn't appeared by Friday afternoon, Emma was unexpectedly troubled. No specific reason could account for this unease. Nevertheless, she felt compelled on both a professional and personal level to reassure herself of Mary's well being.

Without fully examining her motivation, Emma was aware of a sympathetic connection with the young prostitute. There was a quality to her that touched Emma. They were of a similar age. Perhaps it was no more than the recognition that, but for a random twist of fate, she could be living Mary Kelly's life. Although she shuddered in distaste at the thought of selling her body, Emma was enough of a pragmatist to admit to herself that faced with similar circumstances, she might very well make that same choice rather than die a pauper in the gutter. She appreciated the young woman's independent streak, her refusal to rely on a man to ultimately take care of her, and her high spirits and often self-deprecating humor.

Glancing to the left, Emma barely deciphered the smudged street sign proclaiming Dorsett Street. Narrower and dingier than she remembered, it was hardly larger in width than an alleyway. She turned to the entrance lane where the lodging house known as Miller's Court stood. The building, in various stages of dilapidation, stretched all the way to the back of the street. It was in this direction that she proceeded, searching for number thirteen.

The paint on the front door of Mary Kelly's flat was chipped and eroded. Emma carefully avoided the jagged splinters extending from the doorframe as she raised her hand to knock.

When there was no answer, she tried again, louder. *Probably lying in a drunken stupor*, she ruefully thought.

"Mary. Mary, are you in there?" she called.

"She's in there all right. Saw her come home late in the night."

Emma turned to survey the speaker. He was elderly but by no means frail-looking. Noticing Emma's attire, he asked, "She sick or what?"

"Who are you?" demanded Emma curtly. "A friend of hers?"

"Hardly that," the man chuckled. "Though Mary does have a lot of friends." He winked slyly. "No, sadly, I am only here to collect the rent for the landlord. Thomas Bowyer is me name. I live in No. 37 Dorsett." He gestured towards the front of the building.

Emma nodded. "Well, I'm following up on a missed appointment."

Bowyer laughed again. Surprisingly for a man of his age, he still had most of his teeth. "Ah, the only appointment I've known Mary to keep is with a man or a bottle, preferably both." He winked a second time.

Emma sighed. "Then I guess I shall have to return another time."

"You're not giving up so easy, are you?" the man inquired.

Emma glanced at him in irritation. "What do you suggest I do, Mr. Bowyer? Break down the door?"

"No need for that is there?" He gestured for Emma to move closer as if intending to impart a great secret. Emma was having none of that. She stood her ground.

"You can use the window over here." He moved to the right of the door, beckoning for Emma to follow. "There is a pane of glass that's broken."

Emma looked uncertainly at the shabbily-curtained window.

"Go on," Bowyer urged. "All you have to do is reach in and push the curtain aside. You will have a clear view of the bed by the far wall."

Emma stared at him with a stern look. "Obviously, you have taken the liberty of spying on Miss Kelly before," she said reprovingly.

"Well." Flustered, he rushed to get his words out. "It isn't like she did something to fix the window. Everyone around here knew about it. It wasn't like I was the only bloke that took an occasional peek, let me tell you."

Emma shook her head in exasperation. "Your excuses are tedious, Mr. Bowyer. However, since my motives are nowhere near as questionable as yours, I shall use the opportunity to ascertain if, indeed, Mary is there."

So saying, she stepped decisively over to the window a few feet away. Reaching to brush aside the curtain, it occurred to her that such a large gaping fracture in the pane must cause the room to be inordinately chilly at night. A split second later, she was aware of a strange odor. Cheap alcohol, yes, that was there, but in combination with a darker, rancid odor.

The curtain parted. Emma's eyes strained to adjust to the gloomy interior. The lack of sunlight made it more difficult to penetrate the shadows, but before her vision could accommodate itself, her shocked body reeled back from the window as she winced at the nauseatingly powerful smell. The stench rivaled that of a butcher's slaughter room.

She glanced behind her, but Thomas Bowyer had stepped away from the window, obviously holding out little hope of catching a quick peek at Mary while Emma was there. He was busy lighting his pipe, head bent over it as he carefully tapped the tobacco into it. Thus, he missed her anxious tight-lipped expression.

Cold tendrils of dread blossomed along her spine. Her nerves screamed at her to run, track down a constable, let him deal with whatever monstrous occurrence had taken place in that room. Yet even as she registered this message, her muscles tensed in preparation for flight, and she knew she couldn't leave without ascertaining Mary's fate.

Despite the fear churning in her stomach, she was compelled to follow through with her original plan. Fierce loyalty to her profession and to Mary, her patient, would not allow her to shirk her duty.

I owe her this much, she thought. She was not at all clear from what source this idea sprung, even as she subconsciously acknowledged the bond which existed between herself and Mary Kelly.

Taking a deep breath to steady herself, Emma turned back to the window. Her hand trembled as it reached for the curtain. She steeled herself to the stench, willing herself to believe it was not worse than the average postmortem. This time her eyes adjusted to the gloom more quickly. The interior of the room shed only shadowy light, but that light was sufficient to reveal the travesty that had occurred within those walls.

The figure lay stretched out on the bed in seeming repose, although its legs were obviously splayed. The left arm was bent and positioned across the waist, while the right arm extended at the figure's side. Dark, uneven patches stained the wall and headboard as if a demented artist, forsaking canvas, had decided instead to hurl his color at the walls, heedless of pattern or coherence, reveling in a frenzied discord which chilled not only the eye but the soul as well.

Clad in a nightshift, long hair spread out on the pillow, the figure was a woman. Being the sole occupant of the room, there was little doubt that this was Mary Kelly. However, Emma's mind first refused to accept the grim reality that the occupant of the bed was, in fact, a young woman, as any resemblance to a human being had been cruelly obliterated.

It was a freshly slaughtered carcass, giving the distinct impression that the murderer had deliberately mutilated the body to illustrate his conviction that the young prostitute was no different from an animal rendered in a similar fashion. The body was split open from neck to pelvis, and the abdominal cavity gutted, its contents arranged to surround the corpse. The darkly rancid reek of organ meat was overpowering, mixed with the thick stink of fecal matter from ruptured intestines.

The skin over most of the body had been flayed, in some areas down to the bone. The chest cavity was equally decimated.

Pieces of skin, fascia, and muscle lay neatly on the bedside table in a grotesque parody of wares displayed in a butcher's shop. Numerous deep lacerations had been inflicted on both arms and legs. Both thighs were severely slashed, the right one exposing the pallor of gleaming bone. Its whiteness offered an unsettling contrast to the crimson that dominated the scene of carnage.

Emma's gaze was drawn inexorably upwards along the body, registering the ragged wound to the neck, by now a familiar Ripper trademark. Her eyes traveled past the face, momentarily blocking out that horror, and focused instead on the hair fanned out on the pillow. Mary's golden halo of locks, once her proudest trait, was reduced to a matted tangle of clotted blood and bits of gore.

Nor had the victim's face been spared. The ferocity of the attack was beyond comprehension. The decimation was complete and had been savagely wrought. The flayer's knife had wreaked its terrible wrath upon the delicate features of Mary's face. Eyes, nose, and mouth had been hacked and slashed until all that remained was a ruined pulpy mess. Once again, all traces of human identity had been brutally annihilated.

Emma gagged, unable to turn away from the hellish tableau. Her heart beat wildly, the muscles in her throat straining. She couldn't utter a sound. Paralyzed with sheer horror, she was unable even to gasp. A suffocating pressure in her chest prevented her from drawing breath.

She might have stood thus transfixed forever, but Thomas Bowyer, his voice seeming to reach her from a long distance, demanded impatiently, "Well, is she there?"

When Emma failed to answer, he shoved her aside none too gently, so he could look. That contact plus the acrid tobacco smell of his pipe intruded upon Emma's senses sufficiently to galvanize her into action. Balance precarious, she stumbled backwards, still helplessly mute. She whirled to face the old man, a scream trapped like a cotton wad in her throat. Her stricken expression stopped Bowyer in his tracks.

"What is it?" he cried, pipe faltering in its rise to his lips. "For

God's sake, girl, what…?"

Emma was deaf to his words. Eyes wild, hands outstretched before her as if to feel her way out of this terror, she tottered away from the window. After the first tentative steps, her footing steadied. She wasted no time, the pace increasing to a run.

She fled the lodging house as if an entire legion of Satan's demons were in pursuit. A high-pitched keening finally burst from her throat as her lungs painfully gulped in air. She didn't think, reacting only to the panicked urge to put as much distance between herself and the slaughterhouse that was 13 Miller's Court.

Several people stopped to gawk at the bizarre specter of a woman careening madly through the streets. It was an odd occurrence, even for Whitechapel. One man attempted to intercept her, stepping in front of her and grabbing her arms. But with a strength born of sheer terror, she loosened herself from his grip. She clawed at his face with maddened fury, gouging deep scratches along his cheeks, aiming at and narrowly missing his eyes. He let her go immediately, screaming angry curses at her retreating back.

Emma ran, oblivious to all things external. The images in that room were etched like acid in her mind. They burned through every other perception. She cared not where she was headed. Her need was simply to escape, her feet racing along the labyrinthine roads, never stopping to get her bearings. She would not, in any case, have recognized the familiar landmarks, so bereft of coherent thought was she. Finally, exhaustion about to overtake her, she came up against a more formidable barrier to her marathon of madness, the river Thames.

She'd reached the docklands, and unless she intended to throw herself into the river, she was obliged to stop. She sank wearily onto a stone step, the first of several that led to a small wharf where barges were moored. There was no one in the immediate vicinity, and for this, Emma was grateful. A few stevedores were at work further along the pier, but they appeared too busy loading goods onto a freighter to mind her presence there. The relative quiet was a respite to the din in her head, the water lapping at the bottom steps soothing in its gentle rhythm.

She lowered her head to the ground, giving in to the urge to vomit. Her stomach heaved painfully, but all she managed was some dry retching. She had not eaten breakfast that morning, downing only a cup of tea before embarking on her visit to Mary. After the spasms subsided, she cradled her head in her hands and began to rock to and fro. The motion was vaguely comforting, complementing the lulling effect of the river. Her shocked state temporarily numbed her emotions, but she couldn't banish the monstrous scene of carnage from her mind, the vivid images playing over and over.

Time lost all meaning. At some point, she ceased rocking and sat instead as one in a trance, her gaze unblinking. Some of the dockworkers cast curious glances her way, but as she was so quiet and unobtrusive, they went about their business, leaving her to herself. More time passed for Emma in this twilight state.

The clouds had parted sometime during the afternoon to allow weak rays of sunlight to reach the earth. They were now quickly streaking towards the west, and evening would soon be upon the city. She flinched as a hand gently touched her shoulder. Muscles clenched, her body once again ready to flee despite the leaden feeling of fatigue in her limbs, she looked up fearfully.

A woman of middle age, lined face creased with concern, stood over her. She was dressed in drab brown calico with a white apron and bonnet, the standard garment of women who tended the workhouse soup kitchens. Her warm smile exuded motherly kindness.

"A couple of the lads saw you sitting here and wondered if you could use some help." She gestured in the direction of the dockers. "So, they sent me to find out." Her gazed traveled appraisingly the length of Emma's figure. "You're a nurse, aren't you?"

Emma nodded dully, her glance returning to the river.

"Look," the woman continued. "You have been out here for hours. Something's obviously amiss. You're paler than me apron, and you look ready to jump out of your skin." When Emma failed to reply, she added, "Why don't you come back to the kitchen for a spot of tea? You'll catch your death if you stay any longer in the cold. I promise I won't ask no questions, only you look like you could use a good cuppa."

Emma nodded again. With a weary sigh, she struggled to her feet, wordlessly accepting the woman's help. Her legs were stiff and sore from running. She allowed the woman to put an arm around her shoulders and lead her to the poorhouse.

CHAPTER 39

Sarah-Jane gloomily contemplated the noisy crowd of humanity squeezed between the walls of the pub. Her stomach was aflutter with a sick excitement and a dread anticipation. Somewhere outside the safe confines of the Princess Alice lived a menace, the likes of which she had never imagined existed. From her vantage point behind the bar, she felt somewhat protected, but once she ventured into the room itself, she was deluged from every angle. Snatches of conversation, tantalizing tidbits of sensation, news maddingly cut off in mid-flow when someone hailed her attention elsewhere in the room.

The Princess Alice, like every other pub in Whitechapel, was ablaze with news of the latest Jack the Ripper atrocity. The body of a whore had been discovered earlier in the day, but unlike the previous murders, this woman had been killed in her own flat, not out of doors. Also different was the severity of the mutilation, rumored to be more extensive than the other victims suffered. There was much confusion as to the exact nature of these mutilations, and speculation ran rampant—all sorts of fantastic and macabre tales circulated throughout Whitechapel.

"I heard he cut off her 'ead and placed it on the table beside her bed," one fellow, a large beefy laborer, offered.

"That so?" asked his mate in the next seat. "I have it on good authority that the 'ead was missing and could not be found nowheres, though the coppers searched high and low."

"They say she was gutted like a pig and her insides strewn all over the place," said another.

"It's true that there was so much blood that the coppers

slipped and fell in it," declared a fourth. The others looked at him askance. "Least, it's what I heard," he muttered defensively.

Sarah-Jane was inundated with these and other tales as she went about her tasks of taking orders and fetching drinks. At times, she thought her head would burst from the mighty effort in trying to assimilate all the information coming her way.

Her attention was drawn by a woman at one of the tables. Unlike everyone else at this bar, this woman was not engaged in the animated conversation around her. Her face was drawn and tight lipped, both hands firmly gripping her cup of gin. As Sarah-Jane worked her way towards that corner of the room, she saw that the woman's expression was lusterless and her eyes red-rimmed, as though from weeping.

Sarah-Jane approached the table and was immediately beset by alcoholic requests. After she registered all the orders, she turned to the silent woman.

"Another round for you, missus?" she asked.

Julia slowly turned her eyes to look at the young barmaid. She nodded her head mechanically. "Aye," she responded dully. "Another would be fine." She had a slight accent that might have been German or Austrian.

Sarah-Jane began to move away when she heard another woman say, "Come now, Julia, don't blame yourself, ducks. It wasn't your fault poor Mary got herself murdered."

Sarah-Jane paused and turned her attention to this exchange.

Julia's gaze rested briefly on the speaker before returning to a neutral spot on the wall opposite. "You can say what you will, Maria, but if I'd 'ave been with her last night, she'd be alive today. I still don't understand why she never showed up at the Frying Pan."

"Ah, you know Mary," another woman said. "Probably changed 'er mind at the last minute and went somewhere else."

"She was here," Sarah-Jane volunteered. The group of women turned as one to stare at her. "For most of the evening, she was. Sitting right over there at that table." She pointed diagonally across the room.

"You don't say," Maria said, perplexed. "Then why would she tell you, Julia, to meet her at the other pub?"

"She even said she was waiting for her friend," Sarah-Jane said eagerly. "Maybe it was you she was waiting for." She nodded at Julia.

"Then why would that woman 'ave told me...." She trailed off, lost in thought.

"What woman?" one of her friends asked.

"The woman that said she had a message from Mary Kelly saying I was to meet her at the Frying Pan. The woman described Mary like she knew 'er, so I left 'ere and walked over to the Frying Pan."

"Wait a moment!" Sarah-Jane exclaimed. "What did the woman look like?"

Julia frowned in irritation. "I don't know what she looked like. What does it matter anyway?"

"Could be important," Sarah-Jane insisted. "Was she young, attractive, and well-groomed? Did she have dark curls and bright red lipstick, and were her teeth really white and perfect looking?"

Julia gaped at her in surprise. "That describes her exactly, especially them white teeth, not that I'd forget them." She slapped a hand against her brow. "You saw her too then?"

"Aye. I noticed because she came and sat at Mary's table. At first, I thought she was the friend that Mary said she was waiting for, but afterwards, she said she'd only just met her."

"Why would she have lied to you about Mary?" asked Maria.

"Don't know," Julia responded musingly. "Maybe for some reason, she didn't want me and Mary to get together. Did you 'ear anything they said?" she inquired of the barmaid.

Sarah-Jane's brown furrowed in concentration. "Not so's I can recall, but I think they must have been discussing Jack the Ripper."

"What' makes you think that?" one of the women asked.

"You mean aside from the fact that the Ripper's all Mary talked about the last few weeks?" Maria Harvey said sarcastically.

"Well," Sarah-Jane continued. "At one point, Mary raised

her voice and shouted for all to hear, 'Mary Kelly's not afraid of Jack the Ripper,' or some such thing."

The women fell silent as they pondered the sad irony of those words.

"'Tis queer," one of them said in a hushed tone. "Mary being so obsessed like by Jack the Ripper, and then getting herself killed by him."

"Isn't so strange at all," Maria countered roughly. "Seeing as the Ripper only kills us whores. And do you think Mary's the only one that is worried?"

Julia shook her head, preoccupied with Sarah-Jane's account. "If this whore didn't even know Mary, how could she have described her so well?"

Maria Harvey sighed. "'Tis a mystery for sure, and likely to remain one."

"I only know that if Mary and me 'ad been together, she would 'ave been alive today," Julia fervently reiterated, biting anxiously at her chipped and ragged nails.

"More likely, it would have been a 'double event,'" Maria commented darkly. "What makes you think the Ripper wouldn't have killed you both?"

No one had an answer to that, and the silence stretched on. Sarah-Jane lingered a few moments, but the women sat wordlessly, staring morosely at the table, the walls, their empty glasses, anywhere but at one another. None dared to voice the question that lurked in each of their hearts. How many more of them must die before the killing stopped?

CHAPTER 40

In another corner of the crowded public house sat a man hunched over his drink. He had managed to carve out a small niche, his chair squeezed in between two tables. He'd also successfully repelled any attempts to engage in a conversation, his dark scowl unequivocally warning others not to bother him. A slight tremor of hand caused his glass to shudder as he lifted it to his lips. Despite the worn patches at the elbows of his jacket, the general shabbiness of his attire, unshaven face, and unkempt hair, he lacked the aura of a regular Whitechapel denizen.

Montague John Druitt's eyes kept returning to the front of the pub every time the door opened to admit new revelers. It had been a close call, he thought wretchedly. Beads of perspiration broke out on his forehead as he recalled just how narrowly disaster had been averted. Even now, he expected Carruthers to come bursting through that door and make a spectacle of them both.

Damn Carruthers and Hastings. What had their hansom been doing in the East End? Incompetent driver most likely was inebriated and got lost carting them off to one of their insufferable soirees. It was only sheer good fortune that he happened to notice them first, and that was only because Carruthers, insolent bastard that he was, leaned out of the cab's window to hurl abuse at the driver. Luckily, Druitt had ducked into a shadowed doorway at the last possible moment. Otherwise, they'd have passed right by him on the street, and it would have been his misfortune to have Carruthers' hawk-like gaze fix on him immediately.

He pulled out a handkerchief and mopped his brow. Yes, he

would have been in a sorry state indeed. Imagine trying to explain to them what he was doing in Whitechapel, this most disreputable district, and in such sorry attire. They would never understand. Carruthers would smile in that infuriating supercilious way of his, all the while formulating the salacious tale he would gleefully impart to his cronies at the barristers' offices.

Even Hastings, who was a decent enough sort in his own way, would be shocked, perhaps even horrified. The area was notorious for catering to every imaginable perversion, and those who frequented it from outside were there for one reason only. Hastings' well-bred sensibilities would be severely offended.

On second thought, Hastings might even pity him. Oh, he was too tactful to say anything, but it would be evident in his expression, the curve of his effeminate mouth, and that, by God, would be intolerable. He slammed his glass forcefully on the table, but in the chaotic din of the pub, his action went unnoticed. He didn't want or need anyone's pity.

The only one who would understand him and not pass judgment was Andrew. They went back a long way, to Oxford days, and though he'd never actually discussed his intimate preferences with his friend, he had been convinced that somehow Andrew was aware of them. Druitt pursed his lips thoughtfully. Andrew would never be shocked or condescending. He wouldn't condemn Druitt, but simply say, "Well, Monty, if this is what satisfies you and no one is getting hurt…." The trouble was, Druitt wasn't so sure no one was being hurt.

Lately, his mind was playing tricks on him. Granted, he was drinking more, but he knew instinctively that alcohol wasn't the major cause of the blackouts he had been experiencing. They were occurring more frequently, even when he wasn't drinking, sometimes accompanied by massive headaches. They'd only started a couple of months ago on an occasional basis; was it late August or September? He wasn't certain—somewhere around the time the Whitechapel murders began.

No. He squeezed his eyes shut, willing his thoughts to stay clear of those waters. It was a preposterous idea. Why, he liked whores! He would never harm them. After all, they fulfilled his needs quite suitably. Everything was anonymous; no worries, no explanations, not having to account to someone else—not to mention how obliging they were. They never rejected him or refused to comply with his wishes. They never made him feel ashamed or abnormal. In fact, they were more than eager to please him, and he paid them handsomely in return. So, of course, it was ludicrous to even entertain the idea that he might harm these women. To be sure, on occasion, things could get a little rough and out of hand, but whores understood that. It was simply a risk of the trade. But murder—murder was bad for business.

That set him thinking about the whore who was murdered last night. If only he could remember what happened after he left the last pub. Was it the Britannica? He couldn't recall for sure, but he vaguely remembered the pretty whore with the dancing blue eyes and the wistful laugh. What was her name? Something French, Marie-Antoinette or something equally affected. Said she lived in Paris for a while. She had been delighted when he'd spoken a few phrases in French and clapped her hands in pleasure. He remembered going back to her flat, some dingy room near Thrawl Street. She did as he asked. They sang, or rather she sang Irish ballads while he smiled drunkenly and hummed along.

His mind drew a blank. No more details were forthcoming. He had come to his senses early this morning at the Ten Bells public house on Church Street. He didn't know how long he had been there, but he had the impression he had fallen asleep over the tabletop. The landlord had prodded him none to gently and told him he would have to order up more liquor if he wished to remain on the premises. Wearily, he dismissed the landlord and staggered to his feet.

CHAPTER 41

Outside, the crisp autumn air revived his sluggish senses. He started tentatively along Church Street, concentrating on moving one foot in front of the other, well aware of his unsteady gait. At the intersection with Commercial Street, he turned onto the larger avenue. A lot of people were out and about, and a fair number of police as well. He frowned and then recalled a celebration was to take place today, and all of Whitechapel would be out to partake.

His attention was snagged by a group of people congregating near a small side street. They didn't look festive at all—in fact, they seemed agitated and upset. He heard exclamations of shocked dismay. As Druitt approached the gathering, he saw some women with handkerchiefs pressed to their faces weeping unabashedly. The men wore tight-lipped angry expressions.

Druitt tapped the shoulder of a man standing in front of him. "What's going on?" he asked.

The man, a leather tooler by the tangy smell of him, spat on the ground before replying. "There's been another foul murder. The Ripper struck again."

Druitt's stomach clenched. It felt like a block of ice was slowly melting in his gut. "Do they know for sure it is the Ripper?" he asked.

"Aye, not much doubt—the coppers said as much. The poor woman was 'acked to bits, so they say."

Druitt craned his neck to see, but the crowd impeded his view. "Over there on that street?" he pointed.

"Aye," the man nodded. "That building right there, Miller's Court, Number 13."

Bile now churned his stomach, mingling with the ice. There was something familiar about that address. If he could only remember where and when he had heard it before.

"Found her lying stretched out on the bed, she was."

"Wait," Druitt interjected. "She was murdered indoors?"

"It's true, so the coppers say." Another man, wizened faced resembling an old prune, joined the conversation.

"I heard that even some of the coppers was sick when they come upon this scene. Mighty green about the gills they was. Ha." His cracked lips parted in a parody of a grin, toothless maw agape, emitting a foul stench of rotting gums. "Don't have the stomach for nothing, them young coppers," he chuckled.

"You disgusting old bastard. How could you laugh at such a horrible thing?" A woman with a nose as red as her bloodshot eyes snapped at him. "The poor girl, and her so young and pretty. Be off with you before I lose my temper and give your ears a good boxing."

The old codger chuckled again, but less confidently this time. He definitely moved out of the woman's reach, not willing to risk further provocation.

Druitt lightly touched the woman's arm. "Missus, did you know the girl?"

"Aye," the woman nodded, sniffling. She reached into her battered purse and pulled out a well-used handkerchief, and noisily blew her nose. "Just neighbors, mind, but a nice girl, always pleasant, had a nice smile too. She could have men eating out of her hand; she was that charming. Of course, I heard stories that she had a bad temper sometimes, but I didn't see none of that."

"Her name, what was her name?" Druitt asked her urgently.

"Mary Jane it was, Mary Jane Kelly." The woman shook her head. "Mind you, she had a few fancy airs on account of her living abroad. France, I believe. Insisted on making her name sound exotic like. 'Just call me Marie Jeanette,' she'd say. Told me I should call meself Marie Anne instead of plain old Mary Anne. Ah, she had quite the imagination," she sighed.

Druitt's heart, which had been pounding uncomfortably, suddenly lurched and fluttered in his chest. For one agonizing moment, he feared that it would simply stop, but then it sputtered along erratically before finally resuming a more regular though accelerated beat. His vision blurred, and there was a muffled sound in his ears.

Not another blackout. Dear Lord, don't let it happen here. He must keep his wits about him. Squeezing his eyes shut, Druitt focused all his energy on circumventing the blackness threatening to engulf him. His hands balled into tight fists, nails gouging his palms until blood seeped between his fingers.

"Are you all right?" The woman peered at him, more fear than concern in her expression. She backed away a few steps.

His face dripping with sweat, Druitt opened his eyes and slowly unclenched his fists. His monumental effort had defeated the descending darkness, but he knew he had only succeeded in holding it at bay. Poised to strike again, it would lie and wait to catch him in a weak moment. He managed a smile that he hoped would reassure the woman. Taking out his handkerchief, he mopped his saturated brow.

"Yes, yes," he said hastily. "I am recovering from a recent severe fever, and I still suffer the occasional attack."

"Oh, well, if that's it, then." The woman appeared mollified and turned away as a friend claimed her attention.

With trembling hand, Druitt returned the handkerchief to his pocket. His legs felt wooden, and his mouth like it was filled with sawdust. Marie Jeanette, that was the name he had been trying to remember. He had come back here with her to Miller's Court. He remembered them sitting on the bed together and her singing, and then nothing. The pages of his mind went blank, memory erased. The only facts he knew for certain were that he had been with her and that she was now dead, the latest victim of that fiendish madman, Jack the Ripper.

Druitt shook his head, trying to clear his muddled thoughts. How much longer could he endure this torment? The uncertainty, the gut churning anxiety, and the gnawing suspicion that the diabolical Ripper was none other than himself, Montague John Druitt? As implausible as it seemed, he could not dismiss the nagging idea, fast becoming a conviction, that he was the foul murderer.

If that were the case, he would only be fulfilling his destiny, heir to a legacy of madness that held his family in a ruthless grip. But if he was truly mad, why couldn't he be blissfully unaware instead of tortured and anguished, haunted by his own phantoms of fear? That was a common misconception about madness. Very few of the insane were oblivious to their plight—something his mother once said to him in one of her lucid moments that he now recalled vividly.

"There is no oblivion in madness. The worst agony is knowing that your mind deceives you with false impressions and images and that you can't trust your mind ever; knowing that there is no way out of insanity, that you are doomed to exist forever in this shadow world."

Tears sprang to Druitt's eyes with the wisdom of his mother's words becoming clear to him. Little by little, he felt himself slipping into that world of shadows, and despite his best efforts, he was daily becoming more lost and confused.

Suddenly he turned on his heel and pushed his way back through the crowd. He felt claustrophobic, constricted, as though a great weight threatened to crush him. His pace quickened, and he had to restrain himself from breaking into a run. He took the side streets, avoiding people as much as possible. His footsteps slowed a little as he wound his way down to the waterfront.

The wharves were deserted today, everyone off celebrating the lord mayor's show. Druitt relaxed a little, feeling some of the tension easing as he walked along the docks, hands in his pockets. His eyes narrowed as he spotted a figure hunched on some steps leading down to the water. The dark cloak wrapped around its shoulders made it impossible to tell from this distance, whether it was a man or a woman.

As he neared the figure, he recognized the navy cloak and bonnet of a nurse. She had her back to him so he couldn't see her

face, but he didn't need to see her face to realize that here was
another soul in distress, someone whose pain seemed as great as
his own. He hesitated as he passed her, wondering if he should
stop, but she showed no sign that she was aware of his presence.
What comfort could he offer anyway? He watched the steady
rocking of the woman, heard the rhythmic noise she emitted. Best
to leave her to her own devices, wrapped tightly in her misery.
With a heavy heart, he walked to the stone balustrade and leaned
against it, peering into the murky depths of the Thames.

The river had always held a fascination for him. Its secret
waters beckoned as though the answers he sought could be found
lurking just below their surface. The river exuded a seductive
essence, displaying a raw beauty to those who wished to see it.
The oily waters threatened danger, yes, but they also promised
solace to those lost and weary souls who desired nothing more
than to cast themselves into the river's depthless embrace. The
Thames calmed his troubled spirit, providing a soothing balm to
his tumultuous thoughts.

For most of that afternoon, he continued his somber vigil by the
river. By the time he wandered back to the center of Whitechapel,
the sun was low in the western sky, and civic celebrations were
in full swing. He wandered the streets, not caring where they
might lead or what dangers lurked in blind alleyways and dead
end lanes.

CHAPTER 42

Andrew stood before the fireplace in the drawing room. A fire burned in the grate to combat the chill of the November evening. He was deep in thought as he stared into the flames. He had been dining at his club earlier in the evening when he received an urgent summons from his mother. He turned at the sound of the door opening. Henrietta entered, her expression sober. The fine lines around her mouth were accentuated by worry.

"How is she, Mother?"

Henrietta sighed, shaking her head. "It's hard to say. Sometimes she is deathly quiet, lying there pale and trembling, and then suddenly, she will bolt upright, babbling incoherently. She's suffered a great trauma, that's evident. She was in absolute disarray when she arrived here, Andrew. She looked like a madwoman."

"Is she sleeping now?"

"She was earlier if one can call that fitful tossing sleep. She's taken only a few spoonfuls of soup. That's all she'll accept." Her eyes filled with tears, "Andrew, I am so worried. I thought of sending for Dr. Hawthorne, but I wanted to wait for you."

Andrew approached his mother, enveloping her in his arms. He kissed her lavender-scented cheek. "I shall go to her. Don't fret, Mother. We shall uncover the mystery soon enough."

He climbed the spiral staircase to the spare room and paused in the doorway. In the soft lamp glow, Emma lay sleeping, looking slight and vulnerable. She was indeed waxy-colored, a faint sheen of perspiration on her forehead.

Upon her flustered arrival at the Hewitt-Brown house,

Henrietta had initially surmised that Emma had suffered from a severe fever delirium. However, instead of her brow being hot to the touch, her entire body had felt icy and clammy. Wisely, Henrietta had refrained from asking too many questions, recognizing the fragile emotional state of the young woman. After ascertaining to the best of her ability that the source of trauma did not appear to be any physical injury, Henrietta had soothingly escorted the young woman upstairs and tucked her under warm blankets.

Andrew, after a few moments of silent contemplation, crossed the room and sat by the bedside. He watched her uneasy slumber, noting the fluttering of eyelids and the spasmodic twitching of the delicate veins in her neck. Gently he reached for the pale hand resting on the counterpane.

"Emma," he murmured softly. Her eyes flew open and stark terror reflected in them. She struggled to snatch her hand away, but he maintained a firm grip. "Emma," he repeated in the same soft tone. "It's Andrew. You are safe. I'm here with you." He watched her absorb his words. The terror resolved into recognition, quickly followed by relief.

"Andrew," she cried, and threw herself, sobbing, into his arms.

He held her close, tenderly stroking her hair, silent as the painful sobs wracked her body. Despite the temptation to probe her mind to discover the source of this trauma, he restrained himself, chastising himself for his impatience. He must allow her to speak in her own time. At last, after several minutes of violent weeping, the torrent began to subside. Energy spent, Emma hiccupped a few times and then was quiet, with her head buried against his chest.

"It's all right, my love," he whispered soothingly. "Whatever terror you have endured is passed. You are safe with me. You know that, do you not?"

Emma nodded, head still leaning against him. He continued to caress her hair, his words a gentle cadence.

"Emma, you know I love you with all my heart and soul. I

shall do everything within my power to help you through this ordeal."

Emma nodded again, sniffling.

Andrew retrieved a handkerchief from his pocket. "Here, let me wipe your face."

With childlike obedience, Emma raised her head. He wiped away the remnants of her tears and then held the handkerchief to her nose.

"Blow," he instructed. She complied, and when she was done, still cradling her, he examined her face. His critical eye noted the strain and fatigue, the fear that lay just below the surface of her eyes, threatening to rise again.

Cupping her chin in his hand, his eyes locked onto hers, his gaze sharpened intensely as he looked through and beyond her eyes to the hidden chamber of her soul. Instantly he was assailed by a kaleidoscope of fragmented images of half-formed thoughts. The sensation was akin to being tossed about in a maelstrom, a maelstrom of terror so great it could drive one to madness.

Accustomed as he was to receiving such images at will, Andrew nevertheless felt a pang of dismay that his beloved had undergone an ordeal of this magnitude. She must be persuaded to speak of it, and soon, if she were to avoid serious emotional consequences. Yet, he was cognizant that the human psyche had a remarkable capacity for function and survival.

Though the study of psychology was still in its infancy, Andrew's skills allowed him to delve into and interpret the mysteries of the mind. He knew that a common mechanism employed by the psyche was to effectively erase the memory of the traumatic event from the conscious awareness. However, this dissociative response was not without a price, for the psyche's banishment of the trauma to the nether regions of the subconscious resulted in a wounding of the soul. Despite the mind no longer recalling the event, the soul retained its own kind of memory, an imprint of the experience that would remain with the individual always. Unlike the psyche, the soul lacked the capacity to deceive or hide from the truth. In an effort to communicate with the mind and thus initiate the healing process, the soul used the most convenient instrument, the physical self, as a conduit.

To that end, the body might be plagued by mysterious aches and pains, illnesses of unknown origin, or disabilities of sudden and intense onset, often disappearing and recurring without sound medical basis. One might also be subject to nightmares and night terrors. Despite these phenomena wreaking havoc with sufferers' lives, the victims were still able to maintain an existence that afforded them some sense of normalcy, for aside from the specific affliction, they functioned as best they could. These protective mechanisms were not foolproof and not as fully developed in some as in others. There were instances where the psyche collapsed under the tremendous stress of the trauma. Unable to banish the horrific event or reconcile it to reality, the psyche had no other resource but to sever its ties with that reality and create a substitute world of madness; hence the many asylums filled with the hopelessly insane, those with souls too battered for redemption.

Andrew was determined that Emma would avoid this fate. As he continued to gaze into her soul, he removed some of the fear that had frozen her mind. He would not interfere with the experience itself, but through his magic, he could lessen the impact of this terror and allow her to retain the ability to heal herself in time.

"Now then, Emma," he said quietly when it was done. "Tell me what happened."

"I can't. Oh!" she wailed, hiding her face once again.

"Shh, shh, it's all right. Nothing can harm you; no thought or deed."

Emma lifted her head tentatively, tears again glistening in her eyes. Her mouth opened, and she strained to get the words out. "Soooo horrible, unspeakable." Her entire body was trembling. "I should never have looked. Oh, why, why did I look?" She swayed back and forth, eyes brimming with torment.

Andrew waved a hand in front of her face to help her focus. "Emma, look only at me. Concentrate your attention on my eyes, nothing else."

Her gaze wandered back to him.

"Good. Now keep looking at me and listen to what I say. You shall tell me what happened. Simply look into my eyes as you speak, and you shall be able to tell your story. Ready?"

Emma nodded, staring into her fiance's solemn eyes, "It's Mary," she whispered. "Mary Kelly. I went to visit."

"A patient of yours?"

"Yes, I was concerned about her, so...." Her voice trailed away.

"So you paid her a visit," Andrew gently prompted. "To check on her?"

Emma nodded once more. "Yes. I'd been having bad dreams, so had she. She was frightened as if she knew what was to happen to her." Her hands twisted in her lap, knuckles as white as bleached bone.

"Of what was she frightened? Do you know, Emma?"

"Yes," she replied in a hushed tone. "She was afraid of... him."

"Who?"

Emma shuddered and shook her head. "There was no answer when I knocked." She raised her hand and mimed, knocking on a door. "Someone told me the window was broken, and I could look inside." She fell silent, a glazed expression in her eyes.

"Emma," Andrew directed. "You are doing well. Keep your focus—look right at me." Emma's eyes flickered. "That's good. Now then...." He took her hand and tenderly enfolded it in his own. "Tell me, darling, tell me what you saw."

"Blood," she whispered, eyes widening. "So much blood everywhere. One could drown; so much blood." Fresh beads of perspiration broke out on her brow. "She was dead." Her voice became raspy, harsh. "Butchered, slashed, gutted like an animal." Her hand in Andrew's clenched spasmodically. "The stench — worse than a slaughterhouse." Her mouth twisted in revulsion. "I can taste it, the foulness seeping into me." She gasped and clapped a hand to her mouth.

"There, my love, you are doing splendidly," he soothed. "Take a deep breath. That's right, and another. Good."

Emma complied, her trembling calming a little.

"Now," Andrew said. "Continue your story."

Emma bit her lower lip. Eyes closed, she intoned as though in a trance. "Pieces of her, parts hacked off, her face gone. Evil in that room — hideous, despicable, loathsome. I sensed it reaching out to claim me." Her eyes flew open, a beseeching and anguished expression in them. "I knew."

She hunched forward, arms folded in on her stomach as though by making herself smaller, she might also lessen the pain. In a barely audible voice, she continued. "It could only be him. Only he could have inflicted such brutality, such carnage." She stared at her fiancé, the dread in her expression chilling him. "Jack the Ripper. I couldn't move or make a sound. I was mesmerized by the evil in that room. I feared that once I started to scream, I should never stop." She stifled a sob with a clenched fist to her lips. "Suddenly, the paralysis was gone, and an unpleasant jolt raced through me. I stumbled from the window and began to run. I neither knew nor cared where I went. I felt sheer terror, my one desire to flee. I had to outrun the evil or succumb to it.

"I must have run through the city. I don't recall that journey. Finally, I could run no further. I found myself at the docks. I thought of casting myself into the river. I was that distraught. The frigid embrace of the Thames seemed preferable to the terrifying nightmare of being.

"Gradually, I became calmer, the soothing lull of the water a welcome balm to my nerves. The acute panic quieted, to be replaced by a gnawing fear that caused my stomach to heave and twist into knots. Hours must have passed. I had no sense of time. I was oblivious to the cold, to everything except my misery. A woman from a nearby soup kitchen offered me shelter from the elements. She was kind and didn't press me when I could not speak. She must have recognized that I was in a shocked state.

At last, I recovered my senses enough to blurt out your address. The woman persuaded one of the dockers to escort me to obtain a hansom. When I arrived at your door, Henrietta welcomed me warmly, even though my appearance must have given her a fright." She indicated her bedraggled, mud-splattered cloak and gown carelessly heaped on the floor at the foot of the bed. "I can only imagine how terrified Mary must have felt. She was so afraid of the Ripper, Andrew. He haunted her nightmares, so she said, and to think of how…oh!" Emma wailed and buried her face in her hands, once again overcome by sheer horror.

"If it is any consolation, she didn't have time to suffer any physical pain. The Whitechapel murderer always slashes his victims' throats first, which causes a swift death from massive blood loss. The subsequent wounds are inflicted postmortem," Andrew stated.

Emma's expression was bleak. "I take no comfort from the fact that she was spared physical pain," she said harshly. "She would still have had time to feel overwhelming terror at what was to be her fate. She knew what horrors had befallen his previous victims. But that is precisely what he wanted; for her to have felt more terror than she had ever imagined possible." She pounded her fists against the bed, fresh tears streaming down her face. "What manner of fiend is this?" she wailed in anguish.

"I am aware of the rumors circulating," Andrew responded quietly. "But rest assured, he is no phantom that vanishes into thin air. He is housed in a human body of flesh and blood, just like you and I, Emma, and he is bound by the rules and limitations of that flesh. Having said that, however, it is true that he is no ordinary human. He belongs to Satan, and therefore has access to evil abilities that go a long way to protect him in man's world."

Emma stared at him with some confusion. "How is it that you can so confidently state such a thing, Andrew? You speak as if the Ripper has made some kind of pact with the devil."

"And is the concept so difficult for you to contemplate?" Andrew countered. "Men make choices every day, and at a very basic level, those choices encompass elements of good or evil. We have many examples of people who have performed great works of good, who have not sought glory or reward, and who have sacrificed themselves, some literally and some spiritually, for the benefit of others. Why then is it not just as simple to acknowledge those who have done the opposite, who have embraced evil?"

Emma shook her head. "There is much I don't understand about this world, Andrew. Of course, I know evil exists."

"It is just that you never expected to come face to face with such a pernicious example of this evil," concluded Andrew gently. Emma nodded miserably. "Humans seldom do expect it, but it happens more frequently than you might like to think. The fight for men's souls occurs every single day, Emma, between forces of good and evil, or if you like, God and Satan."

"Today feels like a victory for Satan," Emma said in a small weary voice.

"It may feel that way to you," Andrew conceded quietly, "but one thing I can tell you is that this so-called Jack the Ripper is about to meet his match."

Emma's eyes widened. "What do you mean, Andrew? Do you know something about the case? Something you have been keeping from me?" Her hand flew to her mouth, and she gasped suddenly. "Have you been secretly working with Scotland Yard, Andrew? Is that—?"

"Now, my love, I haven't said such a thing," her fiancé soothed. He gazed at her pale face with its pinched pained look, at the dark circles of weariness beneath her eyes. "No more talk tonight. It's time for you to rest." Gently he disengaged Emma from his embrace and helped her settle in a supine position.

Emma's eyes brimmed with love now instead of tears. She reached for his hand and kissed his palm. "Darling, I don't know what I should do without you. Your love always reassures and protects, even helps my anguish recede, so I know that despite the horror of today, Mary's death, such a love exists between us to banish despair and give me the courage to face tomorrow."

Andrew smiled tenderly, the flinty look gone from eyes now luminous with emotion. "Love is a powerful balm, I agree. It makes the impossible possible." He bent and kissed her lips softly. "Sleep now, my dear. I shall stay with you."

He sat beside her bed, an inscrutable expression on his face as she drifted into tranquil slumber. The gaslight burned lower, and shadows gathered in the recesses of the room.

A turning point had been reached today. The Whitechapel murderer had, at last, revealed his previous hidden dark agenda. Not only had he aptly demonstrated to what depths of depravity and abomination he could sink, but he had also calculatingly ensnared Emma, manipulating events so she would be a witness to his horrific deeds. He had reached out to her with his tainted evil touch.

The entity was aware of Emma's connection to Andrew, and this was its way of letting him know it, an act of defiance and challenge that Andrew could neither forgive nor forget. The Ripper had deliberately upped the ante in a deadly game of poker in which not merely lives but souls were at stake. It was not in Andrew's nature to retreat from a challenge. The very fact that the entity had sent this test for him meant he was not quite certain of the Avenger's determination. It was waiting for his response.

Andrew smiled to himself, a smile so chillingly cold that the temperature in the room plummeted several degrees and ice crystals formed on the windows. Emma shivered in her sleep as Andrew hastily pulled up the quilt at the foot of the bed and tucked it under her chin.

The Ripper was flirting with a terrible danger, for if he assumed the Avenger's capacity for anger was limited, then he had vastly underestimated his enemy. For no one in this world or any other threatened that which belonged to the Avenger, especially the Avenger's most beloved. And the Ripper may have committed a further error, this one even more grave. He may have thought that no hatred or blood lust could surpass his own.

He was dead wrong.

CHAPTER 43

As evening fell, the fog rolled in from the river. Druitt thought of the fog as an extension of the Thames itself. Rising nightly in ghostly rebirth, the earthbound manifestation of the river crept over the land, covering everything in its cool, moist blanket or shroud. No wonder Whitechapel was notorious for its treachery, a place in which any vice could be indulged with little risk of discovery. The fog concealed so many of the dark deeds and black hearts hidden in its midst.

It was only fitting that as loathsome a creature as Jack the Ripper should spawn from such a cesspit. So, if Druitt was indeed the Ripper, it would mean his affinity for Whitechapel was not mere chance but of destiny intrinsically linked with his legacy of madness. And if he was not the Ripper? Druitt shook his head, perplexed. He was wrestling with a conundrum to which there seemed no solution. Unless he was caught in the act, he would never know for certain. His brain was faulty and unreliable, stubbornly refusing to fill in the memory gaps.

Thus immersed in thought, he wandered into the nearest pub, the Princess Alice. Although boisterous and crowded, the presence of other people helped to normalize his perceptions. The fact that life continued despite the worries and fears of these East Enders served to calm Druitt's agitation. Though the respite was brief, it brought welcome relief from his tormented thoughts.

Of course, talk of the sensational murder was on everyone's tongue. He listened to the flow of conversation for a few moments, then tuned out as his internal dialogue resumed once more. The room faded from his vision, the sound of voices blurring until it resembled nothing more intelligible than the humming of bees.

Anew, he saw the laughing eyes and pretty face of Mary Kelly as she serenaded him in the dingy flat. The image, slightly out of focus, was suffused with a dreamlike quality. If only it had been a dream! If only he could turn back time and change the events of last night. *What a sorry soul I am*, he thought bitterly. *Feeling such remorse for a crime which I don't even know if I committed*. But madness could do that, he knew, hiding the awful truth from one's self.

A physician who attended his mother at home before she had been placed in the asylum had told him that the deranged mind practiced all sorts of deceptions, distorting one's perceptions until truth became lies and lies were the truth.

"Anything else, sir?"

The face of Mary Kelly wavered before his eyes, then underwent a subtle metamorphosis. The blueness of the eyes deepened, the blonde hair was longer and fell in a wavy cascade, the expressive features lovely in their innocence. Druitt blinked a couple of times and found himself staring at the fair countenance of a girl in her teens. She looked back at him expectantly, and he realized she was waiting for him to respond. For a moment, the scene before him dimmed, and he hesitated, waiting for his mind to emerge from its fog. Had he experienced another blackout? Where, exactly was he? Perhaps in his favorite house of ill repute about to be entertained by this fresh-faced beauty?

An anticipatory smile spread across his face, but the fantasy was rudely interrupted when a gruff voice bellowed, "Hey girl, over here. This is a thirsty lot, right mates?" More voices joined in agreement.

The girl sighed impatiently. "Just wait your bleeding turn," she yelled at the man. "Well," she said to Druitt, "do you want something or not? I haven't got all night, you know."

Druitt swallowed the dryness in his throat. Things were coming back into focus now. He was in a Whitechapel pub, and this lovely vision before him was the barmaid. Even her impatience was charming.

"Ah, yes," Druitt responded. "Yes, I will have another whiskey, please."

The girl nodded curtly and went to serve the customers clamoring for her attention.

By Christ and by King, that girl was a work of art! How exquisite her features were, delicate as fine boned China, and skin as soft looking as the richest satin. A girl like that could command any price she asked. She could be the mistress of any powerful, wealthy man, and there would be many that would vie for her favors. She wouldn't need to depend on a brothel. Within a week from starting at a bawdy house, she would be snatched up by some prestigious gentleman.

Maybe that's what he would do later tonight; stop at his favorite haunt instead of roaming the streets. He'd only taken to the streets in search of new adventure and titillation. Something about the unsavory aspect of street whores perversely excited him. The women of the brothels were too familiar and predictable. He craved novelty and the thrill of the unknown. Maybe he could convince that little barmaid….

Now, now, Monty, he chided himself, giggling inwardly. *That would be very unwise.* At the very least, he could expect an indignant slap in the face from the girl. At the very worst, he could find himself at the wrong end of a beating by the girl's father and his mates. After all, with a daughter that beautiful, the father had to be watching her like a hawk. More than likely, he was the lanky-haired sharp-nosed bloke behind the bar. Druitt sighed. Well, it was a nice thought. Besides, some of the girls at the brothel were even younger than this girl. Pity though, that none of them wore that same innocence like a brightly jeweled gown.

He became aware of a change in the pub's atmosphere, subtle yet discernible. The volume of conversation was more subdued, while the excitement of the crowd had increased. Druitt lifted his head and gazed slowly around the room. It took a few moments for him to be sure, but then he concluded that the crowd's attention was riveted on a couple of men who had just entered the pub.

One of them was George Lusk, a prominent social activist and recently elected chairman of the Whitechapel Vigilance Committee. He'd also gained notoriety for being the recipient of written correspondence alleged to be from Jack the Ripper. Public opinion was divided, and debate raged as to whether the letters were indeed from the Whitechapel murderer or an elaborate hoax. Some less charitable folk even wondered aloud whether Mr. Lusk had written the letters for the purpose of drawing attention to himself and his cause.

Despite Scotland Yard's dismissal of the letters, many were eventually persuaded as to the letter writer's authenticity when a piece of kidney accompanied the final missive. It was as though the Ripper knew the public would demand more proof than just his word. When medical examination not only revealed that the kidney was human but showed evidence of heavy alcohol use by its former owner, a great number of Whitechapel citizens were convinced that the Ripper was indeed the author of those chillingly taunting letters.

It was understandable, of course, that the police gave no credence to the letters, as they were unflatteringly caricaturized and made to appear as incompetent buffoons. Like everyone else, Druitt was aware of Lusk's connection to the Ripper. A grim smile passed fleetingly across his face as he thought of Lusk's reaction were he to discover that Jack the Ripper now sat just a few tables away.

At first, Druitt assumed that attention was focused on Lusk, but on closer inspection, it seemed the crowd's interest was directed towards his companion, an elderly yet robust looking man. He walked slowly, but with a straight gait, no stooped shoulders for him, and his shock of white hair lent his features a somewhat distinguished look. It was evident by Lusk's deferential manner that this man must be an individual of some note.

***

Lusk led the man to a table in the center of the room, where a group of men greeted them and ushered them into waiting chairs. Lusk remained standing, however. He raised his hand, gesturing for the crowd to quiet down. Used to addressing large throngs and commanding attention as he was, the response was immediate. Conversation simply didn't fade away. It was halted in mid-sentence. An anticipatory silence descended upon the room.

"Ladies and gents," Lusk began. "As you are all aware, another murder was committed last night by the fiendish Jack the Ripper. This was a most horrible deed, as the poor woman was brutally killed in her very own home! This indicates to me that the Ripper is so confident of evading capture that he is now bold enough to enter people's houses to satisfy his blood lust. So while the coppers are out there walking the streets dressed as tarts, the murderer is inside with the real whores. I guess the coppers think the Ripper don't know the difference between a copper and an actual woman."

A snicker of derision from the crowd greeted this remark.

"Some of you knew the unfortunate Mary Kelly, but whether you knew her or not, or some of the other victims, these horrific murders affect all of us who live in Whitechapel. And what do the coppers do? Throw up their hands and complain that there aren't enough clues. Well, maybe I'm daft, but it seems to me that the coppers are waiting for Jack the Ripper to just surrender himself, to do the coppers a favor, so they don't have to work their bleeding asses off."

More laughter issued from the onlookers, accompanied by comments such as, "Here here, Mr. Lusk," and, "Too true, George." Many heads nodded their assent.

"I tell you one thing for certain," Lusk continued. "If these murders were happening in London proper, the coppers would have caught the bastard by now. He'd be safely locked away in jail. But Whitechapel? So a few East Enders are murdered—so a madman is loose on the streets. It's only whores he's killing. That's the attitude of our politicians. We have to make them pay attention," Lusk's voice rang out. "We have to demand results! Scotland Yard and the politicians must be held accountable!"

Several voices murmured in agreement.

"Tonight with me is the man who discovered Mary Kelly's lifeless body. He wants to speak to you, the hardworking people of Whitechapel, and tell just what he saw with his own eyes, and what really happened to Mary Kelly. Not the watered-down police version, but the terrible truth. He feels it is important for people to know just how horrible this crime was. Let us not forget this is the sixth brutal murder. If his story doesn't convince you to rise up and demand justice from our elected officials, then I don't know what will. Here's Mr. Thomas Bowyer."

Lusk stepped back as the elderly man rose to his feet. He surveyed the crowd with a somber expression.

"Thank you, Mr. Lusk, for inviting me here tonight." His voice was strong and even. "Like Mr. Lusk said, I just want people to know what happened and to understand that this murderer is unlike anything that has come before. I've heard talk that he is a madman, but even madmen have their limits. As God is my witness, I don't think this monster does! Monster. 'Tis the only word that actually describes him. What he did to that poor girl...."

His voice faltered, and he lowered his head. After a few moments, he composed himself enough to continue.

"It was around ten o'clock this morning. I was collecting the rent like I do every week. When I got to Number 13, Mary Kelly's flat, there was no answer at the door. I saw a pane of glass and the window was broke, so I moved the curtain to get a look inside. I figured Mary would be sleeping soundly after carousing through the night like usual, and sure enough, she was lying in the bed, but she wasn't sleeping."

Bowyer paused, and a hush fell over the crowd. "It was kind of gloomy in the room, so it took me eyes a bit of time to get used to the dimness, but when I saw what that demon done to her...." His voice faded momentarily. He cleared his throat. "It was a slaughterhouse scene, sure enough. Blood everywhere—on the walls, the bed, the floor—and her stretched out on the bed like a stripped carcass she was, flesh ripped right off so you could see the bone underneath."

A shocked gasp from the audience greeted these words, along with horrified exclamations.

"I would never have recognized her," resumed Bowyer. "Her face wasn't there no more. It was hacked and torn to ribbons, so all that was left was a bloody mess."

Women cried out in dismay as angry epithets issued from the men in the crowd.

"It's the truth. In all my days of service in the army in India, I never seen nothing like this. I thought I'd seen wickedness before, but she was so badly mutilated even the coppers wouldn't believe it. Saw it with me own eyes. One of them come from that room, his face the color of curdled milk, eyes nearly popping from his head. And another copper was shaking so badly all over he had to sit down, right on the doorstep he did. It was like a wild animal attacked her, except for one thing. In spite of the blood and gore, the parts of the body that he hacked off were arranged neatly in piles, almost as though they were museum pieces on display."

From somewhere in the room came the sound of retching.

"Now, I don't mean to give too much detail, but Mr. Lusk here convinced me that people got the right to know and understand the horror of these crimes." Bowyer shook his head. "But I wonder if that is really possible because I saw firsthand the results of this gruesome deed, and I have to say that I don't understand. I don't think any decent sort could fathom what a monster like that is capable of."

The silence kept on for a few moments after Bowyer's last words. Then someone from the crowd asked, "So I guess her 'ead wasn't missing after all?"

Bowyer regarded the man with an intense gaze. "No, it wasn't her 'ead what was missing."

An excited buzz swept through the room.

"What do you mean, Thomas?" another man shouted. "Something else missing then?"

"What?" Other voices echoed this question until the entire crowd demanded an answer.

Bowyer waved his hands in resignation. "All right, all right," he exclaimed, vexation playing on his face. Clearly, he felt uncomfortable, as though perhaps he'd offered too much information. Out of the corner of his eye, he glanced at Lusk, who nodded back.

"Well," he hesitated, surveying the expectant faces surrounding him. "It's not a public fact—the press don't even know yet—but I heard two coppers talking just after the coroner was in, and they said that he said that the wretched girl's *heart* was missing."

Another sharp gasp was wrenched from the crowd. Bowyer waited for the furor to die down. He was about to speak again when Julia Vanturney stood and walked over to Bowyer's table. Her mouth trembled, and an angry storm roiled up in her eyes.

"Mary Kelly was my friend." Despite a quiver, her voice reverberated in the surreal silence. "What I want to know is, who's going to stop this fiend? The coppers? Ha!" Her whole body shook with passion, and she banged her fist on the nearby table. "What about our own men? Surely to goodness, the Ripper can't escape all the able-bodied men in Whitechapel. Or are we supposed to sit idly by while the creature murders in cold blood again and again?"

Many voices joined in support and scattered applause for Julia's remarks.

George Lusk stood and gestured for silence. When the indignant words faded to a low rumble, he said, fixing Julia with his keen gaze, "My good woman, that is an excellent point. It's time the people of Whitechapel stopped waiting helplessly for the coppers to do their job. As chairman of the Whitechapel Vigilance Committee, I can assure you that many men in this district have already given up their own time, volunteering to patrol the streets from sunset to dawn, offering protection to women on the streets. But while I know that these efforts have helped tremendously, more resources are needed. I suggest that we petition the government to make the capture of the Whitechapel murderer their number one priority. People in the

East End are scared and angry, and that, ladies and gents, is a potent combination.

"A lot can be accomplished through fear and anger. If Sir Charles Warren and the rest of the boys in London think they had it bad last year with the Bloody Sunday riots, just wait until they see what this community will do to get justice!"

The crowd enthusiastically expressed agreement as Lusk continued.

"If we have to march to the parliament buildings to get their attention, then by God, we will. If riots in the streets of Whitechapel and London Central is what it takes, then riots there will be. We will not be silenced!"

Cheers erupted spontaneously from the crowd. People shouted, clapping vigorously, animated whistles and remarks accompanying the cheers. Lusk surveyed the onlookers with satisfaction.

"Justice for Whitechapel!" he yelled, arms raised above his head in a victory gesture.

The crowd echoed the slogan, everyone now on their feet applauding wildly.

***

Sarah-Jane looked over to where her father stood with a group of men at the bar. All of them were clapping and shouting their approval. She felt caught up in the wave of excitement, and for the first time since this nightmare began, she felt the faintest stirring of hope that it would end with the capture of Jack the Ripper. If only Emma were here tonight. She wondered what her friend's opinion would be of Mr. Lusk's ideas.

Emma had confided to her the disturbing nightmares she was experiencing about Jack the Ripper. Sarah-Jane wasn't privy to every detail, as Emma told her she deliberately omitted some aspects because they were too disturbing to share. Regardless, Sarah-Jane was aware that her friend was very troubled about the murders. On a couple of recent visits to the Princess Alice, Emma had spoken to the whores present, urging them to take advantage of the vigilance committee's offer to escort them home, reminding the women that there were always members outside the pubs every night waiting to see any woman home safely. The committee members remained as unobtrusive as possible, not wishing to propel the murderer into the woodwork because of their presence. The last thing they wanted was to have the Ripper go into hiding and thus avoid capture — therefore, they didn't announce their presence to the women but simply hovered at the doors. They sported red handkerchiefs hanging loosely from their jacket pockets, a sign indicating that they were official representatives of the vigilance committee.

Sometimes instead of walking with the women, they followed at a discreet distance to see if any suspicious looking characters approached them. Of course, being whores, this frequently occurred, and when necessary, the members posted themselves at entrances to alleyways and waited patiently for the whores and their customers to complete their transactions. This way, if anything untoward happened, the vigilance committee would respond promptly.

Sarah-Jane's attention drifted back to George Lusk. He finished his speech and announced that the vigilance committee welcomed suggestions from the people of Whitechapel. The members present this evening would relay the public's ideas to the next general meeting scheduled for the following evening. Their goal was to incorporate as many suggestions as feasible into the formulation of a plan of action. Lusk promised that he or one of the other representatives would report back on the committee's progress. These progress reports would be held in rotating order at five of the most frequented public houses in the East End, namely the Britannica, the Frying Pan, the Queens Head, the Ten Bells, and of course, the Princess Alice. All were welcomed to attend the public meetings and to be part of any subsequent action to be taken.

After Lusk and Bowyer took their leave, the conversation continued at a fever pitch. Spirits and hopes were raised as lively discussions sprouted up, and people felt that at last, they had a part to play in the apprehension of Jack the Ripper. Many vowed that they would be ready at any time to march to London with the vigilance committee and demand an audience with parliament, and perhaps even the queen herself. After all, it was rumored that Victoria was quite disturbed by the events in Whitechapel and wished for an expedient resolution to the case.

***

As Druitt watched the groups coalesce around him, he decided that now was a good time to make himself scarce. It saddened him a little that he wasn't part of this community or any community for that matter, and never would be. He was destined to live out his existence alone, and he would take his shameful secrets to the grave with him.

It was true that he could surrender himself to the authorities. He could have handed himself over to Lusk and the vigilance committee this very evening, but to what avail? He could offer no incontrovertible proof that he was Jack the Ripper. He couldn't produce a murder weapon or even recall any details of the crimes. The police would laugh and dismiss him as a pathetic and deluded individual — unless, of course, they were so desperate to solve the case they would accept the first scapegoat who offered a confession.

But no, on second thought, they would want to be damned sure they had the real killer, for if he was incarcerated and the killings continued, it would be obvious that they had charged the wrong man. They would then be held in more contempt by the public than they were presently.

Druitt's eyes lit up as he suddenly realized there was a way to determine if he was indeed the Ripper. It was so simple yet brilliant that he hadn't thought of it before now. If he, Druitt, was in jail and the killings continued, then that would prove his innocence. All he had to do was have himself arrested, which in Whitechapel should an easy accomplishment. His brow furrowed in concentration as he pondered how he could engineer this.

Then another thought occurred, which put a bit of a damper on his enthusiasm. There was a pattern to these murders of a significant time lapse between the crimes, sometimes extending to four weeks. He didn't particularly relish the prospect of a month or more in prison; however, if it once and for all would prove his innocence or guilt...

He shook his head, ambivalent about how to proceed. He had to break the law seriously enough to be arrested and detained in jail, yet not something so bad that he would be incarcerated for months. He needed more time to think this through. He must restrain himself from acting impulsively. He had to invent a plan guaranteed to bring about the desired result.

Druitt rose from the table and hurriedly exited the pub. Unmindful where his steps led him, he began to walk, his mind busy turning over threads of ideas in the hopes of weaving together a course of action to answer his tormenting question and finally extinguish the flames of anguish which burned relentlessly inside him.

CHAPTER 44

Emma stared listlessly at her cup of tea. The morning sun shone weakly through the dark green muslin curtains in the drawing room. Although she had slept undisturbed through the night, she felt exhausted and heavy-headed. A dull pain throbbed just behind her eyes.

The door to the drawing room opened, and Henrietta entered, followed by Alice. The housekeeper carried a large pewter tray, which she deposited on the small table beside Emma's chair.

"Good morning, Miss Emma. I have fresh scones and cream for your breakfast." She smiled kindly at the young woman.

Emma endeavored to return the smile, but the effort was a ghostly imitation of her usual bright expression. "Thank you, Alice," she murmured.

Henrietta examined Emma's face, noting the sallow complexion. "How did you sleep, dear?" she asked, taking her favorite armchair.

"I slept as one oblivious to the world," Emma replied. "I remember Andrew sitting by my bed and my head resting on the pillow, then nothing until morning. No dreams, no fitful awakenings, as if I had fallen into a deep chasm where only sleep existed."

"And yet you are still exhausted," Henrietta remarked as she poured herself tea from the silver service. She gestured towards Emma, who nodded and handed out her cup for replenishment.

Emma nodded. "Still suffering the effects of yesterday, I should think."

"But of course you are, darling," Henrietta agreed. "After

such an unspeakable trauma, it's a wonder you are functioning at all."

Emma risked a tentative glance in her direction. "Did Andrew tell you what happened?"

Henrietta nodded, her expression solemn and full of concern. "Yes, he did, my dear child." She put her cup down and reached across to clasp one of Emma's limp hands. "I can't tell you how sorry I am that you had to endure such an abominable experience. I know you are blessed with inordinate fortitude and courage and that you shall recover from this ordeal, but it shan't be easy, and it will take time. You must be in a loving and nurturing environment. I suspect that you may wish to go to your parents for a while. That is understandable, but I want you to know that you are welcome to stay in this house as long as you wish."

Tears sprang to Emma's eyes, and she rapidly blinked them away, calling upon her strength of will to suppress the sobs which threatened to erupt.

"Henrietta, I thank you so much," she quavered. "It's strange, for although I am close to my parents, I should prefer to stay here with you and Andrew. My family would shower me with love and solace, that I know, but in their efforts to support me, I fear that they might be overprotective and apprehensive. This would result in tension between us, my parents once again expressing their disapproval about my work, my lodging, etc. As well intentioned as they are, I fear my nerves wouldn't cope with such an onslaught right now." She sighed. "At least you and Andrew treat me like an adult instead of a rebellious child."

Henrietta patted her hand. "I'm glad you wish to remain with us. However," she said with mock sternness, "I must warn you that I too am a parent and can certainly appreciate the concerns of your family. But I promise that I shall try to act more like a friend than a mother."

Emma smiled tremulously. "I have a feeling that I might require a little mothering now and then," she said wistfully.

"And if you want to talk about the incident?" Henrietta paused.

Emma shook her head. "No, I have already spoken to Andrew. He knows all the horrid details." A wave of grief swept over her. "I only wish I could have done something to help her." She broke off as sobs racked her body, choking her words.

Henrietta moved to Emma's side and wrapped the distraught girl in her arms. "My dear, don't torment yourself so. What could you have done? It's not as though you knew she would be murdered."

Emma didn't answer but continued to weep profusely. She allowed the older woman to comfort her, although, at that moment, she doubted that she would ever be able to go on with her life, so vastly changed in forty-eight hours. Every time she closed her eyes, images of that horrid nightmare stabbed at her like the sharpest blades.

She kept seeing herself and the woman lying on those slabs at the mercy of the fiendish Ripper. Her nightmare had eerily presaged poor Mary's fate. Was she now to infer that the Ripper would come after her next? Somehow she sensed that the only safe place for her was in this house, more specifically in Andrew's house.

Even when he wasn't physically present within its confines, a strong essence of him permeated the air so that she felt immediately calmer and less fearful. If there was any hope for her salvation, a chance for her to heal from this trauma, she knew it would only be achieved if she were to remain near Andrew. It wasn't a rational deduction, but just now, it was the only thing that prevented her from collapsing into a torrent of despair.

Eventually, after several minutes, Emma's sobs quieted, and she was able to compose herself. Her handkerchief was completely soaked, and she gratefully accepted the one proffered by Henrietta. She blew her nose noisily and disengaged herself from the other woman's comforting embrace. "I'm sorry, Henrietta—" she began.

"Nonsense," the older woman interrupted. "There is no need to apologize. I daresay it is good for you to have a solid cry or two. Besides, as a mother, I am very used to drying away tears. I only wish I could take away the hurt as easily as that."

Emma smiled weakly. "It helps immensely to have someone as understanding and kind as you, Henrietta," she sighed. "I'm in need of a distraction from my woes. Let us talk of other things."

Henrietta nodded. "As you wish, dear. What would you like to discuss?"

Emma pondered the question a moment before answering. "Tell me about Andrew as a child. What was he like growing up?"

Henrietta smiled fondly. "His was an interesting childhood, to be sure. Andrew and I have always enjoyed a very close relationship. With the others, Amanda, Malcolm, and Reginald, I'm Mother, plain and simple. They don't desire me to be more than that, and I am content to adopt that traditional role. But it is different with Andrew. From the very first, there was a special bond between us that wasn't present with the others. It is difficult to describe except to say that we have a kinship, a connection to one another that extends beyond the mother-son relationship.

"I am his mother, yes. I represent all the aspects of that role—security, nurturing, authority. But I am also his friend and confidante. He has told me things he would never have dreamt of sharing with his father. The other boys, I know, sought George's counsel on a number of issues, but Andrew always came to me, and it is still that way. Even my daughter and I aren't as close as Andrew and I. Of course, Andrew has enormous respect for his father; he just wouldn't share the secrets of his soul with him."

"Did he have that intensity about him then as well?" inquired Emma.

Henrietta chuckled. "Oh, yes. He's always possessed a formidable ability to focus on whatever takes his fancy. An independent child he was, insatiably curious, forever seeking answers; attentive and affectionate, passionate and impulsive at times, fiercely loyal and honest. Indeed, his relentless propensity for telling the truth often ended friendships for him. I remember him saying once—and he couldn't have been older than nine or ten—people shouldn't ask for the truth if they expect to hear lies.

'If they cannot accept the truth, they are not worthy to be my friends.'

"Honestly, Emma, at times, I was greatly taken aback by the things he said, such unusual clarity of thought and wisdom for one so young. It was as if an adult spoke from within a child's body. Other parents and teachers were constantly telling George and me how precocious Andrew was as if we hadn't noticed ourselves. Not that he didn't play and frolic with friends and siblings—of course, he did. But there was a unique essence to his personality, which I have never known a child to possess. The only way I can describe it is to say that it was as though he was used to life, familiar with its patterns, loops and twists like he knew where it would lead him. He showed none of the uncertainty and confusion about his place in the world, emotions that plague the rest of us. It was only much later, of course, that I was able to understand this singular quality."

"Did you know about his spiritual studies with the Indian?" Emma asked.

"Not at first. We found out soon enough when the headmaster at his school informed us that Andrew was absent from many of his classes, and when we finally met Pradeep, Mr. Bhirati, it became apparent that he exerted a very beneficial influence over our son. Thus we allowed the studies to continue, but not to interfere with his regular schooling."

"And if you'd forbidden Andrew to continue those studies?"

Henrietta smiled and shook her head. "You know Andrew. There is no denying him anything to which he has set his mind. I daresay he would have found some way to clandestinely pursue his studies. That was the main reason I persuaded George to view the benefits of such spiritual teachings. I knew Andrew would continue regardless of what George or I might say and, of course, even at so tender an age, I trusted my son's judgment implicitly. If he felt he could learn something of value from this man, then who was I to doubt? George was less than thrilled, but he capitulated when I pointed out that knowledge is never wasteful, and that an eclectic education was an asset for a son who would eventually run the family business."

Emma frowned as she struggled to phrase her next question. "Were you aware of any strange abilities he may have had?"

Henrietta's gaze was direct, her gray eyes reminiscent of her son's penetrating expression. "Yes, of course," she replied matter-of-factly. "I told you that Andrew was different from other children, most strikingly in his perceptions and knowledge. But that isn't what you mean, is it?"

Emma's gaze faltered. "No, not exactly," she replied hesitantly. "I have always known that Andrew was different from other men. The troubles and anxieties that plague them don't occupy him. It's as though he is preoccupied by something other than worldly matters. I suppose it relates to the strong spiritual teaching he received in India."

"Yes, but that is only a part of what makes Andrew different, as I suspect you already know, difficult as you may find it to express," Henrietta observed astutely. She smiled slightly at the younger woman's bewildered expression. "I realize that there is much of which you are unaware, my dear, so trust me when I say that Andrew shall explain his ways to you. Your confusion shall be eliminated soon enough."

Henrietta leaned forward and patted Emma's hand. The strain of yesterday's ordeal was still very evident in the young woman's eyes. "Here, child, your nerves are exhausted. You need rest, not only for the body but the mind as well. However, before I send you upstairs, I shall indulge my prerogative as a surrogate mother and advise that you must attend to your appetite if you are to maintain your fortitude." She handed Emma a plate with two scones and a healthy dollop of fresh cream. "Alice will be terribly crestfallen if we don't enjoy her delicious scones."

Emma sat back in her chair, dully chewing the scone, barely noticing the rich buttery taste and crumbly texture. Her mind reeled from the bloody images of Mary's murder. Her head began to pound mercilessly with the barrage of fearful pictures, and the one that loomed in menace over all the fragments of perception; Jack the Ripper's leering face peering at her, full of vulpine menace as she lay helplessly on the cold slab.

CHAPTER 45

Early evening and all was quiet in the Hewitt-Brown household. Henrietta and George were attending a social function hosted by one of George's colleagues. Alice had finished her chores for the day and retired to her rooms on the ground floor with her knitting and cup of tea.

Upstairs in Andrew's room, the candlelight's soft illumination banished shadows to the farthest corners. Cradled in her lover's arms, Emma basked in the joy she always felt when they lay together. She snuggled her naked body closer to him, savoring the delicious warmth of his skin against hers. She stroked his chin, fingers traveling over the bit of golden stubble, its rough texture tickling her.

"Andrew," she murmured.

"Yes, my love."

"Tell me about the Excala. You promised you would."

Andrew stirred beside her, shifting his weight. "Indeed, I did."

He propped himself up on one elbow and examined her face closely before nodding, satisfied with what he saw reflected there. Sitting up straight in bed, pillow tucked behind him, he proceeded to tell her of his initial encounter with the enigmatic Pradeep Bhirati and the latter's fantastic tale.

"For reasons not understood by me at the time, I felt drawn to this stranger. Despite his bizarre story, I was unable to dismiss him as a madman or charlatan. Somehow I sensed the truth of his words. He only confirmed what I had known all along about myself; I was not like others. Schoolmates, teachers, family friends—I was different from them all, even my own family, with the exception of my mother, whom I sensed shared a unique bond with me, though of its nature I was ignorant. I decided that there was much to learn of this mystery and that Bhirati could provide the answers."

He described his introduction to the Indian's gambling establishment and the time he subsequently spent honing the gambling skills which had at first drawn the man's attention to him. "It was intoxicating to be in the company of other gamblers. Though I was but a lad of twelve, gambling fever was in my blood, and I was in my true element. I was very successful and was considered a wunderkind, which lent Pradeep's establishment an air of intrigue and notoriety.

"It wasn't long before respected high caliber players flocked to the gaming house. Pradeep concocted a scheme whereby these elite players lined up to meet me in the ultimate gambling challenge. It was all very exciting, as well as lucrative for Pradeep and me. As partners, we split the profits equally, and it was a skill that later would serve me well in business ventures, as my teacher had wisely known all along.

"Although gambling was a very pleasurable pastime and helped my insight into the human mind, the time soon came when Pradeep judged me ready to enter the next phase of my learning. I began to study spirituality—not merely skimming its surface as I had been doing, but moving deeper into its substance. Under Pradeep's superb tutelage, I came to discover my spiritual identity and my true purpose in this world. I spent considerable effort mastering one of the great challenges of spirituality.

"Few people realize it, but maintaining a balance between the physical and spiritual existences is infinitely more difficult than it seems. This balance is essential if one is to live in both worlds simultaneously and harmoniously, yet it is a feat not readily accomplished. You see, it becomes increasingly difficult to keep one's focus on worldly issues when those of a spiritual nature beckon so enticingly. And because the spiritual always supersedes the physical, the tendency to ignore physical aspects increases. However, the demands of the physical world must be met all the same, lest the imbalance between spiritual and physical threaten the equilibrium of the self.

"You may be reminded of certain holy men who withdraw from society completely, living their lives in virtual isolation as they strive to attain the greatest degree of enlightenment. That is not my destiny. My purpose requires that I maintain relationships with humankind."

Then he proceeded to speak of the Excala, their origin and history. He explained that although born of flesh and blood, Excala, or Insiders, were special beings, vastly different from their human counterparts or Outsiders. Their purpose, evolved over time, was to guide mankind to a greater spiritual understanding.

As servants of the Creator, the Excala pledged to assist men in their spiritual potential, to develop the gift bestowed upon them by the Creator. To accomplish this enormous task, Excala were permitted to use magic, the ancient craft they had long ago mastered. Andrew briefly described his own meticulous training in magic but did not elaborate upon its uses.

"Prior to the destruction of our world, which I described to you in detail, we lived our lives through the dictates of spirituality. We were peaceful and content. Although our world bordered the human world, we had no real interest in humans, not liking or disliking them, merely considering them inferior because of their focus on non-spiritual matters.

"However, all that changed with the loss of our realm. The Creator gave us the opportunity to continue with a physical existence, the purpose of which was to inspire and assist our human counterparts to develop spirituality. Because, like humans, Excala were given free will, we could choose to accept or reject the Creator's proposal. Some did reject it, choosing to dwell forever in the spiritual realm, never again to adopt physical form. But for those of us who accepted the pledge, free will has always been a part of us. This means that at any time, an Excala may decide to return to the spiritual world, but there is no constraint upon the length of time we serve our pledge. Or one might decline to fulfill a particular task.

"The Creator never demands anything of us, nor does he influence our decisions. Each Excala has an assigned duty or role to play in the Creator's scheme, something that suits us on a spiritual level. Through that role, we may exert an impact upon events that occur in the world of man. We are teachers, healers, leaders, warriors, and discoverers in many forms and guises, and we are given as many lifetimes as we wish in order to accomplish the conditions of our pledge and to increase our personal and spiritual enlightenment."

Andrew paused, allowing an opportunity for Emma to digest the information. He did not wish to overwhelm her with too much too quickly. He watched her closely, seeing the confusion amass like a dark storm cloud in her eyes.

Emma's expression reflected a growing dismay. By the time her lover paused in his narrative, she was sitting bolt upright in bed, body rigid, staring at him in shocked bewilderment. She could barely hold back the tears.

"Oh, Andrew!" she exclaimed. "Why do you torment me with this cruel jest? What have I done to merit such mockery? When you spoke previously of the Excala, I assumed you alluded to a particular selective and discreet club of gentlemen who were anonymous benefactors of society. Instead, I am treated like a child, to be frightened by tales of magic. What next? Goblins, witches, and wicked elves?"

Andrew reached for her cold hand and wrapped it tightly in his own. "Emma, I assure you this is no jest, cruel or otherwise. Do you really believe I would stress you like this for mere frivolity? It pains me to see you so troubled. Yet these are things you must know—the time has come when they should no longer be kept secret from you. You know in your heart I have always treated you with the love and respect you deserve. Tell me, have I ever deceived you?"

Emma gazed at him in consternation, shaking her head. "No, you haven't, but—"

"But what?" he prompted. "You don't believe your own

accusation, for if you really and truly thought this a hoax perpetrated at your expense, you would be angry, and rightly so. However, there is no anger in your eyes, only fear."

Emma started. "It isn't fear exactly," she said defensively. "It is more like trepidation."

"You may call it what you like, but I recognize fear when I see it. A typical human response to my tale of the Excala would involve various emotions, perhaps the aforementioned anger as well as total disbelief, maybe even derision; certainly a question of my sanity. Yet none of these has been your initial response. Why are you conflicted, Emma? Why do you recognize my words of truth, yet flinch away from them?"

"I don't know what you mean," Emma said frankly.

Andrew smiled gently. "Of course, you know what I mean. A part of you does, at any rate. Your heart responds to the truth because it cannot be misled by human deception. Your heart, Emma, wishes to embrace the truth of who you really are." His voice and smile grew very tender. "You are as much Excala as Henrietta and me, for I could never love a human, only one of my own kind."

Emma was very still and pale. Her lips moved, but no words came out. The hand in Andrew's grasp began to tremble. He reached across and stroked her hair.

"There is no reason to fear, dear one. Fear is a man-made obstacle to spirituality. It has no meaning for Insiders. To overcome it, you must stop thinking as a human and allow your Excala responses to guide you. Your heart shall not fail you. It is the mind's connection to the world, the instrument through which the spiritual and physical selves communicate.

"Like all Excala, you possess discernment, a characteristic so innate that you may have taken it for granted. But now, it can serve you as an important tool as you fully enter the next stage of your development. All Insiders experience this phenomenon at some point in their human existence, a process which is repeated in every lifetime. We call it the 'spiritual reclamation,' for it is a reacquiring of all your Excala skills."

Emma appeared transfixed, eyes wide and staring. The look of fear was gone, replaced by a glassy blankness, but Andrew knew she heard every word he spoke.

"You see, my love, the soul retains spiritual memory much as the brain restores physical memory. In the pre-reclamation, or dormant state, Excala aren't aware of the soul memories' existence, but once the reclamation begins, we gain access to this unique memory, enabling us to recall other lifetimes. We also develop an understanding of our legacy and purpose in man's world. We learn to recognize and reclaim the skills we perfected during our time in the realm of the Excala. We may learn to access the most powerful and sacred elements of magic, which can be used for personal growth.

"If we abide by the rules of our pledge, each lifetime allows us the opportunity to acquire new skills, perhaps, while attaining a deeper and more fulfilling spiritual state. The dormant period from which you are starting to emerge is akin to having amnesia on the spiritual level. We know from experience in the physical world that one who recuperates from amnesia is unable to recall memories spontaneously and completely. Rather, one uncovers fragments of memory. Details often remain ambiguous and non-chronological during the recovery phase.

"Caution, however, is advised. The initial phase of the reclamation is unpredictable in duration and invariably, a tumultuous experience. It is necessary for another Excala to guide you and to offer support through the emotional and spiritual turmoil. All Insiders have mentors. Pradeep was mine, I was Henrietta's, and I shall be yours should you choose to continue the process." He smiled reassuringly. "Now, what questions have you?"

Emma pulled her hand out of his grasp. Agitation once more replaced the catatonic-like stillness she'd endured the last few minutes. She wrung her hands and then jumped from the bed. Heedless of her nakedness, she began to pace.

"I don't know what to think!" she exclaimed in dismay. "This is so overwhelming. I believe I must be in a dream. Granted, my dreams of late have been strange, and I can't believe I possess the imagination to concoct something as bizarre as this tale. You say it isn't a deceit; therefore, that only leaves the truth. I know you are sincere, but a madman's truth does not extend beyond the confines of his own mind."

She shook her head, gnawing her lower lip. "Oh, Andrew, I know you are not mad; in fact, you are the sanest person I have ever encountered. Logic dictates, therefore, that if *you* aren't mad, I must be for manufacturing these delusions. Perhaps the trauma of discovering Mary's corpse was more than my mind could bear, and I have descended to the dark nether regions of madness with occasional surfacing to lucidity."

Andrew rose and draped her robe over Emma's shoulders. "You shall catch a chill," he said gently. He drew her to him and kissed the top of her head. "You are not mad, my love. There is no need to torment yourself with that fear. You are allowing your mind too much control when it should be your heart upon which you rely. Come and sit with me while I continue to explain."

Emma allowed him to lead her back to the bed. As soon as she was seated, she exclaimed, "I can't accept your words when they border on blasphemy! This strange sect practices magic and beliefs in past lives, all contrary to Christian teaching. When our mortal lives end, we join our heavenly Father in Paradise. That is our reward for living good lives here on earth. This talk of reincarnation is a religious concept of your adopted country. Perhaps living in India and studying with that Indian philosopher has influenced your belief more than you realize."

Andrew shook his head, a patient expression in his eyes. "No, my dear, it has nothing to do with India. I would have discovered this knowledge wherever I happened to reside in the physical world. This knowledge is true, and the source of truth is never external. Truth can be recognized only within one's self. It can only be clearly seen through spiritual eyes. As for multiple lives, I don't subscribe to the belief of reincarnation as is commonly accepted in eastern religions, for that idea is based upon a reward and punishment theme.

"There are as many different interpretations as there are religions. While all of them claim to be the true religion, logic dictates that this is not possible. Do they all contain some element of truth? Perhaps, in as much as man is capable of understanding truth. What I am saying, Emma, is that anything man-made is inherently flawed, as man himself is imperfect.

"Does it really matter to the Creator what religion man embraces? How many battles are waged, how many lives lost in the name of religious righteousness? Don't you see that these events are the direct consequences of man's beliefs and actions? The Creator never counseled men to shed one another's blood in His name, yet such occurrences have tainted human history from its beginnings. Why do you suppose that is?"

Emma pondered a moment. "I should think it must be the influence of evil in the world."

"Precisely," agreed Andrew. "Combine man's vulnerability to corruption with his penchant for self-deception, and it's no wonder that his spirituality is in such peril."

Emma reflected upon these words. "So man actually needs to be saved from himself, his own weaknesses, which means that evil is only as powerful as man's susceptibility to it allows it to be."

"That isn't completely accurate, Emma. True, the weaker a man is, the more easily he falls under evil influences. However, the stronger one is spiritually, the more enticing is his corruption. For as a thief will reject a flawed jewel in favor of one brighter and of better quality, so is evil attracted to a soul of superior quality. Thus, the more spiritual one is, the greater the assaults and challenges to one's soul.

"And please avoid the error of reducing evil to an intellectual concept. It has become popular among certain clergy to refer to evil as an abstract phenomenon residing in the recesses of the mind. Such men scoff at the idea of a horned entity who lives in a place called Hell and schemes to steal unwary souls." Andrew's eyes blazed with contempt. "The devil exists, and he is mankind's greatest enemy. Evil does not live in men's minds but in their hearts. Because the heart is the conduit to the soul. If it is poisoned, the toxic effect is spread to the soul. It is exceedingly dangerous to minimize the threat of evil. Those who do shall be led to their doom.

"Excala know better. We understand that evil is a force that has always existed independently in man's world. In fact, we are well acquainted with evil in all its many guises, for we are confronted by it relentlessly. So you now can see that it doesn't suffice to save man from himself. Were it not for our interventions on his behalf, man would long ago have succumbed to evil, and this world would have become annexed to Satan's domain, a literal Hell on earth. If humans only knew how close this world has come to such an event, they would never sleep peacefully again. Make no mistake, the earth is the devil's hunting ground."

He looked at Emma's pale face, the usual bright green eyes dulled to a muddy sea color, the pained expression as she strained to understand the magnitude of his words. "Dearest one, do you know how much I love you?"

Emma nodded. "Yes, I do," she whispered.

"Then look into my eyes and beyond them to my soul. Our love has endured for many lifetimes. We have laughed and sorrowed, felt joy and pain, always together. We are a part of one another, sharing a bond which transcends the physical and encompasses the spiritual. Long after our bones have turned to dust, we shall be together, our spirits joined through eternity. Listen now as I recite the old words, the words of love we pledged to one another long ago in the realm of Excala. Open your soul to these words, and you shall remember.

"Body and soul
Blood and bone
We belong to one another
Two hearts. One beat
Keeping the rhythm through Eternity."

He placed Emma's hand against his chest, over his heart. "Can you feel it, Emma?"

Emma did as he directed. Staring into his eyes, she was

reminded of a vast depthless sea whose gray surface concealed untold mysteries. As she listened to the rhythmic cadence of her lover's voice, she entered that sea, letting the waves surround and carry her to a place glimpsed only in her dreams. A world fresh and vibrant with color opened up before her eyes, an exotic flower unfolding to her wondering delight. Dazzling light from a hot sun beat down upon her, forcing her to raise a hand to shield her gaze from its intensity. Turning from the light's direction, she began to run through a field of savory scented grass, barely aware of the blades that tickled her bare toes. Clad only in a shift of lightweight material which just brushed her ankles, she headed towards the woods looming in front of her. Her heart pounded with anticipation, and she heard the unfettered laughter of children ringing out nearby.

From the shadowed woods issued the sound of horses' hooves heralding the approach of a handsome black steed. At a gesture from its rider, the horse paused as the man raised his head to the sunlit sky. Emma's pace increased, and she ran swiftly to greet him, the joy in her heart bubbling over into her eyes and face. As she drew alongside the glistening onyx flanks of the horse, the man laughed and leaned down towards her. With one swift motion, he grasped her waist and lifted her up to sit with him.

She looked into his sparkling eyes, no longer the color of storm clouds, but a beguiling blue-green shade. He bent his head to her, their mouths tenderly meeting. The kiss lingered for several sweet moments, then the young man murmured in her ear, "It is good to be home again. I have missed you so, my Evangelina." With those words, he kicked his heels gently against his horse's sides. The steed began to trot at a leisurely pace.

Emma turned to face the direction from which she had run. For the first time, she saw the town spread out below them, nestled in a lush valley. Towering above all the other structures was a turreted castle whose façades were a silvery gleam in the sunshine. She recognized that castle, her home.

The scene abruptly vanished, and once again, she was drifting in the sea. Submerged in love, she allowed its gentle waves to caress her. So complete was the joy she knew at this moment, she could happily drown in this love. She sighed, savoring the sensation, but gradually the intensity waned, and suddenly she was back in her lover's bedchamber, back in London of 1888.

A delicious warmth tingled in the hand that rested upon Andrew's chest, and she gasped in delight as the sensation traveled up her arm and began to radiate through her entire body.

Andrew lightly touched her cheek. "Describe to me what you experienced," he whispered.

Emma opened her eyes, blinking away tears of joy, overcome by the marvelous lightness traveling inside her.

"I saw you and me," she replied, voice soft with wonder. "Where we began, in the realm of the Excala. Though physically changed from ourselves of today, I recognized us without a doubt. You had black curly hair and beard, and your eyes were a different color, lighter. A tremendous love existed between us, and I was overjoyed to see you."

She frowned in concentration. "We had been parted for a time. You were away on the king's business. You were a close friend of his." She looked at him. "You called me Evangelina."

Andrew nodded. "That was your name in that lifetime. Our very first."

"It was like being in Paradise; at least I can't imagine Paradise being any more beautiful than that world," Emma said.

He smiled. "And who is to say it wasn't Paradise?" he murmured. "The reclamation has fully begun, my love. Your spiritual memory is returning. A few weeks, even days ago, you would not have been able to feel these urges nor understand their meaning. But now, have you remarked that your fear is gone?"

Emma was startled. "Why yes, you're right, Andrew. I am no longer afraid."

"Your heart remembers and rejoices, and happiness has replaced fear. Welcome to the realm of magic."

"Can I really learn magic, Andrew?"

He laughed at her wistful tone. "What do you think that trip back into time was, if not magic?"

"Yes, but that was your magic. You allowed me to take that trip."

"Perhaps I did, but how do you know that you didn't help yourself a little as well with your own magic?"

"Did I?" she asked, bemused.

He chuckled once more. "You shall learn all the skills you desire, but it will take time and confidence. Now it is best that we stop here for tonight. Your human mind is unable to process information beyond a certain point, and I don't wish to overtax you." Emma started to protest, but he stopped her in his firm manner. "We shall continue our discussion in the morning."

"But Andrew," Emma said dejectedly, feeling like a child who's been told there will be no more bedtime stories this night. "How do you expect me to sleep after all I have seen and felt tonight?"

"Believe me, love, you shall sleep soundly. You don't realize it, but this evening's experiences have been quite emotionally exhausting for you."

"But—" Emma began.

Andrew placed a finger to her lips, then leaned over to blow out the candles by the bedside. Then he gathered Emma to him, holding her close in the semi-darkness.

As he lay listening to Emma's breathing as she slumbered in his arms, he thought about the coming day and the further knowledge he must share. This evening's revelations had been difficult enough, but he knew that the morrow would bring further challenges to Emma's fortitude and trust in him.

CHAPTER 46

The next morning after breakfast, Andrew and Emma sequestered themselves in the drawing room. Henrietta was plainly aware of the issue being discussed, but she made no comment other than to remark that she was off to one of her women's meetings. Alice, however, gave Andrew a puzzled look when he requested that they not be disturbed for any reason before luncheon. Nevertheless, her discreet nature prevented her from asking any questions.

Once they were comfortably ensconced in front of the fire, fresh cups of tea in hand, Andrew examined Emma's face for any signs of strain. There were none, her complexion fresh and her eyes bright. The dark circles which had recently appeared in the hollows of her eyes were less apparent today.

"Any disturbing dreams last night, my dear?" he asked.

Emma shook her head. "No, I slept soundly as you had predicted, but a question has been on my mind."

"Well, by all means, ask it now."

"When you spoke of the Excala's interventions on behalf of mankind, what exactly did you mean?"

"Ah, just the subject I plan to address first thing this morning."

"Something confuses me. You stated that free will is a gift from God which all men possess, yet any intercession on your part would affect a person's free will, for presumably, it would override that person's choice. Don't men have the right to make the wrong choices?"

"Absolutely," replied Andrew. "In fact, men often make adverse choices. Free will isn't necessarily in conflict with our interventions. Whenever possible, Excala try not to supersede the individual's freedom. We use our magic to influence events, but what we are really doing is expanding the options available. It remains the choice of the individual as to how he will respond to events; only when it is essential do we actually manipulate his will to bring about the desired consequences.

"For example, if a particular human in a position of power, let's say a politician, is about to make a decision that will set in motion a chain of events that will have a deleterious effect not only on his own people but other nations as well, then I might consider an adjustment to be necessary."

Emma frowned in consternation as a thought occurred to her. "But that means you can foresee the future," she said faintly.

Andrew nodded, spreading his hands in an expansive gesture. "I can foresee what *may* occur depending upon the free will and actions of those involved. For the skill of foresight to be truly useful, one must be adept at analyzing all the possible outcomes. This includes not only the short term effects but long-term repercussions in particular.

"It isn't acceptable to me to initiate a response of which the effects may be immediately beneficial, but which could cause harmful consequences sometime in the future. All this adds up to intricate, precise, and painstaking calculation on the part of the Excala, for one must not only be able to anticipate the potential responses of an individual but to also project how those responses will lead to other actions and consequences. Each one must also be evaluated for their positive or negative impact. I call this the Ripple Effect of magic, and the reason discernment is so vital prior to casting even the simplest spell. Much misery has been initiated in this world by those magicians whose judgment has been corrupted. They might delude themselves into believing their interventions will benefit mankind, but invariably they result in detrimental consequences."

"But there are those who willfully do harm, are there not?"

"Of course. Magic is a force, Emma, neither good nor evil. It can be accessed by those who wish to harm as well as those who wish to help. So-called 'black magic' is that which is used for wicked purposes, but it isn't the magic that is black, only the heart of the practitioner. Those who align themselves with evil may access and use magic for destruction; however, they pay the dearest price of all by forfeiting their souls to Satan. In fact, it is not surprising that the most powerful of the wicked mages were once Insiders who cast their lot with the devil, having fallen prey to the human vices of greed and pride."

"So Excala are not infallible then?" Emma queried.

Andrew chuckled slightly. "How can we be? Are we not born of the flesh, the same as humans? We are bound by the limitations of this mortal vessel; illness, injury, and ultimately death can claim us at any time. We are also susceptible to emotional and character flaws, although our spirituality equips us to overcome these flaws. Still, the existence of the flesh is antithesis to perfection, for eventually it decays and putrefies."

Emma frowned. "But you have no flaws, Andrew. Not that I have detected anyway."

Andrew smiled ruefully and shook his head. "I must disagree with you, Emma, and so would a lot of others. When I interact with humans, my impatience and quick temper rise to the surface."

"You are never quick to anger," Emma protested.

"Not with you, my love. When we are together, there is no need for me to be anything other than loving and gentle. I have another side to me, which I shall presently explain in more detail. But first, what other questions have you?"

Emma thought for a moment. "When you intervene in a situation, do you have any sense of what a person might decide? I know you said that you have to consider all the possible responses."

"Yes, as a matter of fact, an excellent method of determining what choice may be favored over another is to simply listen to the person's thoughts."

Emma gasped. "You can't read thoughts as well?" she asked, aghast.

"Certainly. It is a highly useful skill when planning viable choices to present. It isn't always pleasant, for example, to hear the thoughts of humans, to know what petty vices, shameful secrets, and ill will they store in their hearts. One must develop the spiritual fortitude to avoid becoming disgusted or demoralized by these things."

"They can't all be negative," Emma objected. "Surely you encounter good decent people who wish only to live their lives as best they can."

Andrew eyed her indulgently. "Granted, there are some humans who strive to overcome the baser aspects of their nature. They are what I call In-Betweeners; neither Insiders nor Outsiders, but somewhere in the middle. Depending upon their choices in life, they may gravitate more towards one end of the spectrum than the other, but they have sustained a certain amount of spiritual damage, some of which may never be corrected."

Emma flushed, as an unwelcome thought struck her. "Are you able to read the thoughts of Excala as well as Outsiders?"

He smiled, amused by her slight indignation. "Yes, I have that ability, and while I might perform the occasional adjustment for you, it is not because I have listened to your thoughts. It's simply that I know you so well I understand what options are most palatable to you. However, I never influence your decisions, for I don't allow myself to manipulate the desires of Insiders or to eavesdrop upon their thoughts."

Emma was somewhat mollified. "I believe you, Andrew, for you are a man of honor; nevertheless, I should like your reassurance that you continue to respect my privacy."

"You have my word, Emma," Andrew replied, a gleam in his eye despite his solemn tone.

CHAPTER 47

Emma rose and began to pace, though not in agitation this time. Her pose was thoughtful, her stride measured as she walked about the drawing room.

"I wish to explain in more detail, so you will understand that my purpose to the Creator, while unique, doesn't render me any more special than other Excala, for we all have responsibilities that are important. It's merely that I was created to perform certain functions that no one else may." Andrew looked at her appraisingly. "Something troubles you." It was not a question.

Emma's brow furrowed. "Yes. I want you to explain why sometimes it is necessary for you to overrule free will. I find it distasteful that men are really no more than marionettes whose actions are controlled by a select few."

"Perhaps it would be easier and more palatable to regard humans as ignorant, willful children who require guidance and direction," Andrew answered. "Insiders play the role of parents. Children don't always choose what benefits them. They need discipline and teaching, skills their parents supply. And what parent wouldn't take whatever measure is necessary to protect his children from dangers against which they are ill-prepared to defend themselves?"

"I can agree with that, but children also need love, nurturing, and comfort if they are to develop to the best of their potential," Emma pointed out. "How is that provided?"

"An excellent question, Emma. You remember when I briefly described the various roles of Excala. Those aspects of human nature to which you refer are addressed by Excala who specialize in such skills—for example, the caregivers, the healers, and the teachers."

His expression became inscrutable. "I won't conceal from you my distaste for humans. I have duties to perform that necessitate my involvement with them, but I am continuously frustrated and intolerant with Outsiders. I don't understand basic human motivations and distorted perceptions, for I have had to remain untainted by those things in order to maintain my usefulness to the Creator.

"I am incapable of self-deception, nor do I need the petty artifices humans instinctively employ in their interactions with one another. I must retain my ability to clearly and objectively assess any situation. I can't afford to harbor illusions or moral dilemmas. My decisions are based upon what is required to achieve my goal. Emotional aspects of my character mustn't be allowed to supersede my loyalty to my pledge, no matter what the cost may be, to others and to myself.

"You, Emma, have a completely different purpose, however. It will soon become apparent just how different. Tell me, when was it that you decided upon nursing as a profession?"

Emma was slightly taken aback by the question, for it seemed unrelated to the topic of discussion. "Well, I suppose that I always had an interest in medicine as long as I can recall. As a child, I was teased by my brothers for wanting to play doctor roles in their games. They would laugh and create such a fuss, telling me that I could never be a doctor because I was a girl. Until I was old enough to know better, I would argue with them, telling them I would become a doctor when I was all grown up. When I finally realized the pervasiveness of society's limitations upon women and the discrepancy in educational opportunities between boys and girls, I began to think I could be a nurse instead."

Andrew nodded. "It is no coincidence that you chose nursing, Emma. You are a natural healer, not only in the physical sense but the spiritual as well, and you shall learn just how powerful this healing can be. What does physical health matter if one doesn't have spiritual well-being to match? Do you think it was mere chance that you were sent to nurse Henrietta when she experienced her health crisis?"

Emma's eyes widened. "Why, I don't know. I never really thought about it, but if I had, I suppose I might have surmised exactly that; coincidence, fate, sheer good fortune—not for Henrietta, but for myself. If she had not required a nurse, I should never have met you."

"She didn't require a nurse. She required *you*. If her ailment had been physical in nature, any qualified nurse would have sufficed. But we both know that Henrietta suffered from a spiritual malaise, and only a spiritual healer could have restored her well-being; in other words, Emma, only you."

He chuckled softly at her bemused expression. "The Lord works in mysterious ways," he quoted. "I do not believe in coincidence. Events occur for a purpose. Humans can't understand this concept, so they invented a term like 'coincidence' to explain it."

Emma was contemplative. "Then perhaps such a purpose has led me to Whitechapel," she reflected. "I have always believed there was a compelling reason for me to nurse there. It's as if somehow I recognized that I was needed."

"That was discernment guiding you, for what more appropriate place for you as a healer of souls than one which breeds despair, resentment, and other negative emotions that damage and eventually destroy spirituality? Your skills would be wasted tending those whose only ailment is physical. But for those whose ability to help themselves is severely impaired, or for Insiders who, like Henrietta, come under spiritual attack, the exceptional skills of a healer are required to nurture that ailing spirit back to health."

Emma nodded, a gleam of excitement in her eyes. "Yes, Andrew, that makes sense. Now I can understand the difference between the knowledge in my mind and the truth I carried in my heart, and it was my heart that directed me to Whitechapel. I never fully realized before today that I do offer spiritual and emotional comfort. In fact, one of my patients sends for me whenever she is melancholy. She says I am more help to her than her clergyman."

"That's not surprising," Andrew remarked. "You would be dismayed to discover how many religions are not the slightest bit spiritual. Your skills are one of the reasons destiny led you to Whitechapel. However, your value as a healer may not be the most important."

Emma frowned, perplexed. "To what other reason do you refer, Andrew?"

"The role you have played in the events that have menaced Whitechapel these last few months."

"Jack the Ripper," Emma murmured.

"Precisely." Andrew eyed her speculatively. "I told you there is no such thing as coincidence. The fact that you and I, both Excala, have a connection to Whitechapel at a time when a great evil threatens the populace is not mere chance. Were it not for your work among the destitute, I would have not been so quickly alerted to the presence of such a danger, and thus may have missed the opportunity to intervene at this early stage."

"Six deaths hardly constitute an early stage," Emma objected.

"Five murders, to be exact. The so-called 'double event' is a misnomer. Jack the Ripper only killed once that night, as was his custom. The first whore—"

"Liz Stride," Emma interjected.

"Is that the name? She was not a victim of the Ripper. Her throat was slashed by an ordinary human killer."

"You're saying that the Ripper isn't human?" A shiver coursed down Emma's spine.

"Not in the true sense. Like us, he was born of the flesh, but all resemblance to humanity ends there. He exists in this world for one reason only, to destroy man's equilibrium and claim souls for his master in Hell, and he is very adept, causing terror and despair; in essence, ripping the spirituality from them.

"The name by which he is known was not an idle choice, by any means. By using physical means and destroying the body, he has demonstrated his insight into the nature of humankind. A simpler form of attack would be less effective and would escape the awareness of the majority of men. In choosing to inflict physical suffering and death, he has exposed man's deepest fears. Death of the body remains the single and collective greatest fear of mankind, and the Ripper has taken great pains to demonstrate just how monstrously and horrifically death can claim one."

"But the letter he sent boasting about the double event?"

"Was not written by the Ripper, Emma. An entity of this magnitude wouldn't waste time taunting humans in this manner as a lesser demon might. No, whoever wrote those letters has fallen under the Ripper's influence. He may genuinely believe himself to be the Ripper, but in the end, he is only an unfortunate soul whose susceptibility to derangement has rendered him easy prey for the likes of the Ripper. However, it is of no consequence now. That individual is already doomed to Hell, though he still lives and breathes."

Emma stared penetratingly at him as a realization struck her. "John Dennys is the Ripper."

"Yes," Andrew nodded. "However, the Ripper's human disguise is irrelevant, for there is nothing human about him. A shell who walks and talks like a man, but who is pure evil; a soulless demon."

"A demon, yes," murmured Emma thoughtfully. "That's how I saw him in my dreams. A demon dressed in human garb, hideously grotesque with misshapen features."

"The reclamation allowed you to see him unmasked, in his true form. By revealing the information in a dream, it allowed you to accept the truth more readily. Haven't you wondered why those dreams of Jack the Ripper were so vivid and disturbing? Or that one of them presaged Mary Kelly, whose mutilated remains were discovered by you? Or after all this, do you still believe in coincidence?"

The color drained from Emma's face, and her expression was pained. When she spoke, it was but a whisper, dry as old bones. "I have never spoken of that particular dream, not even to you, Andrew."

"There is very little that remains hidden from me if I care

enough to explore the issue," he replied gently. "I know that the dream distressed you greatly at the time and that after Mary's murder, you were fraught with guilt. You allowed yourself to believe you might have saved Mary from her fate if only you'd shared your dream with her."

His usually intense look was softened by tenderness. "It was terrible to watch you suffer so, but there were no words of reassurance I could have uttered to you then. You lacked the spiritual insight to understand. But now the insight has been restored to you so that what I have to say shall make sense. Mary Kelly's destiny was never in your hands. Nothing short of direct intervention by the Creator could have prevented her demise."

"You could have," Emma whispered.

"The time for intervention wasn't at that point. However, the time now, fast approaches."

"Why now?" Emma's voice was harsh with anger. "Why couldn't you have foreseen these events and thus prevented the murders in the first place? Why did these poor women have to die?"

"Precisely because they were poor, wretched, and spiritually impoverished, the perfect magnets to lure evil to a place where it would be welcomed. You see, Emma, some locations, be they houses, graveyards, any physical site, can be receptive to evil influences. In fact, some serve as portals of entry for the manifestations of evil into the human world. Whitechapel is such a place. I am aware of the existence of all the portals and their exact locations in this world. I monitor them regularly for signs of activity. For a while now, I have sensed that something was going to transgress the portal barrier right here in Whitechapel. I just didn't know the exact nature or time of its appearance.

"Let me explain further about my pledge. My main focus in the human world concerns the balance between the forces of good and evil. To fully appreciate this, you must understand the fundamental concept of the universe.

"Our universe is based upon the existence of opposing forces. We see plenty of examples of this in nature and its elements.

However, these forces also affect the spiritual plane. The phenomenon of duality is so pervasive that most humans cease to be aware of it in their daily lives. The most crucial balance in the spiritual level is that between good and evil. Ages ago, many cultures espoused the belief that the birth of twins heralded danger for the particular village involved. Even today, in some cultures, we deem primitive, that belief remains widespread. It addresses the duality of man's nature, for the premise is that twins represent opposite forces, meaning that one twin is good while the other is evil. Since it is impossible to discern at birth which is which, both children are put to death. This practice is meant to ensure that the evil one doesn't reach maturity and bring disaster upon the village."

"But that's barbaric," cried Emma, appalled. "To kill innocent babes for the sake of an old wives' tale."

"It all speaks to what lengths man will go to protect himself against evil, which in turn indicates how much man fears evil. But evil is an intrinsic component of man's world, and the interdependence between good and evil is essential to the existence of both. My function is to ensure that equilibrium between these forces is preserved, for both of them are linked to spirituality.

"Think about this for a moment. If there was no evil and only good existed, how would men define 'good,' let alone possess a true understanding and appreciation of it? There wouldn't be an opposite with which to compare good, and there wouldn't be the opportunity for free will. One might argue that the world would be a more peaceful, contented place, but in spiritual terms, it would amount to a barren existence. How can spirituality develop fully in the absence of diversity and challenge?

"In a world devoid of evil, there wouldn't be a need for spirituality, but this is not a perfect world. It is a testing ground, a preparation for the soul so that it may successfully complete the transformation from the physical to the spiritual. In human terms, it is referred to as death, the cessation of physical existence which so many humans dread. Humans accessed this knowledge as long ago as the Excala did, but due to their flaws, they distorted and mystified the phenomenon so that death has become an event to fear rather than anticipate, to fight against rather than accept.

"For those who have been deceived into believing there is no existence beyond the physical, the prospect of death is, of course, terrifying. Even the idea of living may seem futile. If one is exclusively occupied in attaining material acquisitions, then one is bound to conclude at some point that life is a disappointment. One realizes that every aspect of life, all that one values, is rooted in the physical existence and thus shall disappear when one dies. My task might seem straightforward enough, except that free will complicates matters and constantly threatens the balance.

"The choices made by men, both individually and collectively, affect that balance. If, for instance, the balance were to be tipped in evil's favor and not promptly restored, its power would grow incrementally. Eventually, evil would grow to catastrophic, irreversible proportions, then darkness would envelop and destroy the human world amongst much terror and suffering. The prophecies of Armageddon are not mere tales told by old men to frighten children into submission. They are the warnings of the Creator, possibly the only words of His not misinterpreted or altered by man. It's imperative that men understand unequivocally what consequences would ensue if they forfeit their spirituality and reject their Maker. He has left no margin for doubt."

"But God is merciful and compassionate!" Emma protested.

"Yes. And because of His compassion, men have been given the opportunity to learn about spirituality through the intercessions of Excala. Evil manifests itself in a variety of magnitudes, some easier than others to combat. Most can be neutralized; however, there exists one evil that is so monstrously malignant that, if unchecked, it will cause cataclysmic damage, not only spiritually but on the physical plain as well. When the threat is this grave, then I alone have the ability and the authority to act. In spiritual terms, I am known as the 'Avenger,' the only being on any plane in existence with the power to destroy this type of evil."

"And Jack the Ripper is such an evil," Emma whispered from dry lips, already aware of the answer.

Andrew nodded. "A deadly evil, yes. Fortunately, I have the opportunity to intervene at this early stage."

Emma shook her head in disbelief. "A demon stalks the streets of Whitechapel, five women have been savagely butchered, yet you consider this an early stage."

"In comparison to the damage that could and may yet be inflicted, yes," he replied soberly. "The purpose of evil is the destruction of the spirit. Sometimes it is accomplished through physical terror like torture and death, but more often, the most crippling damage isn't immediately apparent, for the source is internal, not external. Five women have died, but how many more are terrified to venture out on the streets alone, even during daylight? How many of Whitechapel's citizens retire to bed each night praying that they won't have to scream and claw their way out of nightmares? Many have recently witnessed strange phenomena; shadows which move and follow them, whispers and rustling in the darkened corners of their rooms. Others have observed long dead relatives appearing to them in the middle of the night or materializing on a crowded street or deserted alley. How many are beginning to fear for their sanity? Spiritual attacks can occur in various ways and involve the physical and emotional aspects. This evil is adept at targeting weaknesses wherever they exist.

"Just consider the insane asylums of our world. How many are populated by those whose spirituality is intact? Whitechapel did not escape spiritually unscathed. Remember Sodom and Gomorrah, those biblical cities so vile and depraved that the Creator decreed they must be destroyed. Such an evil as Jack the Ripper was at work there as well. Believe me when I tell you that Whitechapel has the potential to make Sodom and Gomorrah look like a child's playground."

Emma bit her lip, troubled. "The magnitude of this is overwhelming. It's true the East End is under siege. I have heard vague tales of disturbing occurrences, but people are generally closed-mouthed and watchful of their neighbors, reticent to share their concerns. And this is in itself strange enough because most of the time everybody knows everybody else's business." She nodded thoughtfully. "You are quite right, Andrew. This evil has had an insidious effect on the populace, including, I daresay, the rest of London as well." She cast a speculative glance towards her lover. "Is my reclamation linked to Jack the Ripper then?"

"Undoubtedly, your close proximity, both in the physical and spiritual sense, to this great evil has influenced the process, perhaps triggering it to begin sooner than otherwise. Your spirituality came to your assistance by initiating a self-protective mechanism, mainly the reclamation. The reclamation is designed to occur when the Insider has reached a state of spiritual readiness.

"However, certain conditions may trigger a premature commencement of the process; a significant evil threat, a profound emotional or physical trauma, even an epiphany or positive revelatory experience; any stimulus, in fact, which resonates within and touches the soul. In your case, your involvement with the Whitechapel murders was sufficient to cause the reclamation. But if you had been alone without other Insiders present, the process might well have faltered for lack of guidance. In that instance, the extreme disruption and turmoil you experienced would have rendered you very susceptible to a spiritual attack. You would certainly have suffered severe damage."

"More severe than I have already incurred?" Emma asked with bitterness. "I have forever been scarred by my experiences of November 9. They can never be erased or forgotten."

"I know, my love," gently replied Andrew, wrapping her hand in his. "Though it may be difficult for you to believe, those events have strengthened your spirituality immeasurably. Harsh lessons, to be sure, but exceedingly valuable nevertheless."

Emma's laugh was short and mirthless. "I should have preferred much gentler lessons."

"That's why it is so important to take the time and thoroughly ponder all you have learned thus far. You should be cognizant not only of *what* you choose but *why*. The quest for spiritual growth is a challenge like no other. There are no shortcuts, no easier quick process except through the lessons presented."

Emma frowned. "I believe I understand, but I am puzzled by your allusion to my having a choice in the matter. If the reclamation, as you assert, occurs spontaneously, how can I stop it?"

"Free will is the answer, Emma. It's easier than you think. All that is required to terminate the reclamation is that you ignore your heart's counsel and return to your original ways. If you allow your mind to rule your heart, you would be surprised how quickly you would forget your spiritual identity and reclaim your dormant state. It has been achieved by Excala from time to time. However, I can't guarantee that forsaking your spirituality would make this life any easier or that you could ever find great happiness. For though you might forget your spiritual identity, you would always be aware of a great void within yourself, which would not lessen with time. You would remain restless, searching for a deeper meaning to life, almost catching a glimpse of it, yet ultimately failing to find it."

"That sounds like a horridly unappealing existence," Emma remarked with a distasteful expression.

"And it's the way a good portion of humans live their lives," Andrew responded. "Except they don't feel the void as acutely because it was never filled in the first place. One can't truly appreciate what one has never had. But an Insider has felt the spiritual energy inside, and once it departs, his soul yearns for it forever."

"But if I were to renounce the reclamation, what would become of us?" Sorrow stabbed her heart as he replied.

"There would be no us," Andrew said in a sober tone. "You could not be with me if you chose to become an Outsider."

"You mean you would just leave me?" Emma asked, hurt and incredulous.

He shook his head. "No, Emma. *You* would leave me. Without your spirituality to anchor you, you would quickly drift away. Our sacred connection would be severed. You would forget me. I would make sure of that by removing all memories of me from your mind. That way, it would be much easier for you, no thoughts of what might have been to torment you in the night. And I would continue on with my life and my pledge, but with an everlasting sorrow and an empty aching hole in my heart where you should be."

"Andrew, I couldn't bear to be parted from you!" Emma cried passionately.

"This is what you believe now." He smiled sadly. "But if you made that choice, it would be because you *could* bear it, and you wouldn't recall our relationship, so there would be no remorse or self-recrimination."

"But I can't imagine not having you in my life. You are a part of me," she protested.

"Nor is it something I wish to imagine," he said. "Nevertheless, you must be made aware of this possibility in order to exercise your free will. I shan't lie to you and promise that your life as an Excala will be filled exclusively with joy. New challenges, tests of spiritual fortitude will always be encountered. Some changes shall require an attitudinal adjustment on your part. For example, you shall lose the ability to deceive yourself. No longer will a shield of illusion protect you from the baser emotions of other humans, either. You shall see them as clearly as you see yourself. You will never view humans in the same way again."

"You mean I shall become frustrated and impatient, like you?"

With a slight smile, Andrew shook his head. "As a healer, you shall always possess a certain compassion for humans. However, it may be that you shall find yourself less kindly disposed towards them, less willing to overlook their shortcomings."

"What of the Ripper?" Emma inquired anxiously.

A gleam of anticipation shone in his eyes. "The Ripper shan't escape the Avenger's wrath."

"But in the meantime, he is still out there, looking for more victims."

"No, my dear. The women of Whitechapel have no more to fear from Jack the Ripper."

"You mean he shall simply stop killing?" Emma asked, clearly perplexed.

"No, I don't mean that. No further murders shall occur in Whitechapel, of that you can be sure."

Realization had dawned on Emma. "He's left Whitechapel. But where is he bound?"

"It shall be revealed, all in good time." Andrew rose from his seat. "Come, it will soon be luncheon. I have many issues that require my attention; therefore, I won't be joining you. I trust you shall amuse yourself for the remainder of the day. There is much for you to ponder." He took Emma's hand and helped her to her feet. "I shall see you at dinner then." He guided her towards the door.

"But I still have many questions," Emma protested.

"Good. Save them for when we speak next." He kissed her lips.

After the door closed behind him, Andrew shut his eyes, standing very still. He felt the forces gathering around him. His protectors, entities not belonging to man's world, were becoming increasingly restless, anxious for the confrontation with Jack the Ripper to begin.

Andrew opened his eyes; they had undergone a startling transformation. Gone was the gentle, reassuring expression he had worn with Emma. Instead, a hard and predatory look was reflected in his eyes, the flinty gray color enhancing the impression that here was a will of granite, harsh and unyielding. The sharpness of his gaze was like a scythe so that one could easily imagine him cutting down his enemies with one glance.

"Soon," he whispered to the protectors. "Very soon, the Ripper shall be within our grasp. In the meantime, you should all be doubly vigilant."

He gestured to one of the wraiths who materialized at his side. Now that Emma was aware of the reclamation, she was in even graver danger than before. The Ripper's minions would look upon her as easy prey. "Nihalaya." He turned toward the silent figure beside him. "You shall go to her to provide extra protection. Stay with her night and day." The wraith bowed and vanished. "The rest of you come along. We have much to do before nightfall."

CHAPTER 48

Night was fast approaching. Emma stared out the window of her bedroom, the familiar sick apprehension tingling through her body. Even before her grisly discovery of Mary Kelly's corpse, she had been plagued by nightmares, one of which had presaged the fate of the latest victim of Jack the Ripper. However, since the dreadful November ninth morning, her dreams had become even more vivid and disturbing.

When, drenched in terror-sweat, she eventually fought and clawed her way out of the nightmare scene, she was so limp with exhaustion and relief that she would fall into a profound slumber. Pounded by a persistent restlessness, she had great difficulty sitting still and focusing her thoughts during the day.

Intensely frustrated and prone to bouts of weeping, she longed for the strength she always thought she possessed, but about which she now had grave doubts. As night crept over the day, her anxiety grew until she dreaded the approach of sleep. She delayed retiring to bed as long as she could, but sleep inevitably captured her, and she'd awaken, cold and stiff-limbed, to discover that she had fallen asleep in her chair next to the window. Sometimes she felt like she was two conflicting persons; her waking self, rational, practical and in control, and her sleeping self, beset by creeping fear and a sense of helplessness.

Her stay at the Hewitt-Brown's during the tumultuous week since the incident had helped to steady her overwrought nerves. The love and concern that emanated from Andrew and his mother were vital to her healing process. It had taken a few days for her to reluctantly acknowledge the scope of her fear and to recognize that she was prey to an unshakeable feeling of impending doom. Along with most Londoners, she had been swept into a maelstrom of chaos, her inner turmoil reflected in the upheaval and distress of Whitechapel itself. In this new and strange existence, the setting of the sun heralded a profound disquiet, and fearful souls tarried behind locked doors in a futile attempt to keep out the night fog and its phantoms.

Even though Andrew had assured her last evening that Jack the Ripper's reign of terror was over, she still doubted that a creature so vile would simply stop killing of its own accord. She recognized that much of her agitation was caused by fear for Andrew as he prepared to confront this evil. Even though she believed his story of the Excala, namely because she couldn't fathom any other explanation for the bizarre occurrences of the last couple of months, it was difficult to envision her fiancé in this role of Avenger. What did the man she loved have in common with a fierce and relentless warrior intent on obliterating his enemy, even if it meant following him to the ends of the earth? In her assessment, Andrew Hewitt-Brown was the quintessential gentleman—well-bred, civilized, highly educated. She couldn't easily imagine him confronting a monster as dangerous and despicable as Jack the Ripper.

A sudden and welcome anger surged through her. How dare this fiend disrupt their lives in such a manner? She and Andrew should be planning their marriage, discussing a date for the nuptials, talking about their hopes and dreams for the future. Instead, the future was uncertain, a yawning chasm that, when one peered down into it, revealed only empty darkness, all the result of the intrusion of Jack the Ripper.

Emma turned from the window, emotions in turmoil. How she detested this uneasiness. She was not a weak individual, not given to fits of swooning or attacks of the vapors, as were some women. It was disconcerting that her self-assurance could be so swiftly compromised. Naturally, she understood that she had suffered a trauma, and it would take time for her to recover. Nevertheless, it was uncomfortable to have to endure the chaos of her emotions. She felt driven to resume her normal routine and reclaim her life before it slipped away from her completely.

Leaving her bedroom, she descended the stairs to the main floor. Henrietta was in the drawing room, a piece of embroidery in her lap. The fire crackling in the grate extended a welcoming warmth. Andrew was nowhere to be seen, as was his habit of late, and he was most likely absent from the house.

Henrietta looked up from her needlework and smiled as Emma entered the room. In the glow from the gas lamp suspended above her chair, the plains of Henrietta's face looked less chiseled, her features softened by the angle of the light. *How striking she still is,* Emma thought. She must have been quite a beauty, indeed.

She returned Henrietta's smile and sat beside her, retrieving her own embroidery from the basket on the floor. She stared unenthusiastically at the piece of cream colored linen, which was destined to be a pillowcase for one of her nieces. From the room at the end of the hall came the sound of male voices and lively conversation.

"George and his colleagues," Henrietta remarked, inclining her head in the direction of the voices. "No doubt debating the merits of Parliament's latest policies."

"Is Andrew amongst them?" Emma inquired.

"I should think not," Henrietta replied. "As far as I am aware, he hasn't been home all day. Sometimes, of course, he is in the house, and I don't know it. He comes and goes without one's awareness if he desires. It is entirely conceivable that he has been here all day, only we haven't seen him."

"No, I don't believe so." Emma shook her head. "I passed by his room on several occasions. When there was no answer to my knock, I opened the door and peeked inside. There was no one there."

"Ah, but did you know there is more than one room in this house that belongs to Andrew?"

Emma was puzzled. "I never really considered the matter."

"He has another room located in the basement," Henrietta

informed her. "It is to this chamber he retreats when he desires absolute solitude. I have learned that when Andrew locks himself in his subterranean refuge, he will accept no disruption or distraction."

"Is that where he practices his magic?"

"Indeed," responded Henrietta. "It's really quite a wondrous room, an environment he designed with the utmost attention for the purpose of working his most powerful magic, and where he receives visitors who might cause somewhat of, shall we say, a disturbance were they to be encountered elsewhere in the house." She saw Emma's shudder and hastily added, "They pose no threat to anyone, at least not while they are Andrew's guests. It's simply easier for all that they remain anonymous."

"Hidden, in other words," Emma said sharply. Privately, she wondered what manner of creature these visitors were that it was necessary to conceal them from view.

This time Henrietta sighed at Emma's tone. "Andrew is only taking into account our level of comfort, dear. I daresay you may not be ready to meet some of his associates."

"Doesn't it trouble you that these activities occur in your very home?" demanded Emma.

Henrietta's tone was tinged with irony. "I'm quite accustomed to these 'activities.' I have lived with Andrew's abilities since he was a small child. He always had playmates that weren't from this level of existence. Sometimes they were visible to me, other times not.

"From a very young age, he was surrounded by beings called 'protectors.' They were and still are fiercely loyal to Andrew and would interfere in any situation they perceive is harmful to him. Granted, there were a few, but only a very few, uncomfortable incidents involving the overzealous actions of the protectors, particularly before Andrew was old enough to adequately protect himself. But every now and then, something minor might occur to cause me slight uneasiness; certain unexplainable noises and strange manifestations. The rest of the family used to joke that our house in India was haunted. None of them realized it was their own brother who was responsible for the disturbances."

Emma shook her head, her expression a mix of admiration and distaste. "I can't understand how you cope with such equanimity in the face of such daunting phenomena. Weren't you at any time fearful of your son's ability?"

Henrietta contemplated this a moment. "No, I can't say that I was ever fearful of his abilities; apprehensive as to the ultimate purpose of them, perhaps, for I understood that it wasn't an idle coincidence that had bestowed these abilities upon him. Even before I was aware of the Excala, I knew that his magic was linked to some monumental destiny that he would be requested to fulfill, but never for one moment did I doubt my son or his intentions."

Her penetrating gray eyes fixed on Emma, who had the grace to blush and cast her glance downwards.

"You wish to know how I feel about Andrew's intention to confront Jack the Ripper," Henrietta stated flatly.

Emma looked up quickly, meeting the older woman's unwavering gaze. "How did you know?" she asked, surprised.

"Magic," Henrietta whispered, a grin spreading across her face in such an infectious manner that despite her serious demeanor, Emma was forced to smile in return. Henrietta's expression quickly turned sober, however. "I am concerned for my son every time he embarks upon a dangerous quest," she said quietly. "Yet, I never question his actions, for he answers not to me, but to the God who created him. Although I am his mother and the person other than you who is closest to him, he belongs not to me but to God, and every day I thank our Lord for granting me the joy and fulfillment I have experienced for being a part of Andrew's life. The legacy of the Excala is also very new to you, Emma. You haven't yet truly comprehended the depth and breadth of what this legacy consists of, for it is awe-inspiring, to say the least.

"In spiritual terms, Andrew is the most special of Excala, though I know he wouldn't describe himself as such. But it is a fact that without Andrew, other Insiders couldn't successfully fulfill their duties, for only one who is an Avenger has the supreme power to vanquish the vilest, most pernicious evil. The Avenger acts as God's warrior and defender of man on earth. Therefore his abilities are staggering, his magic phenomenal."

"But are there not other Avengers who function in a similar capacity to Andrew?" Emma asked, hopefully.

Henrietta shook her head, and a shadowed look crept into her eyes. "I don't know whether it is a blessing or a curse, but there is only one Andrew who exists throughout time. I believe this is because the Avenger is the right arm of God himself. Thus maximum power, the most any being can tolerate, is transferred from the Creator to the Avenger. Therefore, as God has only one right arm, so He has one Avenger. There is no need for more. The role was expressly created for Andrew; he is the sole being capable of functioning in it."

Emma clapped her hand over her mouth in distress as an appalling thought struck her. Her face slowly drained of color as she whispered, "That means he can never stop. If he is the only one, he won't ever give up being an Avenger, for as long as this world exists, the threat of evil is present, so Andrew must continue in his role until the end of the world." A sob of dismay escaped her.

"Yes and no, for it isn't that black and white," Henrietta cautioned. "If Andrew chooses to return time and again to this world, in theory, he accepts to continue his pledge. But due to the inherent risks of taking on human form, his chances for an optimum existence are no more favorable than those of others. If he should succumb to a childhood illness or be burdened with a physical or mental disorder, that particular life for him is completely wasted, for he would not be capable of fulfilling his pledge.

"Furthermore, should he survive to adulthood, a myriad of temptations and obstacles are thrown his way, more than any other Excala has to endure. The forces of evil stop at nothing in their relentless efforts to destroy him, for they fear the ultimate danger he presents to them. For instance, they tried several times to destroy him while he was still in my womb. Once by my contracting a virulent fever, which nearly induced my physician to deliver him prematurely, a delivery he would have never survived, and another time, I was pushed down a flight of stairs. Of course, I was alone at the time and was presumed to have slipped and fallen, but I felt the force that propelled me down the stairs as strongly as I have felt anything in my life.

"On another occasion, my food was poisoned. One of the kitchen servants was blamed and summarily arrested, but until my pregnancy with Andrew, this man had appeared completely normal. After the incident, when the authorities were taking him away, he ranted and slavered like a wild beast. It was obvious he had taken complete leave of his senses. But for the intervention of my personal physician, who was fortunately quite skilled in these matters, I should surely have perished, and Andrew with me."

Emma was shocked into silence by these revelations.

"Remember," Henrietta continued, "lest you think it is easy for Andrew to make his choices or that his life is without its own unique pain and sacrifice, even though he is a spiritual being, he is yet flesh and bone. He doesn't possess an immunity against evil, for he too must be permitted to exercise free will. As I am sure Andrew would have told you, Excala may succumb to temptation and forfeit their spirituality. They may also choose at any time to stay in the spiritual world and not return to man's world. Excala may decide upon this option and be released from their pledges and spend eternity in spiritual form."

Emma's short laugh was devoid of mirth. "You can't really believe that Andrew has a choice. You said it yourself. He is one of a kind. He serves a unique purpose; God's right arm, didn't you say? So tell me then, would God be so willing to give up His right arm? If He is concerned about the welfare of His children on Earth, would He leave them without an Avenger?"

Henrietta shrugged. "I can't presume to know the Creator's thoughts, although I am sure He knows exactly what He would do if such an occasion arose."

"So is it possible that Andrew might 'retire'?"

"Yes, of course, but if and when only he can answer." She leaned forward to clasp Emma's hand. "It is through acceptance that we find peace. I have accepted who and what Andrew is and, by extension, my own identity as an Excala. And dear child, if you intend to be Andrew's wife, you too must accept the legacy."

Emma's eyes clouded with pain. "And what of the future? If…." She corrected herself. "*When* Andrew has won his victory over the Ripper, what then? It isn't as though there won't be other evils for him to conquer, other dangers. Yet surely a man must think of his family before all else. I have pondered these questions repeatedly, and I am not convinced that I am strong enough to accept these conditions." Her bottom lip trembled, and tears sprang to her eyes.

"Emma, darling, listen to me." Henrietta clasped Emma's hand even tighter. "First of all, you must believe that Andrew's love for you is steadfast and absolute. He could not love you more than he does. Trust me, for I know my son's heart and the love of which he is capable.

"Secondly, you must begin to realize that your life has been altered by the knowledge of Excala. Whether or not you choose to embrace your legacy, your heart has been awakened, and this means that nothing in life will be the same for you. If you cast your fears aside and allow the reclamation to continue, I promise you it shan't be in vain. You will gain understanding and knowledge of the spiritual level, which will enable you to cope with matters you presently perceive as overwhelming.

"In a way, it is similar to a blind man gaining vision, or a crippled man learning to walk. When one is blind, one can not imagine what it is to see, but how different is reality from imagination! It is impossible for you to imagine becoming a more spiritual being, yet the very process of spiritual development makes one strong enough to handle the issues which arise."

Emma shook her head. "I don't know what to think," she said miserably. "And I abhor this feeling of confusion. But since that wretched Jack the Ripper came to Whitechapel, everything has been fouled by his loathsome presence. He is a blight, not only to the people of Whitechapel but to me personally. His intrusion into my life has placed in peril all which I cherish and hold sacred, and I despise him for that." She burst into tears, burying her head in her lap and pounding her clenched fists against the chair.

Henrietta waited in silence for the stifled sobs to subside. "It is a bitter lesson indeed," she said with compassion. "This evil you've encountered is so malignant that it strips you of your illusions and offers in return only doubt and fear. It introduces you to your special brand of torment and tries to ensure that you and that torment become lifelong companions. But believe this, Emma—you have the ability to resist this evil. Have faith in your love for Andrew and his for you. Be mindful that nothing can destroy your love except doubt."

Emma dabbed at her tear-soaked eyes. "I fear I am not strong enough to meet this challenge," she whispered. "I am so afraid, so uncertain of things I once took for granted. Andrew shall soon realize he has made a terrible mistake in bestowing his love upon me, for I am not worthy to fulfill his expectations." She looked ready to weep again.

"No, dear one. No mistake has been made," Henrietta reassured her. "You are Andrew's chosen love. The bond between you is unbreakable. He could no more stop loving you than you could vanquish your love for him."

"Body and soul. Blood and bone," Emma murmured to herself. Nevertheless, she continued to look troubled. "I don't wish to lose Andrew or feel that I am undeserving of his love, but it is so hard to live with the fear that accompanies the knowledge that evil as monstrous as Jack the Ripper abides in this world. How ironic it is that we counsel children not to fear the dark. We tell them there are no such creatures as monsters so that they may sleep securely. We tell them that even if there were monsters, we would protect our children from them. Why do we lie to those innocents? Darkness should be feared, for it is evil's hiding place. Monsters do indeed exist, and we are powerless to keep our children safe. It is only God's good grace which allows them to escape such peril as this."

"Men lie out of fear," said Henrietta. "As Excala, we teach our children how to recognize evil, but we do not teach them fear. Fear is strictly a human invention and has a detrimental effect on spiritual growth. Fear reflects the frailty of the human heart and has no place in the spiritual realm. Excala never distort the truth."

Emma sighed deeply. "I must excuse myself now, Henrietta." She suppressed a yawn before continuing. "I am very fatigued and must rest." She rose from her chair a little unsteadily. "Thank you for your thoughtful words. I know they are heartfelt."

The older woman rose also. She embraced Emma, kissing her lightly on her pale cheek. "Don't worry yourself, child. Just follow your heart's counsel."

Emma smiled wanly as she exited the room.

George Hewitt-Brown and his companions were still discoursing in animated fashion behind closed doors. Emma ascended the stairs slowly, as though the burden threatening to crush her was a physical one. She couldn't remember having felt so miserable. With fresh tears streaming down her face, she entered her bedroom. She flung herself onto her bed, head beginning to throb, but that ache was overshadowed by the pain that pierced her heart.

CHAPTER 49

Andrew hastily threw some clothes into a suitcase. He'd awakened only minutes earlier at the first light of day to the urgent conviction that his quarry had fled. Jack the Ripper was on the run; London no longer serving his purpose. Loathe to engage in a deadly confrontation with the Avenger, his only recourse was to outrun and try to outsmart his adversary; but where would he go? Andrew pondered this question as he finished packing.

The Ripper desired to put as much distance as possible between him and his pursuer. Therefore the continent was not an option. As well, it hadn't been that long since his activities in France. The authorities in Paris were still searching for an unidentified fugitive wanted for the barbaric murder of a young prostitute. With Europe out of the question, that left Africa, Asia, or America. Although he had no clear idea of the Ripper's destination, it wouldn't take much for his superb tracking skills to focus in on the murderer's whereabouts. It was sufficient at the present to know that the Ripper had vacated London in search of safer, if not greener pastures.

Grabbing his gray coat and hat, he hefted the suitcase and descended the stairs two at a time. He heard Alice humming to herself in the kitchen as the fragrant odor of baked bread greeted his nostrils. A pang of hunger stabbed his stomach, but he could spare no dallying for breakfast. He tried not to slam the front door as he exited the house.

A light rain was falling, the sky over the city a mottled gray. He quickly donned his coat, turning up his collar against the sharp wind. This November morning was a grim reminder that the cold breath of winter would soon blow over London. A hansom cab responded to his hail, and as he climbed inside, he issued the instructions, "To the docks, posthaste."

He arrived at the docks as the rain increased in intensity. The wind was stronger also, whipping the masts of the great ships to attention. The foul weather failed to disrupt business. Crews loaded cargo ships with wares destined for faraway countries, while crates of produce, spices, and tea were emptied from those ships arriving from distant lands. Dockworkers and laborers, oblivious to the damp, sweated and shouted to one another as they completed their tasks.

Andrew entered the old and cavernous Marine Building. Travelers aplenty milled about, some with sleepy children in tow. The adults, with their anxious, eager, or indifferent faces, tolerated the passage of time, ears attuned for the boarding signal for their respective ships. He surveyed the interior of the building, heedless of the human cargo surrounding him. The only thought in his mind was to locate the Ripper's trail.

His eyes finally rested upon an unassuming clerk who was perusing the ledger and appeared unengaged. Andrew strode purposefully toward the desk.

"Good morning, sir," the clerk greeted him in a soft spoken, mildly deferential manner. He was clean shaven with thinning hair and unremarkable features in a round face.

"Good morning," Andrew replied briskly. "I require information regarding the schedule of all ships which have sailed within the last forty-eight hours; destination Africa, Asia, and America."

The clerk blinked rapidly. "It may take some time to arrange a list for you. If you would care to take a seat—"

"I have no time for that, my good man," Andrew interrupted impatiently. "I simply wish you to recite the list of ships, departure times, and destinations. Only those which have sailed within the time I stipulated."

The clerk gaped, nonplussed. "You wish me to recite...." His voice trailed away when he noticed Andrew's intense and thunderous expression. Nervously clearing his throat, he began sifting through the voluminous ledger before him. "Let me see all the ships which have sailed to Asia, Africa and America. Ah." He licked his dry lips. "Would alphabetical order be acceptable?"

Andrew shrugged indifferently. "If you like, just get on with it, man."

The clerk cleared his throat once more and began to read from the list. Halfway through the Africa schedule, Andrew interrupted him. "No, no, no," he said impatiently. "Leave the rest of Africa and proceed to the next destination, if you please."

The clerk risked a brief glance at Andrew before returning his gaze to the ledger. "As you wish, sir. This is the timetable for ships sailing to America." When he reached the entry for the Anna-Lucia, departing November 18 destined for New York City, Andrew slapped his hand on the desk.

"Stop there," he commanded. "I require all the details concerning that ship; the exact time of departure and its expected arrival in New York Harbor. Furthermore, I wish to book passage to New York for myself."

"Which line, sir?" the clerk inquired, briskly transcribing the requested information onto a leaf of paper.

"Line? I care not which line. Whichever one departs the soonest for New York."

"And what date would you wish to sail?" the clerk asked in an efficient tone, some of his confidence returning with the familiar routine questions.

"Today," Andrew answered shortly.

The clerk stopped scribbling and stared mouth agape. "Today, sir? Well, I am afraid there are no accommodations available for passage today," he stammered. "There is a ship scheduled to leave in—let me see…." He scanned the ledger in his most professional manner. "Ah, here we are. Yes, a New York bound steamship sails at the beginning of next week." He smiled tentatively.

Andrew's gaze narrowed, causing the clerk's smile to falter. An intensity emanated from those eyes, which produced a profound unease in the clerk. An image of a poisonous snake, a pit viper, poised to strike, intruded sharply into his mind. "If you would be so kind as to check your passenger list for today's departure," Andrew said quietly.

The clerk licked his lips. "But sir, I know for a fact that the ship sailing today for New York is completely booked. I personally recorded the last reservation yesterday; an elderly gentleman."

"Check your list again." Andrew leaned closer to the desk, and the clerk flinched involuntarily at the close proximity. If ice were gray, it would be the color of Andrew's eyes, so frosty was their expression. All protest died on the clerk's lips.

"As you wish, sir," the clerk replied, fighting the rising panic in the pit of his stomach.

How would this man react when he was told unequivocally that there was no room for him? He flipped through several pages of the ledger before reaching the information that he sought. He ran a steady finger along the numerous entries, faltering just once. He bent his head to peer more closely at the page. A flush crept into his cheeks, and he looked up at Andrew, a light sheen of perspiration glittering across his forehead.

"It appears that there has been a last minute cancellation," he said in a strained voice. "There is one passage available today, sir."

Andrew nodded. "Splendid. I shall require a first-class accommodation."

"Of course, sir," the clerk replied meekly.

After the transaction was completed, he stood and watched Andrew's retreating back. He knew beyond a shadow of a doubt that when he left the building yesterday, all the passages on that ship had been filled, and since he had been the first clerk on duty this morning, he would naturally have handled any cancellations. How then was it that this space had mysteriously appeared just as this Mr. Hewitt-Brown had made his request?

The clerk shook his head. He didn't understand the events which had just occurred, but he knew in his core that something unnatural had taken place. It left him feeling strangely unsettled, as did the expression in Andrew's eyes. An even more disturbing thought struck him, and he shuddered. Just what had happened to the elderly man who was so looking forward to seeing his granddaughter in New York?

Four hours later, Andrew boarded the ship destined for New York. The rain had stopped, but the sky still looked threatening. In the relative quiet of his cabin, he arranged his belongings. Willing himself to be patient, he reminded himself that Jack the Ripper had no more than forty-eight hours' head start.

Given Andrew's tracking expertise, it would take little time for him to pick up his enemy's trail once in New York. The Ripper wished to avoid detection; therefore, he would endeavor to remain as unobtrusive as possible. He would camouflage himself, try to blend in with the masses and wrap himself in a cloak of anonymity. In the past, such means had proved highly successful. Would he practice medicine again? Possibly. But perhaps he would immerse himself in a new identity and a new trade. All options were still open to him as the authorities in London had failed to discover anything about him. Nevertheless, some instinct told Andrew that his enemy was determined to shed the identity of John Dennys, physician, and adopt a completely different persona and profession.

A fiery vengeance flared up in Andrew's heart as he silently repeated his pledge to destroy this evil. It would be a complicated and perilous endeavor, for the entity which occupied the body of John Dennys was a demon of the highest order, as clever as it was deadly. As such, it possessed a unique ability for self-preservation; namely the transference of its energy, its essence between human beings. The skill of changing physical identities rendered the demon's destruction a considerable challenge, one which he hadn't mentioned to Emma for fear of overburdening her with anxiety.

So powerful a demon could sustain its existence under certain conditions beyond the expiration of its host body. If, in the final moments before the demise of John Dennys, the demon were to locate a substitute body to inhabit, it would continue its existence in this world to propagate mayhem and terror.

High order or greater demons posed a significant threat of harm or death not only to the hosts they occupied but to others within their environment. These possessions occurred more rarely due to the lack of suitable hosts. A human had to be mentally strong enough to withstand occupation by so powerful a force and, at the same time, be lacking in spiritual awareness and receptive to corruption.

Andrew knew that if the Ripper was unable to escape or destroy him, the demon would not hesitate to employ such a method of self-preservation. However, when initiated as an act of desperation, the process was a considerable risk to the entity itself. Specific essential factors had to be present for the energy transfer to succeed, and under pursuit, those factors could not be guaranteed.

The greatest acquisition host-wise, and easier to obtain than the child, was the unborn infant in its mother's womb. But for that possession to occur, the mother must be the spiritual port of entry, a woman whose selfishness and lack of empathy would impair her ability to protect the child she carried. These women were not difficult to find, for many were prey to unwanted pregnancies, perhaps even a botched abortion attempt.

Andrew was aware that John Dennys had been the unfortunate product of a failed abortion. The truth was that he had been doomed from the start. Recipient of a deep and destructive hatred while still in his mother's womb, unloved, he was born into cruelty and rejection, thus affording a perfect vessel for the powerful demon who awaited such an event.

The demon's capacity to generate evil was so great because it was an innate part of John Dennys. As the child grew to adulthood, the demon was within him, testing and perfecting its skills. Human and demon were locked in a symbiotic relationship, each unable to exist without the other.

In an adult or older child host, the energy transference process was fraught with danger even under optimum conditions. Timing was of the utmost importance. There was no margin for miscalculation. The energy must exit the host body in the very last moments of life just before energy left the body, or the demon perished along with its host, trapped by the symbiotic bond it had failed to sever.

Andrew was determined to circumvent the Ripper demon's attempts to possess another host. That meant isolating the demon, a difficult task. Yet unless he assured that he was alone with John Dennys, the demon stood a reasonable chance of escape. This was a risk the Avenger didn't care to consider.

Furthermore, the encounter would be a struggle to the death. If he succeeded in killing the Ripper while the demon resided within, its human form would be condemned to return to its spiritual domain. Once deprived of corporeal form and back in Satan's realm, it could never again return to the world of man. Nor was it of any more use to its evil master, so massive was the damage it had sustained.

As with good, so it is with evil. The same rules, with few exceptions, apply to both. Thus, to enter man's world, a demon, like an Excala, was born of the flesh and needed to develop as any human from infancy. The exception was that those belonging to the lesser demon category weren't required to undergo this process. Their possessions of humans were often short-lived, especially if the host was seriously damaged by the demon's occupation of him. Therefore, these demons tended to possess multiple hosts rather than one and to discard them when the humans became too impaired to function reliably.

The greater demons, on the other hand, went through the same birth process as their counterparts, the Excala. But once a demon of this magnitude completed the initial birth of entry into man's world, it could avoid repeating the process by choosing to possess an alternate host. This was another fundamental difference between demon and Excala, for an Excala could not trade hosts.

The entity in John Dennys had a power of great magnitude and had used its cunning to hone its diabolical skills to near perfection. The transformation from John Dennys to Jack the

Ripper was merely the final step in a process which began before birth. John Dennys, the man, had never in any true sense of the word existed. He hadn't developed any of the qualities that define humans as a species unique from others. He simply adopted the pretense of humanity, mask firmly in place, moving through the various stages of life. But it was a well executed façade, the only essence in John Dennys being pure, undiluted evil.

His sole reason for existence was to cause as much suffering and destruction of the human spirit as his abilities permitted. Though this goal was often achieved through physical pain, even death, it was because these methods were highly effective in producing the agonizing torments of the soul, which precipitated severe spiritual damage or total spiritual disintegration. Most humans were acutely vulnerable to physical torture and deprivation. Therefore the Ripper cleverly employed these tools against them.

Unlike humans, who might derive sadistic pleasure from such acts, there was no similar gratification for Jack the Ripper. His purpose was to achieve glory and victory for his dark master. The corrosive pernicious evil within him, which defined him, could not be eradicated by manmade weapons. Only an Avenger could defeat such monumental wickedness.

Andrew possessed an innate understanding of this entity, for he had encountered its similar incarnations in previous lifetimes. Whatever the final outcome, their battles proved fierce and exhausting, and ended in the annihilation of one or both. He expected nothing to be different this time.

CHAPTER 50

Deep in thought, he shook his head. Sometimes he felt his lifetimes blur into one continuous life, watercolor images bleeding into one another so that eventually none was distinguishable from the others. Often he was forced to remind himself of his present circumstances, reorient himself to time and place. His physical appearance, with minor alternations such as changes in the color of eyes and hair, remained intact. However, once in a while, when he was feeling particularly homesick for his spiritual realm, he referred to himself by his original name, the spiritual name that had been his in the kingdom of Excala.

Now, as the ship slowly eased away from the dock, he gazed out of the porthole of his cabin. Out of habit, he looked first to the sky and clouds to see if any messages were there. Air and water messages seemed to enjoy a particular affinity to him in this life. The afternoon sky was a flat cast-iron gray, the clouds dark and taciturn. He scanned the cosmos quickly, seeing nothing of significance.

He sighed and rubbed his eyes, suddenly aware of a bone-weary fatigue. The limitations of the human body were a constant source of tribulation, a bane at which he rebelled in every lifetime. He was in conflict with his physical self, the demands of the body clashing with the desires of the spirit. For instance, right at the moment, his body was telling him it needed rest, urging him to get some sleep, but this nagging drain on his energy only raised his ire, causing him to be even more determined to resist its demand. Eventually, his body would simply collapse of exhaustion, as it had on many occasions. Often he went days on end without sleep until at last he was dragged, protesting, into the realm of sleep.

This time, however, even though his body might be at rest, he would continue to employ his spiritual energy to perform the sacred rituals necessary to prepare him for the confrontation with evil. It was essential that he purge his mind of any thoughts that might distract him, especially those with negative connotations.

The greatest challenge right now was to avoid worrying about Emma. He knew he had done all he could to keep her safe and protected. His trusted servant, Nihalaya, would destroy any harm that threatened her. Nevertheless, the human part of him tried to get him to think about all the happiness he was potentially risking in this upcoming encounter with Jack the Ripper. If he perished during the battle, he knew he wouldn't die alone. He would make sure the demon returned to its fiery domain. However, that would be of small consolation if he lost the opportunity to live out his earthly life with Emma. For not only would he be deprived of that joy, Emma too would suffer, not only emotionally in grieving the death of her lover, but more importantly, on a spiritual level.

Without Andrew to guide her, she would never fulfill her true spiritual potential. Henrietta could assist her to a certain extent, but beyond her limitations, there was no one who could fill the gap. He'd lived through too many lifetimes to be tempted into giving up the chase and returning to a life with his beloved. He would not abandon his pledge no matter the cost to himself and ultimately to Emma.

Nevertheless, his multiple lifetimes never rendered these decisions any easier. The human part of him had to endure the sorrow, sometimes even agony, which accompanied such choices. He had come to understand that knowing and doing what was right to maintain his spiritual integrity did nothing to alleviate the great sorrow and heaviness of heart which accompanied such decisions.

Andrew cursed in frustration. This was his burden to bear and had been repeated in every lifetime thus far. Sacrifice was always demanded of him, and knowing it was inevitable, in a sense waiting for it to present itself, induced a special brand of pain like no other he had endured.

Sometimes he felt like he was torn in two, the internal pressure so intense that it would surely blow him asunder. At these times, he knew he must be especially vigilant, for the forces of evil were all too cognizant of his human frailties and would exploit them mercilessly.

Also, when he was physically as well as emotionally exhausted, temptation was harder to resist. More energy output on his part was necessary to repel the distractions. Sensing this, the forces of evil would strengthen their assault, drawn to his weakness as sharks drawn to blood. Fortunately, his protectors were all on alert for evil attacks, and they provided additional fortitude to help him to recognize and tend to his physical needs before his body rebelled and shut down.

If Andrew had one Achilles' heel, it was undoubtedly his lack of attention to his physical self. As the Avenger, his single-minded focus, intensity, and the ability to ignore physical and emotional intrusions were essential to his purpose and his survival. He would make any sacrifice required in order to honor his pledge, including sleep deprivation, starvation, physical illness or injury, or punishing his body to its limit, often beyond that which an ordinary human could endure.

There was a price to be paid for such intensity, however. The human body was not designed to contain this phenomenal amount of spiritual energy. Without his protectors to remind him to attend to his physical needs, Andrew would have burnt out his body long ago. This premature demise of the physical self had occurred with regularity in his first two lifetimes before the Creator compensated for his Avenger's eccentricity by dispatching entities to watch over his trusted servant.

Even so, Andrew observed that he never lived to a ripe old age. Some misadventure invariably conquered his human resistance, often when he reached the so-called prime of life, or he would fall prey to some pestilence which decimated the population. He had succumbed to the Plague or the Black Death in several of his lives.

Magic and materialism were like oil and water; they did not mix. Magical energy was not meant to be confined or restricted, and certainly not meant for a vessel as frail as the human body. A perpetual discord existed between the physical and the spiritual. Most humans who attempted to combine the two destroyed themselves in the process. The terrible fiery energy in magic consumed them, their spirituality corrupted as their bodies were broken and battered. Andrew and the few remaining Excala who managed this precarious balance were aware that time would eventually defeat them. A day would arrive when their bodies no longer responded to commands, and their human lives would end.

Andrew turned away from the portal and lay down on the narrow cot, which served as his bed. It was time to banish all extraneous thought and prepare for the journey ahead. He soon entered a trance state while his body slumbered, allowing his spirit to drift where it would.

***

Far out at sea on a similar steamship bound for America, the demon within John Dennys became aware of another presence in the ether around him. It instantly recognized the familiar and detested essence of the Avenger. He had known it would not take long for his enemy to follow his tracks. The snarl on the Ripper's face turned to a malignant smile as he thought what he would do to Emma Hollander after he destroyed the loathsome Avenger.

That in and of itself would be worth returning to England to accomplish, just when the traumatized citizens of Whitechapel had begun to breathe easier once again, believing the nightmare of Jack the Ripper was behind them. For the demon realized and gloated in the fact that in its present incarnation as Jack the Ripper, it possessed abilities that rendered it more dangerous and deadlier than ever before. Although the Ripper had caused the death of only a handful of disease-ridden prostitutes in London, he'd succeeded in terrorizing an entire nation, even intruding into the royal chambers of England's venerable ruler.

In an era and location where human life was cheap indeed, the heinous crimes of Jack the Ripper had shocked people out of their torpor. He'd forced them to recognize on a subconscious level that a vast difference existed between the petty evil of men and the darkly abominable evil that emanates from the depths of Hell.

It was no coincidence that the famed writer, Jack London, would refer to Whitechapel as the abyss, for he was discerning enough to recognize that a sinister stain was engrained in the heart of Whitechapel, an imprint of evil that would never be eradicated. Tainted forever by Jack the Ripper, a monster whose spectre would continue to haunt the fog-shrouded streets, Whitechapel was heir to a legacy of terror that history would never forget.

CHAPTER 51

"Miss Emma, Miss Emma!"

"I am in the library, Alice," Emma called in reply.

The door to the library opened, and the housekeeper bustled in. The room felt cheerful thanks to the fire Emma had lit to dispel the remnant of the bitterly damp November morning.

"This just arrived for you, miss," Alice announced, presenting her with a letter.

Emma, sitting at the polished mahogany desk, reached for the correspondence. She intuited immediately that it must be from Andrew. She looked up to see the housekeeper watching her intently. "Thank you, Alice," she said, her tone even.

After the housekeeper's departure, Emma stared thoughtfully at the envelope as though she could decipher the contents without actually reading it. She closed her eyes, briefly aware of a knot of tension in her stomach. *I know it is not good news*, she thought grimly. Taking a deep breath, she tore open the envelope and scanned the letter in her lover's elegant script.

My dearest Emma,

By the time you receive this correspondence, I shall already be aboard a steamship bound for America. I regret that my departure is so precipitous, for I greatly desire to embrace you and whisper my love.

Alas, my darling, circumstances have otherwise dictated. Remember, we foresaw that this journey would be necessary. It is imperative that I not allow our foe to put too great a distance between himself and me. You may breathe easier to know that London shall be free of further activities. I shall arrive in New York in seven days hence, but I cannot say where else the journey may lead.

I trust that you carry me in your heart as I carry you in mine. I shall write again as soon as opportunity permits.

Yours for eternity,

Andrew

Tears sprang to Emma's eyes as she finished reading. The fear haunting her since Mary Kelly's murder had at last reached full fruition. In vain, she had hoped that the Ripper might just disappear into anonymity, leaving Andrew content to let the matter rest and to start planning their life together. The thought of risking his life in pursuit of this fiend was more than she could bear. In her heart of hearts, she knew that if Andrew was to perish at the hands of the Ripper, she would not tolerate life without him. If what he told her about the spirit realm was accurate, she would rather join him there than endure a meaningless existence in this world.

Despite her increasing understanding of the Excala, her lover's pledge was not any easier to accept. Knowledge of the mind was vastly different than that of the heart. As she listened to and felt more with her heart, Emma was discovering that it was more difficult to believe the deceptions the mind presented. The heart was steadfast, dismissing the convoluted machinations of the intellect, exposing them for the pathetic lies they were. *I should be comforted being less vulnerable to lies and self-delusions,* she thought forlornly. Yet, the truth did not of necessity bring comfort.

A quiet knock on the door interrupted her musings. Henrietta's voice, slightly muffled through the heavy oak door, said, "Emma dear, luncheon is ready. I told Alice that I would come and fetch you."

Emma cleared her throat. "Thank you, Henrietta. I shall just complete this piece of correspondence before joining you shortly."

"Very well, dear." Henrietta's footsteps faded towards the dining room.

Emma's hand shook as the anger surged inside her. Ever since her discovery of Mary Kelly's corpse, and despite the terror and anguish which beset her, she was prone to episodes of almost uncontrollable anger. Without warning, this terrible rage would smite her, disrupting whatever task upon which her attention was focused. It was an anger fueled by fear and helplessness, blazing to a conflagration of hatred towards the one who had caused her to feel such anguish. She never imagined herself capable of a hatred so fierce, so consuming. Sometimes she wished she were the one to confront Jack the Ripper face to face. She suspected that after all the horror she'd endured, her fear would be consumed by her hatred of this monster, who had nearly succeeded in destroying her, and who continued to threaten her future happiness. As absurd as it sounded, she longed to accompany Andrew so that when the day of reckoning arrived, she too could partake in the battle against the loathsome creature.

As the familiar waves of rage swelled inside her, Emma forced herself to draw in several deep, slow breaths. She was determined to consign the anger back to where it belonged, to a small black box tucked into a corner of her heart. As though to hide it from prying eyes, she jealously guarded her anger. Only she could possess the key to unlock that box, and within this receptacle, her anger was permitted to fester.

By the time she reached the dining room, her usual demeanor was carefully in place. Her facial muscles were flexed and ready to smile. The anger had reluctantly returned to its cage, tamed for the moment, but capable of unleashing its ferocity at any time.

Emma entered the room, her comportment rigid. Henrietta looked at her appraisingly. It was an annoying habit, Emma decided, grating on her nerves. Henrietta seemed perpetually to evaluate one, trying to ascertain one's thoughts. *It is not my mind that should concern you*, Emma thought, *but the turmoil which lives in my heart*. She smiled thinly, slipping into a seat across the table from her hostess.

"Have you had a productive morning? Henrietta enquired.

"Yes, thank you," Emma responded.

Henrietta nodded. She watched as Alice ladled steaming soup into their bowls. She sniffed the fragrant aroma then smiled at the housekeeper. "It smells delicious, Alice."

The housekeeper beamed and returned to the kitchen with a light step.

"We are to have the leftover mutton pie. With only the two of us sitting down to luncheon, it seems pointless to serve anything elaborate. George is dining with his colleagues, no doubt over-indulging in the rich food his club has to offer."

"Yes, that is sensible," Emma concurred. She looked keenly at the older woman before reaching for her water glass. She noted Henrietta's omission of her son and wondered if she was aware of Andrew's departure for America.

"You must try the soup, Emma. It's Alice's special dish. Braised pheasant."

Emma obediently raised a spoonful of the aromatic liquid to her lips. The chunky pieces of pheasant were deliciously sweet, the broth surprisingly spicy. Her lips and tongue tingled pleasantly.

"It's superb," she murmured.

Henrietta smiled. "Alice's special ingredient is curry, which gives it that delightful spicy flavor, a remnant from our days in India. I must confess that I became quite fond of the spices and herbs used in Indian cooking, and of course, the children fancy it as well. Amanda even persuaded Alice to give her cook the recipe so that her family could enjoy it at home as well as here."

Emma listened distractedly, preoccupied with thoughts of Andrew.

"Something troubling you, dear?" Henrietta asked gently.

Emma's gaze was steady. "I think you know the answer to that."

Henrietta nodded. "Yes, I believe I do. It concerns that dreadful Jack the Ripper, does it not?"

Emma sighed heavily. "It does indeed. I just received a message from Andrew. He set sail this morning bound for America. But then you were aware of that, weren't you? Did he discuss it with you beforehand?" She was unable to suppress the bitter inflection to her tone.

Henrietta's expression registered the emotion. "I awakened early today and heard Andrew moving about downstairs. He sounded as though in a great hurry. I watched through my bedroom window as the noise of an approaching hansom caught my attention. Andrew boarded the cab and departed. I was not privy to his destination, nor was I aware of the need for so hasty a departure without so much as a farewell gesture." Her eyes were troubled.

"Apparently, Jack the Ripper has fled to America," Emma said quietly.

It was Henrietta's turn to sigh. She pushed her half-filled soup bowl aside. "Well, he did warn us that this might happen. Nevertheless, it is disconcerting."

Emma stared down at her soup bowl and did not respond.

Henrietta reached across the table and touched Emma's hand. "On a more positive note, at last, London is rid of this vile murderer."

"Yes, and if Andrew should lose his life battling with that fiend, no one in this wretched city would be any the wiser," Emma replied bitterly.

Henrietta's smile was tinged with sorrow. "Do not think yourself alone in these tribulations, my dear. I, too, have struggled with fear, resentment, and, yes, even anger. The life of an Excala is not easy to accept. It can demand of us the sacrifice of desires in order to fulfill our spiritual duties. I found the only way to banish anger and other negative emotions is to understand that one may exercise free will and choice.

"For example, Emma, you may reject the life of an Excala. Nothing holds you to it; nothing binds you to Andrew but your desire. Your life is yours to live as you wish, but you must choose to take control of your destiny. I realize that since that horrible November day, your beliefs and values have been sorely tested. Confusion and betrayal are your constant companions. Your security and future, your ideals, have all been savagely threatened." Henrietta's eyes, so like those of her son, looked deeply into Emma's eyes. "You may question if you possess the strength of character, the spiritual maturity to embrace life as an Excala. But I know, as does Andrew, that you are Excala. You belong to us and with us. However, it is your choice whether you wish to live as one of us."

Emma acknowledged the earnestness of the older woman's expression. "I have heard that adversity makes one strong," she said. "If that is true, then I should not feel helpless and weak as I do." She shook her head, puzzlement and sadness evident. "You speak so loftily of free choice, yet I feel as if choice has been removed from me. You say nothing binds me to Andrew, yet he has told me that we are part of one another." Her tone became more passionate. "And I believe him. I know his words are true. I cannot simply walk away from him, for I am a prisoner of my heart, and my love will not permit me to abandon him."

Henrietta patted her hand. "Then I believe you have made your choice," she said gently.

Emma lowered her gaze. Tears slipped from her eyes and cascaded heedlessly down her face, softly landing in the liquid in the bowl before her.

CHAPTER 52

Andrew stood on the deck of the ship, his gaze intent upon the approaching shoreline. Other passengers crowded the deck, chattering in excited tones, eagerly pointing at the Statue of Liberty looming majestically in front of them. The statue was indeed an impressive sight, in that it symbolized the noble aspirations and lofty ideals revered by men.

It was an irony Andrew sardonically mused. He thought it an interesting quirk of humans, this propensity to erect monuments that embodied the highest of human values. It was as if the monuments themselves safeguarded these values, thus allowing men to abdicate their responsibility for upholding such virtues.

A small boy brushed impatiently against Andrew, trying in vain to catch a glimpse of the famous statue. Finding he was no match for the sheer volume of adults pressing him on all sides, he stamped his foot in frustration. Andrew looked down upon a head of tousled red curls. A small face spotted with freckles and sporting a slightly indignant expression peered up at him.

Andrew smiled at the boy's perturbation and bending in one smooth motion, lifted the child up to his shoulders. The boy, no more than six or seven years of age, hooted in delight as he caught sight of the magnificent lady in New York Harbor.

"It's true, it's a whopping big statue!" he exclaimed.

"The biggest one I've ever seen," Andrew said.

"Me too," the child agreed. "How come we don't have one in England?"

Andrew chuckled. "I daresay because it was a gift to the Americans, given them by the French two years ago."

The boy pouted. "And why did not the French give us one?"

"Because the French don't like us as well as they like the Americans."

The boy accepted this answer and turned his gaze back to the statue. After a few moments, he leaned down and said, close to Andrew's ear, "This is my first trip to America."

"Is it?" Andrew responded. "I trust you shall have an enjoyable visit. New York is an impressive city."

The boy nodded. "I shall visit with my father. He's promised to take me to a zoo, where they keep all sorts of wild animals with sharp teeth and claws."

"Is that so?" Andrew inquired in mock surprise. "I daresay that would be quite an adventure."

The child nodded happily. "Yes, I am looking forward to it."

"With whom are you traveling, lad?"

The boy wrinkled his little nose in distaste. "Uncle Samuel. He is frightfully stuffy and has been known to never have any fun."

Andrew laughed again. "Yes, uncles can be that way. But your father, I gather, is not as disapproving of frivolity."

The boy's expression was serious. "And for that, sir, I am truly grateful."

Just then, Andrew became aware of a man making his way through the crowd, obviously searching for someone.

"Matthew, Matthew," the man called, a deep frown creasing his brow.

The boy turned around at the sound of the familiar voice. "Over here, uncle, over here." He waved both his arms atop his perch on Andrew's shoulders.

The man started in surprise as he caught sight of his nephew and strolled purposefully towards them. Andrew noted the grim expression which, combined with the dark heavy eyebrows and bristling black beard, lent him a stern and dour demeanor. He extended a short, thick fingered hand to Andrew.

"Samuel Thompson, sir. I trust my nephew has not caused you undue inconvenience."

Andrew smiled easily as he shook the other's hand. "Indeed, on the contrary, Mr. Thompson, young Matthew, has been a delight. I was only too pleased to assist him in his first viewing of the statue in the harbor."

"Oh, uncle, it is the biggest statue in the whole world!" the boy declared enthusiastically.

Samuel Thompson appeared unmoved by his nephew's excitement. His expression grew even sterner, and his tone was steely as he said, "I warned you explicitly not to wander from my side. You have completely disobeyed my command."

The boy meekly protested. "But uncle, I so wanted to see the statue, and I could not from where we stood."

"And so you pestered this fine gentleman, Mr. uh…." He turned inquiringly to Andrew.

"Thorpe, Jeremy Thorpe," Andrew replied.

"Quite, Mr. Thorpe," Thompson repeated.

"I assure you, Mr. Thompson," Andrew interjected more firmly this time. "Matthew has been most polite. Far from engaging me, it was I who approached him to offer my assistance. The boy bears no fault at all."

Thompson was somewhat appeased. "Very well, if you say so, Mr. Thorpe." He gestured for his nephew to climb down. "Come along, child. You should be very grateful for Mr. Thorpe's intercession, for were it not for him, you would retire to bed this evening with an empty stomach."

The boy, with Andrew's help, slid to the ground. Without thinking, the child automatically slipped his hand into Andrew's reassuring grip. Andrew looked into the boy's blue eyes, seeing the helpless expression of a small animal caught in a trap. A strong sense of fear and loneliness emanated from him. He squeezed the boy's hand.

"Remember, Matthew," he said, his gaze never wavering from the child's eyes. "You shall see your father very shortly, and the two of you shall enjoy a wonderful time together." He bent closer and whispered in the boy's ear, "Do not despair, lad. You shall see your wish of living with your father soon fulfilled."

The boy smiled tentatively up at him, then let go of Andrew's grasp and walked obediently over to join his uncle.

Thompson watched the exchange with a scowl. Sensing that some secret communication had passed between the two, knowing somehow that he would never be privy to it, with a peremptory nod towards Andrew, he grabbed the boy's hand and led him away. The boy looked back at Andrew once and waved.

The child turned once more to face forward, led none too gently by his uncle's unyielding grip. He looked at his small hand completely enveloped in the meaty fist and marveled how different it felt from the stranger's grasp. Mr. Thorpe had held his opposite hand. That hand now tingled with a pleasant warmth that traveled slowly up his arm and soon flowed gently throughout his entire body, filling the boy with a strength and peace that would calm his fears and render him impervious to his uncle's callous indifference, at least for a time. The boy thought of those last words the stranger had uttered, and he smiled to himself, a smile all the more delightful because it was a secret of his very own.

CHAPTER 53

The ship glided gracefully into port as the sun set. The sky was alive with a kaleidoscope of colors; pink and red streaks a breathtaking contrast to the burnished copper of the sun. Andrew, though aware of the brilliant display above, stared instead at the lights of New York City, his thoughts focused on his quarry. Somewhere in the city lurked a demon-hearted killer seeking to camouflage his wickedness by pretending to be one of the nameless, faceless people passing through on the way to someplace else.

As Andrew's concentration shifted focus, his vision increased in acuity, penetrating the physical layer of existence to a level of reality hidden from humans. A dimension in which the incorporeal overshadowed the material and physical laws were superseded by spiritual ones. Thus was he able to observe the dark mass hovering like a thundercloud above the city, invisible to all eyes but his.

Despite its appearance, this was no thundercloud, for its origin was not in the physical plane of reality. It was a sign of blight, the dark stain of evil suspended over New York. Black Jack might be able to hide somewhere amongst the crowded streets, but his presence was evident to one such as the Avenger. A similar mass had tainted London's atmosphere while the Ripper menaced that city. It was irrefutable proof of enormous evil.

Andrew knew only too well that the longer the Ripper remained in New York, the larger and more ominous the mass would grow, accompanied by the manifestations and disturbances that signify the transgression of the barrier between these two dimensions of existence. Servants of evil waited patiently at the gate, looking for a vulnerable moment when the barrier could be breached. A catalyst was required, one of sufficient malevolence and depravity to set things in motion.

Once the Ripper began to hunt and kill, New York would greatly resemble London at the height of the Whitechapel murders. The streets of New York would become the feasting ground for other entities and lesser demons drawn as magnets to the presence of the master evil. Not only would they fight to extinction to protect the Ripper from the Avenger's wrath, but they would also wreak their own havoc and destruction on the populace. Therefore, it was imperative that Andrew destroy Jack the Ripper before he left another corrupted, devastated city in his wake.

Andrew blinked a few times rapidly in succession, and his vision snapped like an elastic band back to the physical plane.

The ship had completed its docking maneuvers, and passengers lined up to disembark. The casual observer might have remarked upon the scant baggage carried by Andrew in comparison with the other passengers, most of whom were laden with heavy trunks. No matter his destination, Andrew traveled light, for if a swift or clandestine departure was necessary, it could be achieved with minimal preparation and risk of discovery.

He waited in line to leave the ship, keeping impatience in check. His sharp eyes were alert for anything amiss, his other senses also vigilant. It was certainly within the Ripper's nature to set a trap, to attack him in a surprise move before he entered the city proper. The Ripper would not risk such an assault himself but would send one of his demons to engage the enemy. In the Avenger's experience, these entities were not possessed of sufficient strength to destroy him but nevertheless were nasty and troublesome and capable of causing enough of a disturbance to draw unwanted attention his way. Besides, these fiends cared not whether anyone else might be injured or killed. Some were known to deliberately provoke such chaos for the sheer satisfaction of watching humans suffer. Andrew heartily desired to avoid a debacle; nevertheless, he was prepared to encounter it.

As he stepped off the landing ramp onto American soil, he was greeted by a commotion of sight and sound. Whereas activity at the London docks tended to decrease towards evening, New York's harbor bustled and teemed with people engaged in all manner of interaction, transaction, and reaction. Stalls vied for crowded spaces, their vendors frantically peddling their wares. Wagons and carts were in abundance to assist weary travelers with their baggage, the entrepreneurs only too happy to relieve the newcomers of any available coinage. Newsboys prowled the area calling out the headlines of the day, voices raised in strident competition.

At first glance, the scene appeared overwhelmingly chaotic, but if one examined it more closely, it was clear that it was cleverly orchestrated mayhem, designed to make the senses reel. As passengers disembarked and stood momentarily stunned by the frenzied activity and sheer volume of people, they were descended upon by news vendors, baggage handlers, cab operators, and others, all vying with one another to offer their services. Like birds of prey swooping in for the kill, they easily targeted their victims, whisking away the bewildered travelers in their eagerness to make a sale. They offered everything from food and drink, rides to destinations, even lodgings to those whose prior arrangements had gone awry.

Andrew was approached by several cab drivers, all trying to outbid one another for his patronage. He was reminded of the rickshaw drivers of Bombay, whose competitiveness was so fierce that physical altercations routinely occurred, sometimes resulting in serious injury. On rare occasions, death resulted, not only for the rickshaw drivers but for their unfortunate passengers as well. Andrew noted with mild interest that Americans conducted themselves with appreciably more civility in these circumstances, notwithstanding voices raised in anger and the odd insult hurled. Andrew dismissed them all with a wave of his hand and a peremptory "not interested."

The autumn night was so fine that he decided to walk to his

lodging house, which was not a great distance from the harbor itself. The air was surprisingly milder than London at this time of the year. Despite its location on the Hudson River, the city lacked the pervasive bone-gnawing dampness of its English counterpart. He was glad to leave the noisy crowd behind him as he proceeded up the street. The sun had just set, twilight claiming the sky, deepening the previous rosy shades of the tableau with blue and violet.

As with most industrialized cities in the west, the waterfront remained an underdeveloped area, home to the seedier and poorer citizens; drunkards and prostitutes, society's dregs. In fact, this part of New York uncannily resembled Whitechapel minus the tenaciously thick fog. Of course, there were structural and architectural differences, but the streets were similar in their narrowness and squalor.

The familiar potent odor of poverty and disease was palpable in the air. There was no question; the Ripper should feel right at home here. But it would be a temporary haven at that. Andrew smiled at the thought. His smile was far from pleasant and would have sent a chill shuddering into anyone who saw it, for it was the Avenger who smiled, and there was no mistaking the menacing and predatory quality of his expression.

Had any human been about who possessed some spiritual awareness, that individual might have sensed the presence in the city of a great evil, for an entity as powerful as the Ripper could not avoid impacting the environment. However, that discerning human would also have detected another presence equally as formidable, but much harder to categorize. It was not evil, it was not good, but a hybrid of the two. It defied description, and for that reason alone, it was unknowable and immeasurably unsettling.

After a twenty-minute walk, Andrew arrived at the lodging house, carefully selected to suit his specific requirements. A plain, unobtrusive structure, originally designed as a boardinghouse, it was located on a secluded side street, yet not far from the main thoroughfare.

The proprietress, a woman in her sixties, explained that this was both a blessing and a curse.

"Thank goodness we are close to the port. Otherwise, we'd have been forced to close the hotel," she told Andrew as she showed him to his room. She explained that she and her brother had bought the old boardinghouse on a whim, hoping that the refurbishings they added would make the hotel an appealing place for visitors. "It's modest, but tidy and clean, I assure you. Theodore and I earn enough to support ourselves. Our needs are few." She smiled.

"Your establishment meets my needs superbly, Mrs. Plummer," Andrew replied. "The room is immaculate." He nodded in satisfaction as he surveyed the plain but functional room.

"There is a sign posted downstairs, Mr. Thorpe, which states the time meals are served. The dining room is of a size to accommodate all our guests at once, although that need seldom occurs. The food isn't fancy, but I trust you will find it appealing."

Andrew flashed a bright smile. "Please, Mrs. Plummer, do not trouble yourself on my behalf. I keep erratic hours and may not avail myself of the hotel's meals all that often. However, there is one thing about which I am insistent, and that is a steaming cup or two of strong black tea in the morning. I am an early riser."

Mrs. Plummer smiled again, nodding. "No trouble at all, Mr. Thorpe. I, too, rise before the sun. I bake my bread every morning at five o'clock."

Andrew rubbed his hands together. "Splendid. I foresee no difficulties whatsoever, Mrs. Plummer."

Her smile was less tentative this time, and she left her guest's room thoroughly charmed by the young gentleman from abroad with the wonderful eyes and courtly manner.

CHAPTER 54

Andrew wasted no time in tracking the whereabouts of his prey. After a light meal thoughtfully provided in his room by Mrs. Plummer, he was ready to begin. He had ascertained from the proprietress that the hotel was only half occupied, and as he had requested in his prior correspondence, his room was a corner one, and the room beside it was vacant. Andrew required absolute privacy. Mrs. Plummer was paid a handsome stipend to ensure that the other room remained unoccupied throughout his stay.

Heaven help anyone who dared intrude upon his chosen sanctuary, no matter how innocuous the motive. Circumspect in his human guise was Andrew Hewitt-Brown. When he functioned as the Avenger, he had neither the time nor patience for distractions of any kind. Those who threatened impediment to his purpose were dealt with summarily. In this instance, he made no distinction between friend and foe, for any who interfered with his actions forfeited their rights as friends. He waited, listening to the hotels' occupants as they settled for the night.

At midnight's approach, he lit some candles and extinguished the lamp. His candles accompanied him on every journey, an integral component to his rituals. He listened now to the silence, felt it sink deeper, pulling him down with its gravity. It was another presence, an ally, senescent and tangible; like cold sand slipping through his fingers, it surrounded him in a protective embrace.

At last, it was time to summon his magic. He drew a pentagram in the air around him to serve as a deterrent against anything which might attempt to thwart his purpose. As he focused his energy, drawing the magic from the core of his being, a change occurred within the room. Subtle at first, it grew more palpable as the Avenger's concentration intensified. A human observer would have difficulty describing the quality of that change, but he would be aware of a heightened energy in the air, an anticipatory excitement which built to an expectant crescendo. The sensation would be akin to how one might feel observing a great beast emerging from its lair after a long hibernation. And like an unpredictable and feral beast, magic, if mishandled, could turn on its master with dire consequences. A magician must remain focused if he was to retain control over this capricious and highly volatile force.

The air in the small room was alive. It crackled with energy, seeming to shift physically. The Avenger sensed the individual molecules coming to life and rejoicing in a new frenzy of motion. The increased speed of air caused a wind to spring up inside the room. It ruffled Andrew's hair and clothes, causing the curtains to billow and the candle flames to flicker.

Andrew sat in his chair, eyes closed, feeling his mind expanding and entering into play with the dancing molecules of matter. He directed his will toward the huge well of energy inside him, summoning up that energy to do his bidding. His respiration and heartbeat at first accelerated, then began to slow to normal, and then below normal as his consciousness shifted from the physical to the spiritual body. Senses preternaturally alert, he allowed his awareness to expand until he felt the universal energy flow reach out and engulf him.

Now ready to leave behind physical form, he poured his essence into the spiritual realm, his passage after so many times smooth and effortless. His entire being resonated with the pure rush of energy surging through him, bringing the sense of freedom not possible to duplicate on the physical plane. In fact, the experience was so powerful that were his spirit not tethered by the receptacle of his body to the physical world, it would be swept into the vortex by the sheer violence of the energy bombarding it.

Despite Andrew's enormous skills, there was always some risk involved when embarking upon such an endeavor. If he failed to maintain his razor sharp focus or if he underestimated his level of physical fatigue, his spirit could be in danger of severing its connection to the physical body, resulting in the death of the body from the enormous trauma of having the spirit precipitously severed.

The spirit would also undergo massive shock. Confused, disoriented without the anchoring balance of the physical, it would be trapped between these two planes of existence. Though futile, the spirit would attempt to re-establish its symbiotic bond with the body. With the body no longer alive, this, of course, could not happen. The spirit's efforts would become more frantic as it repeatedly tried and failed to connect with the body. Manifestations of these attempts were sometimes visible in the material world and commonly referred to as ghost or spirit phenomena.

According to those who subscribed to the increasingly popular spiritualist movement of the nineteenth century, spirits of the dead were presumed to attempt to communicate with the living. Often it was believed that some urgent message was the reason that these particular spirits wished to communicate with others, particularly loved ones left behind. Reality, unfortunately, was more straightforward and less romantic. Lost spirits, such as those who suffered an abrupt, oftentimes unexpected severance from their physical forms, most commonly through sudden or traumatic death, did not possess the conscious will to even consider communication with the living. Their confusion at suddenly finding themselves in another existence, of being dead, as it were, was so overwhelming that their only focus, their only desire, was to reunite with the physical.

Because time in the spiritual existence does not pass as time on the physical plane as measured by humans, any amount of time may elapse before the spirit attempts to rejoin its body. Failing either to relocate or rejoin its body, a spirit would then gravitate towards familiar surroundings, hoping to find the elusive object of its search, thus the phenomenon known as haunting.

Another untoward effect of such powerful magic, though perhaps not as dramatic as the one just described, involved the effects of time itself. As Andrew aged, his body would become increasingly susceptible to the infirmities time inflicted on all humans. Eventually, it would weaken to the point where it no longer possessed the strength to carry out his will.

It was yet another of the prices Excala paid for accepting the burdens and restrictions of man's world. Time, as measured by men, was merely an illusion around which they constructed their lives. Although finite beings, they did not truly understand the concept of mortality, behaving instead as though life would continue indefinitely. Only the Excala understood time. No matter a man's allotted time in this world, it would never feel enough.

These thoughts traveled through Andrew's mind fleetingly, for he needed to focus on his magic. He opened his eyes to see the molecules swirling and tumbling about him. They began to dance around him purposefully, weaving a synchronized pattern, a cloak of concealment around him. The cloak shimmered as it took form, drawing substance from the abundant energy source. His eyelids closed again, feeling heavy, his body as though encased in lead. The sensations marked the figurative disregarding of the body as he left it behind and transcended the physical barrier.

With the spell now completed, the Avenger could travel wherever he wished without fear of discovery. He would evade detection by all of the most evolved of the Ripper's minions and, of course, the Ripper himself who, if as yet unaware that the Avenger had followed him to America, would soon become aware of the presence of his arch enemy. But in Andrew's non-corporeal form, he could move more quickly, and without all the physical limitations to track the Ripper's whereabouts and to the demon's chagrin, the Avenger posed an even more dangerous adversary while in that manifestation.

***

Andrew was up and about the city streets early the next morning. After a cup of tea and a plate of scones shared with the amiable Mrs. Plummer, he departed the hotel in search of the daily newspapers. He had not long to wait, for as in all major cities of the world, the news vendors of New York were on the streets just as dawn broke.

It was his intention to check all the dailies, and in the case of the more popular presses, the second editions as well. This would be helpful in gaining a sense of New York; more importantly, he hoped to gauge the activities of the Ripper. Reports of unusual murders or tragedies which generated a high degree of fear in the populace would be an unmistakable indication that the demon was on the prowl.

Armed with several newspapers, Andrew walked over to the New York Public Library, where he could peruse the stories at his leisure. The building, even at this early hour, was crowded with other gentlemen similarly engaged. He managed to find a chair in a more secluded area. Amidst the smell of pipe smoke, the rustling of turning pages, and the occasional cough, the city began to wake.

New York was booming and prosperous, fully enjoying the fruits of industrialization. Businesses earned considerable profits, and there were jobs aplenty. Immigrants flocked by boatloads to New York harbor. For some, the city was a transition point, an access to America on their way to another location in that vast country. For others, New York was the place they would henceforward call home, setting up communities, establishing family businesses, dreaming of prosperity and a solid future in their new country.

In his mind, Andrew traveled through the city streets, conjuring up images of the various districts he encountered. Compared to London, New York was a well-defined, organized city. Individual ethnic groups claimed the various sections of the city for their communities. They tended to remain within their specific cultural milieu, preserving language and customs from their country of origin.

London, on the other hand, was essentially divided into two main parts; central London, including the North, South, and West sectors, home to the middle and upper classes. And the East End, which housed the poor and derelict. The slums of Whitechapel and Spitalfields knew no distinction between cultures; poverty embraced all and sundry without bias. It was commonplace for Eastern Europeans to live side-by-side with Cockney homegrowns and to hear Polish, Russian, Hungarian, and German all spoken along the same street. Jewish laborers worked alongside Bulgarians, as well as English, Scottish, and Irish tradesmen.

Andrew's interest was suddenly snared by a story that occupied a moderate space on the second page of one of the dailies. Apparently, several children had gone missing from the Italian area over the last couple of days. No trace of them had been found, the police describing them as having "vanished from the face of the earth." Extensive searches of the district and surrounding neighborhoods yielded no clues. Fear bred paranoia, and the Italians closed themselves off from other communities in an attempt to keep the perpetrator at bay.

Andrew frowned thoughtfully as he finished reading. The Ripper's blight of evil had spawned those mysterious disappearances. The Avenger knew with a cold certainty that those unfortunate children would never be found, for in this way, would the parents of the children endure the maximum suffering. The slow, agonizing day-by-day erosion of their hopes as no definite answers emerged, before the final plunge into a despair so profound they could never recover from it.

This divergence from his usual victim pool only confirmed the Ripper's brilliant lethality. Andrew would be the only person to connect the murders of several prostitutes in London with the unexplained disappearances of children in New York. And he knew one additional piece of information.

Jack the Ripper was still in town.

CHAPTER 55

Over the next few weeks, daily life in Whitechapel resumed an uneasy routine. November ended, and December ushered in colder temperatures. Christmas preparations, such as they were in this impoverished district, went ahead, albeit with a cautious and subdued air. The specter of Jack the Ripper still haunted the streets, and mindful of the gap between previous killings, people waited in trepidation for news of the next murder.

The Metropolitan Police and Scotland Yard doggedly pursued the Ripper investigation, producing numerous theories and suspects, all of which led to the same result; a dead end. Many a finger was pointed, and accusation declared, some evolving from good intentions, others of spurious origin as acts of vengeance against troublesome neighbors or relatives. For a while, speculation focused on Joe Barnett, the former lover of Mary Kelly, who left their shared lodging at Miller's court two weeks before her murder. However, in the absence of any concrete evidence, this line of inquiry was not pursued, it being the private opinions of the detectives involved that while it was possible that Joe Barnett's temper could have driven him to murder Kelly, it was highly improbable that he possessed the nerve or cleverness to have avoided detection in the other murders.

Thomas Bowyer, the man who had alerted the police about Kelly's murder, enjoyed his notoriety for a period of time. But after his testimony at the Kelly inquest, his name slowly faded from public attention. The dampness and cold attacked his old joints with a cruel ferocity. He soon found himself unable to leave his lodgings, his knees crippled and swollen with pain. A few of his neighbors pooled their resources to assist as best they were able, but for the most part, Bowyer spent the long winter days and even longer nights alone, his mind unable to stop replaying images of Mary Kelly's gruesomely mutilated body. He suffered through sleepless nights, plagued by shadows that whispered and rustled in the corners of his room. He didn't understand the soft and sibilant words they spoke, but he knew they were malevolent in intent. He also knew he would never again enjoy a peaceful night's sleep, and it wasn't long before he bitterly cursed the day he looked through that window in Miller's Court.

Briefly, he wondered what had happened to the young woman who had been there with him, the nurse who fled the scene like a mad thing, leaving him to confront the police. He fervently hoped she suffered as much as he and that her dreams were as greatly disturbed as his own. In his heart, he blamed her for his misfortune. If she had not been at Mary Kelly's flat that morning, he would have never looked through Mary's window; thus, he would have been spared the sight that would haunt him to his dying day. He was an old man, not as robust as once he was, and somehow he intuited that he would never recover from this ordeal. Time would not be that kind.

***

Emma kept busy working, which helped her through a good part of the day. Nights were more problematic, for though she didn't once think of Thomas Bowyer, the midnight hours found her contemplating with much anxiety the well-being of her fiancé.

Toward the end of November, she received a message from Andrew. Tantalizingly brief, it stated that he had arrived safely in New York but had not yet encountered Black Jack. He promised to write whenever there was an opportunity but cautioned Emma not to be concerned if she heard only sporadically from him in the next while ahead.

Emma sighed in disappointment as she acknowledged that there was no possibility of her lover returning in time for Christmas. Foolishly she had entertained the hope that they might still celebrate the festivities together, as they had in previous years.

Now she was certain that she would spend the Yuletide with her family in part, and with Henrietta. She understood that Andrew's mother would miss her son terribly, despite the presence of her daughter's family. Somehow Emma's own sadness was eased by the fact that she wasn't the only one who desperately longed for Andrew's return.

The Whitechapel Infirmary continued to be a haven for the downtrodden, especially as temperatures plummeted. Those without a roof over their heads sought temporary shelter at night within the infirmary walls. Though always a busy environment, particularly in the winter months when cold-related infections such as pneumonia and bronchitis were rampant, the pace had slowed from the frantic response during the autumn typhoid outbreak.

Still, no matter how much work there was to be done, there was always time for gossip, and gossip there was aplenty regarding the mysterious disappearance of the apprentice physician, John Dennys. Rumors abounded that he had run off to the continent with a wealthy widow he had met at one of Dr. Mackenzie's soirees. Another was that he had been banished from London's medical elite for an ill-considered dalliance with the niece of Sir William Gillespie. A third popular story was that Dennys had accrued a considerable gambling debt while indulging in his secret vice at some of the highly disreputable gaming houses in Whitechapel. Alas, unable to pay back his large losses, he met with foul play. No doubt his remains would eventually surface somewhere along the Thames.

No one had seen hide nor hair of the erstwhile Mr. Dennys since early November. However, if anyone other than Emma noticed that his unexplained absence coincided with the weekend of Mary Kelly's murder, they did not state the obvious. Probably, Emma reflected, because it was not an obvious connection to anyone other than Emma.

John Dennys had failed to appear at the infirmary on the Monday following the murder, yet curiously enough, when any and everyone was regarded as a suspect, not one person at the infirmary even raised the question of John Dennys being the Whitechapel murderer. *But perhaps that shouldn't come as a surprise*, thought Emma. Dennys had guarded his secret masterfully, choosing her as the sole individual to whom he revealed a glimmer of his true identity. And Andrew, of course. He probably guessed long before Emma the identity of Jack the Ripper.

Emma wondered if she had discovered the truth about John Dennys earlier on but had chosen to banish the knowledge to the murky depths of her mind. She now realized that although her mind may have been deceived, her heart never was, and it was that realization, along with Andrew's protective influence, that had saved her from becoming one more victim of Jack the Ripper. She now had no doubt that the Ripper's intention had been to harm her, for she had seen the roiling evil in his eyes. She felt to her marrow the cold hatred that emanated from him. The simple fact was that time had run out on him. He had been forced to vacate Whitechapel, his work unfinished, in order to flee the Avenger.

Emma shuddered as she realized his hatred of her must be even more intense now, for no doubt he would blame her for alerting the Avenger to his presence. The fact that such monstrous wickedness existed in real terms, not simply as an abstract subject for philosophers and clerics, was not a matter she could share with anyone other than Andrew and Henrietta, and perhaps one day, Sarah-Jane. For she intuitively recognized that her young friend, with her astounding ability to gently subdue the Princess Alice's boisterous clientele, was a peacekeeper and also an Excala, albeit in a dormant state. But when the time came for Sarah-Jane's reclamation to begin, she would be there to support her.

It would be useless to approach the authorities with her knowledge, for even had the Ripper remained in Whitechapel, they would have continued to be powerless against him. There would not have been one shred of evidence she could offer to incriminate John Dennys, and she would only have brought ridicule and ignominy upon herself. She shook her head. It was best this way. She simply need bide her time until her lover returned, triumphant with his victory over the demonic Ripper. It did not occur to Emma that the danger to her might not yet be past.

CHAPTER 56

Christmas Day came and went. Emma dutifully carried herself through the motions of enjoying the festivities. Only with Henrietta could she put aside the pretense. The women gravitated towards one another, becoming even closer. They shared solace and comfort, gaining strength from each other. Life was not pleasurable, but it was bearable.

Henrietta instructed Emma in the reclamation process. It was slow going and frustrating for Emma due to her general malaise and fatigue. Henrietta understood that the young woman's recent ordeal with the demon, coupled with her anxiety for Andrew's welfare, were draining her energy. Yet energy was essential for the casting of magic spells. Therefore Emma's training was dependent on her energy levels. Henrietta cautioned her against unrealistic expectations, reiterating that Emma must develop according to her ability to focus and learn.

She tried her utmost to reassure Emma and to nurture her soul and mind as best she could. Like her son, she had learned that magic would not be rushed. It was a force not subject to mere human dictates and whims.

The two friends sat companionably in front of the roaring fire in the Hewitt-Brown's drawing room. It had been unusually cold throughout the holiday period, and the dawning of the first day of the New Year was no exception to the intemperate conditions. Emma had rekindled her interest in knitting, as she discovered it produced a soothing effect on her overwrought nerves.

She was knitting a muffler and hat for another one of her nieces. Absorbed in an intricate bit of stitching when she heard

Henrietta gasp, she looked up in alarm. Henrietta, who had been perusing the daily newspaper, gazed at her over the top of the *London Star*, a stricken expression on her face.

"Whatever is the matter?" Emma demanded, rising from her seat.

The older woman gestured for her to sit down. "It has nothing to do with my well-being," she said in a strange voice. "Just some rather disturbing information I have come across."

A look of dread twisted its way into Emma's eyes. "Is it about...does it concern Andrew?"

"No, no child," Henrietta hastily replied. "Not Andrew. Rather a friend of his, someone with whom he attended Oxford. You may even have been introduced to him, Montague Druitt."

"Monty," Emma repeated. "Well, yes, I recall the name. Andrew referred to him as Monty, and I remember thinking how odd that such a distinguished name as Montague could be reduced to a silly sounding diminutive. I may have briefly met him. Quite serious and morose-looking, if I am not mistaken."

Henrietta nodded. "Apparently, he was as morose as his appearance indicated. The news item says that he drowned himself in the Thames, up near Keswick; at least that is the location in which his body was recovered."

"How tragic!" Emma exclaimed. "The poor man. Had he been distressed about something in particular?"

"That is the truly shocking aspect. The news article claims that Monty has been the subject of a police investigation for some time. As a suspect in the Whitechapel murders."

It was Emma's turn to gasp. "Are they serious? Why on earth is he a suspect?"

Henrietta sighed. When she spoke, her voice shook slightly with emotion. "There is a significant family history of mental imbalance and suicide. As a matter of fact, his mother was recently committed to an asylum. Despite this terrible familial affliction, Monty managed to do quite well for himself. He graduated from Oxford and enjoyed some success as a barrister. However, I recall Andrew saying — oh, it must have been back in September — that

Monty had left that position and had instead obtained a teaching post at some boys' school. Andrew's impression was that Monty suffered from mental anguish and that he accepted the teaching position because he believed it would cause him less stress than the other. You see, he confided to Andrew that his greatest fear was of going mad like his mother."

"How profoundly sad," murmured Emma. "What torment that unfortunate man must have endured. Still, it doesn't explain his connection to the Ripper murders."

"No, it doesn't," Henrietta agreed. She resumed reading the article. "It says that Mr. Druitt's increasingly erratic behavior was brought to the attention of the police by an anonymous family member. This person expressed concern on behalf of several other relatives that Mr. Druitt exhibited bizarre personal habits, wildly fluctuating mood, and by his conversation gave the impression that he suffered from a sexual insanity as well. Moreover, he displayed an intimate knowledge of the infamous brothels of Whitechapel and was obsessively preoccupied with Whitechapel. The anonymous family member further reports that Mr. Druitt would read the newspaper accounts of the murders over and over, sometimes laughing to himself in apparent glee. This person went so far as to say that the family members themselves became fearful that Druitt was none other than Jack the Ripper himself."

"What utter nonsense!" Emma stated emphatically. "The poor man was obviously seriously deranged. He required medical intervention, not condemnation."

Henrietta shook her head as she continued to read aloud. "According to Inspector Abberline, the authorities have been interested in Mr. Druitt for some time and were aware that the suspect disappeared around the time of the last murder. However, they did not suspect that Druitt had killed himself. No actual suicide note was found amongst the deceased's possessions. However, of particular significance to the authorities, hidden amongst Druitt's items of correspondence was a letter, verifiably in Druitt's own handwriting. While not precisely a confession, the contents strongly suggest that Druitt himself might have committed the atrocious murders. The note is undisputed evidence of a pitifully deranged mind, the words at times rambling and incoherent."

Henrietta continued. "However, the deceased at one point refers to Miller's Court, the scene of Mary Kelly's murder. The police have refused to release any other details of this letter, leading to speculation that there may be more incriminating evidence therein, which the police, for their own reasons, do not wish the public to know at this time. Postmortem examination of Mr. Druitt's remains shall be conducted in the next day or two, although it is virtually certain that death was caused by drowning and was self-inflicted." Henrietta leaned back in her chair. "Goodness," she said. "How perfectly awful for the Druitt family, as well as poor Monty himself, to go to his death with that vile suspicion in his mind. I wonder why Andrew never mentioned it. He must surely have known that Monty was under scrutiny."

"Undoubtedly," Emma agreed. "However, regardless of what the unfortunate Mr. Druitt believed or feared, Andrew would have known that his friend was not Jack the Ripper." A frown creased her brow. "But now that I think about it, I believe Andrew did know of some involvement on Monty's part.

"Yes, I remember now," she said eagerly. "We were discussing the letters Jack the Ripper allegedly sent to the press. Andrew said the letters weren't written by the murderer himself, but someone who was enthralled to the demon within the Ripper. Although Andrew wouldn't confirm it, I suspect that he was aware of this individual's identity. I had the impression he felt some emotion akin to sympathy for this person, despite his words that whoever it was would be doomed to Hell." She shuddered at the memory. "He said the person was as good as dead, though he still lived and breathed."

Henrietta sighed once more. "It seems the repercussions of Jack the Ripper's evil continue to manifest themselves, even though he no longer stalks Whitechapel."

Emma said nothing, but as the two women sat in silence, she

wondered what other ripple effects were yet to be encountered from the devastating impact of the Ripper's evil.

CHAPTER 57

It was as he finished writing a letter to Emma that Andrew was overcome by the familiar sense of urgency he had experienced that morning in November, the one that precipitated his journey overseas in search of Jack the Ripper. It could mean only one thing; his enemy was on the move once again. An image of a speeding locomotive flew across his mind. He felt the shuddering rails beneath him, heard the thunderous pounding of the engine.

Andrew jumped up from his desk, quickly gathering his possessions. He ran out of the room and down the stairs, maintaining a light and graceful stride despite the breakneck pace.

Mrs. Plummer was humming to herself in the kitchen as she prepared pastry for the pie to be served at dinner that day. Her plain face lit up as the young Englishman, after a peremptory knock, entered the room.

"Why, Mr. Thorpe!" she exclaimed, hastily wiping flour-coated hands on her apron. "Is something amiss?"

"Forgive my intrusion, Mrs. Plummer." He reached into his coat pocket and extracted his billfold. "I am afraid that I must depart immediately. I regret this precipitous leave-taking, but as we agreed when we made our arrangements, the length of stay was unspecified." He held out some money. "This should adequately cover my rooms and recompense you for any inconvenience."

The proprietress gaped at the large amount. Nevertheless, she reached for it without hesitation. "Mr. Thorpe, you are too generous," she said, blushing slightly.

"Nonsense. Please accept it without reservation."

Mrs. Plummer smiled gratefully. "Of course, Mr. Thorpe. It has been a pleasure doing business with you, and I hope that we may oblige you when next you visit New York."

"Indeed, to be sure." Andrew bowed and quickly took his leave. He knew he would never see the proprietress or her hotel again.

***

As the front door closed behind him, the smile vanished from Mrs. Plummer's face. She sighed as the buoyant feeling she'd enjoyed over the last few days abruptly vanished. She'd rather hoped that Mr. Thorpe might decide to extend his stay at the hotel. Instead, he had done the opposite, seeming in a frightful hurry to get someplace else. Something about the gallant Jeremy Thorpe made her forget the middle-aged, dowdy widow she was. She'd felt younger, lighter in his presence. He had touched her heart in some indefinable yet powerful way. He'd made her smile, and she would miss him.

***

Andrew, for his part, spared no further thoughts on Mrs. Plummer. He arrived at the train station sensing there was no time to lose. He swore inwardly, angry that his nemesis had almost slipped away from under his very nose.

The city's train station seemed even busier than its harbor. He scanned the hordes hurrying to and fro, fighting back a growing impatience. Jack the Ripper was here, of that he was certain—but where? His finely tuned senses leapt to an even more heightened awareness, registering the myriad stimuli, disregarding superfluous sights and sounds.

In an instant, he was as though in a vacuum, his mind instructing his ears to deaden all sound. The very atmosphere around him rippled with intensity as his eyes penetrated the chaos of the station. Time slowed down, allowing him to see every movement of every person in a deliberate, exaggerated fashion. He spent several moments scanning the crowds but did not locate the enemy he so desperately sought.

His gaze shifted focus to the many sets of stairs, each leading to a separate platform above where trains awaited boarding. It was impossible to guess which city the Ripper had chosen as his destination. America was a vast country, and to one as clever and creative as the demon, a true land of opportunity where he could continue his murderous spree.

Still no sign of his quarry. Perhaps the Ripper was already on some platform, about to board a train. Andrew allowed his senses to return to normal, as amid a growing frustration, he pondered his next move.

Out of the corner of his eye, he glimpsed a woman with a flower cart wending her way through the throngs of people. She maintained a steady pace as she navigated around the mass of humanity, heading, in all probability, to a spot where she regularly sold her wares. Andrew frowned as he watched the flower seller's progress. There was nothing remarkable about her appearance, nothing to warrant his attention. Why, therefore, were his eyes drawn to her? Could she possibly be in thrall to the demon, one of his minions sent by the master to distract the Avenger?

The woman continued to approach, swerving her cart to avoid running into a woman with a young boy in tow. As she came abreast of Andrew, she lost her footing slightly, swaying into him, her shoulder brushing against him.

Andrew instinctively reached out to steady the vendor, becoming aware of two things simultaneously. As his hands made contact with the woman, a jolt shuddered through his body, signaling that he was face-to-face with the demon itself. At the same time, he felt a hot, searing pain under his ribs.

Glancing down at his left side, he saw a scarlet patch begin to blossom and spread across his shirt. Even as he tried to stanch the flow of blood, he registered the bright, lethal gleam of the scalpel as it disappeared beneath the voluminous folds of the woman's skirt.

The demon paused long enough to flash a feral sneer of triumph before twisting out of the Avenger's grasp. Then it fled into the crowd.

Andrew felt a rage burn inside even as the wound pulsed out his life's blood. Damn the Ripper for outsmarting him! He should have anticipated such an underhanded attack. After all, although the authorities never discovered it, that was how the demon had ambushed his victims in the back alleys of Whitechapel.

Never taking his eyes off the fleeing figure, he stumbled in pursuit, the blood still in his veins aboil with a fury born of pure vengeance.

The Ripper ran up a flight of stairs leading to a departure platform. So focused was the Avenger on his prey that he completely blocked out the agony of his wound. Whether the injury would prove fatal did not concern him. All that mattered was destroying the Ripper before the demon could escape to the heartland of America, where it might never be found.

However, the continuing blood loss caused the Avenger to falter, losing precious seconds in his pursuit. He gritted his teeth, fighting back the blurred vision and increasing light-headedness. Despite his tenacious determination to reach his enemy, he knew it was only a matter of time before his body succumbed to the shock of the injury.

Several passersby gaped in horror as he lurched ahead like a drunken man in their midst. Some tried to offer help as they noticed the blood-spattered shirt front and the trail of scarlet drops in his wake. But the fierceness of his expression, the vengeful gleam in his eyes, daunted even the heartiest of these. They instinctively backed away, sensing that the figure before them was infinitely more dangerous than a wounded beast.

Oblivious to everything but his need to destroy the enemy, the Avenger focused on one painstaking step at a time, dragging himself to the set of stairs up which the Ripper had vanished. The cacophonous roar of a locomotive assailed his ears as its engine fired, signaling imminent departure. He just had time to glimpse the sign before a pall of blackness obscured his vision.

Chicago. The Ripper's next destination.

He collapsed to the floor, becoming aware of the presence of his protectors in the rapidly encroaching darkness pressing in on him. Their voices washed over him, but the wave which bore them was far from gentle. Instead, it worried at him insistently, like a shock of cold water trying to revive him. The message swelled in urgency, the voices berating him to gather his failing strength, to get up from the floor, to continue the fight. He gathered them around like a cocoon, but he was deaf to their exhortations.

His last conscious thought as Andrew, the human, was of his beloved Emma. She was and would always be the one true love of all his lives, the woman for whom he would risk his soul. Emma, who made existence worth the price he always paid.

His last conscious thought as the Avenger, most powerful of all Excala, was to curse the human frailty that always brought him to this fate.

***

The mist was cool and inviting. He was cocooned, wrapped in soothing tendrils that quelled the fever of rage coursing through him. He drifted for a time before the swirls of mist parted slightly, enough for him to view a scene unfolding below him.

A group of people milled about on a train platform, gesticulating and pointing at two constables, who were lifting an inert form onto a stretcher. Through the veils of mist, he saw the stretcher loaded into the back of a police wagon. Just before a tarpaulin was pulled over it, he registered, without surprise, that it was his own body.

At once, understanding flooded him, and he realized that his spirit had vacated his lifeless body. Obviously, the knife wound from the demon's attack had proved lethal. Unlike most mortals, Andrew did not experience the disorientation, confusion, and fear that accompanied the transition from the physical to the spiritual existence. Nevertheless, death was an inconvenient thwarter of his current aspiration.

Once more, anger flared within him, threatening to consume him. He had been so close to his quarry. Now he was obliged to wait for the entity to manifest itself in the spiritual world. Until then, it would continue to prey on men in its human guise of Black Jack.

A feeling of dismay as sharp as a knife gash gripped him. What of Emma? His beloved would be devastated at his demise. Only now was she starting to heal from the psychic and spiritual trauma wrought by the demon. How would she cope with the added blow of the loss of her true love? Even with Henrietta's guidance, she might not have the strength to withstand the onslaught of sorrow to her mind and heart.

As he endeavored to control the waves of wrath surging internally, he heard the calming voice of the Creator address him.

"My son, there is a choice before you. You have served me long and well, and always faithfully. You may now leave the earthly realm behind and journey to the paradise for which your heart and soul long. There, in the kingdom of Excala, you shall dwell amongst your brothers and sisters until it is time for your love to join you. Or, you may return to the life that was interrupted and once again expose yourself to the hardships and sacrifices of human existence. I grant you this choice in the name of free will."

Anguish trembled throughout the Avenger's being. He had not anticipated such a choice would prove so difficult. How he longed to shed the shackles of the flesh and all its limitations, to abandon mortal existence and its attendant suffering. How he ached to flourish in his natural form, to embrace the wonders of his lost world, to become a being of pure spirit and magic.

But…there was Emma to consider. She needed to continue to experience his fathomless love in order to navigate the treacherous waters of her reclamation. If not, she would fail to achieve her spiritual potential in this lifetime. She would be forced to return for yet another cycle of earthly existence, and in so doing, risk further concerted attacks to her reclamation process.

And, of course, there was the demon. If left unchallenged, Black Jack would continue to wreak havoc and destroy souls wherever he journeyed. Ultimately he would pave the way for other monstrous entities of the dark one to follow.

The Avenger's loyalty, both to his beloved and to the Creator, would not allow him to reap any rewards while others were still in peril. He would honor his pledge and fulfill the destiny for which he was put on earth.

"Father, send me back. I still have work to do."

The joy and repose he desperately craved would have to wait. Only *he* could restore the balance between good and evil in the human world.

Black Jack thought he had vanquished his foe. He would soon learn the magnitude of his error. The Avenger would hunt him to the ends of the earth. And if it took until the end of time to find and slay him, then so be it.

Black Jack had best beware.

The Avenger, in all his wrathful glory, was coming.

Gina Easton is a writer who, after working for many years as a registered nurse, has finally decided to pursue a career as an author. She has had several short stories accepted for publication in horror anthologies and magazines.

Black Jack is her first novel.

She adores the weird, the macabre and the magical aspects of life. She lives in Toronto, Canada, with her husband.

www.ingramcontent.com/pod-product-compliance
Lightning Source LLC
Chambersburg PA
CBHW070359260626
47161CB00001B/204